CW00508119

THE
ONLY
FISH IN
THE SEA

ELIZABETH GANNON

Text Copyright © Elizabeth Gannon 2014
All rights reserved
Cover Image Copyright © Elizabeth Gannon 2014
All rights reserved

Published by Star Turtle Publishing

Visit Elizabeth Gannon and Star Turtle Publishing at
www.starturtlepublishing.com or on Facebook for news on upcoming
books, behind the scenes details, trivia and promotions!

Or email Star Turtle Publishing directly:
starturtlepublishing@gmail.com

We'd *love* to hear from you!

Books by Elizabeth Gannon

The Consortium of Chaos series
Yesterday's Heroes
The Son of Sun and Sand
The Guy Your Friends Warned You About
Electrical Hazard
The Only Fish in the Sea
Not Currently Evil

The Mad Scientist's Guide to Dating
Broke and Famous

Other books
The Snow Queen
Travels with a Fairytale Monster
Nobody Likes Fairytale Pirates
Captive of a Fairytale Barbarian

You may also enjoy books by Elizabeth's sister, Cassandra Gannon:

The Elemental Phases Series
Warrior from the Shadowland
Guardian of the Earth House
Exile in the Water Kingdom
Treasure of the Fire Kingdom
Queen of the Magnetland
Magic of the Wood House
Coming Soon: *Destiny of the Time House*

A Kinda Fairytale Series
Wicked Ugly Bad
Beast in Shining Armor
The Kingpin of Camelot
Coming Soon: *Happily Ever Witch*

Other Books
Love in the Time of Zombies
Not Another Vampire Book
Cowboy from the Future
Once Upon a Caveman
Vampire Charming
Ghost Walk

To my friend Grady,
The best dog (or person) I've ever met.
Who wasn't afraid of anything or anyone... except the smoke alarm.
Who met each day with a happy smile and a pure heart.
Who even dying from cancer and fresh from surgery still mauled a pit bull that was attacking me.
There was never a moment of your life when you weren't adored, and there will never be a moment of mine when you aren't missed.
This world won't see your like again.
Goodbye, buddy. Thanks for always being there.

PROLOGUE

"MANY MEN GO FISHING ALL OF THEIR LIVES WITHOUT KNOWING THAT IT IS NOT FISH THEY ARE AFTER." - HENRY DAVID THOREAU [ATTRIBUTED]

1912

The fuel tank exploded in a fireball, lighting up the docks with a shifting angry brilliance. He stood back for a moment to watch the flames destroy the holding tank and its foul contents. The sickening smell of burning bodies filled the air.

He wiped his face and slowly focused on his new enemies.

He jumped up onto the wooden crates filled with corpses and raised his voice above the blaring emergency siren and the sound of the inferno, as this terrible place burned.

"HEAR ME MORTALS!" He held his golden trident high over his head. "I am Lord Julian Thalassic Sargassum! Ruler of the waves and sovereign king of the seven seas!" He pointed his weapon at the crowd of soulless adversaries before him. "Your rape of my lands *ENDS NOW!*"

He swung the pointed weapon and smashed a crate filled with cans of 'Happy Sailor Tuna' to pieces.

Around him stood the industrial buildings and storage tanks which fulfilled the terrestrials' evil purposes. They used this place as a base of operations for their unyielding murder spree. Year after year. Decade after decade. His people suffered because the surface-worlders hungered for the flesh of the innocent.

These decrepit buildings were the nest from which they struck. These men had blood on their hands, and always would.

They were soulless killers.

All of them.

"Did you really think that I would allow you to get away with this unpunished!?!" He pointed at the cans, trying to keep from crying again. "That I would allow *murderers* to go free to kill again!?!"

The dock workers fled the scene in terror.

Julian almost smiled at their obvious cowardice. His birth mother's people were *all* like that. His father had always told him as much, but he had never before had the opportunity to see them firsthand for any length of time. But now they had attacked him. They had struck at him without warning and with insidious and calculating cruelty, firing the first devastating shots of this war.

A war which he would now END.

"That's right! FLEE!" His voice boomed out over the dock. "Run for your insignificant lives! I am not innocent sea life which you can murder for your own dark pleasure, barbarians! I am protector of the ocean depths! I am retribution on an oceanic scale! Justice made flesh! A tide of blood will..."

He trailed off as a figure strode through the flames, softly singing something that must pass for "music" among the surface people. Julian had heard sailors singing it before, but could not say that the experience was a pleasure. *Singing* murderers were still murderers.

This man's deep voice echoed through the screams though; calm and clear. He simply sang his relaxed sea shanty, as if he didn't have a care in the world.

"Oh Shenandoah,
I love your daughter,
Away, you rolling river.
For her I'd cross,
your roaming waters..."

The man was dressed in a variety of leather and armor pieces, joined together with intricately decorated buckles. Across his deeply tanned chest was a tunic of light fabric, and strapped to his loincloth was a strange looking net. Clutched under his arm was an ancient looking Roman-style gladiator helmet, in his hand he held a fishing spear, and he wore over-the-knee gladiator sandals.

The man was a fisherman. A *mortal* fisherman.

Julian looked down at him in silent rage, as if this man were singlehandedly responsible for everything wrong in Julian's life. He was the personification of *everything* about the world which Julian now *despised*.

The man stalked across the pier and stopped a few paces from the boxes on which Julian was perched, his song ending. "I'm The Retiarius." Said the Roman fisherman. "You from the sea?"

"I AM the sea!" Julian bellowed back.

"*Outstanding*." The fisherman said, looking oddly pleased. "So, how about you just calm down and let these people go?"

"Did they let *my* people go!?!" Julian gestured to the boxes of the dead which surrounded him. Coffins made of tin, filled with the bodies of the innocent, taken before their times. "Why should I give them mercy when they have shown *none!?!*" He pointed the trident at the fleeing cowards. "I will drench this land in blood! I will rule this dry world above! I will…"

The fisherman sighed. "I can't let you do that, my aquatic chum." He slipped his helmet over his head and put his hands on his hips. "I am a *protector* of this world. How about you just go back to the ocean and forget all about…"

"'FORGET!?!' You think I could ever POSSIBLY forget the evils of you terrestrial swine?!?" He let out a sharp bark of laughter. "HA! I will remember your treachery until the end of time! I will make it my MISSION IN LIFE to destroy all which your kind holds dear! Feel the pain that I FEEL! I will make your world WEEP!" He pointed his trident at the other man. "I am the watery fist of justice! I will shatter this puny facility to pieces!"

"This facility is worth tens of thousands of dollars and employs hundreds of men."

"And it kills tens of millions of my people!" He pointed at the boxes. "How can you put a cash value on their innocent lives?"

"There are better ways to go about this, chum."

Julian laughed haughtily. "It's far too late for *talk*." He sneered the word out. "I *refuse* to debate such a clear issue with you, *especially* while my people suffer and die. Terrestrials know *nothing* about life under the waves, *least of all* ones girded as an *executioner*."

"Executioner? I think you're being a little melodramatic." The man heaved a weary sigh. "I know you probably don't want to hear this, but they're only fish."

Julian bellowed with rage at hearing those words again and charged the man, jumping down from the pile of crates and landing in a crouch on the pier.

The man threw the harpoon, but Julian dodged to the side to avoid it. The sharp barb stuck into the wooden plank of the container behind Julian instead. The man tugged the line, yanking the board free and smashing it into the back of Julian's head, stunning him, and causing the entire pile of crates to collapse. Julian let out a small cry as the stack tumbled down on top of him, crushing him beneath.

The fisherman prowled forward and stood over his prone form as Julian tried to pull himself free of the wreckage. "How about you just settle down, chum. I think the globe is big enough for…"

"I will bury this entire world at sea!" He bellowed over the man's next words, shoving cans of tuna bodies aside. "Do you hear me!?! ALL WILL DIE FOR WHAT HAS BEEN DONE TO ME! *ALL WILL DIE!!!*" He jumped to his feet and swung his trident at the man's head. "I will yet gaze upon your grave!"

CHAPTER 1

KING: "GOOD EVENING, I'M PAIGE KING AND YOU'RE WATCHING 'KING OF CAPES AND COWLS,' YOUR SOURCE FOR HARD-HITTING NEWS FROM THE WORLD OF SO-CALLED 'HEROES.' ON TONIGHT'S EPISODE, I WILL BE DISCUSSING THE CONSORTIUM OF CHAOS, AND WHETHER OR NOT THEY HAVE DOOMED US ALL WITH THEIR FINAL TREASONOUS ACT OF UNBELIEVABLE COWARDICE. I WILL BE JOINED BY FORMER CITY PROSECUTOR GWEN HARDY, WHOSE OWN NEPHEW WYATT FERRAL RUNS WITH THE GANG, AND WITH ME AS ALWAYS WILL BE MY CO-HOST, CONNIE STORMS.

(INTRO MUSIC AND TITLE ANIMATION)

KING: "NOW THEN, LET'S GET RIGHT TO IT. THE CONSORTIUM OF CHAOS, THAT FOUL DISEASE, SPRINGING FORTH FROM THEIR PESTILENT HIVE DEEP BENEATH THE EARTH IN NEW JERSEY..."

STORMS (INTERRUPTING): "PAIGE, I DON'T THINK THAT'S REALLY THE..."

KING (WAVING HER OFF): "SAVE YOUR BIAS FOR SOMEONE WHO DOESN'T KNOW THEM, CONNIE. OR SHOULD I SAY, 'USED TO KNOW THEM'? THANKFULLY, THEY'VE BEEN ALL BUT WIPED OUT NOW. OFFHAND, I CAN'T THINK OF A SINGLE CRIMINAL THEY EVEN HAVE LEFT IN THEIR FELONIOUS BAND."

STORMS: "WHAT ABOUT LORD SARGASSUM?"

KING: "WHO?"

TRANSCRIPT OF "KING OF CAPES AND COWLS," MEDIA: TELEVISION, SHOW: 1407, NEWSCHANNEL 6, FRIDAY 21:00-22:00 EST, NETWORK SEGMENT-ID: 918000606

Present Day

Julian stared impassively at the gravestone in front of him.

He couldn't think of anything more horrifying than being entombed forever under the dirt of the surface world. Surrounded. Trapped in its dry and lifeless filth.

Dying was bad enough, but sentencing someone to the hell of the surface world was a fate too harsh for even someone in the *Consortium* to deserve.

No one deserved this place.

He put his head back and let the water falling from the cloudy gray sky hit his face. The rain was possibly the only thing about the surface world which Julian actually liked. He found it restful. It was a reminder that the parched land which surrounded him wouldn't last forever. That no matter how arid it seemed, one day soon, the water would rise and all would be put right. The burning sun of the surface world could evaporate the waters of the ocean and drag it away from paradise, but it would escape its prison in the clouds and find a way to fall back to the seas once again. It would *always* come back.

Home.

Not that Julian really had anything *against* the people of the surface world, per se. True, they were savages, and yes, they all deserved to die screaming, but he didn't hold those facts against them. He was too magnanimous to ever blame them for the unfortunate circumstances of their existence. They couldn't help that they had been born. The terrestrials were perfectly *fine* in their own way... he was just on a sworn mission to kill them all.

But it wasn't *personal* or anything like that.

His quest for vengeance was merely the clashing of cultures. His glorious aquatic nation's *correct* way of doing things, versus the terrestrials' asinine world and its parched and waterless landscape.

But he held no malice against them. Why would he? That would be petty and beneath him. He was a god-king! He rose above the slings and arrows of their actions and slights.

They couldn't hurt him on a personal level, even if they tried.

His ever burning hatred was a completely *rational* way of thinking.

But it *wasn't* personal.

At all.

He was simply the only one who was still fighting the surface-dwellers' illegal occupation of the globe. The last defense the planet had.

Julian was used to being alone though. His father Neptune had died when he was still a boy, and his mortal birth mother hadn't even made it that long. The little he knew about them, he didn't particularly like. Julian was always alone, even during the few short years he had known them. He had been on his own almost his entire life. The ocean was the only home he'd ever had. The fish and sea life, his only family.

Luckily, life under the sea was filled with far more excitement, enriching experiences and deep values than anything the surface world could have provided. The sea had its own mores and principles. The sea taught a man how to be a MAN! Not some weak little surface-dweller, stumbling around his scorched perverted land on absurdly tiny legs. The ocean taught a man how to stand on his *own,* and that he didn't need others around getting in his way or hindering his plans.

True, some people would probably be lonely if they were in a similar situation...

But those people were morons. *Weak* morons, who didn't understand how *glorious* it was to be free of the necessity of others.

Julian didn't need to be loved. He never had been before, so why would that change now?

He didn't need children. He was an only child, and he had resigned himself to the fact that his only offspring would be the new aquatic world he left behind.

He didn't need a woman in his life. He was the only one of his kind, and he was fine with that. He was *done* chasing mermaids.

And... and even if Julian *did* occasionally feel loneliness, that was only his dead birth mother's weak surface-dweller DNA clouding his judgment. She had passed onto him a nagging feeling that he needed a companion. That he needed to be loved by *someone* before he died.

Because no one ever had.

Not his birth parents, or his friends, or his subjects.

Julian was alone. He always had been, and he always would be.

All his life, he'd sometimes found himself thinking about how nice it would be to have someone to share his kingdom with though. He often stared off into the darkness of the sea floor, towards the light which trickled down through the waves, and he'd daydream about having someone there with him. Someone who *understood* him...

But that was nonsense. Nonsense which he blamed his birth mother for. It was her final attack on him, when all her others had failed.

Again, Julian had nothing against the surface-dwellers, but to even have a single drop of their polluted blood flowing through his noble veins was a never-ending source of embarrassment. If Julian had friends and if he cared what they thought, the knowledge of his half-humanity would bother him. Luckily, he didn't, he didn't, and it didn't.

True, the other Eternals of the world never let him forget his parentage, but Julian was totally at peace with his contaminated blood and the lamentable circumstances which had brought him into this cruel world. He instead chose to focus on more positive things, such as laying waste to the surface world and exterminating the hordes of air-breathing, fish-murdering savages which infested its lands.

The worst mistake life on earth ever made was leaving its home in the sea. Their so-called "evolution" was their expulsion from a true Edenic paradise; a blunder of *epic* proportions which many species were still being punished for. Julian felt sorry for them. Yes, he was on a mission to eradicate them, but that didn't stop him from almost pitying them.

Almost.

When you really came down to it, the sea was the only thing this planet had going for it. He couldn't imagine living away from its embrace. Without even the water to keep them company, how could the surface people bear the crushing solitude? How did they keep from just killing themselves to end their torment?

Perhaps that was the escape his birth mother had been after. Julian had no way of knowing what was going through the woman's mind as she left this world the way she had. At the time, he had had other concerns.

In either event, the sea was the source of all life and the architect of man's successes and tragedies. The sea WAS the planet, and Julian was its protector. He was the only one willing and able to stand up for it and to shield it from harm.

The *sea* was his mother, his lover, and his only friend.

He paused, thinking about that for a moment.

...It sounded *really* creepy.

He made a mental note to come up with a better way of phrasing that.

He slouched down in his metal folding chair, his eyes remaining fixed on the grave. Julian disliked funerals. He'd been to too many of them, especially in recent years. Sometimes it seemed like his entire *life* were a funeral. Everywhere he went, there was yet another testament to his failure. Another of his people dead. Billions of them every year. The terrestrials mounted his murdered kinsmen on their walls and posted images of their crimes on their 'Facebook' ...whatever *that* was. And no matter how hard he tried, he just couldn't stop them. His quest for vengeance would evidently never be realized. The surface-dweller's offenses against the innocent would never be punished.

The innocent would die and the guilty would thrive.

And it was all Julian's fault.

Every day that went by, Julian became more and more alone. Soon, *all* of his people would be gone, and he would be the only one left swimming the now empty waters of his home. But the surface-dwellers would just find some other beautiful place to exploit and ruin, and some other people to exterminate for entertainment. That was their way. That was all they *ever* did.

He was so tired of failing. Of losing friend after friend. Of being dismissed.

Of... of being alone.

He was so very tired of having his grand vision thwarted by *lesser* beings, and watching as they exterminated the only things he'd ever really cared about. Watching as terrible people did terrible things, and were rewarded with success after success, and by finding people who loved them.

Their evil was rewarded with love.

Julian's nobility was rewarded with misunderstanding. His royalty was rewarded with loneliness. His heroism was rewarded with being overlooked and ostracized. His life's mission was rewarded with failure. Crushing and unmitigated failure.

Julian didn't understand this world.

His ways were the *old ways*. And Julian just couldn't adapt. He was beginning to understand how Everett had felt in the end. He had always thought the old man had just been melodramatic, but Julian understood him now.

The old world had changed, and Julian was the only one left who even remembered how things used to be.

How they *should* be.

The old man's "Golden Age" was truly dead.

Sometimes it seemed like Julian had never won in his entire life. What was his purpose if not to rule over a flooded earth? But events and the surface-dwellers seemingly conspired at every turn to foil his glorious quest. Why had he been given powers and the noble burden of protecting the seas, if he could never win?

Sometimes, he wasn't even sure why he bothered. Hell, he wasn't even sure who he *was*. He was part god and part mortal, and yet felt at home with neither. He looked like a surface-dweller, but he could breathe underwater and found terrestrials repulsive. His domain was beneath the waves, but he was in a constant struggle to protect his kingdom.

Julian was a stranger and an outcast no matter where he was or who he was with.

But today's memorial was nothing new for him. It was just another day, and another dead associate. On the bright side, at least in the current instance, no one had broiled and eaten the deceased. Not all of Julian's friends could say the same.

The man had gotten off lucky.

No matter how many of them he attended though, funerals always reminded him of... other things. *Personal* things, which were in *no way* continuing to bother him. They didn't bother him, because he was used to his life and accepted the incontrovertible central fact of his existence.

Julian would *always* be alone.

That is of course, if you discounted the people sitting near him, which he *always* did. His coworkers were *easy* to ignore. They were annoying and loud, but they were simple to tune out once you knew how. *All* terrestrials were. Sometimes when they were talking, he'd just stare at them unseeingly and imagine the sound of the waves was drowning them out.

Drowning *them*.

The rain dripped down his face unnoticed as he watched the grave, and Julian thought about living and dying beneath the indifferent sky. The sea and the land. ...The loved and the alone.

And grey socks.

Load after load of Everett's horrifyingly grey socks.

The old man had been right about that too.

The rain continued pouring down on the funeral, soaking the few people in attendance. All that was, except Montgomery Welles, AKA "Robber Baron," who was staying dry under an umbrella held over his head by his ever faithful flunky Higgins, who was getting drenched in the effort.

Julian didn't like Monty. He was the ice-cold center which lurked at the heart of *all* surface people, no matter how hard they tried to hide it. Monty was unadulterated *humanity*, in all its selfish, grasping, underhanded, dastardly glory. When you looked Monty in his soulless eyes, you could tell that in his mind, you meant *nothing*. Not a damn thing. He was truly the most coldhearted and hate-filled man Julian had ever met, and since Julian himself was planning on drowning every man, woman, and child on the planet, that was really saying something.

Monty casually readjusted his small silver wireframe sunglasses and glanced at the vacant chairs arranged around the grave at the empty service, and at the protesters screaming from the gates at the edge of the cemetery. The citizens were less than happy over the fact that the Consortium had basically started a war this week, and so they were currently picketing the funeral service as a result. Normally, such people would be unceremoniously escorted from the Crater Lair's property by the Consortium's security detail, the Excessive Force, but most of them were currently missing in Agletaria. As such, there was simply no one left to move the public back.

Monty continued to survey the scene and nodded to himself. "It's really at the end that we can see how much we were *truly* valued." He said with mock seriousness, looking out over the dozens of empty chairs of the service. "How many lives we touched."

McCallister MacReady, AKA "OverDriver" readjusted the sling which held his injured arm in place. He had been hurt in the Agletarian attack and had not yet recovered.

Julian didn't like Mack. The man was a brutal thug and not worth Julian's time. Julian was fighting a heroic crusade against surface-worlder oppression; *Mack* was more likely to be on the evening news for stealing beef jerky from a convenience mart someplace or getting into a brawl at some sort of mortal sporting event. He had engine grease under his fingernails and bloodstains on his threadbare clothes. In any case, the man looked weary, wary, and morose, which wasn't unusual for him.

Mack bowed his head. "Today we gather to bury Mangle, a good man and a good friend."

"He owed $6,200 in unpaid alimony and child support." Monty pointed out conversationally, as if adding a bit more information to that incomplete interpretation of the dead man's character. "Plus court costs."

Everyone turned to glare at him.

"What?" Monty sounded both insulted and confused. "*I'm* not the one who turned my back on my responsibilities. It makes no sense to transform the man into some kind of martyr *now* simply because he had the good sense to die young." He looked down at his gold repeater pocket watch as it chimed to the tune *Bringing in the*

Sheaves; the tiny enameled automaton men arranged on its face swinging their hammers down onto a small golden anvil in time with the bells. "...And *now* I'm running late."

"We're at a *funeral,* Monty." Mack reminded him in disbelief.

Mangle had been one of the members of the Consortium who had been killed in Agletaria by a group of disgruntled Capes and villains led by Reece Proffit, AKA "Reciprocity." Julian honestly had no idea why the man was trying to kill everyone, and he didn't particularly care. Terrestrials were a violent species. They didn't need a reason to murder innocent things. They seemed to trod on *all* miracles, consume beauty like some horrible plague, and leave behind only bodies.

Killing things was all they *ever* did.

And all Julian could ever do was watch it happen.

Mangle had gotten out on a helicopter with a handful of others before dying of his injuries, but the rest of the Consortium was still MIA. The job of defending the world in their absence had fallen to Julian, and his group was currently running on a skeleton crew made up of the injured and the unimportant. The useless parts of the company that no one wanted.

...And *Julian*, of course, whose magnificence transcended all terrestrial terms for resplendence and power.

Water continued running down the granite surface of the headstone, pooling in the etched letters, and Julian thought once again about the relationship between water and stone.

"And you expect me to be a hypocrite and weep for the man now simply because he's dead?" Monty brushed droplets of water from his lapel and turned to glare at his underling with cold flat eyes. Higgins quickly moved the umbrella so that more of his boss was under it. Monty promptly went back to ignoring him. "I disliked the man while he was *alive*, and *death* has certainly not improved my opinion of him any, with the possible exception of this being the only action he ever took which I *approve of*. Other than that though, his early demise has merely robbed the world of a few more bastard children coming into the world which would have further drained the social service system, and half a dozen spools of copper wire which will now go un-stolen from inside the walls of abandoned homes." He heaved a disinterested sigh. "*Somehow*, I think we'll all manage just fine without him. After all, if he were *that* good at his job, he wouldn't have died in the first place."

The group gaped at the man in silence.

Multifarious leaned back in his/her chair, resting his/her white combat boots on the back of the seat in front of him/her and gestured to Monty. "Personally, I'm just shocked that the rest of you were really looking for human compassion from a man who dresses like 'Snidely Whiplash.'"

Julian didn't like Multifarious. The person was insane. He/she never took off that stupid mask with that stupid Kilroy doodle on it, and hadn't for as long as Julian had known him/her. Of course, if Julian were a surface-dweller, he'd feel the need to hide his face from the world as well.

"What if this were *your* funeral?" Oswald Dimico AKA "OCD" asked Monty, unwilling to let the issue drop.

Julian didn't like Oz. The man wasted entirely too much water washing his hands so frequently. Plus, he generally disapproved of any new people being added to the team, and despite being with them for months, Julian still considered the man "new."

Oz gestured to Monty. "Is that how you would want people to act?"

"My good man, whatever gave you the peculiar notion that you people would even be *invited* to my funeral?" Monty sounded appalled at the very idea of his co-workers attending the service. "Besides, I *fully* intend on outliving you all." He looked down at the grave, the beginnings of a cruel smile crooking the corner of his mouth. "So far, so good."

"What are you? Some kind of robot or something?" Quinn Aguta, AKA "Tupilak" asked in amazement. "Hell, Polly's a *machine* and even *she* has more feelings than you." He pointed at Polybius, the computer hologram representing the program which ran the Consortium's IT Department.

Julian didn't like Polly. She was rash, impatient, temperamental and surprisingly innocent despite her chronic smug passive aggressive demeanor. In fact, Julian wasn't a fan of *any* surface world technology, least of all ones which were so discourteous. A synthetic surface-dweller was *still* too close to an *actual* surface-dweller for his comfort. On the other hand, her contempt for the terrestrials—though thinly veiled—rivaled his own, so she wasn't the *most* annoying person of his acquaintance.

"No, she has been *programed* to have the *appearance* of feelings." Monty slipped his watch back into his pocket and leaned against his walking stick with both hands. "That is an entirely different situation."

"You're an asshole, Monty." Mack rounded on him, his

temper visibly on the verge of snapping. "Shut your mouth." His voice took on an edge of warning. "*Now*."

Monty shrugged. "Fine. Live in whatever dream world you like. The fact remains that this organization is currently on its last legs." He gestured to the small group surrounding the grave. "We are down to a mere *thirteen* employees, a tiny fraction of our normal membership and nowhere *near* enough to function successfully, as only a portion of *those* are capable of field missions. With the exception of me, our entire remaining staff is useless, and *none of you* have any experience with being a leader."

That snapped Julian out of his meditative thoughts.

"I am king." He informed the other man. "I have *billions* of subjects."

"Yes, of *course* you do." Monty cooed humoringly. "And we all appreciate every parmesan crusted and cocktail sauced one of them."

Behind him, Seth Van Diemen smirked. The man had showed up for Cynic and Marian's wedding, and had simply not bothered to leave yet. His reasons for attending the funeral of a man he had never met were known only to himself.

"Your friend has a point on both counts, Julian." Seth informed him, slipping a funeral card into his pocket for some reason. "Your little club is certainly falling apart, and your subjects are *certainly* quite tasty. You can tell your snow crab friends that their sacrifice keeps my casino's buffet in business." He put his hand over his heart. "They died martyrs for the noble cause of flaky deliciousness."

Julian turned to pin the man with a vicious glare. "Do *not* tell me how to run this organization." He jabbed his golden trident at him, the only thing he kept of his father's belongings. "I am a god and a king and now *I* am in charge of this group, and *I* will be the one who decides what we do and when."

"Uh-huh." Seth didn't sound convinced. "Not to quibble over semantics, but you're a *demi-god,* Julian. That's the genetic equivalent of nepotism: you're only an Eternal because your daddy got you in the door and the rest of us just had to ignore the fact that your mommy was from the wrong side of the tracks." He reached into his pocket for a flask. "Just for giggles though: what *is* your plan now that all of the 'big fish' have been caught and you're left with the little ones that got away?" His brow furrowed in curiosity and he gestured to Julian's less than ideal grouping of co-workers. "If you intend to play 'Triton of the Minnows,' just how *will* you be getting your team out of this jam?"

Julian paused, thinking about that for a moment.

He had absolutely no idea. Surface-dwellers were so much harder to deal with than sea life. If they were *sturgeon*, this whole situation would be handled by now. But that didn't matter. Julian had no idea what to do. ...But he was *still* in command.

"My plans are none of your business. I *refuse* to discuss proprietary information with an *outsider*." He straightened. "If you wish to join us, you can petition Human Resources when Gabe returns, but until then, *stay out of this*."

"I'm *touched* that you would ask me to join your little club. Truly, I am." Seth leaned forward in his chair. "I know a lot of people, Julian. I've been around a long time and I *fully* intend to be around awhile longer. I've outlasted your father and most of the other silly gods who got involved in matters which were not their own." He gestured to the protesters. "*You* might have suddenly decided to care about these creatures, but I yet have *some* sense." He rolled his eyes. "So, I *don't* think I'll be petitioning anyone for anything. There are only two things in this world that I would die for, and neither of them is this city." He paused. "...Or *you*, just in case there's any misunderstanding on that front." Apparently satisfied that his point had been made, he leaned back in the chair again and began pouring the contents of his flask into a martini glass he produced from somewhere. "To be perfectly honest, I don't know *what* you hope to accomplish with this endeavor anyway."

"What do you mean?"

"How can I say this gently?" Seth thought for a moment and casually ate the cherry from his glass. "Let's put it this way: did I ever tell you that I know the god of the Neanderthals?" He nodded. "Disagreeable chap; utterly uncivilized and wild. The man makes the Unabomber look like Emily Post. The point is that he controls mammoths and other forms of mega fauna." He pointed the red plastic toothpick shaped like a sword at him. "Think about that, everyone who ever even knew the man's name is dead, and his powers have been utterly useless for over thirty-thousand years, as all the animals he controls are extinct." He downed his drink in one gulp. "...And he's *still* more useful than you in a fight."

Julian advanced on him, looming over his chair. "I am *more* than willing to demonstrate the true extent of my powers."

"*Tempting*, but alas, I didn't bring my swimsuit with me on this trip, Julian. Besides, I wouldn't want to mess up your 'formal' speedos." He pointed at Julian's black lorica squamata scale armor pants, then pressed a hand over his heart. "I'm only telling you this because you and I have always been so close. Please don't ask me to stand by and watch as my dear friend throws his life away." His concern sounded utterly fake, reaching a level of mockery just shy of pointing and laughing. "Don't make me watch you die, not after I've had to watch so many of our kind die already. There are so few of us left as it is."

Mack rolled his eyes. "Yeah, I'm sure that just breaks your heart."

"Oh, *indeed*. Being a god is like being part of a brotherhood, no matter the pantheon. And to watch so many of my *dear* brothers and sisters cut down before their time..." Seth paused as if imagining the horrors he had witnessed, and jauntily poured himself another Manhattan from his flask. "...Why, it's all just simply *ghastly*." He added another cherry to his drink; piercing it with the plastic toothpick sword. "I still have *nightmares* about how those poor people all died." He took a sip. "Truly, I do."

"I don't care what one dickhead claiming to be a god does to another dickhead claiming to be a god." Mack ran a hand through his hair. It was odd seeing the man without his ever-present baseball cap, which at the moment was tucked under his arm as a show of respect to the deceased. "The fact remains that we still only have thirteen people in our entire organization, and that's *not* good."

Oz cleared his throat. "Perhaps this is an opportunity to change the very nature of heroics itself. Personally, I've always thought that fighting crime was foolhardy without first rooting out the *causes* of crime. Since we no longer have the manpower to go head-to-head with villain groups of any real size, this is the perfect time to institute a new way of doing things and involve more of the private sector and the community. Social programs, diversion initiatives, mentoring opportunities..."

"Wait," Mack looked horrified about something, "you want Monty to mentor someone? *Monty?* The goal is to *stop* crime, not create better criminals."

"While studies indicate that social programs can temporarily help alleviate the effect of crime to some degree, it will do little to stop Reece's men and their efforts to kill us all. Their goal is to eliminate all non-superpowered people, and they will destroy the city to accomplish it." Polly chimed in. "I think that we..."

Monty cut her off. "Perhaps the *real* people should be the ones to determine our new direction and not electronic personal assistants, and their carefully encoded synthetic emotions." He straightened his collar. "'Teddy Ruxpin' does not set governmental policy on the management of *actual* bear populations. He has no voice in the process, despite his ability to 'speak' and the fact that children everywhere *delight* in the whimsical belief that he is somehow magically *'alive,'*" he made jazz hands, as if drawing attention to the absurdity of that idea, "and is speaking to them about his *'thoughts.'*"

She closed her eyes and words sped across her digital skin. "You are now a registered sex offender, Mr. Montgomery." She told him sweetly. "If I were you, I would stay away from any schools."

"Well, there goes my career as a mentor then." He sighed dramatically. "Pity. I was *truly* looking forward to turning their little lives around."

Higgins looked sad. "You... you would have been an *inspiration* to them, sir."

Monty nodded solemnly, agreeing with his underling. "Well, their loss I suppose."

Ramble Maxwell, AKA "Rampant" ignored them and continued watching the protestors for a long moment. "I'm done." He announced, and got to his feet. "*Done.*" He pointed at the grave. "We're fucking DYING and what's the reward we get?" He gestured to the crowd of people. "*This* shit." He picked up one of the vases of flowers and angrily threw it at the mass of people crowding around the fence to the cemetery. The vase shattered against the iron gate and showered the mob with dirt.

The yelling got louder.

A man with a sign showing the C of C logo with a red 'X' through it started chanting, and was soon joined by the rest of the crowd. The man pointed an angry finger at them. "Pigs! Cape-wearing pigs! Go home!" He turned around to address the crowd. "*Boo!*"

Someone threw a large stone at them, which Rampant easily caught in midair and tossed back at the crowd, hitting the man who threw it in the head and knocking him down.

The man with the sign led the crowd in booing louder.

"Um..." Oz raised his hand, looking at Rampant. "Perhaps that's not the *best* way to win back the..."

"How many times do we have to have this conversation?" Rampant made an annoyed sound. "TALK FASTER!" He pointed at Oz. "DO YOU HAVE ANY IDEA HOW LONG IT TOOK YOU TO SAY THAT? *HALF AN HOUR!*" He ran a hand through his hair in agitation. "I just... I can't..." He pointed at the protestors. "I'm THROUGH WITH THIS SHIT!" He raised his voice so that the crowd could hear him. "FUCK ALL OF YOU!"

Julian didn't like Rampant. The man was always testy, as he had the unfortunate power of living his life in slow-motion. Everything took an inordinate amount of time in his world, and he seemed to be able to move in fast-forward as a result.

Oz cleared his throat. "To be fair, they are upset because they believe that we assassinated a foreign head of state and destroyed their capital. The diplomatic headache they think we caused has pushed the entire country towards war."

"Well, *that* wonderfully observant thought was certainly worth an hour and a half of my life. Thanks, Oz." Rampant stormed off. "Consider this my resignation, guys. I *quit*."

"*Twelve*." Monty calmly informed no one in particular.

Multifarious raised a gloved hand; rain beading on the white faceplate he/she wore. "How do you figure? I still get thirteen."

"That is because you are including *Polybius* in your estimate, while I am not." Monty rearranged his long black overcoat on his shoulders. "I am *also* not counting my pocket watch, the refrigerator, or any of the other delightful *things* which fill our lives."

"Please wait while I plan your directions to Hell, Mr. Montgomery." Polly smiled at him pleasantly, a small map of their current location projecting above her hand and showing a little icon with Monty's image traveling downward into animated cartoon flames below. "Estimated time of arrival... 12:23 EST."

Mack ignored them. "We're going to need more people, guys. Simple as that." He shook his head. "We can't do this on our own."

Tupilak slouched down in his chair, trying to use the hood of his traditional fur-lined parka to shield himself from the driving rain. "I think Manny had the right idea." He gestured at the gravestone, indicating the deceased. "Get the fuck out of Dodge. I mean, with us as the only line of defense, the world has days left *at most* anyway. At least Manny died before the rush."

"No one is dying!" Julian snapped.

Everyone turned to stare silently at the grave for a moment.

"...Well, no one *else* anyway." He added. "The losses we have suffered were the result of bad leadership, and now you have a *new* leader! At long last, I have taken my rightful place at the head of this organization. Ferral's reign of terror has finally ended."

"I feel safer already." Monty shifted in an effort to keep his meticulously shined shoes from sinking into the mud. "Who better to lead us than someone with no experience, who hates the people we're trying to protect, and who has never won a fight?"

Tupilak snorted. "Do you really think it'll make a difference? Fuck, we could have *Julius Caesar* leading us, and we'd still get crushed. There are only *thirteen* of us now!"

"Twelve." Monty corrected.

Standing a short distance away, Cynic's headless brother Ceann removed his spelling toy from behind his black leather clad back, and typed something into it. "YOU HAVE SPELLED: STAY." He pointed at himself.

Julian didn't like the man. He didn't know anything about him, but he didn't like him. He was Cynic's brother, and *anyone* associated with the Dullahan was worthy only of contempt.

Seth turned around in his chair to stare at Ceann in amazement. "And just what do *you* hope to get out of helping these morons?"

"YOU HAVE SPELLED: GLORY."

Seth snorted in dismissal.

"*Thirteen*." Tupilak announced smugly.

"Fourteen." Mack readjusted his sling. "It was *always* thirteen, and the headless fella makes it fourteen." He began ticking them off on his fingers. "Me, Polly, Jules, Monty, Arn, Oz, Mull, Roach, Doug, Ban, Quinn, Bee, the headless fella and..." He paused. "...Wait. Who am I missing?"

"Oh, who cares?" Tupilak began trying to wring the rain water from his thick fur mittens without taking them off. "The point is that our glorious army now contains a crippled old man, two people who are catatonic at all hours of the day, a man whose specialty is betrayal, an incorporeal computer projection, several people with no useful powers, an asshole with no powers *at all*, a dude with no head, and an agoraphobic who refuses to talk to anyone. And as scary as that is, a quarter of *those* people are not active heroes and won't take any part in doing anything *anyway*, which makes it even scarier." He nodded. "I think the Earth is doomed."

"The only thing that is doomed is the surface world!" Julian cried.

"...Yeah." Tupilak blinked at him. "That's kinda what I just said, boss."

"Oh." Julian cleared his throat. "Force of habit. Sorry."

"Well, I think I'll just leave you all to the dying, and squeeze out of the doors of the Alamo before you barricade yourselves inside." Seth got to his feet. "I have another appointment this afternoon, and as much as I enjoy spending time with all of my friends, I'm afraid this will have to be goodbye." He toasted the grave with his glass and sauntered away like he didn't have a care in the world. "I'll pray for you though."

Julian didn't even bother to turn his head. He never liked Seth. Not in all the time he'd known him. Honestly, Julian never particularly liked *any* of the gods.

Or the mortals.

Or *anything*, really.

The only thing that mattered to Julian was the sea and its life. They were his only family. The only things which reminded him that he wasn't as alone as he often felt.

Always felt, actually.

...And he would *have* his revenge. A revenge which would be all the simpler and come all the sooner now that he was the only Cape left standing; a very large shark in a tank filled with very small fish just *waiting* to be devoured. The surface world was populated with brine shrimp and he was a fucking *Megalodon*.

There would be no survivors.

He would *FEAST ON THEM*.

There was a certain poetic justice in that.

He sank down in the uncomfortable folding chairs as the other members got into another argument about a subject which Julian didn't understand. The surface-worlders were such a *baffling* species.

He didn't even *try* to understand them anymore.

He stared sightlessly at the grave and thought about the sound of the ocean. Unbidden, he began to hum "*Shenandoah*" under his breath, his mind a million miles away...

Tupilak glanced over from the seat next to him. "We're in deep shit, man." His voice was utterly serious. "You and me been through a lot, but I don't see a way out of this." He shook his head gravely. "We don't *do* field missions, boss. You *know* that."

Quinn was his second-in-command at the undersea base, and together with Bubonic, the three of them were basically its entire roster. With almost everyone else out of action though, they were also pretty much all that was left of the Consortium.

"The job of saving the world is now in our hands, and I *refuse* to let Ferral's remarkable failures as a leader spillover into my stewardship of this organization." Julian tried to sound sure of himself. "*He* may have been afraid to do what needs to be done, but I am not."

Quinn nodded and was silent for a long moment. "...You're *totally* going to take us back to villainy, aren't you? Finally destroy the surface world?"

Julian smiled evilly.

"Oh, Julian would never do something like *that*."

Julian turned in his chair to see Prometheus strolling through the rain towards the scene, somehow managing to keep the mud from staining his white linen suit.

"Why, Jules is on the verge of becoming this organization's breakout *star*. Every person in the country is going to know his name soon." He paused to stare down at the grave for a moment, removing his straw hat in respect. "Pity that Reece chose the path he did though. Betrayal always stings." He glanced at Julian. "So, was Wyatt *ever* friends with anyone who hasn't tried to kill him?"

"To even *meet* the man is to begin plotting his demise." Julian heaved a weary sigh, feeling his own pain at having to put up with Wyatt's difficult antics. "Are you here to join us, Prometheus? I'm told our membership is in the decline."

"Me?" Pro snorted in amused dismissal. "Good grief, no." He laughed again, as if the idea was the silliest thing he had ever heard. He glanced down at his pocket watch. "I have a lunch appointment, and I *don't* think you'd like it if I missed it."

Julian made a disinterested "Mmm" sound. He honestly didn't care about Pro's characteristic references to his prophesized future. Julian didn't like him. The man was a surface-dweller, and thus, not worth listening to.

None of them were.

They watched the grave in silence for a long moment.

Pro cleared his throat. "Oh, before I forget, I got a line on some badness about to go down. Crime to fight, and all that."

Julian didn't bother to turn his head. "I care not what happens to this world. It shall all be in my grasp within days anyway."

Pro ignored him. "Turns out, some baddies are about to blow up a dam and kill some people."

"Good." Julian said disinterestedly. "I hope the surface-worlders *suffer* before they go."

"The dam happens to contain the outer edge of Lake McKenzie." Pro let that news sink in, as if Julian should care for some reason. His smile faded slightly. "...As in, the 'Lake McKenzie Trout Hatchery?'" He tried.

Julian considered that for a moment.

The surface-dwellers were once AGAIN trying to destroy his innocent kinsmen. Their heartless evil was spreading from the seas to the blameless rivers now.

Every ocean, waterway, estuary and inlet on the planet, from the mightiest river to the smallest creek, *belonged* to Julian and Julian belonged to them. If one of them was imperiled, then he was *honor bound* to defend it.

Luckily, he wouldn't have to guard the innocent aquatic creatures of this world much longer. Soon, the terrestrials would be gone and all would be put right. His people and his lands would be safe.

And then no matter where he was, he would feel at home. He wouldn't be an outcast or a stranger ever again. He would *belong* and would be understood by everyone.

His loneliness would soon be *ended*, one way or the other.

He got to his feet. "We are leaving." He pointed to the vehicles. "We are needed. The innocent shriek for justice and we shall *answer their cries!*"

Mack put his face in his hand. "I can't believe you really just said that."

"*Get in the car!*" Julian snapped. "Tell the others."

They all filed into the rundown vehicles, and pulled through the gates and out onto the main road. Protestors massed around the cars, blocking their way.

"Cape wearing fascist *SWIIIIIIIIIIINE!*" The man with the sign drew the word out in a scream. "Freedom from super-powered oppressors!" He began to beat his fist against the window, raising and lowering his placard in time with the action and his words. "DEATH TO CAPES! DEATH TO CAPES! DEATH TO..."

Mack rolled down the window. "Get in the car, Arn." He deadpanned.

Arnold Benedix, AKA "Traitor," nodded and handed his sign to the man next to him. "Gotta go." He patted the man on the shoulder and held up his fist in a show of solidarity. "Stay strong, my brother. Keep up the struggle." He dashed off towards the car whistling merrily.

Traitor wasn't immoral; he was *amoral*. There was a difference. He wasn't violating any moral principles, because he simply didn't have any. He was possibly the only member of the Consortium who had no personal code, guidelines or rules. He'd do anything if he felt like doing it in that moment, and rarely gave any thought to a larger plan or strategy. But somehow, no one seemed to blame him for that. Julian wasn't sure if that was a result of the man's powers, or because it would be like trying to ascribe 'morals' to a snake. The snake wouldn't understand them, and it wouldn't listen to them even if it could. It would continue to behave according to its essential nature, no matter how right or wrong you thought its behavior was. Traitor was Traitor. You had to accept his moral emptiness and move on, because he didn't do the things he did and said out of malice, and besides, he wasn't going to change.

Julian didn't like him.

The vehicle sped from the scene, leaving the graves of fallen comrades behind. But Julian didn't care. He had other things on his mind at the moment.

Right now, those poor fish needed a hero.

CHAPTER 2

STORMS: "...ALL I'M SAYING IS THAT MAYBE WE
SHOULD GIVE THE GROUP THE BENEFIT OF THE DOUBT
FOR THE TIME BEING, AND SEE HOW WELL THEY CAN..."

KING (INTERRUPTING): "WELL, SURELY NOT EVEN YOU
ARE SO BLIND THAT YOU COULD POSSIBLY DEFEND
THEIR HEINOUS AND CRIMINAL ACTIONS AT THE DAM?"

STORMS: "...NO. NO, I DON'T THINK ANYONE COULD DO
THAT. YOU WOULD HAVE TO BE INSANE TO EVEN WANT
TO WATCH THAT FOOTAGE. ...IT'S SOMETHING THAT
WILL HAUNT ME FOREVER."

TRANSCRIPT OF "KING OF CAPES AND COWLS," MEDIA:
TELEVISION, SHOW: 1407, NEWSCHANNEL 6, FRIDAY
21:00-22:00 EST, NETWORK SEGMENT-ID:
918000606

Bridget Haniver didn't believe in heroes.

Not in the sense that she thought they were fictional, as she was certainly *aware* of their existence– hell, she had been president of their *fan club* at one point– just in the sense that she thought there was a difference between being a hero, and being *heroic.* In her entire life, she had only seen one *truly* heroic act, and it sure as hell wasn't performed by a Cape. Since then, the idea of professional hero-ing just left a bad taste in her mouth.

Not that she gave the matter much thought anymore though. She had long ago put away that notion, along with the other trappings of childhood.

No, Bridget lived in the *real world,* where super-heroes were just another group of over-the-top annoying pseudo-celebrities, who fought each other for space in the public consciousness by *physically* fighting each other in the streets. Their various drunken tirades, DUI arrests, sex scandals, secret identities, and inappropriate use of super powers against the paparazzi, filled the news almost every night. They were like reality TV stars, but they wore capes and fought crime. And since the Freedom Squad had had their fall from grace, things had gotten even *worse*. Now, everyone and their brother was claiming to be either the city's savior or the city's doom, and the whole field seemed to be changing into something else. She wasn't entirely sure what it was changing into, but it certainly wasn't the heroism her grandfather had told her about, or that she had grown up with. This was something new. Something not nearly as interesting or... *grand*. The majesty had been lost at some point, and now the heroes were all cape and no valor.

Bridget was honestly sick of even thinking about them. True, some of that could have been related to her past experiences with them, but mainly, it just had to do with the field as a whole. Plus, the TV news' "Special Reports" were beginning to interfere with her shows, and that was really annoying. The talking heads on screen never stopped blathering on, regurgitating their stale talking points about the same tired cast of characters, and at this point, it was all just white noise to her.

The Consortium of Chaos were the go-to Capes for the city now though, despite their troubled past. It was a sad state of affairs when a group of villains could take over the city and it seemed like a breath of fresh air compared to the other guys. At least the villainous heroes were *honest* about being terrible people. Still, she wasn't a huge fan of Capes in general anymore. Imagine the cast of *Jersey Shore* if they were granted fantastical cosmic powers, and unleashed upon an unsuspecting world which couldn't *possibly* stop them from doing whatever the hell they wanted.

If you were tied to the railroad tracks, would you really be screaming for Snooki to rescue you from the train bearing down on you as she flew by overhead? *Hell no*. You'd be better off getting run over.

Capes were like children with handguns; total power in the hands of immature creatures which couldn't be trusted. THAT'S why Bridget didn't believe in them. Thinking about them for any length of time would just ruin your day.

Bridget was sick of thinking about a lot of things though, so she was used to the feeling.

She absently ate another handful of bar peanuts and waited for her burger to arrive. Bridget ate lunch at the same bar every day. Not because she particularly *liked* the food– truth be told, it was dreadful– just because it was the closest place to her job, and it was simply what she *always* did.

She was currently working for a small firm as a press agent

and image consultant. She'd never really felt that it was her calling or anything like that, but it was fun sometimes and paid the bills.

Well... *some* of the bills anyway.

She'd always thought that she'd do something important with her life, but it was beginning to look like she'd been wrong about that.

At the very least, she had wanted to be *successful* at her career, but she'd been wrong about that too, and despite the talent she had assumed she had when she went into the field, she was wallowing at the bottom rung of the company. That was one of the disadvantages of not being related to someone in upper management, or having an impressive degree from somewhere amazing. For that matter, it was also the problem with not being amazing at the job itself.

There really wasn't *anything* amazing about Bridget.

She didn't have an extraordinary business accruement. Hell, a *salamander* could do her job as well as she could.

She didn't have an extraordinary mind. Despite years of study and countless attempts through trial and error, Microsoft's "Excel" program was still a baffling mystery to her. ...So many little boxes.

She didn't have any extraordinary talents. She tried to play the cello once in middle school, and had ended up breaking the music teacher's foot by dropping the instrument on him during the recital, and then as an encore, she fell off the stage. Her attempt at painting had ended up with her visiting the emergency optometrist to remove the "cadmium yellow" from her eye, and she had spent her junior year wearing a cast on her leg due to her only foray into sports.

She had no extraordinary friends. The only time she had a large circle of associates and actually met her idol... it hadn't gone well.

Hers was also not an extraordinary beauty, and she didn't have an extraordinary body. ...Well, it was extraordinary only in the bad sense. It was like saying that the ruins of the house which burned down was "extraordinary" compared to the other pretty and perfect little houses which surrounded it. It *was* certainly out of the ordinary, but it also wasn't anywhere someone would want to live.

She was several dress sizes overweight– if not more– and her face had a rounded Rubenesque or Greek Hellenistic sculpture quality to it. ...Or any other way of saying "chubby" without quite coming out and saying it, as she preferred to think of herself as a piece of art rather than merely being out of shape and too lazy to join a gym. Her job was to control the perceptions of the public, after all, and the "art" thing sounded better. She had planned on losing the weight over the summer, but she'd been wrong about that too, and had actually *gained* weight. As it turned out, ice cream was not a diet food, despite its all-natural ingredients and the happy cows on its label.

Bridget got a *lot* of things wrong, but she didn't care.

She was too bored to care. Nothing interesting ever happened in her life and unfortunately, in recent years, nothing interesting seemed to be happening in anyone else's either.

Bridget was an observer by nature, and there was nothing she enjoyed more than watching something curious which she had never seen before. But nothing had happened in years which caught her imagination, and so, she was bored most of the time. Not that she was depressed, as she was always in a fairly good mood, just that weird things amused her, and always had. She found people funny, but now their stand-up act was getting tired. Everyone told the same jokes lately, and Bridget was getting bored with the entire show.

Not that she *herself* was fascinating or anything. If her own life were a movie, Bridget would somehow *still* be a costar. Some insipid little stick-thin girl would be shoved to the forefront to play her, and Bridget would be recast as the vapid fake-Bridget's overweight but jolly friend. She would be there to make sure the audience recognized how thin and beautiful the actress playing "Bridget" was, and Real-Bridget's only scenes would be comic relief which showcased her own stupidity, to really drive home the message that being beautiful and thin also– by definition– meant that you were intelligent.

Bridget was her own fat comic relief.

But she didn't care.

She was fine with that, because it meant that she wouldn't be in every scene, and could instead focus on watching the other actors and critiquing their performances. Besides, everyone liked the "color" characters, right? It was the zany supporting cast which really completed a story, and they were the ones who everyone wanted.

...Well, except *men*, apparently. Bridget had always thought that there was a man out there for her, but once again, after years of bad experiences, she was beginning to think she had been wrong about that too.

Luckily, she didn't care. Bridget wasn't the type of person to dwell on setbacks or dreams of what she didn't have. Honestly, she didn't even give it much thought. She was a collector of human eccentricities, and the fact that she couldn't watch *other people* doing interesting and amusing things, bothered her much more than the fact that no one found *her* interesting or amusing.

It made no sense, but that's just the way it was. In fact, it was almost funny, but not in a good way. If the skinny bland actress portraying Bridget in "Bridget Haniver: The Movie!" could capture some of that— in what would no doubt be an otherwise uninspired and lackluster performance— Actual-Bridget would enjoy watching it while she waited to return to the set to look fat and say something stupid— which would probably involve hitting on some guy who would never go near her— which audiences would undoubtedly find amusing.

Oh, Movie-Bridget's fat friend. You'll never find love, you're too fat and stupid. It's funny that you'd even try.

Cue the laugh track.

Skinny-actress-Bridget shakes her head at Actual-Bridget's hijinks with what passes for "gentle amusement" in her limited acting range. Actual-Bridget exits the scene so that Skinny-Fake-Bridget can go back to making out with the muscular and *insufferably* hot male model playing the utterly fictional boyfriend that Skinny-Movie-Bridget is dating in the movie but Actual-Bridget has never met in real life, and debating whether to accept his pledge of *complete and total devotion*. Actual-Bridget will probably advocate sleeping with hot-male-model in her typical sassy and sexually charged way, with advice to Fake-Movie-Bridget like that she should "totally hook up" with that "yummy" Male-Model-Action-Star because "his bod is *slamming!*" or "ripped" and "girl, just check out those *pecs!*"

Skinny-Fake-Bridget is too focused on her burgeoning career as an astrophysicist or something though, and has no time for love, even with an *utterly* unobjectionable and empirically *perfect* man, willing to devote himself to her completely, and asking for absolutely nothing but the opportunity to make her already easy life even easier. Skinny-Movie-Bridget needs to focus on her needlessly complicated but impressive sounding job though, because audiences would *never* accept Actual-Bridget's real career.

Thin, beautiful— and thus *intelligent*— people shouldn't work in dead end jobs, they should be off doing exciting things which would lead them to both academic and financial success. Your worth as a human being is defined by your appearance and your job, after all, so Movie-Bridget would need to look like a Victoria Secret model and have a doctorate from Yale in something that audiences couldn't spell but were still impressed by for some reason. She would need to be a super serious scientist, and spout meaningless technical sounding nonsense, because Lord knew that no one wanted to watch someone who was something mundane like a press agent or a nurse on screen. There were the *children* to think about, and little girls needed to be told that if they studied hard, they could one day also achieve what Fake-Movie-Bridget had. ...Provided they were gorgeous, nineteen years old and built like a pin-up model. Otherwise they were screwed, because that meant they had lost the game of life, and no one would ever love them. Girls needed to be warned that they shouldn't strive to be happy, they should instead concern themselves only with their waistline and their salary.

In that respect, Fake-Movie-Bridget would really be inspiring for all the potential aspiring Little-Fake-Movie-Girls of the future. She was a role model, and the future would no doubt now be *filled* with scientifically minded sexpots, who somehow had stunning success and fame in an obscure and purely theoretical academic field, and who randomly and inexplicably found gorgeous and dedicated boyfriends wandering around isolated small towns, who mystifyingly hadn't been snatched up by someone else, despite their underwear ad good looks and tendency towards expressing their deepest emotions in tender scenes around desert campfires, before going off to fight giant killer robots from space in the film's climax.

Thanks to Fake-Movie-Bridget's efforts to tear down the barriers holding brilliant teenage models with great jobs back though, the future belonged to *them* now. Actual-Bridget and the rest of female humanity were just the fat comic relief who added levity to the scene. Their only use to the world was to convince Fake-Movie-Girl that she *deserved* love and that she's just had it so *hard* being thin and brilliant and successful and unaccountably adored by everyone she meets, and needs to focus on *her*.

Don't give up on love, Fake-Movie-Bridget. Allow yourself to *feel*.

It was like natural selection; the Fake-Movie-Girls would now just out-compete normal women, because they were simply not thin and sexy enough to be worthy of screen time in the movie of their own lives. They were just the rarely seen costars, only added when the scene was dragging and needed someone funny to arrive and spice things up with a sexy remark or superficial flippant attitude about the drama or craziness happening around them.

They had no storyline of their own. They didn't get billing on the movie's poster or do interviews with the press. They probably didn't even have last names in the film.

They were the rejects.

The fat comic relief.

Still... all in all, it did sound like a fairly entertaining film though.

Bridget especially liked the fat girl in the movie who played Bridget's best friend. You know? What's-her-name? She was funny. Someone should make a movie about her. ...They'd have to *recast*, obviously, but it would be a hoot.

She picked up her hamburger and took another bite.

"Bartender?" A man dressed in a weird straw boater hat and white linen suit seated a few stools away from her called. "I wonder if you would be so kind as to please turn on Channel 6? I don't want to miss my stories."

The man behind the bar reached up to switch the channel on the flatscreen suspended overhead, and the image immediately shifted to show a blonde woman with too much makeup, standing on a dam.

"...anks, Trevor." She said into her microphone. "This is Connie Storms at the new Weisinger Dam in Curry County." She gestured over her shoulder. "As you can see, authorities tell us that seven are believed dead, as members of the terrorist group known as the 'Mourning Haze' seized control of the dam an hour ago, and are threatening to blow it up unless their demands are met."

The image became a split screen, showing Connie Storms on one side and the anchors at the news desk in the studio on the other. Connie was the *poster girl* for Bridget's scary Stepford vision of the future. She was a perfect little blonde with a spunky 'can-do!' attitude, a great body, and she simply *oozed* an 'intrepid girl reporter' vibe straight from central casting. She'd won all kinds of international journalism awards, but still found the time to do 'on the scene' local reporting, just so people didn't forget how pretty her insipid little face actually was.

She was a fucking bitch. It was women like *HER* who made NORMAL women like Bridget look bad. They set the bar *impossibly* high, and made Bridget either want to hit an actual bar to get drunk, or grab the metaphorical 'impossible to top' bar and start beating bitches to death with it.

"Did you have any information on what the terrorists want, Connie?" The male anchor asked, with what sounded like carefully rehearsed concern. "Have they issued any demands?"

Connie shook her impeccably quaffed head. "No, Trevor. Authorities have evacuated the area around the dam and the communities downstream, but have released no information on..." She was cut off as someone pushed past her, blocking the entire screen for a moment and then continuing on their way.

Bridget chewed thoughtfully as the camera moved to focus on the man in question.

Dressed like one of the *300* at a pool party, the image of Lord Sargassum was *unmistakable*.

She smiled in spite of herself.

The Consortium didn't really let that guy take the lead on much. In fact, they didn't really let him take the lead on *anything*. ...Most likely because he was insane, but for a *connoisseur* of the ridiculous and bizarre such as Bridget, he was an *endless* source of amusement.

Besides, the man had his moments. ...Not lately, and certainly not many, but when he had them, they were incredible.

And if nothing else, he was certainly more fun to look at than the rest of them. Hell, *Chippendales* dancers wore more than he sometimes did, and his tiny costume showed off all the impressive angles and bulges which came with being a god and a superhero. Swimmers really did have the *best* bodies, and his tanned skin set off his black hair quite nicely. His eyes shown with the color of the waters he called home. Even his *teeth* were perfect. The man was like a painting of a Roman god brought to life... which was probably understandable, as she was pretty sure that's what he was. ...Or something. Honestly, she'd never really been entirely clear on that, and he appeared in public so rarely, it wasn't really widely known. It was the equivalent of trying to figure out Bigfoot's ancestry by waiting to ask him directly. He wasn't around a lot to do interviews, and on the rare occasion when you *were* looking at him, wondering about his history was the *last* thing on your mind.

Connie Storms watched the man for a moment, trying to weigh the chances that he would talk to her.

Bridget put her odds at "shit outta luck." Connie would simply receive a curt dismissal, and most likely an insult about her job, her appearance, and her ground-based lifestyle.

Bridget ate another French fry.

Good.

She found herself *eagerly* anticipating watching Sargassum cut that bitch down to size. She was about to meet the *one man in the world* who wouldn't be affected by her perfect face and her pert little body. Sargassum would hate her simply because she wasn't a fish.

This was going to be *beautiful*...

Sadly, Connie evidently came to the same conclusion as Bridget about her chances of an interview, and scanned the road for someone else to speak with. The camera panned back around to focus on a masked figure a short distance away, who appeared to be transparent.

The reporter hurried across the street, holding the microphone up to the individual. "...*Multifarious*, right?" She asked, obviously trying to place the obscure Cape's name.

...Okay. Bridget had to give her credit for that one. That was pretty impressive. Bridget had *no idea* who that person was. She knew most of the Freedom Squad, but the Consortium was still a mystery. There were way too many of them, and they were all insane. She recognized *Sargassum,* obviously, but the rest of them were kind of a blur.

The transparent figure turned his/her Kilroy etched facemask to look over at her. "I am not Multifarious. Today I am..."

"I'm Connie Storms with Channel 6 Action News," the reporter interrupted, "can you tell us what the terrorists are asking for?"

"How the *BLEEP* should *I* know, lady?" The masked Cape asked, his/her words censored by someone at the network who was very good at their job, since the broadcast was live. "Do I really look like someone who pays attention to what other people want?"

Connie cleared her throat. "Well, what can you tell us about the situation?"

Multifarious shrugged. "Well... there's a dam involved. And terrorists. And the hot chick from the news is here."

Bridget snickered and ate another fry.

These heroes were *way* more fun than the usual group.

Connie was undeterred. "Well, can I at least ask you what your powers are, exactly? Are you made of diamond or something?"

"Glass." Multifarious informed her calmly. "Today, I am *Glass Hammer!*" The Cape raised a glass war hammer high over his/her head. "The light of justice shines through me! Crime will break, and evil will shatter!"

The reporter blinked. "...You want to go into a fight, even though you're made of *glass?* Is that a good idea?"

"Hey, leave Mull alone, lady." A rough looking man in a trucker hat and wearing a sling on his arm snapped. The guy had a heavy and muscled build, dark hair and obviously hadn't bothered to shave in several days. He looked like a rugged mixture of a truck driver, a mountain man, and a street thug. His voice was deep, with a southern drawl, and his nose looked like it had been busted more than a few times. "Some days the powers kind of suck, but even made of glass, Mull could still kick *your* scrawny lil' ass." He gestured towards the dam's control room. "So, unless you wanna try *your* luck against some terrorists, butt the *BLEEP* out and let us work, okay?"

That guy in the control booth at the censor button was really, *really* good.

The trucker leaned closer to his companion. "...She has a point though. Figure you should prolly sit this one out. One good hit and you're *done*. Maybe tomorrow you'll have a power that don't handicap ya."

Multifarious looked pointedly down at the sling on the man's arm, and then back up at him, as if pointing out that he wasn't exactly 100% today either. "Those in glass houses, Mack."

The reporter let out a long breath of annoyance and looked around the street as more Capes with the Consortium trickled onto the scene with the enthusiasm of teenagers showing up for detention after school. Most of the actual team was currently MIA in Agletaria, so this was evidently kind of the B-squad.

For some reason, Bridget found that idea rather appealing.

She ate another fry.

The camera zoomed in on a conversation taking place between Lord Sargassum and a smaller man dressed in a top hat and long 19th century looking black overcoat and suit. There was something rather sinister about the second man, but Bridget couldn't put her finger on what. Something... *wrong*. It wasn't the fact that his one eye was injured or the fact that he was missing a finger and walked with a limp, it was something *else* which made her fearful of him. Something hidden. Something about the man himself; his soul, or lack thereof.

He didn't have the usual Cape physique of bulging muscles, sparkling eyes and chiseled jawline. His skin was on the pale side and he had a lean and hungry look about him. His eyes were like a shark's; dead cold and utterly emotionless. If his face had ever once been handsome, it now indicated only a sly menace, as if he were always cooking up some new ruthless scheme. He had an unpleasant smile, and he carried himself with a sort of murderous mixture of shrewd craftiness and lethal boldness. He spoke with a husky, whispering, somewhat broken voice, but one with an edge of educated refinement and culture, as if he had grown up in serious old money somewhere. It was difficult to imagine any words of kindness ever passing his lips.

There was something displeasing and unsettling about him, and whatever it was, Bridget had never seen anyone she disliked so much, so quickly.

"...leadership?" The evil looking man in the top hat finished his thought, the rest of which was lost. "No. You do not. I am the only one here who has *any* experience with it, and therefore, I'm not about to take orders from you. If *you* want someone to circle around the building, I suggest that you do it *yourself*." He gestured nonchalantly with a gloved four-fingered hand. "Call in a school of fish, or lead a cavalry charge of seahorses or something."

Sargassum drew himself up to his full height. "I am KING!"

"So was Louis XVI at one time, but the world has moved on since then, Julian." 'Ebenezer Scrooge: Year One' said as he started strolling towards the control center where the terrorists were lurking, limping on a bad leg. "I have no desire to engage in heroics. Frankly, I couldn't *possibly* care less what happens here today, and view all of this as a *tremendous* bother..."

Bridget's eyebrows shot up, surprised that a Cape would ever say that on live TV, no matter how obviously evil he was. The man *knew* the camera was there, he just simply didn't care. Bridget wasn't sure if she should be impressed by the man's confidence, or scared.

"...but I will be damned if I will allow someone as useless as *you* to order me around. *I* should be in charge of this mission and this organization. Until then, I am merely here to watch you fall flat on your face." He made a show of checking his pocket watch. "And I *sincerely* doubt I will have to wait very long for that opportunity."

Bridget's eyes narrowed, silently willing Sargassum to club the man to death like a baby seal.

Sargassum grabbed him by his arm and spun him around. "I am third in command after the Commodore and Ferral. ME." He brought the trident in his hand closer to the other man's face. "And *I* will be damned if I will allow a powerless *surface-dweller* to try to usurp my rightful position, *especially* as this particular crime involves the waters of..."

"Maybe we should argue 'bout this *later*, boys." The man in the battered trucker cap snapped. The hat read 'Burton's Arcade' in a colorful 1980s looking font, and had seen better days. "We could just go..."

"What's going on?" Called another man. The camera swept around to show OCD standing in the middle of the access road a short distance away, evidently staying off of the dam itself for some reason. "Why aren't you going in there to stop them?"

"Why aren't *you* going in there to stop them, Oswald?" Asked the evil Monopoly man. "If you're so desperate, feel free." He made a sweeping motion with his arms towards the control room, inviting the other man forward. "Have at it."

"I told you, I'm not crossing that line." OCD pointed at a jagged red line spray-painted onto the cement street in front of him.

"Red is a *bad* color. You cross red lines on the ground, you get brain cancer."

The man in the trucker hat put his face in his palm. "Aw, Jesus."

A person dressed in a medieval plague doctor costume was crouched inside the Consortium's battered car, arms held up over their masked face, slowly rocking back and forth. A man who appeared to be in his early twenties and was dressed as an Eskimo was trying to talk to the person and coax them towards the scene. He tried the handle. "Unlock the door." He pulled on the handle several more times. "Come on. You're going to have to get out of the car *eventually*, you know." His voice took on a comforting tone. "There's nothing to be afraid of out here. Just your friends... and some terrorists and their bombs, but *mainly* your *friends*."

The camera swung back around to where the fight over the leadership of the team was still raging.

"I AM IN CHARGE!" Sargassum roared, pushing the smaller man backwards. "I AM THE MONARCH OF THE SEAS AND LEADER OF THIS TEAM!"

"*Are* you now?" The top hat man asked calmly and snapped his fingers. "Let's *vote on that*, shall we?"

The area around him suddenly filled with a dozen burly men dressed like industrial workers from the nineteenth century. Just how they had arrived on the scene was anyone's guess, but they moved to threateningly surround Sargassum.

He spun his trident around, as the situation spiraled out of control. "You WILL follow my commands!"

"Will I?" The top hat man asked calmly. "Funny, that doesn't *sound* like me."

Bridget gave up even *trying* to eat her meal, and focused all of her attention on the scene.

A new figure stalked onto the dam, ignoring his battling teammates and prowling towards the control center like Death himself. He was dressed all in black leather, a tattered long black fabric cape blowing behind him in the breeze. His heavily muscled right arm was bare and covered with ancient looking red and black Celtic tattoos, from his shoulder to the edge of the black leather gloves he wore.

The camera zoomed in on the place where his head should be... but it simply wasn't there.

Wow.

Bridget took another bite of her burger. This team was

soooooo much more interesting than the other one.

The cameraman whispered something to the reporter who emphatically pointed back to the fight between Sargassum and Scrooge McAsshole.

The man in the trucker hat and the sling was trying to get between them. "Come on fellas, put them away, okay? You're *both* pretty. Maybe we should focus on the bad people fixin' to kill all these nice folks and..."

"I DON'T CARE WHAT HAPPENS!" Sargassum snapped. "THE SURFACE WORLD ABOVE *DESERVES* TO BE DROWNED IN FEAR! ALL WILL SUFFER!"

Wow.

"*Unlock the fucking door or I'll set the car on fire!*" The Eskimo shouted from somewhere off screen, still trying to get his friend to exit the car. "What on Earth are you even afraid of? Huh? It's just..."

"Lasciami in pace!" Squeaked the muffled voice from inside the car, cutting him off. "*Vattene!*"

"I don't speak FUCKING *ITALIAN!* I DON'T KNOW..." The Eskimo paused. "...Are you hyperventilating? You *know* you're not supposed to do that! Breathe into a paper bag or something before you pass out again!" The microphone picked up the sound of his fist smashing against the car's roof repeatedly. "*RELAX, GODDAMMIT, RELAX!* RIGHT FUCKING NOW!!!"

The camera shot back around to where the headless guy was continuing to stalk towards the control room.

"Where do you think *you're* going!?!" Sargassum yelled after the headless man, closing the distance between them. "Did I *tell you* to go in there!?! No!" He pointed at his evil top-hatted companion. "I told *Welles!*"

The headless man turned towards him for a long moment... then pulled out a *freaking broad sword!* The weapon burst into flames.

"HOLY SHIT!" Gasped the cameraman.

Obviously the network censor couldn't catch everything.

Bridget laughed in amused excitement and dipped one of her fries into the ketchup. If she had friends, she'd be texting them right now to turn on the TV to watch this. Finally, something *interesting!*

When she looked up again, the headless man, the trucker, several of the top hat man's stooges, and Sargassum were tussling like eight year old little girls. There was some pushing and shoving and shouted name-calling. Someone pushed the trucker and the man was knocked clean through the door of the dam's control room and into the structure itself.

The headless man and Sargassum continued yelling at one another, the headless man using what appeared to be an old spelling toy for his side of the argument. Then both of them yelled at the top hat man. The top hat man said something which seemed to just piss them off *more*, and a moment later, they were once again locked in childish combat. Sargassum and the headless man tussled with each other and crashed through a window in the control room at the center of the dam.

The camera zoomed in closer on the area as shadows moved inside... then a fiery sword blade cut clean through the wall and into the road surface, gouging a deep swath of destruction.

One of the top hat man's henchmen was shoved through a *different* window, then raced around the structure to the door to rejoin the fight.

The trucker pulled himself from the building as it rapidly got destroyed around him, and looked down at the road. "We got a SERIOUS problem here, boys!" He pointed down at the dam, apparently seeing something which concerned him. "I think we should *deal* with this before..."

"I AM IN CHARGE!" Sargassum roared over him, utterly ignoring his warnings. "I will destroy these meaningless terrorists for endangering the innocent trout of this river, I will destroy *Welles* for not going in there to destroy the terrorists, I will destroy *Ceann* for *trying* to go in there to destroy the terrorists without my order, and *then* I will be able to focus on the destruction of the *entire surface world!*"

The fight erupted again.

Bridget snickered.

The man in the trucker hat yelled into the structure at his quarreling teammates . "Can you PLEASE stop that? I don't give a shit WHO is in charge, but it needs to be SOMEONE! 'Cause this is..."

The headless man and Sargassum crashed through the side of the building and back onto the street, scattering plaster and bricks around the area.

Bridget gasped in astonishment.

The man in the top hat disinterestedly checked his pocket watch, as though bored.

Several people– who could only be the terrorists formally hidden inside the building before it was destroyed– ran from the structure in an effort to escape its collapse. One of them made a frantic movement with his hands, gesturing for his companions to flee the area for some reason.

As the first terrorist ran by, the headless man absently decapitated him, the way someone would swat a fly away while staying focused on more important things.

The cameraman swore again.

The terrorist's body turned to ash and its momentum carried it forward another few feet, before it crashed into the pavement and disintegrated in a shower of glowing embers.

The top hat man stepped to the side to avoid the cascade of fiery terrorist.

There was a muffled sound from inside the destroyed control room of the dam, followed by several other louder explosions. Presumably, the altercation had inadvertently set off the terrorists' bombs or perhaps the fight *itself* was now bringing down the structure.

Whatever the reason behind it, the headless man turned to look back at the noise.

Sargassum and the top hat man paid no attention, beginning their argument again.

The man in the trucker hat swore quite artfully, the censor unable to catch everything due to the sheer density and creativity of the rich tapestry of profanity he effortlessly wove.

The Eskimo and the Plague Doctor continued their bilingual argument.

Multifarious/Glass Hammer casually dropped a quarter into the tower viewer binoculars set up on the dam, and absently scanned the surrounding area, taking in the natural beauty of the site.

The noise got louder and was followed by a strange ripping sound as the concrete began to separate around the control room.

A French fry stopped halfway to Bridget's mouth.

Uh-oh...

The headless man took off, trying to make it off the dam before the whole thing came down. He raised his spelling toy, and a black stallion appeared at the other end of the dam and raced towards him. He somehow managed to pull himself onto it despite the fact that it didn't slow down, and galloped towards land.

Everyone else followed suit.

The cameraman swore again and the image became a confusing jumble as the man dashed towards safety. He dove the last few feet, and there was a horrifying sound of twisting metal and shattering concrete, as the ruined dam was swept away by the power of the rushing water behind it.

The party got back to their feet.

The sinister man in the top hat began to clap very slowly at Sargassum, sarcastically commending him for a job well-done.

Several police officers standing at the end of the access road joined suit, mockingly applauding the *entire* Consortium for completely bungling the situation.

The camera swung around to focus on OCD as he stood in the center of the road a short distance away. "What happened?" He craned his neck in an effort to see over the edge of the cliff without crossing the red line on the pavement. "Did we win? That didn't sound good."

The person dressed as a plague doctor peaked out through the window of the car behind him, saw the camera, and hid again.

"...We don't have to pay for that, do we?" Asked the Eskimo worriedly. "...'Cause it looked expensive."

The terrorists slowly started backing away while everyone was distracted, and then took off.

Multifarious/Glass Hammer absently swung the glass war hammer at one of the terrorists as he ran by, and knocked him off of his feet from the force of the impact. The weapon shattered but not before driving the six inch glass spike on one end of the war hammer straight through the man's head. The masked Cape then turned to casually stab the broken handle of the weapon into the other man as he dashed by.

The reporter swore as she and the camera lens were showered with the terrorist's blood. The man staggered away, the huge shard of glass sticking out of his chest right below his collar bone. He grabbed at the reporter, trying to hold himself on his feet and plead for help.

The reporter screamed in horror.

The group absently turned to watch the man's death struggles, looking either mildly intrigued by the scene or annoyed at the noise.

Bridget found that she simply didn't care about the man's pain either. Fuck him. He killed *seven innocent people* today. His death was making for good TV.

Sargassum continued looking down the valley as the released water swept away everything in its path; houses, roads and trees.

The man in the trucker hat pointed at Multifarious. "What the hell!?! Huh!?!' He flicked a finger against the Kilroy mask covering his friend's face, producing a 'ting' sound. "You're made of *glass* today and you STILL can't just sit still!?!"

"You're a 'glass is half empty' person, you know that, Mack? *MY* glass is half *full...* of *justice!*" Multifarious shoved him in annoyance, knocking him backwards into the mortally wounded terrorist, who then fell onto the reporter's feet. The terrorist hit the ground face first, driving the shard of glass clean through his body and splashing more blood onto the reporter.

Her screams were hysterical now; blood covering her from head to toe.

The Capes didn't appear to care. Multifarious snickered.

After another moment of silently contemplating the scene of the disaster, Sargassum turned back to his companions. "I blame the city for this." He told them seriously as if it were an important realization which he had long deliberated on. "They never should have built those houses there."

The remote satellite feed went to test pattern, and was replaced with the talking heads at the station. The anchors stared at their monitors in slack-jawed amazement.

Bridget very slowly put her forehead down on the bar in front of her and began to beat it against the smooth surface.

That was just a public relations *nightmare.* Offhand, she couldn't think of *anything* worse they could have done, and since they were all currently accused of basically singlehandedly starting a war with another country this week, that was really saying something.

She just... She just...

Wow.

The TV began running video of Sargassum from a 1940's newsreel. The grainy black and white footage showed the man standing on top of a submarine, poking holes in it with his trident in an effort to drown the men inside.

She let out another sigh.

He was... well, he was clueless. *Utterly* incapable of dealing with people. With him in charge of the Consortium, it would be a matter of days before the villagers stormed the Lair with torches and chased all the Capes into a burning windmill or something. He was TERRIBLE at dealing with the public, had no idea what a Cape was actually supposed to do, and was the proverbial fish out of water in surface world culture.

The man was impossible.

He was a walking media *disaster.*

She let out another sigh and tossed a handful of bills onto the bar for her meal. She marched from the restaurant and back onto the street.

Sadly, she owed the man. *Big*. So, she felt responsible for helping him with this.

Whether he liked it, or not.

She arrived at the spot where she had parked her car... and found only an empty space. Beside it, the man in the white linen suit from the bar lounged against the parking meter.

"I think someone stole your car." He shook his head sadly. "Looks like you're going to have to take a cab, miss."

Bridget's eyes narrowed in silent rage. Criminals in this city needed to be taught a lesson. A *serious* lesson. And luckily, she knew *just* the ex-criminals to do it.

CHAPTER 3

KING: "I DON'T KNOW WHY YOU ALWAYS ARGUE WITH ME ON THIS, CONNIE. THE FACT REMAINS THAT CAPES ARE A TOOL OF THE STATUS QUO. THEY ARE THE UNCONSTITUTIONAL FIST WHICH BIG GOVERNMENT USES TO KEEP THE AVERAGE TAXPAYER DOWN, AND THE DISTRACTION IT USES TO KEEP THEM FROM REALIZING HOW BAD THINGS HAVE GOTTEN. THEY ARE BIG GOVERNMENT'S HAMMER TO QUASH DISSENT, AND THEIR 'BREAD AND CIRCUSES' TO KEEP THE MASSES COMPLIANT."

STORMS: "OH, THAT'S NOT TRUE, PAIGE. CAPES WORK WITH THE GOVERNMENT, NOT FOR THE GOVERNMENT. BESIDES, SOME OF THESE PEOPLE ARE JUST TRYING TO HELP, AND ARE THEMSELVES DEALING WITH ALL MANNER OF PERSONAL..."

KING (INTERRUPTING): "I DON'T CARE WHAT THEY'VE DONE IN THEIR PASTS, ALL I CARE ABOUT ARE THE CRIMES THEY'VE COMMITTED."

TRANSCRIPT OF "KING OF CAPES AND COWLS," MEDIA: TELEVISION, SHOW: 1407, NEWSCHANNEL 6, FRIDAY 21:00-22:00 EST, NETWORK SEGMENT-ID: 918000606

16 Years Ago

Julian staggered backwards as the fist impacted his face, causing him to trip over a park bench in the process. His opponent took the opportunity to attempt a killing blow. The shirtless masked Cape who went by the name "Sledgehammer" raised his namesake weapon high and brought it down at Julian's head.

Julian rolled to the side so that the hammer crashed into the pavement, and he kicked his opponent's legs out from under him. Julian pulled himself back to his feet just in time to see his companions racing towards the midway.

Half an hour before, Julian, Poacher and the New Guy, who

went by the absurd moniker "The Cynic" had been part of a Freedom Squad transport destined to take them to the SeaCastle Asylum. While on route, the armored van had been taken out by the Consortium's resident rescue operative, "Harlot." ...Who was an eleven year old girl. The surface worlders evidently taught their young how to use missile launchers early though, as the child had managed to disable the vehicle and free them with no difficulty.

Sadly, her escape plan had not actually included an *extraction* per se, and thus Julian was sprinting through this terrestrial amusement park in a running battle with seemingly *everyone in the Freedom Squad*.

All in all, his morning could be going better.

He'd *certainly* had worse though, so he wasn't complaining. Yet.

When he got back to the Lair, he was going to have words with the Commodore about this matter though. The man had no business sending his daughter out on dangerous missions unless she was old enough to actually *drive* a getaway car. Otherwise, the entire endeavor was *preposterous*.

Poacher leapt over a decorative planter like an Olympic hurdler, despite the fact that he was currently carrying the girl in question and brandishing an elephant gun. He spotted Julian and called to him. "Hey! 'Jacques Cousteau!' We gotta *haul ass!*" He ducked under a sword swung by a man dressed as a medieval knight, and immediately kicked the man in the groin with one large combat boot, somehow managing to keep his own body between his attacker and the girl in his arms the entire time. The knight fell to his knees groaning and Poacher swung the heavy elephant gun like a club, knocking the man to the concrete and leaving a very impressive dent in the knight's helmet.

Julian ignored him and continued running for the park exit. The Freedom Squad theme park stretched over 160 acres of Coney Island, and Julian was finding that he didn't much *like* this place.

Terrestrials were "amused" by the oddest things.

Behind them, "The Cynic" continued laughing manically. No matter what name he was currently going by, Julian didn't like the Dullahan either. The Irishman was insane, and had once basically destroyed the world, if only for a few hours. Not that Julian was exactly *in love* with the world to begin with, but the man's thoughtless use of his powers had endangered the seas, and thus, he was Julian's enemy for life.

As they ran through an intersection of the park, where a

colorful recreation of "Supertron, Captain Dauntless' Home Planet" intersected with "The Honey Badger's Burrow," a group of park employees dressed in large fiberglass heads designed to look like the Capes in question appeared from behind a door marked "Heroes Only."

The Dullahan laughed again and charged at the characters, who saw him racing towards them and took off running. This just made the other man laugh louder, and he threw himself at them, trying to wrench the heads off, either because he thought owning one would be funny or because he was crazy enough to believe them to be the *actual* heroes. In either case, the costumed employees continued tussling with him, as more and more park employees dressed in fiberglass Cape heads emerged from behind the door and began to try to aide their endangered comrades. The Dullahan smashed his fist into a fiberglass "Fabricator" character, knocking the employee to the ground, and then he pounced on top of him, continuing to pummel the mask with reckless delight and maniacal giggling. The mob of costumed characters surrounded the Dullahan and began to return blows with whatever makeshift weapons were handy.

Julian ignored them, not bothering to slow down to help the Dullahan extricate himself from his predicament.

Screw him.

Julian didn't risk himself for surface-dwellers, *least* of all the Eternal people who had mocked him in his youth. ...Not that the Dullahan had actually *been* one of those people. Truth be told, the Dullahan had been persona non grata in the Eternal community for as long as Julian could remember. Not even the *Irish* wanted to talk about that psycho, and they were his family.

But it was the *principle* of the thing.

All his life, Julian had been forced to endure the disdain of those people. Had to listen to their whispers as he passed.

How his mother was a lowly *mortal* and how he would never amount to anything.

How his father's powers had evidently skipped a generation, and how it was for the best that Julian was alone, lest he pass on his mortal *deformities* to future generations.

Listen as they told Julian that he was the bastard son of a heartless son-of-a-bitch and a mortal whore.

Listen as everyone he knew told him how much *better* it would have been for the world if *his father* had been the one to survive the war, and not Julian. How much better it would be for the oceans if *any* other god of the sea, from *any* other pantheon had survived instead of Julian. How much better it would have been for all involved if Julian had never existed at all.

How he was a *failure*.

Useless.

Weak.

That he was some kind of genetic half-breed, who *should* have been killed at birth.

That no one had ever loved him, and that his mother had chosen the ill-fated path she did rather than be burdened with him for the rest of her short mortal life.

No.

The only thing Julian hated more than being alone, was being around *those* people. He had long ago chosen solitude rather than their company, and he didn't regret that decision. Not in the *slightest*.

The masked park employees raised the Dullahan up on their shoulders and began to carry him off as he struggled and cursed against the mob of caricatures.

But Julian didn't care.

Let the man hang.

The Dullahan might not have *technically* been one of those people, but he was close enough for Julian.

All surface-dwellers and *all* Eternals were alike.

They were Julian's *enemies*.

Everyone was.

Poacher hesitated for a moment, obviously trying to decide whether to go back for the man or not. He looked down at the small dark-haired girl clutched in his arms, swore in a manner that *no one* who was holding a child should swear, then continued barreling forward.

Julian raced to keep up with him. If he could just make it to the ocean, everything would be fine. He'd be home. *No one* could touch him in the water.

Poacher turned his head to call back to him. "The exit's up ahead! I took Harl here a few weeks ago, and the gates are..."

The rest of his words were cut off by an explosion which rocked the area and sent them both sprawling. Julian was knocked through the window of a building and he tumbled down a flight of wooden stairs into a subterranean theater of some kind.

Surface-dwellers and their children scattered in fear as he landed in a heap at the bottom of the auditorium.

Good.

They *should* fear him.

Everyone should fear him, as he was a being of irresistible might and *overpowering* vengeance. He was punishment made flesh! He was the justice of his people!

He pulled himself to his feet with all the dignity he could muster, sweeping his black seaweed inspired cloak over his shoulder and eyeing his enemies.

"Watery *death* has come to your shores, mortals!" He raised his trident. "The time of reckoning for your crimes against my people has finally arrived! Make your peace with whichever gods will still have you!"

Half of the audience stubbornly refused to budge from their seats though, despite the fact that this obviously *wasn't* part of the show.

Julian pointed at them. "All who remain to face my retribution shall receive *no mercy*!"

They continued eating their popcorn.

He rolled his eyes.

Fucking tourists.

"I will *kill you* if you stay here." He reiterated, trying again to carefully explain the situation to them. "Understand?" He pointed towards the doors to the theater. "Run! Run, fools, *run!*"

The mother snapped a picture with her camera.

Julian threw his hands up in exasperation.

Unbelievable.

Surface-worlders were just so...

The sledgehammer caught him in the side of the face and all but took his head off. The force of the blow spun him around and sent him sprawling several feet away. It was just a glancing blow, but it had done the trick.

The Cape emerged from a side room, weapon in hand. "Come quietly, or come *apart*." He said emotionlessly.

Julian reached a hand up to straighten his jaw, a thin stream of blood already oozing from the corner of his mouth. He was *not* a god of war. He was by *no means* impervious to injury.

He pulled himself to his feet again, trying to maintain his regal dignity. "Do you know who I *am*, mortal?" He waved his trident at him again. "I am Lord Julian Sargassum! King of the Oceans and..."

The sledgehammer hit him in the stomach, harder this time.

Julian staggered back from the force of the blow, and impacted a wall. Another shot like that, and Julian was *done*.

He reached out his hand to support himself against the wall's strangely cool surface, his vision swimming. He blinked rapidly trying to focus…

And his breath caught in his throat.

A vision floated before him like some aquatic dream…

He blinked again, assuming that it was merely some kind of hallucination, but the vision remained.

Behind the glass wall he was leaning against, an honest to god *mermaid* was gently floating in the cool water. Her dark hair drifted around her face, highlighting her porcelain skin and soft curves.

…Julian had never seen such a thing in his entire life. He had often dreamed of it though. Imagined that *somewhere* in his kingdom, there was hidden a woman of his kind. A mate. Someone who would *understand* him…

The meaningless battle was *instantly* forgotten.

Julian pressed his hand to the glass, hypnotized by this ghostly visitor's spell. She was wearing a top made to look like seashells, and had a fish-like tail, which was oddly sparkly. Julian had *certainly* never seen any sea creature with a tail like that before, but he was beyond caring.

Bubbles gently floated to the surface from the mermaid's nose and mouth, as she watched him through the glass with wide intelligent eyes.

…Strangely, Julian found himself unable to communicate with this incredible woman though. Normally, the glass would not interfere with his ability to converse with sea life, but in this case, he tragically was unable to make himself heard.

The stunning woman continued watching him silently.

At first, she had appeared almost scared of him, but now she appeared… curious? Amused? Julian had no idea. He had never met a mermaid before, so he had no idea what their facial expressions were like. They were a magical species, which up until today, had been entirely fictional.

She was young though, that much was evident. *Far* younger than *Julian's* eternal years. Had she been a surface-dweller, she would only be in her late teens. …Just a child.

Since she was of an enchanted race though, there was really no way of knowing how old she was.

Julian pressed his other hand against the glass, forgetting it was even there.

The woman did the same, and Julian imagined that he could feel the warmth of her soft skin through the cold glass.

In his mind, this strange dazzling woman and he were already exploring the depths of the ocean together. …Sharing the beauty of his kingdom. Sharing the wonders of the untamable sea, and his deepest thoughts which he had never before shared with anyone.

The mermaid's dark green eyes seemed to sparkle and dance like the water she floated in. Her full lips parted slightly in a hint of a smile and she gave him a slight wave with one elegant hand.

His heart melted.

The woman was simply...

The sledgehammer hit him in the side this time, tearing him away from the window and propelling him through the first row of wooden bleachers in the theater.

He smashed into the seats, dazed for a moment but still conscious. It felt like he had broken several ribs, and it was now difficult to breathe without pain.

His bleary eyes focused on the banner proclaiming the theater to be "Retiarius' Aquatic 'Sea-ater.'" The image on the sign was that of the Roman fisherman, *long* familiar to Julian.

He almost smiled, his vision instantly clearing again.

Typical.

Leave it to his *mortal enemy* to have his own theater to celebrate his exploits, and his own *mermaid*. The man was the greatest foe the oceans ever had. His entire *existence* was dependent on plundering the waves and murdering its peaceful inhabitants.

He was Julian's *nemesis*.

...And *now* he had the only thing that Julian had ever wanted.

The mermaid in question brought her small hand up to her face in astonishment at the unexpected attack which had knocked Julian off his feet, and for the first time ever...

Julian felt...

Pissed off.

Not hurt, or wracked with grief, or weighed down with his noble duties and the knowledge that he could never fulfill them.

He was *angry.*

All of his life, he'd been told that he was a loser. That he was a half-breed. That he was a mutant. That his powers were useless. That he had too much of his mother in him. That no one would ever love him or ever could. That his life's work was stupid and that his people were unworthy of life because some Divine power had made them taste good to savages. But he patently *REFUSED* to suffer the indignity of defeat in front of the only woman he had ever seen who might understand his loneliness. The only one who could see how isolated life under the sea could sometimes be when you were an outcast. The only woman above or below the waves who had *ever* made him feel like this. The only one who could see... him. Plain and simple.

The only one who could see *him*.

He pulled himself to his feet again, not even bothering to appear graceful or dignified. He was out for blood, and he didn't care *how* he appeared to the surface-dwellers or anyone else this time. His opponent had *DARED* to lay his hands upon the King of the Ocean, and more *importantly*, had frightened the mermaid. Some things were just simply *not done* in the super-powered trade, and frightening such a magical creature was one of them. In the *old days,* no self-respecting Cape would have *ever* hit Julian in front of a woman, *especially* not while his back was turned. It was one of the main unwritten rules! Everyone knew it!

The man would pay *dearly* for that.

Sledgehammer swung the weapon at him again, but Julian simply caught its handle on its downward swing before it could make contact.

He eyed the man coldly, then ripped the weapon from him and tossed it aside. The man stared at him in astonishment for a moment, then moved to hit him. Julian didn't give him the chance. He slammed his fist into the man's stomach, doubling him over, and then punched him in the face as hard as he could.

The man went sprawling, and was propelled through a nearby door to the janitor's closet. He impacted the far wall, cracked the cement from the force of the blow, and knocked the shelves of cleaning supplies down on himself.

Julian eyed the man coldly for another moment, silently *daring* him to rise, then bent to retrieve his trident from the ground.

He turned to look at the poster which featured his nemesis' smiling image from his more youthful days. Julian thought about how *satisfying* it would be to do the same to Retiarius. The man was *far* more deserving of a throttling than this surface-dweller had been. But Julian had never been able to best the other man, despite countless attempts. His archenemy was seemingly *always* one step ahead. His was an evil which could never be bested, no matter how many times Julian tried.

...In fact, offhand, Julian couldn't recall *ever* besting a Cape before.

He was surely simply failing to remember the events because there were so many of them though. His career was *studded* with successes, as befitting a god-king. ...He just couldn't recall them all right now.

The tourists snapped another picture.

Julian turned to the side so that they could get a better shot of what *true* splendor and power looked like, as this might be their only opportunity. The surface world had no hope of *ever* producing someone as glorious as himself.

As he turned though, his vision fell on the mermaid again. ...Or rather, where the mermaid had *formally* been.

He raced over to the glass, his heart about to beat out of his chest.

...Had he merely imagined her? Was she simply some angel come to guide him to long-sought victory?

He pressed his face against the glass and glanced towards the top of the aquarium in an effort to see where she may have gone. To his surprise, the woman in question was exiting the water, an air hose in her mouth.

...Why would a mermaid need an air hose?

Then it came to him, and his heart sank. The mermaid needed an air hose because she *wasn't* a mermaid at all.

...She was an aquatic mammal, and thus breathed *air*. Like a dolphin or a whale.

Unfortunate, but Julian protected all creatures of the sea, whether they breathed water or air. It was his *duty* and one he...

The mermaid's stunning gaze locked with his through the water again, and he completely lost his train of thought.

...Such an *exquisite* creature. He'd never seen anything so graceful in the water...

"Yo! 'Moby Dickhead!'" Poacher's gruff voice called from the stairs. "You coming, or should Harl and I forward your fucking mail here?"

Julian glanced away to glare at the man in contempt for a moment, and when he turned back, the vision was gone.

His world was empty and alone once again.

His head sunk against his chest, and he felt as if he had been hit with the sledgehammer. All he could manage was a weak nod to his idiot companion, and began climbing the stairs towards the exit with rubbery legs.

He had never felt more defeated in his entire life.

But Julian would *find* that woman.

He was *sure* of it.

...Or at least, he *wanted* to be.

Oh, God, how he wanted to be sure he'd see her again...

****

Bridget's plan for the summer did *not* include this.

Nope.

Her plan for the summer had included a trip to Cancun with her friends. Sadly, she didn't have the money for the trip. ...Or the friends who were actually *taking* a trip to Cancun, but the point remained the same. In her head, her summer would have been spent on a tropical beach somewhere, surrounded by her comically rowdy friends and visiting exotic sights which were probably fictional and certainly nowhere *near* the beach.

Sadly, that was not to be.

Instead, she was filling in for her idiot cousin, who had some sort of plastic surgery disaster or something, and would thus be unable to "perform" at her "show."

Bridget knew that was a lie.

The woman had simply gotten a better offer somewhere else, that was all. And so that meant that Bridget... poor innocent Bridget... was the one roped into this job.

A child excitedly waved at her through the glass, and she waved back at her.

For the past six weeks, Bridget had been an extra in the underwater show here. Basically, it was her job to swim in the background while the other "mermaids" did the hard stuff, and to float around and wave at kids while the other "mermaids" were getting ready for the next show.

It wasn't terribly complicated.

The shows themselves involved swimming in front of the glass and entertaining the guests in the theater on the other side. The "mermaids" swam with sequined fishtails around their legs, and remained underwater in the tank for extended periods. The secret behind this feat was a system of underwater hoses which were hidden in the coral around the aquarium's bottom. The "mermaid" entertainers would perform their show, and every few minutes, swim over to one of the hoses and breathe from it. Basically, it was the equivalent of going scuba diving, but taking off your tank, duct-taping your legs together, and then trying to act out an underwater fairytale ballet, while struggling to stay within a ten foot space underwater, entertain people, and not drown.

It required grace, agility, nerves of steel, and an athletic ability which would put Navy frogmen to shame.

...Bridget had none of these things.

What she *did* have was the ability to hold her breath for extended periods however, and the manager of the attraction had hopes that the rest would come in time.

Bridget thought the woman was kidding herself.

Still, if she really pushed it, she could hold her breath for close to four minutes though, which was almost double what the other girls here could do.

Bridget had a big mouth, and she evidently had big lungs to match. ...In fact, Bridget sadly had a big *everything,* which was another reason why the director of the "Underwater Mermaid Spectacular" in the small "Retiarius' Grotto" section of the Freedom Squad theme park, had put her in the *back* of the chorus line whenever the other mermaids were out here with her. Evidently, the woman was under the assumption that if she put her further away from the audience, forced perspective would take over and she would appear thinner.

Personally, Bridget thought she just appeared like a fat mermaid who was swimming further away for some reason, most likely because the other mermaids didn't like her. Not that she was complaining too much though, as the "mermaid" outfits left nothing to the imagination anyway. They really needed to get some new costumes, as the little shell bikinis were *not* meant for someone with Bridget's cup size.

It made swimming... awkward. And occasionally obscene.

But whatever.

Bridget could deal. She could deal with the potential embarrassment of her friends from school seeing her, because she didn't really have any. Besides, the job was *tough.* It had all the worst parts of dancing, swimming and acting, with the added benefit of being seconds away from drowning every moment you were at work.

The little girl waved at her again, and Bridget smiled back.

But it was worth it.

All in all, she actually kinda *liked* this job. She found the water... relaxing somehow. It felt *right.* And besides, it was worth it to see the happy faces on the kids. There were probably *worse* ways to earn some extra cash. And it was *almost* like being at the beach, right?

The kids were...

The sound of an explosion echoed through the space, and even underwater, Bridget could hear it quite clearly. The entire aquarium shook from the force of the impact, and a second later, something crashed through the back wall of the theater.

She swam closer to the glass to get a better look at what was happening.

The audience began to scatter, terrified of whatever it was that had tumbled down the bleachers and struck the wall beneath where she was currently floating. A moment later, a man stood up with his back to her and began yelling something at the audience. She couldn't quite hear what was going on, but she was guessing that he was warning them of the explosion outside.

He was carrying a trident and wearing a cloak of what appeared to be black seaweed. ...Was he part of the show or something? Bridget didn't remember this from rehearsal. Whoever the guy was though, he certainly looked like he could swim circles around anyone here. The dude had a *killer* build.

Another man emerged from a door to the first man's right and Bridget tried to tap on the glass to get the first man's attention and warn him of the impending attack.

He didn't hear her though, and the second man struck him with what appeared to be a hammer of some kind. The first man righted himself and said something to the second man, but was cut off as he was once again smashed with the sledgehammer.

Bridget winced as the blow hit home.

The first man leaned against the glass to catch his balance, and turned to face her for the first time.

...If Bridget hadn't been holding her breath, it would have caught in her throat.

The man was simply... *gorgeous.* On an *unbelievable* level. Like one of those guys in the TV show, who was so good-looking that it just didn't matter what part he played or if he had any talent. You were just watching the pretty; plain and simple.

Granted, he was obviously much older than Bridget. She was going off to college in the fall though, so she wasn't letting that bother her. Older men were *just fine* when they were that hot.

...But she wasn't a huge fan of the man's beard. It kinda made him look like a picture from a mythology book or something.

She *wholeheartedly* supported everything else about him however. His hair was so black that it shone blue in the light, and framed his classical face. His dark hair also made the turquoise of his eyes all the more piercing.

The man had a swimmer's build and an angel's face... Which sounded *totally* lame, but there was something about the man which made her not care.

All her previous ideas of how attractive a man could be were tossed aside, and a new man now stood atop her "hot guy" list.

Her attraction to the man and the cold water in which she

was swimming was *doubtlessly* testing the strength of the thin and barely-there seashell fabric which was currently covering her rapidly tightening breasts, but she didn't care.

Hell, at this particular moment in time, she wouldn't have cared if the whole top popped off. She was *busy.*

If he wanted to look at her breasts, she'd let him. And if he *didn't* want to look at them, then why worry about the fact that her body was rapidly making her wardrobe obscene? He didn't care anyway.

Her eyes stayed locked with his.

Nothing mattered right now.

Not whatever had caused that explosion, or the man who as apparently trying to kill her new male model friend, or the fact that her lungs were rapidly running out of oxygen and she'd die soon.

All of that could wait.

The man pressed his hand against the glass, and Bridget moved forward to press her own hand against his. Strictly speaking, she wasn't really supposed to do that, but she didn't care. This was just a summer job anyway. What was the worst that could happen? If the most attractive man she had ever seen wanted her to press her hand against the glass, she was *going* to press her fucking hand against the glass! Hell, she'd press whatever he *wanted* against the glass and would feel *good about it.*

…She didn't understand why he was carrying a pitchfork though. That was *weird.*

The man opened his mouth to say something but before he could get the words out, he was once again struck down by his opponent.

Bridget almost gasped in astonishment and fear that he had been hurt, which would have been bad, as she was still underwater. Drowning herself in front of this guy probably would be a hard trick to top on a second meeting.

She worriedly swam closer to the glass, trying to see if he had been hurt.

Come on. Get up. …Please be okay…

His eyes locked with hers again, and she all but sighed with relief to see that he appeared undamaged. It would be a *tragedy* if a man with a face like that got it mangled by a psycho with a sledgehammer. …A fucking *catastrophe.*

The man pulled himself to his feet, and Bridget *willed* him to beat the living shit out of the guy who had ruined their moment. She had *no* idea what was going on, and she didn't care. The good-looking

guy hadn't done anything to anyone, and was *totally good-looking!*
That *alone* was enough in her mind to deserve her support. That other
guy was a bully and he *deserved* whatever the good-looking guy was
hopefully about to do to him.

Sure enough, the good-looking shirtless guy decked the bully
with the sledgehammer like the fucking hand of god, and the other
man went flying.

Bridget did a fistpump in support and gave a yell of
excitement. ...And then remembered that she was about to drown, as
she had been without oxygen for four minutes.

She reluctantly tore her eyes away from her new friend and
swam for the oxygen hose, her vision darkening around the edges. She
made it JUST in time and breathed through the hose in relief.

Sometimes this job was simply *too* exciting.

She began swimming towards the top of the tank to see
what the hell was happening out there, when she glanced back down
to see the good-looking guy looking back up at her.

He looked almost... disappointed now.

Bridget's heart sank. She had swum too close to the glass
and lost the forced perspective. He'd seen that she wasn't as shapely
as the other mermaids, unless the shape you were talking about was
an oval.

The man turned away.

And Bridget exited the tank. She wasn't entirely surprised at
how her brief imaginary affair with the good-looking guy had ended. It
was how *most* of her relationships ended, imaginary or not. Bridget
wasn't exactly what anyone would call "desirable."

It had been fun while it lasted though.

She yanked the towel from the rack above the aquarium's
portal shaped exit tube, and began to dry off, doing her best to use the
fabric to cover her body's continued reaction to seeing the man,
despite his eventual dismissal of her.

Stupid breasts. Stupid seashell costume thing. Stupid job.

Stupid *Bridget* for taking said stupid summer job in the first
place, when she knew *damn well* that said stupid costume was too
small for her.

...She should have just gone to Cancun with her friends
instead.

CHAPTER 4

KING: "I REALLY DON'T KNOW WHY YOU CONTINUE TO BE TAKEN IN BY THE CAPE PROPAGANDA. SURELY YOU CAN SEE THAT THE ONLY REASON ANYONE WANTS TO BECOME A CAPE IS BECAUSE OF THE MONEY."

STORMS: "OH, I DON'T KNOW ABOUT THAT. YOU'RE MAKING THEM SOUND VERY MERCENARY AGAIN. I MEAN, I THINK THEY CARE ABOUT MORE THAN MONEY."

KING: "THEY WOULD BEAT UP THEIR GRANDMOTHERS AND YOURS IF SOMEONE PAID THEM A DOLLAR. THEY ALWAYS FIND A WAY TO TAKE ADVANTAGE OF CIRCUMSTANCES TO GET WHAT THEY WANT, NO MATTER WHO GETS HURT IN THE PROCESS. YOU DON'T GET TO BE A CAPE IN THIS CITY WITHOUT THE ABILITY TO QUICKLY PROFIT FROM ANY TRAGEDY. THEIR WHOLE PURPOSE FOR EXISTING IN THE FIRST PLACE IS BECAUSE BAD THINGS ARE HAPPENING. IF BAD THINGS STOPPED HAPPENING, WE'D HAVE NO FURTHER USE FOR CAPES AND THEY'D BE OUT OF A JOB. THINK ABOUT THAT THE NEXT TIME YOU PREACH TO ME ABOUT HOW BRAVE AND AMAZING THEY ARE."

STORMS: "NOW YOU'RE JUST EXAGGERATING."

TRANSCRIPT OF "KING OF CAPES AND COWLS," MEDIA: TELEVISION, SHOW: 1407, NEWSCHANNEL 6, FRIDAY 21:00-22:00 EST, NETWORK SEGMENT-ID: 918000606

Present Day

Three hours later, Bridget was pulling down the long dirt driveway in her rental car, towards a rusting 1950s era looking broken neon sign which declared the site as: "The Enchanted Forest Miniature Golf Course: 18 Holes of Fantasy and Fun." A cartoon knight dressed in rusty armor held his putter high, as if it were a magical sword. In the background, the fading evidence of his painted lady fair, waved to him from the top of her cracked tower, pieces of which were missing.

The facility itself appeared abandoned; weeds filled the courses, and the obstacles were all crumbling and chipped. What had once been the clubhouse and souvenir shop was an empty husk, missing its back wall, all its windows, and half of its faux-thatched fairy tale cottage roof. Around the attraction, the thick woods and wetlands of the Pine Barrens encroached from all sides, threatening to destroy the only sign of civilization for miles.

Despite that though, several people were busily arranging things around the small cracked cement parking area, as if expecting a sudden surge in traffic. A man dressed as an Eskimo climbed up onto a chair and began nailing a sign onto one of the trees.

Bridget pulled into one of the few spaces that looked like it could actually support her car's weight and not have the pavement crumble to dust or sink into the marshes which dotted the area, and turned off the engine.

This was a bad idea.

She had a long history of bad ideas though, so she was used to it.

Besides, this might be fun. It wasn't every day that she had the opportunity to attend a super-villain's yard sale.

She stepped from the rental car into the unseasonably muggy air and readjusted her baseball cap. Around her, the handful of disreputable-looking costumed people stopped what they were doing, and stared at her like she was an alien or something.

Silence filled the clearing as they all stood around motionless and watched each other. Even the crickets and cicadas seemed to stop chirping.

...Yeah, this was a *really* bad idea.

Generally, she didn't have the best track record with Capes. Bad things had a tendency to happen to her when they were around.

She cleared her throat nervously and tried to look confident as she made her way over to one of the folding tables in front of the wreckage of the main office. The elderly man in the wheelchair behind the table readjusted his oxygen line so that it didn't get tangled in the plastic antenna attached to the rubber cockroach headpiece he wore, which formed a sort of hood and connected to the rest of his rubber insect outfit. He watched her suspiciously, as if anticipating her trying to steal something at any moment.

Arranged on the table were half a dozen bizarre and rusting Rube-Goldbergian contraptions which she couldn't identify.

His cloudy eyes narrowed at her in annoyance. "You gonna

buy something, lady? I got shit to sell, and if you're just gonna be a looky-loo, then you can fuck right the hell off. You're holdin' up the line."

Bridget turned around to look at the completely empty clearing again, just to confirm that she was currently the only customer here.

...Yep.

She turned back to stare at the man in disbelief.

A pretty girl wearing a black unitard and sparkly wings was sitting next to the man, listening to her iPod through one earbud, the other dangling loosely at the base of her elegant neck. She had the build of a ballerina; graceful but frail looking. Like Audrey Hepburn, if Audrey Hepburn were still alive, and evil, and in her twenties, and was selling junk in a decrepit mini-golf course perched on the edge of a swamp in New Jersey for some reason. "Papa, it's time for your pill." The woman reminded her father pleasantly.

"Leave me alone, May." The old man pointed at Bridget. "Can't you see I have a fucking customer? She's gonna buy some of this useless shit so we don't gotta haul it all back inside."

"Yes, I can see that." The girl said humoringly, feigning enthusiasm for the man's retail achievement like he was a kindergartener who had finished his finger-painting masterpiece and wanted her to approve of it. She turned the page in her magazine, not bothering to look up. "Take your pill."

"NO! Fuck you! I WON'T DO IT!"

"Papa, *take your pill*."

He made a face at her, but obediently fished a plastic pill bottle from his pocket and swallowed the white capsules, downing them with a shot from his flask.

"*There*." He angrily shoved the bottle back into his pocket. "Happy *now,* you fucking harpy?"

"Yes, papa. Ecstatic." She reached for another magazine. "...Until *three-thirty*, when you have to take them again."

Bridget continued browsing the items arranged on the table, and picked up a strange black tube attached to some kind of battery by ancient looking wires. The machine had a strap fastened to it, as though it were meant to be worn as a backpack or something.

"Picked that up in 1905." The old man nodded to himself. "My parents lived next to that Tesla asshole, and the stupid bastard ran up all his bills and couldn't pay. So, the bank sold all of his shit, right there on the fucker's front lawn."

She stared at him for a moment in silent amazement. "...You

went to Nicola Tesla's *garage sale?* The mad scientist inventor guy who had that feud with Thomas Edison?"

"Yep."

She continued blinking at him. "Just how old *are* you?"

"None of your *goddamn business*." He snapped, then pointed to the device she was holding. "That's the 'teleforce weapon,' some death-ray thing that crazy bastard was cooking up. It sends concentrated beams of particles out at thirty four times the speed of sound. You can incinerate an army from two hundred miles away with that sucker. Works on planes, submarines and neighbor's cats too." He drank another gulp from his flask. "Fifty cents."

She stared down at the device for a moment, then pointed at one of the other contraptions on the table. "Throw in his earthquake machine, and you've got yourself a deal."

"May," the old man turned to his daughter, "wrap these up for the young lady."

"Uh-huh." The girl made no move to bag the items for Bridget. "I'll get right on that, papa." She absently turned the page of her magazine. "You shouldn't be in the sun, it's bad for you." She reached into her bag and handed him something, without looking up. "Put your hat on."

"I don't *want* to." He argued. "It messes with my antenna and makes me look like a pussy."

"I don't care." She said simply, as if that was all the debate which was needed on the matter. "Put it on."

The older man grabbed the hat sulkily and pulled it into place on his head, causing his plastic antenna to get redirected downwards towards his shoulders. He crossed his arms over his chest; pouting.

...He was right. He looked *utterly* ridiculous.

Bridget had seen enough of that table and quickly moved on to the next one. Behind it, a dark-haired man was busily arranging boxes. He was handsome in an entirely generic and utterly unobjectionable way.

"Wanna buy some medals?" He gestured to the table behind him. "I have like ten of them left. We got Freedom, Honor, Peace... Joy... or something. I don't remember, but they're going *fast*." He held up one of the golden objects, flashing a wide friendly smile. "Right now, most of them read 'Wyatt Ferral,' but give me a few minutes with the belt sander, and I can clean that *right off* for you." He held one out to her enticingly. "It would *really* impress your friends. A lot of people think that medals are only worn at formal ceremonies and state dinners, but I just read in *Vogue* about how more and more women are choosing to wear them with their everyday outfits now. Nothing says 'bling' like a Presidential Medal of Freedom around your neck while you're shopping for groceries or rocking out at the club." He put the object on and then proceeded to dance around making bass sounds as though at a dance party. "Umm-tiss-umm-tiss-umm-tiss..." He began pumping his arms in the air over his head, seemingly lost in his imaginary music.

"...Uhh. No, thank you." She shook her head. "I'm just looking."

From the man's left, Sargassum suddenly appeared as if by magic. She had no idea how the man had accomplished that feat, as the building he had walked out of appeared to be a ramshackle shell.

"What the hell *is this*, Arnold!?!" Sargassum threw his arms out in exasperation, gesturing to the tables.

"What does it look like, man?" The other man pointed to one of the yellow poster board signs nailed to a tree. "I'm having a yard sale."

Sargassum shook his head. "You *cannot* just sell everyone's belongings."

"Why?" The other man sounded genuinely confused. "They're probably all dead and I'm planning on subletting their space in the Lair, so there's not really going to be room for this stuff anymore anyway. Besides, it's not like they're going to *need* it again. Like my dad always said: 'You can't take *it* with you, but if you have to die, take *them* with you.'" He took on a serious tone, pressing a hand over his heart. "I think they'd *want* me to have it."

Sargassum shook his head. "No, they wouldn't."

"Yeah-huh!" The man smiled cheerily. "Plus, I've made almost *ten dollars!*" He waved a handful of dollar bills. "...I'll split it with you. You can have twenty percent."

"I am *leader* of this organization. I do *not* want twenty percent of the money you've stolen from our missing and injured comrades." Sargassum drew himself up to his full height. "...I am entitled to *at least* half."

"Thirty." Arnold handed the man the bills. "But I get to keep the concession sales, and anything I can steal from the cars of the shoppers."

"Agreed."

Bridget cleared her throat. "...Umm, Mr. Sargassum?"

"*LORD* Sargassum." He corrected in irritation, not bothering to turn around. "Why is it so hard for surface people to understand that?"

"Whatever." She rolled her eyes. "Listen, I was wondering if maybe you could help me find my car? Someone stole it and..."

"Mortal, do we *look* like LoJack?" He turned around to face her. "We are VILLAINS and..." He trailed off. "...It's you."

She blinked at him in confusion. "How could it be me? I can't steal my *own* car."

He ignored that, walking towards her as if in a daze, and gently reaching down to pull her hat off her forehead so he could see more of her face. He softly put his index finger beneath her chin to redirect her gaze up at him.

She met the intense depths of his turquoise eyes...

She swallowed, suddenly feeling impossibly warm. "...Hi." Was all she could manage to get out.

He moved closer to her and her body immediately responded. "I have been looking for you for a *long* time."

She swallowed again, her mouth suddenly feeling very dry. "...Sorry?" Her breathing was getting faster and it was hard to concentrate. "...I moved... to a new... apartment." She was suddenly overcome with an almost overwhelming regret and anger at herself for not making sure to leave a forwarding address with her old landlord. ...Well, technically she *had,* but she should have made weekly calls back to him or something, just to make sure no one incredibly hot was looking for her.

His eyes skimmed down her body, an action which she usually would have found insulting and awkward, but at the moment found oddly pleasurable. "...How are you surviving out of the water?" He caressed her cheek with his thumb. "You shouldn't be endangering yourself like this. You are too precious."

She opened her mouth to respond to that, then stopped. "...I don't know what that means." She shook her head to clear it, trying to ignore how strangely good it felt to have the man touch her like that. "You're kinda freaking me out here."

He straightened like she had slapped him and jerked his hand away. "My apologies. I was being disrespectful." He cleared his throat. "I'm sorry, what are you the goddess *of*, exactly? I'm not as familiar with my father's world as I obviously *should* be."

"I'm not the goddess of anything. I'm a press agent. I'm just here because someone stole my car."

"...You're...*mortal?*" He said the word like it was horrifying for some reason. "...Oh god. A mortal surface-dweller..." He leaned forward bracing himself on his knees. "...I feel sick."

"Here, let me get you some lemonade." She reached for a

glass from a nearby table.

"Not without $5 you're not." Arnold shot back.

She pointed as Sargassum. "He's like... overheating or something. He's a fish guy! He needs to hydrate!"

"Lady, I don't care if he's on fire and you need it to *douse the flames*." He shook his head. "If I don't see Mr. Lincoln or the Washington quintuplets, no lemonade."

She took it anyway and handed it to Sargassum, who drank it in one long gulp.

Arnold gasped in horror. "Shoplifter!"

She ignored him, and put her hand on Sargassum's shoulder, trying not to dwell on how *solid* the man was built. His muscles were like iron!

Bridget was seriously impressed, and Bridget didn't *get* impressed by stuff like that.

"Hey, you okay?"

He jolted when she touched him and shied away. "I'm... fine." He cleared his throat. "Just... *surprised,* that's all." He stood straighter. "No matter. You were saying? What service do you require?"

"I said: someone stole my car and you guys are heroes, and I need..."

He grabbed his trident and held it high. "I am Lord Julian Thalassic Sargassum, first of my name and strongest of my kind, and I *swear to you* on my eternal ancestors and the lives of my unborn sons and daughters, I *shall* return your vehicle to you, no matter where it is hidden or what monsters conceal it."

She blinked at him for a moment in silence. "...Umm, okay. ...Super. Good to hear you guys are so... umm... *dedicated* to heroism or whatever." She nodded and gave him a thumbs up sign with one hand. "One less thing to worry about then." She paused. "It's a Honda."

"I do not know what that is, but put your mind at ease, fair lady. I *shall* discover 'Honda's' location." He paused. "...You wish it to be *your* car, correct? Because we have a *number* of vehicles in the motor pool which you could choose from. We would be glad to give you one or *all* of them if that would make you feel better and lessen your pain."

She made a thoughtful face. "Yeah, I kinda want mine. I mean, I know it's going to be trouble, but..."

"No trouble at all." He said regally. "That is what we *do* here. Being bestowed with a glorious and noble duty is an *honor*. It is a task which would crush *lesser* men, but merely provides me a chance to once again demonstrate my greatness to the surface world."

"Uh-huh." She was barely paying attention. Her eyes continued to trace the muscular lines of his bare chest. "...Steroids are *so* awesome."

"Huh?"

"Nothing. Forget it. Surface world thing, I guess."

"Your people baffle me as well." He nodded in understanding and commiseration. "TUPILAK!"

She jumped at the sudden sound which cut off her ogling. "*Jesus!*"

A moment later, the Eskimo who had been hanging the signage appeared. "Yo. What's up, boss?"

Julian spun on his heel to address the younger man. "We shall assist this lovely woman in locating her vehicle."

"We will?" The man blinked in confusion, then turned and pointed across the parking lot. "Found it!" He nodded, obviously proud of himself. "Hell, it was *easy* to spot. It's the only one here, so I don't know how she could have missed..."

"Her *stolen* vehicle." Julian snapped.

Tupilak put up his hands. "Whoa, whoa... I'm not going down for 'grand theft auto' again, boss. That third strike would..."

Julian cut him off. "We are going to help her *recover* her *stolen* vehicle!"

"Who are we now? LoJack?"

Sargassum shook his head in condemnation and disgust. "That is a *very* insensitive thing to say to someone on what is *surely* an upsetting day. We are *heroes* and heroes treat everyone– even *surface-dwellers*– with respect." He crossed his arms over his chest. "Don't you think you owe..." He trailed off and turned to look at her expectantly.

"Bridget Haniver." She told him.

"Don't you think you owe the Lady *Haniver* an apology?"

Bridget blinked in confusion at the name. Lady? What the hell?

The Eskimo thought about it for a minute. "No?" It came out sounding like a question. "...Am I supposed to?"

"Yes!" Sargassum snapped.

"Oh, in that case, I'm filled with shame and regret and all *kinds* of tears and stuff." The Eskimo placed his gloved hand over his heart. "You gotta forgive me, Miss Haniver. I'm not usually this insensitive." Apparently satisfied that his apology had been accepted, he wandered over to one of the tables. "While you get the details on the car, I'm going to start moving Syd's stuff out onto the tables so we can sell it now that he's dead, 'kay?"

"I care not what you do." Sargassum turned to look at her. "It's a lovely name, by the way."

"Syd?"

"Bridget Haniver." He said the name like it held deep importance, or was the refrain of some ancient beautiful song.

"Oh, yeah." She nodded sarcastically. "One for the poets." She decided a change of topic was in order. "Listen, the car wasn't the only reason I came over here. I figure, you can help me, and I can help you."

He stared at her for a long moment. "I would *very* much like your help, Lady Haniver. I have needed it for quite a while. It is the only thing in this world which I desire."

"Super!" She began walking back towards the tables. "I figure, with my skills as a press agent, I can help you improve your image a little. I mean, how hard can it be? You're an *awesome* hero, after all, so I don't think I'll have any trouble. Plus, it'll be really good for my career. Now that you're finally allowed to start going on more missions and stuff, I think the city's going to quickly realize how *amazing* you are. And all that attention will help me, as well."

He hurried to catch up with her. "I'm sorry. ...The help you mean to provide me... is assistance in looking good to the *terrestrials?*"

The Eskimo glanced up from his work and laughed. "Why would we need *that?* Hell, Jules is going to *drown* the world in..."

"*Focus on your duties!*" Sargassum snapped, cutting the man off and pointing at the boxes. He turned to look at her, his voice returning to its normal soft but deep tone. "I think this organization would benefit *greatly* from your assistance, Lady Haniver. You should remain with us and help us achieve your *vision*. ...Stay right here with us for *however* long it takes."

She squinted at him in confusion.

She had really expected him to put up more of a struggle before agreeing to her offer. For some reason, he seemed more than happy with the arrangement though. How odd.

Behind him, Arnold began arranging a collection of small figurines on a table while a man in a trucker hat busily tried to get a second table assembled, despite the fact that he only had one working arm; the other still hung loosely in the sling he wore. He was being assisted in the effort by what appeared to be a holographic girl in an old-timey haircut, wearing a toga.

The hologram shook her semi-transparent electric green head. "I have examined the manufacturer's instructions on their website, and Part A is required to be inserted into Slot B before assembly, McCallister."

The man sighed. "The instructions are wrong, Poll." He told her patiently, as though they had been having this argument for a while. "I know it's hard for you to accept that, but you need to deal with it and move on."

"Why would the manufacturer post incorrect instructions on how to assemble their own product?" The girl asked in her soft English accent, sounding genuinely confused. "I do not understand, McCallister." She blinked rapidly, looking upset. "Can you please explain it to me?"

He put down his work to look at his companion. "People make mistakes, Poll. Someone just uploaded the wrong thing, that's all."

She stared at him for a beat, obviously trying vainly to process it. "..But... but the instructions *say* that..."

He nodded. "I know. It's hard to believe, isn't it?" He smiled at her gently. "It'll be okay though. It's not the end of the world."

The hologram didn't look entirely convinced. Her eyes uneasily darted about, as if trying to deal with the ramifications of the world being imperfect. She looked on the verge of panic.

"Hey." He saw her distress and leaned down into her line of sight. "Don't worry about it, okay?"

She met his gaze with large eyes. "...Yes, but..."

"I know." He nodded in understanding.

"...But the..."

"I know. It's okay, though." He gave her a gentle smile. "Trust me. Everything's *fine*. I swear."

"...Okay." She thought about it for a minute more, then brightened. "I am still not convinced you are doing that correctly, McCallister. I suggest choosing another site for the table's construction. My readings indicate that this ground is not stable."

The Eskimo dropped another box filled with statues onto the gravel near them. "How many of these fucking things does Syd *own?*"

"None." Arnold carefully arranged a figurine of a blond boy in lederhosen playing with a small dog, next to a figurine of a blonde *girl* in lederhosen playing with a small *cat,* then stood back, obviously pleased with his selling display. "They're *ours* now."

"Oh joy." The hologram deadpanned.

"Syd's stuff is boring." The Eskimo headed back towards the

golf course again. "I'm going to start gathering up *Holly's* stuff instead. I bet *her* stuff will sell better."

Bridget looked back to Sargassum, who for some reason, was staring at her. She turned around, trying to see if there was something fascinating going on behind her, then faced him again. "Something wrong?"

"Not at all." He said in his deep rumbly voice. "Things are finally looking up."

She nodded. "Yeah, I think this could really work out for both of us."

"That is my hope."

She cleared her throat and pulled a pad of paper and a pen from her pocket. "So, tell me a little about yourself?"

"What is there to know?" He sounded genuinely confused. "I am a god-king and the most powerful man in the world. Isn't that enough?"

"Well, what about your parents?"

"I was raised by dolphins."

The Eskimo struggled to contain his laughter as he emerged with another box. ...And failed. "*Dolphins?!?*" He put his head back and positively howled with laughter. "That's really what you're going with?" He dropped the cardboard box onto the grass. "'Dolphins' my ass. You're a *terrible* liar, boss. At least make it *somewhat* believable."

Sargassum ignored him.

Bridget wrote that down, long accustomed to clients lying to her. "And the water thing?"

"I can breathe underwater, yes." He stood taller. "When I am in the water, I am even *more* astonishingly powerful than I am on land." He paused. "...*Far* more powerful than any surface man you've ever met, and *much* more capable of protecting my hypothetical woman and our offspring."

"Uh-huh." She jotted that down. "Any specifics on how powerful?"

"I can *easily* lift 20,000 tons in the water."

The Eskimo broke out laughing again.

Sargassum ignored him with *visible* effort and continued on as if the other man wasn't even there. "And I can travel quite fast when I am in my native element."

"Such as?" She asked, genuinely curious.

"31,283 knots." He proclaimed with obvious pride.

She stared at him blankly. "...Is that fast?"

"That is *597,464* nautical leagues an *hour*." He tried again, sounding insulted.

"What's a 'league'?" She frowned, trying to remember her high school math classes. "I thought those measured depth or something?"

"You are thinking of '*fathoms*,' which I can comfortably swim to a depth of 3000 of." He made an annoyed sound. "To the *surface world*, 597,464 nautical leagues an hour would mean that I can travel ten miles a *second*."

"Ha!" The Eskimo snorted in amusement and lifted a pair of delicate but sexy looking red lace Santa-themed panties from one of the cardboard boxes and casually slipped them into his pocket. "Only if we dropped you from a plane, boss."

"Shouldn't you be unloading more boxes?" Sargassum angrily pointed back towards one of the mini-golf holes. "Perhaps you should *get back to it.*"

The Eskimo trudged away again.

Bridget wrote down his abilities on her pad. "Personal life?" She cleared her throat, trying to sound sure of herself. "Wife? Girlfriends..."

"None."

"Any crazy exes who might show up and cause us trouble in the tabloids?"

"None." He shook his head. "I have always been alone."

"Good." She said immediately, oddly cheered by that for some reason, then realized how awful it sounded. "...I mean, not 'good' that you're lonely, just good that it will make my job easier."

"I understood what you meant, Lady Haniver." He told her calmly. "You do not need to ever explain yourself to me."

She glanced up from her pad to smile at him, finding that an oddly nice thing for him to say.

A shout from the table startled her out of her moment.

"*Oh, here we go!* Emily's digital camera!" Arnold flipped through the pictures on the camera's memory card for a moment, then put it down in apparent disgust. "Why don't women take more naked photos of themselves and their friends? I mean, what's the point of even *having* an identical twin if you're not going to do that?"

The trucker made a disturbed face. "You're telling me if you had an identical twin, you'd what? Wanna take dirty pictures of them or somethin'?"

"If my identical twin looked like Amy? Fuck yes, I would!" Arnold sounded amazed that anyone would even question that.

"Why would *your* identical twin look like *Amy?*" The trucker sounded both annoyed and rather astounded over the other man's line of thought. *"What the hell kinda sense does that make, son!?! Don't sound too 'identical' to me!"*

"Haven't these girls ever heard of a slumber party?" Arnold asked regretfully, ignoring the trucker's question and affixing a $1 price tag to the object. "Unfair."

"Dude, don't you remember Wyatt's riveting speech about how we all needed to be careful about making sex tapes and stuff, because we have a public reputation now to consider and all?" Asked the Eskimo, still sifting through the box of Christmas themed items, looking for anything of value to steal or a camera filled with pictures of naked female coworkers to appropriate for his own uses

The trucker shuddered at the memory. "Jesus, what an *awkward* hour and a half that was. Fella blushes *entirely* too much for a married man, if ya ask me. Harlot being a mama must have resulted from Divine intervention, 'cause I don't think that boy had it in him. Prolly spent his honeymoon locked in the bathroom cryin' and askin' her why they couldn't just hold hands instead."

Arnold rolled his eyes in agreement and continued to root around in another box. "God what an *asshole* that guy was." He slid the box under one of the folding tables and wrote "50 cents" in large block letters, then grabbed another one. He frowned at the contents. "How many bottles of nail polish did Emily *own*?"

"Well, Wyatt had a point." Bridget felt compelled to point out. "It *is* damaging to reputations for tapes like that to be released. ...Assuming of course that the person has a good reputation to begin with, which most of you don't anyway, and I frankly don't see how it could damage your public image any more than it already is, and the DVD sales could really make ends meet around here because that's a *huge* industry, especially when celebrities are involved, and *most* especially when celebrities with *superpowers* are involved, as I think the public would actually be kinda interested in seeing that."

Arnold stared at her for a moment. "You know... I think I'm starting to *like* this girl. Sure, she seems to have a tendency to use run-on sentences a lot..."

She opened her mouth to argue that fact, then closed it, knowing that it was true.

"...But I respect anyone who realizes that good pornography is the answer to *anything.*" Arnold turned around to look at the hologram. "How about it, Polly? You're a woman... kinda. And we don't have too many of them left. Wanna make us a few quick bucks by shaking what your programmer gave you? It could *really* help us."

The hologram looked confused. "I do not understand why organic people are always so obsessed with seeing each other's fleshy nakedness." She said the words with barely controlled disgust, as though the mere thought of living skin was nauseating. "Surely, you must know what is under your clothes, so why is there all of this drama and mystery attached to it? It's illogical."

Arnold and the Eskimo both slowly turned their heads to look at her in unison.

Arnold nodded sagely, not missing a beat. "You know, I *absolutely* agree with you, Polly." He chuckled in amusement, sounding oddly fake for some reason. "People just get so hung up on such a *little* thing." His smile was one of complete trust and friendship. "Why, take *you* for instance. I bet *you* could take off that little dress thing you always wear, and you wouldn't feel weird about it at *all.*"

The hologram shrugged. "That emotion is not in my programming, no."

"And you certainly haven't *done* that yet, so it would be a new experience for you. ...It might even be *fun.* Freeing, in a way..."

She thought about it for a moment. "I suppose..."

"And it's not like you're among *strangers* or anything. We're your *friends.* We'd be *touched* that you'd trust us like that." Arnold's wolfish smile grew. "So, really... there's nothing holding you back at all..." His hand slowly reached towards the digital camera...

"Just *me.*" The man in the trucker hat stepped in front of the hologram, blocking her from view and glaring at the other man. He held up a finger. "That's *once.*" His voice took on a hard threatening edge, suddenly sounding like the terrifying thug he appeared to be. "There ain't gonna *be* a '*twice,*' ya feel me?"

Arnold held his hands up to show his confusion. "What? I was just having a conversation with my good friend Polly, and..."

"Go find another *'good friend'* to 'converse' with, ya pervert." He glanced at the hologram reproachfully. "And you *know* better. We've talked about this *before.*"

She looked confused. "...I...I do not understand this conversation anymore, McCallister." She shook her head, causing her digital curls to sway. "Can you explain it to me? Please?"

"You don't want to know." He got back to work. "*Trust me.*"

The pair launched into an argument about whether or not she needed to know, and what exactly his duties were in their partnership.

Bridget ignored the byplay, her eyes absently scanning the goods at the yard sale. She pointed at the box of nail polish in Arnold's hands. "I'll give you $10 for all of it."

He paused to consider that offer, and smiled like a used car salesman. "I couldn't *possibly* let these *treasured* mementoes of my good friend go for less than $15."

"$12."

"*Done*."

She handed him the cash, then stacked the box next to all of her other purchases in the back of her rental car. "So, what *is* all this stuff anyway?"

"The few tacky belongings of some classless co-workers." Sargassum sounded bored. "We are doing some cleaning. Nothing to become concerned about, Lady Haniver. It will not affect our business together and this mess will soon trouble you no longer."

"Are they dead or something?"

"Probably." He shrugged. "...Well, some of them."

"And the others are what? Missing?" She frowned. "And you're just selling their stuff while they're away? That doesn't seem very nice."

He thought about that for a moment. "...Which is *precisely* why I've already ordered an end to this *ghastly* spectacle." He rounded on his heel and pointed at the Eskimo as he appeared with another box of Christmas themed weapons, lingerie and handbags. "I thought I told you to return all of these items to their rightful owners! We *cannot* steal from our missing friends. That would be *wrong*."

The Eskimo stared at him in amazement. "WHAT!?! Why didn't you tell me that before!?! A second ago, you thought this was a *great* idea."

Arnold placed a $1 price tag on a Pokémon themed diary, and casually began flipping through it. "I think we're all just going through the stage of grief where you try to profit from the tragic loss. It's a natural part of the healing process. Almost beautiful, in a way."

"*Theft* isn't a stage of grief. ...As far as I know." Julian pointed at him with the trident. "And the Bell girl isn't *even* missing, she's on her *honeymoon*! You heard the Lady Haniver! Put it back, right now! All of it!"

Arnold turned the page, paying no attention to him. "...Oh, this part's getting *steamy*. You kinky little *minx*, you. I had no idea. ...How wonderfully *graphic*." He reached for the price tags again and promptly increased its selling price to $3.99.

Julian refocused on her. "Believe me, I'm as shocked and horrified about all of this as you are."

"Uh-huh." She made a non-committal sound. "I can totally

see that." She wrote that down. "'Shock and horror.'"

Why did people never make her job easy?

CHAPTER 5

STORMS: "I KNOW I TELL YOU THIS EVERY WEEK, BUT WHY CAN'T YOU SEE THAT CAPES ARE SIMPLY MEN AND WOMEN WHO ARE JUST LIKE YOU AND ME? SURE, THEY HAVE SUPERPOWERS AND TRY TO USE THEM TO..."

KING (INTERRUPTING): "THAT'S JUST IT THOUGH! IF THEY'RE 'JUST LIKE YOU AND ME,' WHAT GIVES THEM THE RIGHT TO TELL YOU AND ME WHAT TO DO? WHO PUT THEM IN CHARGE OF PROTECTING THE CITY!?! NO ONE! I DIDN'T VOTE FOR THEM. I DIDN'T ASK THEM FOR THEIR SO-CALLED 'HELP.' THEY'RE NOT THE POLICE, THE GOVERNMENT OR OUR FRIENDS. NO. THEY'RE JUST ACTION JUNKIES AND ATTENTION WHORES, WHO USE THIS CITY LIKE A PORN FILM USES A CHEERLEADING SQUAD."

STORMS (WINCING): "OUCH, PAIGE. THEY'RE JUST TRYING TO HELP US THE BEST THEY CAN. SURE THEY MAKE SOME MISSTEPS ALONG THE WAY SOMETIMES, BUT DON'T WE ALL?"

KING: "WHEN I MAKE A 'MISSTEP,' PEOPLE DON'T DIE. MY 'MISSTEPS' DON'T INVOLVE LITERALLY STEPPING ON A BUILDING BECAUSE I'M A HUNDRED FEET TALL. WE ARE TALKING ABOUT PHENOMENALLY POWERFUL PEOPLE, WHO HAVE LITTLE TO NO OVERSIGHT ON THEIR ACTIVITIES. I MEAN, WHO EVEN KNOWS THE KINDS OF THINGS WHICH ARE BEING DISCUSSED IN THEIR SECRET HEADQUARTERS? THEY'RE PROBABLY PLOTTING AGAINST US RIGHT NOW."

STORMS (LAUGHING): "OH, THEY ARE NOT! THEY DON'T HATE US; THEY'RE JUST TRYING TO PROTECT US!"

TRANSCRIPT OF "KING OF CAPES AND COWLS," MEDIA: TELEVISION, SHOW: 1407, NEWSCHANNEL 6, FRIDAY 21:00-22:00 EST, NETWORK SEGMENT-ID: 918000606

Julian hated surface-dwellers.

He'd hated them his entire life. They'd taken *everything* from him, and he was determined to bring about their extinction. It was the very core of his entire world view.

…And yet, now he had apparently spent the better part of the last 16 years thinking about one of their evil kind.

All in all, it had been a very strange and disconcerting morning.

To make matters worse, if anything, the years had merely made his mermaid woman even *more* attractive. Her girlish prettiness had given way to the full-blown beauty of adulthood, and Julian was finding it very hard to concentrate on anything else.

He might detest the surface people, but not this SPECIFIC surface-dweller. He found the woman fascinating, and he wasn't about to hold her breed's betrayals and sinister nature against her.

He was a proud man, but he wasn't a fool. There wasn't a single ideal or belief he wasn't willing to cast aside to keep her around him. Part of being a king and a god was knowing what you wanted, and being unafraid to go after it.

And he wanted *her*.

For her part, she appeared to only want his assistance finding her car, but if that's what she wanted from him, than he would *die* to see her desires fulfilled. Usually, when someone was looking for something, they… well… *looked* for it. She didn't seem overly concerned with her vehicle however, undoubtedly because she was counting on *him* to solve the matter.

And he would.

That car would be *found*. Period. If he had to burn the world to cinders and then sift through the ashen remains, he would *get her that car*.

…Eventually.

The sooner he found "Honda," the sooner Bridget would leave though. Thus, his best course of action was to delay as long as possible, without looking incompetent. It was a delicate balancing act, but Julian excelled at *everything*.

What exactly his new mission in life had to do with his public image was anyone's guess though. Personally, he didn't understand that.

"It's probably for the best if you just go about your day and let me see how all of this works." The majestic creature sitting to his right waved a hand at them. "Just do what you'd normally do."

Julian shifted in his chair in the Consortium's meeting room, feeling awkward around the woman for some reason. He felt... exposed here. He wasn't one to ever feel self-conscious. Not since his childhood. Not since having to endure the whispers and the harassment of the other Eternal children, and the snide comments from their parents. Not since spending long hours devising ways in which to get the attention of a father who had never acknowledged him and never would.

He shuffled through the random paperwork in front of him on the large table, like he cared what it said. He didn't, but it was probably a good idea to *pretend* that he did. Or at the very least, give the impression that he had actually *read* any of it, which he hadn't. "...Well, I suppose at this time, we usually..."

Shit.

What did they usually do?

Julian had no idea. He never paid attention in these types of situations. Generally, Ferral just sat around and droned on and on about silly non-ocean related things which didn't interest Julian in the *slightest*. Why would Julian care about the insignificant concerns of the surface world? He was above them. ...He couldn't exactly *tell* this woman that he had no idea what he was doing though, or that her people filled him with unfathomable loathing and disgust.

It was just a stupid meeting!

He flipped to a random page of the paperwork and only then realized that it was actually for a meeting from a week ago, because no one was left to type out a new meeting agenda. Ferral's annoyingly terrestrial-looking chicken-scratch covered this particular document. Too bad the man hadn't made himself a notation like: "Remember: don't get killed" or "Note to self: dying in some dusty hellhole is not on the itinerary this week for any of our departments."

Julian tried to hold back his amused smile, then it faded as a realization hit him.

...Ah-ha! THAT was what Ferral usually did at times like this! He called on the other departments to give updates on their status!

He straightened in his chair, feeling victorious. He would be FAR better at overseeing meeting procedure than *Ferral* ever was.

"We usually get an update from the Deadly Plagues Department." He announced.

The Consortium Crater Lair had foisted that particular department off on the Undersea Base. ...Something about them not wanting to be around lethal viruses. Strangely, the Undersea Base seemed to be the place where they stuck *all* the people they simply didn't want to deal with on a daily basis. ...Probably because they knew Julian's leadership would inspire them to greatness.

Thus far, he had met only with disappointment in his efforts though. The small team assigned to the Undersea Base was hopeless, and pairing them up with the regular Consortium crew wasn't helping matters.

Across the table, "Bubonic, the Plague Doctor" readjusted the black medieval plague doctor outfit, complete with eerie bird head shaped mask. "After three and a half years of work, I have *finally* perfected my KM85 pox virus." The voice came out raspy and whispering; slightly scrambled and electronic sounding from the filters in the mask. Bubonic carefully removed a vial of innocuous looking fluid, and placed it on the table with gloved hands. "This is the most deadly plague the world has ever seen. It will make Ebola look like a *tummy ache*." Bubonic cackled with evil glee, like only a demented epidemiologist can. "It will be a pandemic of truly *Biblical* proportions, and *we'll* be there to pick up the pieces!"

Julian rolled his eyes, feeling bored. "That would be a *fantastic* piece of news... if it were delivered *last year*."

Bubonic's head tilted in confusion; the round heavily-tinted eyeholes of the bird mask staring blankly.

Julian absently massaged his temples, wondering why he didn't just go back to being a solo criminal. "We agreed to be *Capes* now. We are charged with *stopping* people from creating things like that, *remember?*"

There was a moment of silence.

"...Wait. We did *what?*" Bubonic watched him for a moment longer, then reached up to remove the wide brimmed leather hat, hood and mask with its long curved beak. Bella D'Peste stared at him in amazement, pure black hair spilling around her exceedingly young face. "Is that a joke? When did *that* happen?" She looked around the table at her companions. "Did I miss a memo? Was there a vote on this that no one invited me to? *Capes!?!*" She held her gloved hands out in disbelief. "Ma questo è ridicolo! *Pazzo!*"

Julian rubbed at his temples, more annoyed with this bunch of losers than he could ever remember being. They couldn't even pretend to be capable for *one afternoon*. "Blame Ferral. *I* do." He pointed at Bridget, still glaring at Bubonic. "*You are making us look incompetent in front of our guest*."

Bubonic turned to face her, apparently just realizing that Bridget was there. She made a small squeak of surprise or fear and quickly retrieved her mask, pulling it back into place, as if hiding beneath it. The hood and hat immediately followed until she was completely covered from head to toe again.

The girl was reportedly hands-down the brightest mind in her field, but unfortunately, she wasn't *in* her right mind most of the time. She was *terrible* at social interactions, spent most of her time reading, wouldn't say more than two words at a time to anyone but Julian and Quinn, had a tendency to hide from strangers and a pathological fear of leaving the base. She didn't understand the surface-dwellers any better than Julian did, and she lacked all traces of empathy.

He respected that.

Tupilak looked up at Bridget and shrugged. "Bee's kind of shy."

"She has Asperger syndrome and is agoraphobic." Oz added from as far away from the girl as possible, apparently trying to avoid the vial in the young woman's hand. He readjusted the surgical mask he was wearing in an effort to shield himself from the germs. "I recognize the symptoms."

"*Vaffanculo!*" Bee pointed the end of her wooden staff at him, which was carved to look like the Rod of Asclepius, the ancient symbol of medicine. The snake winding around and around the staff had its jaws open; tiny wooden teeth bared. She turned to look at Quinn, as if he had been the one who spoke rather than Oz. "I do *not* have autism, and I'm *not* agoraphobic."

Quinn nodded. "I know, Bee." He said reassuringly. "Don't worry about it."

Bee sniffed indignantly beneath her mask, her uncharacteristic anger giving way to her normal gentleness and introversion. "...I just don't like being *outside*, that's all." She whispered. "...Or traveling. ...Or heights. ...Or open spaces. ...Or the water. ...Or the dark. ...Or loud noises. ...Or being around strangers." She huddled down into her chair, pulling the collar of her ankle length black leather overcoat up to the base of her mask, like she was expecting Bridget and Oz to attack her or something. Her scrambled voice became even softer, as if talking to herself now. "...Or crowds of people. ...Or talking to people. ...Or people looking at me. ...Or people touching me. ...Or clowns. ...Or the number three." She was silent for a moment, then picked up the test tube of virus again as if mesmerized by it. "...Tu sei la malattia perfetta, sei *bellissima*..."

Tupilak's smile never wavered, continuing to talk to Bridget as though the other woman had never spoken. "I think she *likes* you though. Just look how much she's talking today. She's becoming *quite* the little chatterbox now that she's finally out of the Undersea Base." He glanced at his companion. "Aren't you, Bee?"

The girl began to tremble.

Quinn nodded, as though that were an answer, and turned back to Bridget, looking pleased. "And she didn't start crying uncontrollably or give you smallpox yet, which is *always* a good sign." He nodded good-naturedly. "It was touch-and-go when Wyatt was in your shoes, but he pulled through like a trooper." He paused. "...After the coma."

Muffled sounds of the girl swearing softly in Italian could be heard from beneath the bird mask, as she huddled down in her chair and pulled her knees up against her chest in an effort to disappear, then began to sob.

The girl was very odd and had *serious* psychological and emotional issues.

Luckily, Julian didn't care.

Tupilak ignored that and extended his hand to their guest. "Hey, how ya doing? I'm Quinn Aguta."

Bridget's eyebrows went up. "You're an Eskimo named 'Quinn?'"

"My parents had an odd sense of humor." His smile immediately disappeared. "I *don't*. That stupid song ruined my life. It's one of the main reasons I went into super-villainy. And I'm not an 'Eskimo.' As a racial group, I'm part 'Alaska Native' and part 'Greenland Inuit.' 'Eskimo' is a pejorative given to us by our enemies because they're racist and we're so badass that we make them feel inferior. And rightly so. Because we *are* so badass that we *make them* inferior."

"...Uh-huh." She wrote that down. "And what can you do?"

His voice took on a 'far off' mystical quality. "I was born into the world where there is nothing but the spirits of all things."

"What does that mean exactly?"

"I have no idea. But it sounds cool, so that's my story." He nodded his head. "But among a few other things I won't mention, I'm immune to the cold and I can hunt seals good."

"'Well.'" She corrected

"You'll notice that I didn't mention the ability to be a grammar Nazi on that list. Thanks for pointing it out though. I forgot that even in casual conversation, I need to remember that everyone is judging me." He pointed over his shoulder. "You can proofread my diary if you want. I have it back in my room, and I'm pretty sure I ended a few sentences with prepositions."

"*Tupilak*." Julian snapped in warning.

The man glanced over at Julian and waved him off, then turned back to Bridget. "I'm filled with shame and regret and all kinds of tears and stuff over my rudeness just now." He placed his gloved hand over his heart. "You gotta forgive me, Miss Haniver. I'm not usually this insensitive."

She ignored him. "And your department is?"

"I'm second in command at the Undersea Base, and I oversee some of the Consortium's artic missions."

"And... are there many of those?"

"Just waiting around for the alien from 'The Thing' to invade or for the Rebel Alliance to set up its hidden base on Hoth, Miss Haniver." He chuckled. "It's going to happen any day now, I'm *sure* of it."

"Doesn't the Consortium have another 'cold' themed guy?" She snapped her fingers trying to remember the man's name. "Blue hair?"

Tupilak's smiled faded again. "Yeah, *Pakk*." He spat the name out with annoyed jealousy and shook his head. "I don't talk about him. He takes all the cool jobs, pun intended. He's at his parents' anniversary party right now."

"So, he's what? Competition?"

"Something like that." He leaned forward in his chair. "Let me boil this down for you, since you're new here and might not have noticed yet. You see, we're the *rejects*." He gestured to his companions. "We're the assholes that no one ever wanted on the team, but it was just easier to stick us somewhere and forget about us than to do anything about it. I been 'downsized' by two different criminal organizations already, and the Consortium only gave me *this* job, because I was willing to work the 4 AM shift, and they can cut off the power to the Undersea Base and won't have to heat it when they're gone. That's a pretty shitty job, and I was their only applicant. I *don't* go on field missions. No one would ever *want me* to go on their field mission. I *don't* have a room at the Crater Lair; I had never even *seen* this fucking place until yesterday. I'm not wanted for any infamous or legendary crimes anywhere, because no one's ever wanted me for *anything*. And most of us can say the same. We are *not* the Consortium's starting lineup, we are the fucking benchwarmers and batboys." He pointed around the table at his coworkers again as if introducing them to her. "We are the forsaken and *the damned*, lady. Welcome to Hell."

She pursed her lips. "'The Rejects.' I like that. That would play well. Everyone likes the underdogs."

"I'm so happy my failures will allow you to sell magazines. I'm pretty sure I can track down some ex-girlfriends who could tell you more embarrassing things about me if you wanted."

"Maybe we should spell it with an 'X'." She sounded Interested in the idea. "Like 'The RejeX.'"

"...And what would our motivation for that be?"

"I don't know." She shrugged. "Just to get people's attention."

"Using improper linkage of an action verb is unforgivable, but spelling things incorrectly is apparently 'hip.'" Quinn rolled his eyes. "I don't understand the media."

"Which is why we need a *professional*." Julian announced. "The Lady Haniver will guide us towards getting the recognition which we so *rightly* deserve." He pointed down the table. "Now then, the Purchasing and Production Department will announce itself."

Quinn leaned closer to their guest. "That's Monty." He pointed to the man in question. "He puts the 'dangerous' in the phrase 'dangerous psychotic.'" Quinn's voice lowered to a stage whisper. "He's the reason that doors have *locks* and innocent people carry *guns*."

"I see." The woman wrote that down.

Monty ignored them all, and shook his head at something he read in his folder, looking disappointed. He handed it back to his flunky. "I cannot do *anything* with this one, Higgins."

"B-b-but, *sir*... you said that you wanted the most pow..." The man stammered.

"I *know* what I said, Higgins." He opened the next file, still paying no attention to the meeting. "I don't need a summary of my own words, no matter how *inspirational* they obviously were. I need a..." He stopped, apparently finding something in the new file which caught his interest. "Now *this* I can work with." He flipped the page over to continue reading, a sinister smile passing over his twisted face. "...Oh, that's just *delightful*. This one will fit my needs *splendidly*. ...How *marvelous*." He tapped the paperwork. "Yes. I want *this* one."

Higgins glanced over his boss' shoulder at the file and paled. "...But how will..."

"Somethin' you wanna *share* with the class, Monty?" Mack asked.

The man looked up from his paperwork. "I don't think so, no." He closed the file. "Just thinking of starting a new hobby, that's all." He pointed to something in the file, and glanced over his shoulder at the other man. "*That's* our way in, Higgins. *That's* how we will gain control. That's how we'll *win*." He closed the file, then wrote something out on a slip of paper, sealed it inside an envelope and handed it to the other man along with the file. "We will need to find something which fits my criteria. It's our price of admission. Go see to it." His voice became stern. "*Personally,* Higgins. I want you to see to it *personally* to ensure there are no mistakes, understand?"

The other man nodded eagerly. "Yes, *sir,* sir." He scampered from the room. "I'll go take care of it right now, sir."

The room watched Monty in silence for a moment.

Quinn chuckled. "Uh-oh, I think Monty finally found the *perfect* species of moth to shove down the throats of his victims before he skins them."

Monty ignored him. "I apologize for keeping you all waiting. I know firsthand how annoying it is to deal with people who waste your time." He opened another file. "Now then, I will..." He paused, frowning slightly at their guest. "I'm sorry. Do I *know* you?"

"The Lady Haniver is going to be helping us improve our image, and in return, we are going to help her find her lost vehicle." Julian told him simply.

"...Why the devil would we ever want to do *that*?" The man paused, obviously pondering the issue in his sinister mind. His one good eye squinted slightly at Julian, then slowly focused on the woman, then back again. He relaxed slightly, looking amused. "Well, *that's* certainly unexpected. Usually, I *hate* unanticipated events, but in this case, I find it almost *comically* doomed to failure, and I look forward to the amusement which that will bring me." His creepy inhuman smile widened. "Miss Haniver, is it?" He tipped his top hat to her. "Welcome to the Consortium of Chaos. I hope you survive the experience. ...Few people do."

"Thank you." Bridget told him politely. "Do you mind if I ask you what happened?" She tapped her face, indicating the bullet wound beneath Monty's eye.

"No, not at all." Monty set about calmly organizing his files. "As it turns out, you can't change a contact lens with a revolver."

She frowned. "And the finger?"

"One day I just decided that I liked the number nine. It's so much nicer than *ten*." He said the word as if the idea of having ten fingers was both disgusting and utterly uninspired. He opened a file. "Any other questions?"

"No." Bridget obviously didn't appreciate the man's lies. "I think I have a full picture of you now."

"Excellent. I'm so pleased when I can let people see the *real me*." He looked down at his file again. "Now then, as the only one of our current group who has *ever* cared about the day-to-day functions of this facility, I've gone ahead and taken control of the Human Resources Department, in an effort to head off our current staffing crisis." He took a sip of his tea. "I sent Higgins to have a meeting with Moxley DeWitt this afternoon, trying to make inquiries into whether any of The Dangerous Loners might wish to join our team to fill in for our missing co-workers."

"Yeah, and how'd *that* go?" Mack asked, seemingly already knowing the answer.

Monty looked down at his paper again. "...Well, you have to consider the *audience*."

"In other words, Moxie told your stooge to fuck off because her team don't wanna be your scabs." Mack translated. "Should have just gone *yourself*, Monty. You usually know better than that."

"I assure you, despite all appearances to the contrary, if Higgins were not the most capable man in this room, he would not be in my employ. I'm only interested in hiring the *best*. If *he* couldn't get it done, then *no one* could." Monty made a face. "Besides, 'Scab' is such an *ugly* word. I prefer to think of them as 'freelance consultants' who will join our company free of the unnecessary *burdens* of contracts, employee benefits, and all of that other *needless* paperwork which tries to prevent good hardworking people from obtaining employment as quickly as possible."

Julian let out a long sigh. "Have you contacted any of the other super-groups in town?"

Monty shrugged. "I really don't see the need, to be honest. Our company has never been especially close with any of them, and recent philosophical *changes* here haven't helped matters. To make matters worse, all of the larger groups are currently in Agletaria with our missing employees. Thus, The Dangerous Loners were our last hope on that front, as they've always been more independent than the others and were small enough to avoid going to Agletaria at all. Moxie smells our blood in the water though, and is in no hurry to push her people in with us." He glanced down the table at Julian. "If you intend to move against her in retaliation, I can begin briefing my Irregulars on when and where to hit them. I already have plans drawn up and estimate 90% completion of the project before The Dangerous Loners even realize what's happening to them."

Bridget gasped. "You can't just kill people because they

don't want to work here!"

"Actually, that is *precisely* what I can do, Miss Haniver." Monty told her calmly. "In fact, I can do *worse.*"

Julian shook his head. "You heard the Lady Haniver: you *can't* do that."

"Very well." Monty sighed wearily and looked down at his paperwork. "Then I suggest we focus on maximizing our *current* resources and view this recent staffing issue as a much needed opportunity to reduce overhead." He pulled out another folder. "Speaking of which, before leaving on her honeymoon, Librarian placed me in charge of overseeing Commodious Corporation business in her absence."

Quinn looked confused. "Why would she do that?"

"Because she didn't trust any of *you* to perform the function, for *obvious* reasons." Monty readjusted his monocle. "Now then, our purchase of the 'Pirate's Galley' chain of restaurants has been finalized, using the former Freedom Squad's assets. As a way to increase business in an otherwise stale industry, I have taken the liberty of having Polybius hack into the largest car GPS navigation companies, and alter their systems so that all dining suggestions offered by their services are now for our chain *exclusively*, and all routes supplied to drivers will now be rerouted by way of the nearest 'Pirate's Galley' restaurant before taking them on to their destinations."

"What if they don't want to eat there?" Bridget asked. "What if they want to eat somewhere else, or they aren't even hungry?"

Monty blinked at her for a moment as if she were speaking another language. "I'm sorry?" He looked genuinely confused. "...Why would *that* matter?" He closed the folder. "Just who *are* you, Miss Haniver?" He glanced around the table. "Do we have any assurances that this woman is who she says she is, or are we just going on the honor system now?"

Bridget looked insulted. "Are you accusing me of...?"

"You have *overstepped,* Welles!" Julian bellowed. "The Lady Haniver is NOT to be bothered!" He pointed his trident at the man. "She is here to improve our public image, and she does NOT have to put up with *you.*"

Sitting several seats away, Laura McPherson crossed her arms over her chest. "As the Consortium's governmental liaison, I can't approve any new publicity campaigns *anyway.*" She shook her head. "You people really need to focus on stopping the Super-Person

Resistance Movement, before they kill us all like they did your friends in Agletaria. This city is in *danger*. Personally, I'm *shocked* at how *blasé* you're being about all of this, when you *should* be out there fighting for..."

Quinn glanced at Bridget, cutting the other woman off. "Ignore her. We all do." He rolled his eyes. "Every time she opens her mouth, all I hear are the adults in the old Peanuts cartoons, you know?" He began moving his gloved hand like a mouth and making a strange honking sound. "Waa-wa-waa waa-waa wa."

The woman extended her hand to their guest, ignoring Quinn's mockery. "Agent Laura McPherson. *I'm* in charge, Miss Haniver." Her expression turned sour. "You aren't needed here. *Go home*."

Bridget shook her hand, but appeared confused. "I thought *Lord Sargassum* was in charge?"

"I am." Julian told her simply. "Anyone who tells you differently is a liar and a charlatan." He sat straighter in his chair. "I am the leader of this group, and *I* will be the one who determines our course of action. If I suddenly decided that we should fight crime through clogdancing, there is *nothing* Agent McPherson could do about it except go out and buy *wooden shoes*."

Bridget chuckled in an utterly charming way. "Well, I mean, I'm not going to tell you how to do your job or anything, but it seems to me that your main problem isn't your shoes, it's your *image*."

He nodded. "Indeed. It's that horrible *King* woman on the television machine."

"For starters." Bridget nodded. "She's not your only detractor, but she certainly doesn't take it easy on you guys, that's for sure."

"To say nothing of her *terrible* addiction to cocaine." Monty added to no one in particular.

"She's a drug addict?" Bridget asked, sounding interested.

"Not yet." Monty held up a small baggie filled with an unidentified white powdery substance. "But she will be *soon*." He flashed a cruel smile. "It's a simple matter of having my Irregulars break into her apartment and lace all of her foods with..."

"Enough!" Julian snapped. "Our staff is already depleted, we do not need to further exacerbate the situation by engaging in unneeded missions."

Monty rolled his eyes. "Honestly, the only impact the departure of the others has really had, is that it's now quieter around here, and my department's supply room no longer has to concern itself with quite so much blatant thievery. Besides, elementary staffing theory will tell you that it's always better to be understaffed than be burdened with too much dearly departed *deadweight*. As it turns out, our associates did us a *favor* by getting slaughtered." He put his hat over his heart, as if in respect to his dead co-workers and friends. "It's true what they say: progress really *does* occur one funeral at a time."

"Well, the rest of the departments actually had people in them *as well* at one point, Monty. It wasn't always just you and your boys." Mack told him, as if the man might not have realized that. "I know that you miss a lot of stuff that goes on around here, what with spending all your time in the basement, but we had staffs *too*."

Bridget frowned. "Well, can you hire some new people to help out or something?"

"With what?" Quinn shrugged. "We're tapped out unless we start selling stuff. Thus, the yard sale. Sadly, crime paid better."

"Speaking of which, are we *finally* ready to admit that this whole 'paying it forward' heroism nonsense is simply *preposterous* and go back to trying to make a *profit?*" Monty asked in annoyance. "Hands?"

Several other members immediately put their hands up.

Julian jumped from his seat. "Enough! We will NOT be voting on that! We are HEROES! PERIOD!"

The woman said she was here because she needed a hero, and so, heroes they needed to *stay*. ...No matter how *distasteful* the occupation was.

Quinn frowned in confusion. "...Wait, I thought we were going to flood the..."

"I said: *enough*." Julian turned to glare at the man.

"I swear to God, I should write a children's book to give to all of you idiots called 'Adventures in Common Sense,' and maybe the happy little cartoon kittens inside could get through to you." Monty leaned forward, taking on an exaggerated slow tone, as if speaking with very stupid children. "Try to understand this: we are a *business*. The essential purpose of *all* businesses is to *make money.* "

"What about charities?" Bridget asked. "*They* aren't about making money."

Monty chuckled cruelly. "It's so cute that people still believe that. It makes taking advantage of them so much easier."

Mack sighed. "Why is it that no matter how many or how few of us there are, all our meetings are always the same?"

"Personally, I *like* this meeting." Polly intoned happily. "Look, McCallister! I have a chair!" The hologram pointed to the chair she was projecting herself into. The empty seat was usually occupied by 'Dysphoria,' who was currently in Agletaria.

Mack smiled despite himself. "Yeah, I can see that, Poll. It suits you. I'll talk to Tasha when she gets back and see if you can use it more."

The hologram beamed.

Julian frowned.

Where was he?

Oh yes.

"So, I think it might be of help if we continued telling Lady Haniver who we are and a little about ourselves." He told the group.

Silence.

He tried to keep from killing them.

Quinn apparently sensed the bloodbath about to take place and rose from his seat. "You know what? I think I can take care of this and save us some time. Let's see, who else we got here..." Quinn looked around the table, pointing people out. "That's Roach, I wouldn't talk to him if I were you."

The old man flipped him off. "Fuck you, ya little commie bastard."

"I'm native *Alaskan*, Hector."

"Which is as close to Russia as you can get without dousing yourself in vodka and caviar, and fucking a polar bear in the ass, *comrade.*" He crossed his arms over his chest. "Back in *my* day, we woulda shipped you back to your commie paymasters in a *box*."

Quinn rolled his eyes. "Big talk for the leading suspect in the *Lindbergh kidnapping*, man." He pointed down the table. "That's Traitor, don't..."

"Wait, what about her?" Bridget cut him off, and pointed at Roach's daughter May. "Why isn't she included?"

"Oh, I'm not a Cape." May didn't bother to look up.

"Well, what *are* you then?"

"Reading." The young woman calmly licked her thumb and used it to turn the page of her art magazine. "Just pretend I'm not even here."

"Already do." Quinn informed her cheerily, then pointed at Arnold. "That's Traitor, don't ever trust him."

"And why *not?*" Arn sounded insulted. "I'm a valuable part of this team. I think you're just biased against me."

"It's not 'bias,' it's *experience*."

"Hey, the *government* trusts me." Arn retorted. "I did wetwork for the CIA for years."

"Really?" Mack sounded doubtful. "'Cause *last* week you said it was for the KGB. And *yesterday* you said it was for PBS."

"A man can't have three jobs in your world?" Arn looked confused. "Is that now a crime?"

Quinn rolled his eyes and pointed at the next chairs. "That's Skullduggery and Prohibition. I wouldn't expect much from either of them if I were you. One's always drunk off his ass and the other has been basically in a coma for months now as a result of his 'girl-frenemy' Gia dying. Very sad."

Several moments passed in silence, and then Skullduggery blinked rapidly as if coming out of a trance. "...What? Did someone say something to me?"

"No, Doug. It's okay; go back to taking *Wuthering* to previously unknown *Heights*..." Quinn rolled his eyes again. "We got Mack and Polly... they're pretty normal."

Polly beamed, evidently pleased with that description for some reason.

Mack stared at Bridget silently for a moment. "I don't much take to new people, ma'am." He finally told her simply. "I don't think I wanna talk to you a lot. Try not to take offense."

Polly made a face at him. "Oh, *real nice*. What happened to 'Southern charm'?"

He shrugged. "This is as charmin' as I *get,* darlin'. Thought you knew that by now."

Quinn ignored that, continuing with his introductions. "Mull, who is probably the craziest one here but is less 'in your face' about it."

The masked Cape nodded at her in greeting and made a gun-firing gesture at her with one gloved hand.

"Oz, who is kinda like *Shaft,* but a Shaft who worries about radiation from the microwave getting into his food, and who washes his hands eight times an hour."

Oz frowned unhappily.

"Cynic's brother Ceann, who I don't know anything about, but is pretty much the baddest-ass looking motherfucker I ever saw."

The headless man didn't move a muscle, continuing to silently loom in the shadows against one of the walls.

Bridget shifted, obviously finding the fact that he had no head unnerving. "...And just so there are no surprises which cause media disasters down the road: how did you... umm... become *disabled?*"

He typed something into his spelling toy. "YOU HAVE

SPELLED: AX."

She waited for an elaboration on that, but when none was forthcoming.

Quinn made a dismissive face, and turned to look at the last man at the table. "...And that's..." he trailed off, "...I have no idea who that is."

The man in question nervously shifted in his chair. "I'm Wendell." He choked out hurriedly. Everyone stared at him in silence. "...From Finance?" He added, hoping to jog their memories. It didn't. He shifted in his seat again. "Dean Willson, she brought me in as a Temp to handle payroll while she's on her honeymoon. I'm a grad student at GSU?" It came out sounding like a question.

"I see." She wrote that down. "And what can you do?"

The man shrugged. "Actuarial tables?" It came out sounding like a question again, as if the man were asking them what his purpose was. "I'm not a superhero, I just place cash values on human life."

"Whenever *I* do that, I'm called an 'inhuman monster.'" Monty rolled his one good eye and made little air quotes with his fingers, obviously feeling unappreciated, but still almost amused with what he saw as his detractors' naive stupidity. "Apparently, I should have come up with a more innocuously named job title, so that it sounds more respectable and less 'cold-hearted.'"

"And this is the entire team at the moment?" Bridget looked up from her list. "Everyone else is busy in Agletaria?"

"Tyrant, Rayn, Hazard, Stacy, Cynic and Marian are all on their honeymoons in Rayn's kingdom." Arnold told her, sounding uninterested. "I wasn't invited." There was a twinge of bitterness in his voice, as though not taking him along on their honeymoons had been a personal slight in his opinion.

"Your friend has her own kingdom?" Bridget's eyebrows soared. "Wow. That's pretty cool."

"...I have my own kingdom." Julian informed her, hoping to spark that same level of approval. Not that he was trying to *impress* her or anything... just let her know how important he was. "The oceans are *far* more interesting than some silly fairy dimension, as you *undoubtedly* realize."

"Uh huh." Bridget was obviously not paying her full attention to him, despite the truth of his words. "Anyone else?" She asked the group.

"Well..." Quinn's brow compressed in thought, "now that you mention it, I still feel like there's someone we're forgetting about here."

Arnold shrugged. "I thought that too, but I got no idea who."

"Maybe you're thinking of Meg?" Oz suggested. "She was here yesterday, but now seems to have wandered off somewhere."

Quinn made an uncertain face. "...Nah. There's someone else we're overlooking, I know it."

"Well, Cory and Holly are in Mexico lookin' for Lexie. I still think we're forgettin' someone, but they're the only other members unaccounted for. Wyatt sent them down there on a search and rescue mission after they lost Lexie in Tijuana." Mack scratched his chin with his free hand. "Which means they're all prolly on a beach somewhere, relaxin' with margaritas."

****

The ground rumbled and a deep throaty roar echoed in the distance. The sound was filled with furious rage.

"Oh, I think he's angry." Cory was on the verge of full-blown panic now.

"Well of *course* he's angry!" Holly yelled back, running along the path ahead of him. "Wouldn't *you* be after what just happened?"

A short distance ahead of them, the hero known as "Jaguar Knight" appeared from the jungle; bare-chested and wearing jaguar spotted fur leggings. He pointed his obsidian macuahuitl ax across the river. "We *must* hurry, my friends." The Aztec warrior disappeared into the tangle of leaves again.

"Shitshitshitshit..." Cory leapt off of one of the large stone blocks scattered around, which had previously been part of the ziggurat they were fleeing from. He landed in a crouch and swore again, firing off an arrow from his bow and hitting one of the crazed monkey warriors as it crashed through the jungle behind them. "Why the hell did you do that, Holly!?!" He fired off several arrows in rapid succession, wiping out a wave of guards as they sprang from behind a boulder. "What the fuck were you *thinking!?!*"

Overhead the sky continued to darken and seethe with furious lightning.

"Oh, sure. Blame me." Holly jumped across a large crevasse, landing in a roll on the other side. "I don't see how this is *my* fault." She dusted herself off and pointed to the woman next to her. "Talk to *her.*"

Trapper Voldar crossed her arms over her more feminine version of her father's safari khakis. "My dad always said you were a *fucking bitch,* and now I see he *understated.*" She ran off into the jungle again, carrying the golden object, which resembled a large gear. "Now I'm *glad* you're dead, Aunt Holly." She yelled back at them. "MOVE YOUR FAT ASS! THE PAST SUCKS EVEN MORE THAN THE PRESENT!"

Cory ran towards the edge, preparing to jump over to the other side. "I don't blame *her* because she's from the futu..." he skidded to a stop; inches from the edge, "...nope."

Holly had made the jump because she had enhanced abilities due to her magical physiology. *Cory* on the other hand, had no such talents. He'd never make it.

Holly frantically gestured with one gloved hand. "Jump! Do it! Stop being such a 'Tiny Tim' about it and jump!"

Cory heard a noise behind him and slowly turned around. The sky over the secret jungle valley was utterly black now, and an endless wave of furious monkeys was rushing towards him, obeying their dark master's command.

He reached behind his back to pull out another arrow... but found that he had fired them all.

He swallowed, taking a step back and finding only air. He pin-wheeled his arms, trying to keep his balance and avoid falling from the cliff.

The monkeys crashed from the tree line in front of him.

He swore again; his words lost in the howl of crazed primates, the echoing laughter of their master and the booming thunder.

The solid wall of monkey guards was upon him now and...

****

"They are unimportant." Julian announced. "Vaudeville, Missile-Tow, and Lexington have never done *anything* of merit, and they have no place in my new organization."

"Gotcha." Bridget crossed something out on her clipboard. "Well, we'll just forget all about them then."

"An *excellent* plan."

She glanced up from her work. "Well, I guess it's my turn." She put the clipboard down and gave them an *adorably* awkward wave. "Hi! I'm... uh... Bridget Haniver. I live in the Village. I'm an only child, I like seafood and country music, and I've been a press agent for five years now."

"Which university did you attend?" Monty asked, pulling a monogramed gold pen from his breast pocket to begin recording her information. "I will also need your parents' names, your social security number, a blood sample, your home address, and a current copy of your resume."

Julian glared at him in annoyance. "I've *warned* you about that already, Montgomery."

The man polished his monocle and replaced it on his face. "Yes, forgive me for doing something as *impertinent* as asking for the qualifications of the woman we are entrusting with our personal information and the future of our company's image." He put the pen down and gestured across the table at McPherson. "I mean, didn't we learn *anything* from Ferral inviting *that* cow to spy on us?"

Polly snorted in laughter.

McPherson didn't look nearly as amused.

Bridget shuffled her feet nervously. "I, uh... I understand that kind of thinking. I mean, if I had... Monty, is it? If I had *Monty's* sterling reputation in this city, I wouldn't trust it to anyone either." She glanced across the table. "Polybius?"

The hologram perked up. "Yes, Miss Bridget?"

"Polybius, can you please see which terms are most associated with Monty on the internet, please?"

The hologram obviously liked being asked nicely for something. "Yes, I can do that. You may call me 'Polly,' Miss Bridget."

Bridget smiled. "Thanks!"

"Please wait..." Words and images sped across Polly's digital skin as she searched, then returned to normal. "The words most commonly associated with Mr. Montgomery include: 'cult,' 'evil,' 'mystery man,' 'gears,' 'who is,' 'shot,' 'crash,' 'heir' and..." she frowned slightly, looking uncertain, "...well, 'motherfucker.'"

Mack chuckled, apparently either amused by someone associating Monty's name with that word, or merely from hearing his rather innocent companion use such a *colorful* term.

"Several people also confuse his name with the 'Montgomery *Ward*' department store." The hologram added helpfully.

"Thank you, Polly." Bridget nodded and turned to address Monty again. "I can see why you'd worry about someone tarnishing *that* reputation, after you've obviously done so *much* to preserve it."

Monty watched her expressionlessly for a long moment, then reached into his coat pocket to pull out his phone. He pressed a button. "Siri?"

"What can I help you with today?" Said the computerized voice of his iPhone's digital assistant app.

Polly gasped in horror and turned to Mack. "McCallister! He's using that horrid *thing* again!" She pouted. "Make him stop!"

Monty smiled evilly. "Siri, look up the street address of 'Bridget Haniver,' in Greenwich Village."

"I can search for that if you'd like, Montgomery." Said the voice.

"Yes, please do."

"Searching for Bridget Haniver Greenwich Village.... Here are the results."

"Ah, thank you, Siri." He turned the phone around so that Bridget could see her home address displayed.

"You're most certainly welcome." Said the phone.

"Well, look at *that*." Monty said with feigned surprise. "I have your address *after all*, Miss Haniver. ...Oh, and *here's* your resume which you helpfully posted to a job search site. Now, all I need to do is call up one of my Irregulars who works for the police department, and get her to find out *everything* about you for me." His smirk grew wider. "I *do* hope there aren't any *skeletons* in your closet."

Mack waved a hand and turned Monty's phone off using his powers, then leaned forward to glare at the other man. "Why do you do that? You *know* it upsets her?"

Monty looked down at his phone in confusion. "Siri? I don't know, she sounded *'pretty normal'* to me." He stressed the words, deliberately repeating how Quinn had described Polly earlier, then smirked. "But then again, who can tell with *mindless* computer programs. They sound however they're *programmed to sound*."

Polly's eyes narrowed in irritation and barely constrained hate.

Mack watched the man silently for a minute. "You and me are gonna have a problem." He finally said, his voice utterly flat. "Aren't we?"

Monty went back to his paperwork. "Considering the number of things you seem to have *'problems'* with, I would say that the odds are certainly *quite good*, yes."

Bridget tapped her fingers on the table in annoyance, then pointed at him. "You know, I just can't work with you." She gestured at him with her free hand. "It's not about you getting bad press, it's about the public having it right the *entire time*. You *are* an evil motherfucker, *aren't* you?"

"*Unquestionably*." Julian agreed immediately, not realizing that that fact had even been up for *debate*.

"Well, if the internet says it, it *must* be true. That was probably the first rule they taught you at…" Montgomery paused, "I'm sorry, *where* did you say you earned your degree in public relations, Miss Haniver? …Oh, wait. According to your resume, you *don't have one*, that's right." Monty's sinister sneer never wavered. "Not that I am criticizing your 'credentials,'" he made little air quotes with his hands again, "I just think we should perhaps hire someone who is actually *qualified* for their job, rather than random women off the street whom we simply *feel sorry for.*"

Julian very slowly rose from his chair. "*Leave.*" He pointed towards the door, struggling to keep his temper in check.

Monty rolled his eyes and continued working.

Julian's knuckles went white around his trident. "*Now.*" He got out between gritted teeth.

Monty looked up at him, as if surprised.

"If I see you again today, you're not going to *like* what happens." Julian warned him seriously.

Monty sighed as if he was the most mistreated person on Earth, and began collecting his files. "Very well. Honestly, I don't know *why* I waste my time with you people anyway." He tipped his top hat to them. "Enjoy your meeting." He limped out the door and into the shadowy hallway beyond. "I have *work to do.*"

Julian took several deep breaths, trying to calm down.

Bridget reached for the glass of water in front of her. "There. That's better, isn't it? Now that he's gone?"

"Oh, yes. *I* certainly think so." Polly chimed in. "Don't you think, McCallister?"

"Anytime Monty's not here is a good time in my book, Poll." He took off his cap and ran a hand through his hair, letting out a tired sigh. "Y'know, I've known that asshole a long time… longer than any of y'all… and he's gettin' *entirely* too big for his britches." He pulled his hat back into place, and looked down the table at Julian as if he had just come to a hard realization. "We're gonna haveta *deal* with him soon, Jules. Ya know that, right?"

Julian nodded soberly. "Indeed."

"And that boy ain't *goin'* quiet." Mack sounded almost sad as he imagined the trouble they would all be in. "He's a *scrapper*. It ain't *in him* to just walk away." He met Julian's eyes. "We're playin' under the anvil tree keepin' him around."

"And just where would you suggest that we *send* Monty and his fanatically loyal and heavily armed private army– which, incidentally, knows *every inch* of our home– where they *wouldn't* be a threat?" Arnold asked in genuine curiosity. "And not to disagree with you guys, but I personally always feel *better* when he's in the room, as at least *then* I know he isn't going to set a bomb off under the table or something."

Julian made a disinterested hand motion. "Welles is a surface-dweller with no powers. He poses *me* no danger, other than ruining my good mood." He pointed at the table with one finger. "But if he insults our guest again, I'm going to feed him to the fucking *sharks*. I give you my *word* on that."

Quinn shook his head. "Monty isn't going to try anything. All his little pieces aren't even on the board yet. He's just acting out because our proverbial 'mom' and 'dad' are out of town, and he wants to throw himself a *righteous* party before they get back."

Traitor continued absently clicking through the songs on one of his missing coworker's iPods. "My dad always said: 'Keep your friends close, but your enemies closer.' He paused to think about it. "...No, wait. That doesn't make any sense, does it? Why would you want to be close to your *enemies?* Who the hell would do *that?* No, I think it was: 'Keep your friends close, but *put your enemies in the fucking ground*.' He nodded to himself, obviously pleased at remembering that charming maxim. "Yep. That was it."

Bridget looked down at her notes again. "Okay, where were we...." She ran her fingertip down the paperwork. "...Oh, yes. Here we are..." She looked up at him. "I found a rumor that you were somehow responsible for those shark attacks in 1916 which inspired the movie *Jaws*? Any truth to that?"

Julian shook his head. "None. I've never bitten anyone in my life."

"What about the shark?"

"Oh, most certainly. But I'm not the one who bit those people, all I did was send the shark." He looked around the table for support. "Is that somehow now *illegal* in the surface world?"

Quinn raised his hand. "I got no problem with it, boss. *Jaws 3D* was awesome. What's-her-name, Michael J. Fox's hot mom, was hot as fucking hell in it. Not to go all weird and freaky on you, but if *I* was in his shoes, I *totally* woulda sealed the deal at the *Enchantment Under the Sea Dance,* and worried about the consequences *later*, you know? I mean, if you're so worried about kids with like birth defects and mutations and shit, wear a fucking *condom*, right? Then you could fuck her as much as you wanted and not have to worry about knocking her sexy ass up with your new little brother or sister." He crossed his arms over his chest, obviously believing that he had the answers to all of the world's troubles. "Problem *solved*."

Bubonic leaned over to whisper something in Quinn's ear.

He nodded. "...And Bee likes Dennis Quaid." Quinn added for her. "Jaws 3 has just got something for *everyone*."

Mack shook his head sadly. "Sometimes I feel like I'm part of some kind of secret laboratory study, and there are scientists hidin' behind hidden wall panels in this room, just watchin' me and waitin' to see how much stupid I can listen to before finally crackin'."

Bridget ignored the byplay. "Well, it'd probably be for the best if you kept from mentioning that to anyone in the press from now on, okay?"

Julian frowned. "Why would your people care about which surface actors my team finds most attractive?"

"Because it's gross?" Polly guessed. "And..." She trailed off, looking for the right word.

"...gross." Mack finished for her. "I got to listen to Arn talkin' about wantin' to take nudie pictures of his twin sister, and now Quinn talkin' about wantin' to fuck his mom in the past, and frankly, this place is beginnin' to scare the shit outta me." He shook his head. "I mean, there's *evil* and then there's just..."

"...gross." Polly finished.

"Not *my* mom, you pervert. Michael J. Fox's Back to the Future mom! I'm just saying that if she was my mom, and I was there, I would have totally hit that."

"*What the hell is wrong with your head, boy!?!*" Mack asked, once again looking confused and annoyed. "How could she be *your* mom, if she's not your *mom!?!*"

Quinn ignored him and refocused on Bridget, his eyes narrowing. "And as an American man, it's my *God given right* to enjoy movies based solely on how hot the women in it are." He shook his head angrily, jabbing a finger against the tabletop to show his resolve on this all-important issue. "I don't know what kind of ass-backwards world you're trying to create here, lady, but..."

"Not *movies*." Bridget rolled her eyes. "I mean not mentioning to people that you and the Jaws shark were friends."

Julian nodded. "Word of it will not pass my lips."

"We have enough troubles without reminding people of the century of disasters that you're responsible for." She ran a hand through her hair. "On the bright side, someone set footage of your dam antics the other day to the 'Can-Can' song, then ended with the footage of Julian's 'I blame the victims for this' line." She looked up from her paperwork. "It has over two million hits on YouTube so far."

She nodded, obviously impressed with those numbers. "I think it just might hit meme status. An *unconventional* marketing strategy, to be sure, but any publicity is good publicity, I suppose. It certainly cements the notion that this is not the everyday team of heroes, and it's definitely getting your names out there."

Julian had no idea what a 'Youtube,' or a 'meme' even was, but if it made her happy, then he was pleased as well.

"*Excellent*."

CHAPTER 6

KING: "MY PROBLEM WITH THE CONSORTIUM HAS ALWAYS BEEN THAT THEY AREN'T THE RESULT OF ANY GOVERNMENTAL OR PHILANTHROPIC AGENCY OR INSTITUTION. THEY AREN'T EVEN PRIVATE CITIZENS STEPPING IN AND TRYING TO PICK UP THE SLACK FOR LAW ENFORCEMENT AND THE UNNEEDED HAND OF BIG GOVERNMENT. THEY'RE SIMPLY TERRIBLE PEOPLE WHO FOUND A WAY TO ELIMINATE THEIR LONGSTANDING ENEMIES, AND AT THE SAME TIME, TAKE OVER THE CITY."

STORMS: "THEY SAVED THE CITY!"

KING: "SURE, ACCORDING TO THEM. I HAVE NO WAY OF KNOWING THAT. NOT REALLY. I MEAN, WHO'S TO SAY WHAT REALLY HAPPENED WHEN THEY TOOK DOWN THE FREEDOM SQUAD?"

STORMS: "BUT I WAS THERE! I SAW THE WHOLE THING! THEY REALIZED THAT THEY HAVE A DUTY TO THIS CITY, AND SAW THAT THEY COULD MAKE A DIFFERENCE."

KING: "VILLAINS HAVE A DUTY TOO, CONNIE. THEY HAVE A DUTY TO THEMSELVES. A DUTY TO DESTROY EVERYTHING THEY SEE. A DUTY TO TAKE EVERYTHING THEY CAN, AND LEAVE THE REST OF US TO OUR FATES. THAT'S THE ONLY DIFFERENCE THEY CAN EVER MAKE TO ANYONE."

TRANSCRIPT OF "KING OF CAPES AND COWLS," MEDIA: TELEVISION, SHOW: 1407, NEWSCHANNEL 6, FRIDAY 21:00-22:00 EST, NETWORK SEGMENT-ID: 918000606

Bridget had an excellent sense of direction, despite getting lost all the time. Most people probably would have given up their stubborn insistence about the impressive nature of their own navigational prowess, but Bridget wasn't a quitter. She *was* good at directions, she just sometimes decided to unintentionally find longer routes to where she needed to go, that's all.

In the instant case though, she probably should have just followed the signs. There was a difference between taking the "unbeaten path" and taking a path which had never even been in the fight. …Or whatever.

Not that she was "lost" in the traditional sense, as the Consortium's Lair only had a couple dozen different hallways, just in the sense that she wasn't entirely sure which one of them she was in at the moment.

It was completely different.

In any case, she was trying to locate her wayward clients in an effort to discuss some of her strategies with them, but they were all missing. She had arrived at the Lair fifteen minutes before, and thus far, no one was to be seen. What kind of heroes didn't bother to show up for work? *Especially* since almost all of them *lived here*, so it was basically like calling in sick to your home office.

And the security here *sucked.* No wonder most of them were probably dead now. Hell, she had just strolled right on in today.

She came to a set of swinging metallic doors, and absently glanced through the small round windows cut into them. Tables were arranged around the large darkened room and their empty plastic chairs were stacked upside down on the tabletops, as though waiting for their occupants to return. It looked like a cafeteria of some kind.

Huh.

She started to walk away and continue her search again, when something caught her eye in the corner of the room. Sitting alone at one of the tables, Sargassum was bathed under the room's only illumination.

She paused in her tracks to watch him for a long moment.

He looked so… *alone.*

Honestly, it was actually kinda sad. Like he was the kid that no one wanted to sit next to in the lunchroom. The man sat motionless; staring off into the darkness of the room with unseeing eyes.

…But he was here, which meant that she could discuss her work with him. …And that overhead light was doing *wonderful* things to the angles of his face…

She took a deep breath, feeling nervous for some reason, and pushed the door open.

He turned in his chair, instantly straightening when he saw

her. "Good morning, Lady Haniver."

She nodded in greeting. "Lord Sargassum."

"You may call me 'Julian.'" He shifted in his chair uncomfortably. "...If you would prefer."

She nodded. "Okay." She held up her notes. "I have a few more suggestions about the team, Julian."

"Excellent. I look forward to hearing them." He leaned forward expectantly.

Her eyebrows rose. "What? Now?"

"Indeed."

"What about the others?" She looked around the room. "Where *are* they, anyway?"

He shrugged. "I have no idea."

"Well, don't you think that's something you should... I don't know... *investigate?* I mean, it seems like a lot of you guys have been disappearing lately."

He shook his head. "They are fine, I assure you."

"The people in Agletaria?"

He shook his head again. "No, they are most likely dead." He sounded almost bored. "I was speaking of my team here."

"Then why are they MIA? Are they out trying to track down that Reece guy and his band of super-crazies?"

"Who?"

"'Reciprocity?'" She reminded him. "You know, the guy trying to take over the city? He was on all the news stations this morning, vowing to kill everyone."

He stared at her blankly.

"You didn't *see* it? Hell, they're probably *still* running the footage! *He set the Statue of Liberty on fire with a laser!*"

He shrugged disinterestedly. "I do not watch the news. It is terrestrial propaganda."

"Well, please don't tell the news people that."

"If that is what would make you happy, I will abide by your wishes and refrain from telling the media that anymore."

"...'Anymore'? Meaning you've told them that *before?* Wait... you know what, I don't want to know." She glanced around the darkened room again. "And why are you sitting in here all alone? It's kinda creepy."

"It is Wednesday." He informed her, as though that was all the explanation which was required.

"Last time I checked." She nodded. "So?"

"The *Book Club* meets on Wednesday."

"Oooh." She nodded again. "Oh, okay. Where are they?"

"Agletaria." He said calmly. "Or on their honeymoons."

"All of them?"

He shook his head, looking almost sad. "No. *I* am still here."

"...And you're what? Just going to have the meeting here all by yourself?"

"Lady Haniver, there is no one left to have the meeting *with.*"

She had no reply to that. There was something almost tragic about that idea. The man was seriously going to sit in the dark alone all morning, because none of his friends were here to talk to him. Even the people who weren't in the club had all gone off to do other things, and hadn't even invited him along.

She cleared her throat, trying to dislodge the lump which was forming in it for some reason.

"Call me 'Bridget.'" She looked down at the table. "Well, what book is it? Maybe I've read it."

"I do not know, Lady Bridget." He glanced down at the book. "*The Remains of the Day.*" He read from the cover as if it was the first time he had ever seen the title.

"Wait, you haven't read it *either?*"

He snorted. "Why would *I* care what happens during a surface-dweller's day?" He shook his head. "This book is the *Bell girl's* doing, as she insists that her husband needs to become better acquainted with his 'foreigner-ness.'" He pinched the bridge of his nose in irritation and dropped the book back to the table in disgust. "Honestly, I question the taste and sanity of the rest of the club. Her nomination of this particular title was the most awkward moment I've been forced to experience since the time we were all required to read *Poacher's* choice of book: '*Are You There God? It's Me, Margaret.*'" He shuddered at the memory. "Since then, he is forbidden from choosing the titles we discuss."

"Well, then why are you even here, if you have no interest in the book?"

"It is Wednesday." He repeated. "I go to Book Club on Wednesday. We have discussed this already."

"*But you didn't even read the book!*"

"What does *that* have to do with anything?" He sounded genuinely confused. "I haven't read *any* of the books which the club discusses."

"Then why are you *here?*"

He stared at her in apparent bafflement. "Because today is

Wednesday..."

"And you go to Book Club on Wednesdays." She finished for him. "You're a difficult man, you know that? Why would you want to discuss a book you've never read, with people you don't like, who aren't even here?"

He watched her for a long moment, then glanced down at the cover.

Then it hit her.

"You have nothing else to *do*, do you?" It wasn't really a question.

His eyes flicked back up to meet hers. "This is not *all* I have to do today." He went back to looking at his book. "...I also have to watch for trouble on the eternal seas. Ocean disasters can happen at *any* time you know, and I need to be prepared for them." He cleared his throat. "...Sinkings. ...Fires at sea. ...Whale poaching..." He trailed off.

"That's like, the saddest thing I've ever heard, you know that?" She flopped down into the chair across from him. "All you have in the world is a stuffy book, and some water."

"In my defense... it is a *lot* of water."

She made an unconvinced sound. "Yeah, I'm sure." She absently tapped her fingers on the tabletop, unsure of why she was even here. ...Probably because she honestly didn't have anything else in her life at the moment *either*. Her eyes drifted down to his book. "So what's it *about*, anyway?"

He looked at the cover. "Well, there is a pocket watch shown. Perhaps it's about watches."

She rolled her eyes. "*Watches?*"

He nodded seriously. "I know several people who carry them."

She pointed at his book. "Well, I'm sure you'll enjoy this book then. Think of all the *fascinating* things you'll learn about pocket watches from it, and you can then share your knowledge with them."

He processed that for a moment. "I do not *like* them though."

"Watches?"

"The people I know who carry them."

"Ah."

"They... they annoy me."

"Well, what about Bee and Quinn?"

"Neither of them carries a pocket watch." He paused to reconsider the matter. "...Unless they are *hiding* them from me for some reason…"

"No, I mean that *they* seem like your friends."

"A god-king does not *have* friends." He informed her, as if imparting an important lesson which she had somehow overlooked all these years.

"What are they then? Family? Coworkers?"

He appeared to think about that for a moment. "…More like 'pets,' I suppose." He said seriously.

She snorted. "*Pets*." She slapped her palm against the tabletop and put her head back to chortle with laughter. "Pets!"

He frowned slightly. "…Are you laughing at me?"

"*Absolutely*."

"God-kings do not *like* being laughed at, or having their dignity impugned."

She laughed harder, putting her head down on the table.

He rose majestically to his feet, looking hurt for some reason. "I shall leave you now. I'm glad you find me so amusing."

She sat straighter in her chair, and waved a dismissive hand. "Oh, don't be like that. We're friends, aren't we? And friends can josh one another every now and then."

"I do not know." He blinked at her in confusion. "…Who is 'Josh'?"

She shrugged. "I have no idea."

"Then why am I expected to befriend him? I do not *like* surface-dwellers."

"Uh huh." She reached for his discarded book. "Well, you certainly hang out with enough of them for some reason."

"A god-king is always alone." He looked down at the floor.

"Is he now?" She began absently flipping through the book. "Well, that must save money on movie tickets. In fact, I bet…" She stopped on one of the pages and pointed at it excitedly. "Wait, wait, wait…"

"I am waiting."

She waggled the book at him. "I know this stupid book! *I saw the movie!*" She cried in victory. "It had what's-his-name in it! You know, that British guy!"

"Merlin?" He guessed, sinking back into his chair.

"No, Anthony Hopkins. He was…" She processed his words and looked up at him in amazement and disbelief. "'*Merlin*'? What the fuck?"

He shrugged. "He was British, wasn't he?"

"And totally *random*, you weirdo." She pointed at the book

again. "The point is that I *totally* know all about this thing now."

"Excellent." He folded his hands on the table with extraordinary dignity. "And what is it about?"

"Butlers and stuff."

He waited expectantly. "And?"

"And *what?* That's what it's about."

"A 300 page book reduced to three succinct words." He flipped the book over to examine the back. "Just *look* at all this wasted verbiage in the summary. The author really should have consulted you before publishing."

She rolled her eyes again. "Well, *excuse me* Mr. 'I think this is about *pocket watches.*'" She snatched the book from him. "At least *I* came to this club meeting with *some* understanding of the book we're supposed to be discussing."

He held his arms wide to show his helplessness. "And just *what* am I supposed to discuss with you? How does 'butlers and stuff' inspire any conversation?"

"It's better than *you* could come up with." She crossed her arms over her chest. "Maybe I'll just reminisce about the book by myself, and cut you right the hell out of my examination of its themes."

He arched an eyebrow. "Which were?"

She opened her mouth to reply, but he cut her off.

"If you are going to tell me 'butlers and stuff' you needn't bother."

She closed her mouth.

He snatched the book back from her and flipped through it. "Why would anyone want to read about *servants* anyway? Especially *terrestrial* servants?" He made a scoffing sound. "I'm a *king*, what do *I* care how a servant spends the remaining hours of his day?" He frowned. "...Unless it's serving *me.*"

"Well, you serve the city, don't you?"

He snorted in a *most* undignified way, then cleared his throat as though trying to cover. "*No*, of course not."

"What do you mean? I've seen you do some pretty damn heroic stuff. You're *obviously* a Cape. You even told me so yourself."

His eyes widened as though he just remembered something. "Oh, yes. I mean, *of course* I serve this city." He shifted in his chair. "The wellbeing of its citizenry is of the... umm... *highest* import to me. I love this city so very, very... umm... *very* much."

"See? So maybe the butler guy in the book feels the same way."

He flipped through the book again, then glanced up at her. "I... I don't think that he fights crime." He shook his head, as though breaking bad and unexpected news to her. "I think he mainly just serves tea to his betters."

"I don't mean that he fights *crime*, I mean that he..." She trailed off and made an annoyed sound. "You're just not going to understand this, are you?"

"I will tell you what I do not understand," he apparently wasn't listening, and continued reading random pages, "I do not understand your surface peoples' insistence on writing in the first person. It is annoying."

"Because it messes with the author's ability to switch character's perspectives?"

"Because then I have to make believe that I am *one of you*, and that is something which I cannot abide."

"Ah." She nodded. "Should have seen that one coming."

He turned the page in his book. "I do not like this man. He is a coward."

"Who is?"

"Your butler." He pointed to the book. "Why does he serve others when he could just take the manor for himself?"

"Because he understands the satisfaction which comes from hard work." She told him, trying to sound wise. "He takes pride in being part of something bigger than himself and helping others."

He glanced up at her from his book, his eyebrow arching again.

She shrugged. "No, you're right. I don't get it either." She shook her head. "Hopkins in 'Silence of the Lambs' *never* would have put up with that shit." She tapped her finger against the table. "First time Lord what's-his-face told him to fetch the cucumber sandwiches, Silence-of-the-Lambs-Hopkins woulda cut his face off and worn it on his date with Emma-Thomson-the-maid."

Julian frowned in confusion. "Why would he cut off his own face?"

"No, not *his* face, what's-his-face's."

"...Whose faces?"

"The *other* guy. Archibald McStuffyPants, or whatever the rich guy's name was."

He thought about that for a moment. "...Why would he wear another man's face on his date with Miss Kenton?"

"*How should I know!?!*" She shrugged helplessly. "The man's *insane!* Who knows *why* he does the things he does!"

He squinted in confusion. "The butler?"

"No!"

"This 'Archibald' person?"

"No, Hopkins in *Silence of the Lambs.*"

He pursed his lips in thought, then skipped several pages. "When does *he* show up? That sounds far more interesting than the events of this chapter."

"He doesn't."

"Then how can he possibly wear Lord Darlington's face on his date with Miss Kenton?"

"He can't!" She waved him off dismissively. "Oh, you're not even *listening*, are you?"

"I assure you that I *am*, I simply do not understand how a character from another book can influence the events of this one."

"I'm not *talking* about a book, *I'm* talking about a movie!"

"Which movie?"

"*Silence of the Lambs,* obviously."

He nodded slowly, still trying to process that. "...And your lamb movie is the *sequel* to..."

She cut him off. "Look, just *forget it*, okay? Just forget I said *anything.*"

"Am I permitted to remember what this book is about?"

"*No.*" She shook her head sarcastically. "No, not even that."

"Very well." He closed the book. "I still believe that it is about watches then."

"Think whatever you want." She crossed her arms over her chest, scowling at him. "You're not going to listen to me, then I don't care what you think either."

"I have forgotten you spoke at all."

Her mouth fell open in shock, and she rose from the table. "*Fine.*" She began to storm from the room. "Then I'm not going to waste my time with you anymore."

"But Book Club is not over for another twenty-two minutes!" He sounded both insulted and shocked that she would try to leave early.

"*Tough.*"

He hurried to catch up. "I have somehow insulted you, haven't I?"

"Really? Ya think?"

"Indeed." He tried to squeeze around her to block her path. "I am not familiar with many terrestrial customs, so I'm not sure what it is that I might have done to upset you, but..."

"You just said you weren't listening to me!"

He shook his head. "That's *not* what I said. I said that I had *forgotten* everything you said." He crossed his arms over his chest. "That is entirely different."

"Oh, yeah." She rolled her eyes. "I feel *much* better now."

"Good." He smiled, as if he had solved everything. "You see? If you would just *explain* the strange social practices of your backward people, this entire misunderstanding could have been averted."

She gaped at him in astonishment. "What misunderstanding? How did I misunderstand you ignoring me?"

"I'm *not ignoring you.*" He repeated as though he were sick of rehashing this issue with her. "I am simply making an effort to forget what you say."

"That's a terrible thing to say!"

"You told me to!" He held his arms out in exasperation. "Why do the surface people *always* do that? They can never just tell you what they want, they always have to have some *scheme* brewing."

"And how is this part of some insidious scheme I'm cooking up?"

"You told me to forget our entire conversation had taken place, and now you are yelling at me for abiding by your wishes." He crossed his arms over his chest again, looking smug. "But I have *uncovered* your plot, and now you are angry."

She opened her mouth to reply, then closed it again. "...You know... I just don't even know what we're talking about anymore. Last thing I remember had something to do with *Silence of the Lambs.* Let's just go back to talking about that."

He shook his head seriously. "I have no recollection of that event."

She pinched the bridge of her nose to keep from hitting him. "Okay. On *that* note, I'm going to call it a day."

He frowned again. "But there are still nineteen minutes left to Book Club."

"But we're not even discussing the book anymore! We're just arguing, and I'm about to hit you with something!"

"Welcome to Book Club." He beamed, as though she was finally catching on. "Next week, we shall be discussing *Robinson Crusoe.*"

She shook her head. "I've never read it, and I don't intend to."

"Me either."

"How in God's name can we have a meeting to discuss a book that *neither of us* has ever read?"

He smirked. "I don't remember."

She put up her hands in surrender, and left the room.

The man was *insane.* No one in their right mind would *ever* want to spend time with him, which, now that she thought about it, was probably why he was sitting in here alone to begin with!

CHAPTER 7

KING: "...AND NOW WE HAVE THIS STRANGE FISH PERSON IN CHARGE OF PROTECTING US, AND FRANKLY, I'M NOT HAPPY ABOUT THAT FOR ANY NUMBER OF REASONS. I HAVE NO IDEA WHO HE IS, AND WHAT LITTLE I DO KNOW ABOUT HIM, JUST MAKES ME FEEL EVEN WORSE ABOUT THE SITUATION. I MEAN, WHAT CAN A FISH-MAN EVER DO TO PROTECT A CITY FROM HARM, EVEN IF HE WANTED TO, WHICH DOESN'T APPEAR TO BE THE CASE. HE'S GOT HIS WET, FLIPPERED HAND ON THE PROVERBIAL BUTTON, AND FOR SOME REASON, YOU'RE FINE WITH THAT."

STORMS: "OH, HIS HANDS ARE PERFECTLY NORMAL, THERE'S NO REASON TO BE INSULTING. AND TO BE FAIR, YOU SAID THE SAME KINDS OF THINGS ABOUT FABRICATOR, AND THAT TURNED OUT OKAY."

KING (SCOFFING): "OH, YEAH. THAT TURNED OUT JUST DANDY. WHAT DID HE EVER DO THAT WAS SO GREAT? NOTHING. AND THIS FISH-MAN IS EVEN MORE USELESS THAN FERRAL WAS. AT LEAST FERRAL HAD A REASON FOR BEING A MANIAC. HE WAS A PRODUCT OF THE WHOLE DISEASED CAPE SYSTEM; CORRUPT AND WEAK. WHAT'S THIS FISH-MAN'S EXCUSE? I MEAN, HE'S GOTTA HAVE ONE, RIGHT? EVERY MONSTER HAS A JUSTIFICATION FOR THE TERRIBLE THINGS THEY DO. WHAT? WERE THE OTHER GUPPIES MEAN TO HIM OR SOMETHING? UTTERLY RIDICULOUS."

TRANSCRIPT OF "KING OF CAPES AND COWLS," MEDIA: TELEVISION, SHOW: 1407, NEWSCHANNEL 6, FRIDAY 21:00-22:00 EST, NETWORK SEGMENT-ID: 918000606

Many, many years ago.

Julian sat in the ante room of the meeting hall, absently tracing the lines and swirls in the marble floors with his eyes and trying to find where they ended. They seemed to move with the effortless grace of the water, but they were stone. Forever still and motionless.

Marble was just what happened to water when it died.

It was the useless shit that no one wanted which was left over when the *best* parts of water went off to a better world.

He had arrived for the meeting between the Eternal pantheons over two hours ago, but Julian was not allowed entry into the meeting room. For one, he was far too young. He was nowhere near the age of maturity, and should technically still be with his mother... But that was *obviously* impossible. The more important reason for his exclusion from the goings-on though, was the fact that he was a half-breed. He was not of pure blood, and thus he was not allowed into the hall to discuss the war. The place was off-limits to mortals. ...Even *half* mortals.

Not that Julian really cared about the meeting anyway. He saw no sense to the endless blood feud, but if these people wanted to kill each other over nothing, he was more than happy to let them. Once upon a time, the Eternals had been just that: eternal and unkillable. In the infinite brilliance that his father's people *weren't* known for though, one of them had discovered a way to somehow put each other down for good. Since then, it was open season and their numbers were rapidly thinning.

But Julian didn't care.

Honestly, Julian didn't really care about a lot, *least of all* the looming extinction of a people he didn't like, who were also too stupid to realize that if they didn't *stop* killing each other soon, they'd *all* be dead.

He looked up at one of the frescoes painted on the wall of the hallway, and the tranquil sea scene which was preserved there. Fish and dolphins and beautiful mermaids frolicking in the peaceful surf.

Julian let out a long breath, imagining that he was there and not here. That he wasn't excluded from meetings which would determine whether he would live or die. That his father would one day *want* him to attend a meeting with him rather than rejecting him because of some asinine ideas about Julian not being fully a god. Julian could just bask in the warm sun and the cool water, and enjoy another wonderful day in paradise, beside all of his loving aquatic friends.

He would have a *place*.

A *purpose*.

A *family*.

And a woman to be his true partner in all three.

Several other Eternal boys walked by, blocking his view of utopia for a moment. The boys were obviously laughing amongst themselves about the fact that Julian had to sit in the hallway, and was the tragic result of his father's mistaken one night indiscretion. They smirked at him and took obvious delight in their ability to simply walk through the doors which held Julian back.

Julian's gaze slid back to the stone in front of him, once again tracing the lines in the stone.

Fucking Eternals.

He *hated* being around his peers. He avoided them whenever possible. It was so much easier to just stay behind and watch over his father's kingdom while his father was away. Solitude was better than being ostracized and reminded of your deficiencies as a son and a god. Sadly, his father didn't always trust Julian to do that. Plus, if anything were to go wrong with the kingdom while the man was away, Julian would look like a failure, and Julian did NOT want that to happen. Thus, he was forced to tag along after his father like some kind of puppy.

The entire thing was *utterly* humiliating, and no other Eternal boy would have stood for it. They had *pride.* They had *dignity.* Sadly, Julian's life meant that he could afford to have neither of those luxuries. He would never inherit his father's mantle. The seas would never be his. That was forbidden. He didn't have his father's powers, and he had no choice but to do what the man asked of him or be thrown out onto the streets.

Quite simply, Julian had nowhere else to go. His only option was to keep his mouth shut and do as he was told.

But Julian was *determined* to make something of himself. One day, Julian would prove himself, and his father would look at him and acknowledge him as his son and tell him that he was proud of him. Julian would do *anything* for that. To feel like he belonged somewhere.

...Anywhere.

He rested his cheek in his palm, going over what he would say to his father when the man's meeting was done. He needed to figure out what his father wanted him to say, and he didn't have much time in which to do it. If he didn't come up with what he was supposed to say soon, a prime opportunity to win the man's respect would be lost.

It would need to be something supportive, but deferential. Something...

Several more children walked by, smirking at him like he was the butt of a private joke. One of the girls pointed him out to her friend and they both had a good laugh before disappearing into the room as well.

Julian really, really *hated* these people.

"Arrogant little pukes, aren't they?"

Julian turned in astonishment to see a man suddenly standing in the darkened alcove to his right. He was wearing a futuristic looking white outfit, and a strange hat made of woven straw. Julian knew who this was, and the man's arrival meant trouble. The entire Eternal world knew that Prometheus was a liar and a traitor and couldn't be trusted. Plus, the man was a Greek and NO ONE trusted those assholes. Their whole pantheon was on a power hungry effort to take over *everything*.

The other man paid no attention to Julian's silence. "Don't worry about them though." He sat down on the bench beside him. "They'll be dead soon." He absently gestured to their surroundings. "And all of this will be gone."

Julian didn't know what to say to that. "...*Good.*" He finally spat out.

His answer seemed to amuse the man.

"Have you come to speak with my father about the war?" If Julian could uncover some vital fact which would aid his father's efforts, it would prove to him that he could be of use.

"Me?" The man snorted. "Nope. I already fought my war." He glanced down at him. "Lots of people are going to die fighting over nothing in this one. You planning on being one of them?"

Julian thought about it seriously for a moment. "If that is what is expected of me."

Prometheus watched him silently. "And that's all you want out of life then? Just dying on someone's orders?"

Julian's eyes drifted over to the mural again.

Prometheus accepted that as an answer. "Ah. Some things never change, I guess." He leaned back against the wall. "You're what now? Eight? Ten?"

"I do not measure age on the mortal calendar."

Prometheus ignored that, treating it like it was a confirmation. "When *I* was your age, I was having some dad issues of my own." He nodded to himself. "That lasted for a long time and didn't get better until I was older and was able to engineer a war for control of the universe and the very fabric of existence itself." He shook his head sadly. "Growing up is hard."

Julian made a noncommittal sound.

The man looked down at him. "It's not going to work, you know."

Julian ignored him, but didn't need to ask what the man was talking about.

"Some people are just like that." Prometheus tried again. "You can't change them."

"It *has* to work." Julian told him after a moment of silence.

"But it *won't*. No matter how much you might want it to, or how much I might want to *see* you succeed." He pointed at the mural. "He's just simply not part of that."

"He *could* be." Julian bit out, sitting straighter in an effort to look more powerful and sure of himself. "I just have to *show him* that..."

"That what?" Prometheus interrupted. "That you can pretend to be *him*? That you're willing to do whatever he wants, just so he'll respect you?" He shook his head again, his voice serious. "Does that really sound like the way to win someone's respect?"

"...No." Julian admitted, slumping slightly.

"No." Prometheus agreed. "You're a proud man, tiny version of Julian. Your caustic pride is one of your defining characteristics, and you shouldn't toss that aside in an effort to get someone that isn't worth it."

"But I *need* to..."

"No. You don't." Prometheus interrupted again. "And even if you *did,* it *still* wouldn't matter because you *can't.* You're a powerful person. Consistently thwarted, yes, but powerful and determined." He pointed to a potted plant a short distance away. "Say I was to take that pot and try to drain the ocean with it. I mean really *dedicate* myself to the task for years. Work at it constantly. Make it my *mission in life* to be the best one-man bucket brigade the world will ever see... Do you think when I was finished that ocean would be one inch lower?"

Julian swallowed and looked back down at the marble floor. "...No."

"No." Prometheus agreed. "Because some things are beyond even the most powerful of us. And making someone *care* when they obviously *don't* is one of them." He leaned closer. "There are hard truths about the world, Julian. Truths that aren't the pretty lies we tell ourselves to help us sleep at night, but ones which will keep us alive when the darkness comes and the rest of the world is caught napping."

"Why are you telling me this?"

"Because no one was around to tell me." He shook his head in warning. "Don't waste your life chasing something you can never have. He may not want you as a son, but I assure you, you're much better off not having him for a father. Go out there and find a family of your *own*. After all, there are plenty of fish in the sea."

Julian thought about the matter for several moments, then squared his jaw. "You're *wrong*." He announced.

Prometheus smiled. "You're stubborn too. That's the other element of your personality that never changes. Pride and stubbornness. I genuinely hope they serve you better this time through, kid. I truly do." He tipped his hat and got to his feet, pointing at the painting. "I just *love* mermaids, don't you? Such amazing creatures. ...Even if they do have a tendency towards treating people like children and using run-on sentences." He smiled to himself. "One day, I'll tell a rather large purple-haired friend of yours that mermaids are like good icebergs."

Julian frowned. "'Good icebergs'?" He repeated. "That's the stupidest thing I've ever heard."

"Hey, it made sense in the moment, okay? I was rushed for time. There's this whole sinking thing, and I needed to make sure his 'heart would go on' in a hurry." He casually checked his watch. "And don't interrupt. Where was I? Oh, yes. Good icebergs. See, they suddenly appear on the horizon and give your boat a direction to sail in. Sometimes they look like the personification of everything you hate, but if you give them a chance, they'll surprise you."

Julian opened his mouth to again point out how stupid that sounded, but before he could, the doors flew open and his father stormed out with his characteristic boldness.

Julian leapt to his feet to stand at attention, holding up his father's weapon, which had been entrusted to him for safe keeping during the meeting. "Sir."

The man yanked the trident from his grasp, not bothering to acknowledge him. "Isn't your voice *ever* going to change, boy?"

Julian cleared his throat, choosing to ignore the taunt. He turned to bid farewell to Prometheus, but found that the man had already disappeared. He hurried after his father. "Did the meeting go to your satisfaction, sir?"

The man ignored him, which told him everything he needed to know. If the meeting had gone the way his father had wanted, the older man would have been crowing about it. His silence meant that the meeting hadn't gone well.

"They will *all* be destroyed, sir." Julian told him, trying to sound regal and proud. "They shall be taught the..."

"And what exactly are *you* going to do to them?" The man took the marble stairs in front of the building two at a time. "*Swim* them to death?"

Julian opened his mouth to curse at the man, then bit his lower lip to keep the insult back. "...Perhaps if we contacted my mother's people, they would assist us in our .."

"Go to the *mortals* for help!?!" The man sounded horrified. "Have you lost your MIND, boy?"

"Maybe they would be our friends?"

"I am a god-king, boy, I do not *have* friends." He heaved a disgusted sigh. "Every time I turn around, you're yammering at me again and again about your precious damned terrestrials. Always mercy and appeasement, mercy and appeasement." He spun around and pointed at Julian. "You're *soft,* boy. Those surface people wouldn't *lift a finger* to help you." He started walking away again. "You can pretend like they'd *ever* accept you, but we both know they *won't*. They'd see you as the same useless little disappointment that the rest of us do. The only difference is that they lack my endless pity for your plight."

Julian looked down at the ground for a moment, trying to hold back bitter words and bitter tears. His father never wanted to try to make peace with the surface world. To Julian, the problem was simple: they needed more people on their side, and the surface world was *teeming* with life. It was simply a matter of harnessing it, and using it to accomplish good things.

From a purely selfish point of view, it would also mean that Julian wouldn't have to hold his head down whenever walking amongst the Eternals. He'd be a bridge between the two worlds, and would have a position of honor.

It was a beautiful dream. ...Which would never be.

He cleared his throat, trying to think of something to say, but the bitter rage would not leave his mind. "I am what you made me, sir." He finally got out. "If I ended up not living up to your expectations, perhaps you should have given me more to work with."

"Not *this* again." His father snorted. "Any other Eternal would have fed you to the *dogs* if you were dropped on their doorstep like the little bastard you are, you know that, right?"

"...Yes, sir."

"You owe me *everything you got*, boy."

"Sir."

"I give you a *home*, didn't I?"

"Yes, sir."

"I give you a *pantheon* to follow. I don't beat or torture you, do I?"

"No, sir."

"I give *purpose* to your otherwise useless little terrestrial existence."

"I'm *not* a terrestrial, sir." Julian snapped, sick of arguing this point with his father. "I belong to the seas."

The older man rolled his eyes, shouldering his way through the crowd of people eager to learn the results of the meeting. "'Belong to the seas?'" The old man chuckled. "Boy, you don't 'belong to the seas,' you're our *burden*. The dead weight which the oceans have to bear because you would be welcomed nowhere else. *Certainly* not amongst your *real* people. Your fellow surface brutes would take one look at you and toss you back into the waves. *Again*. They didn't *want* you. *No one does,* which is why *I'm* stuck with you."

Julian bit back a curse again. His father *delighted* in disparaging the mortals, just to make Julian angry. The man seemed to get a perverse thrill from it for some reason.

"They are *not* my people, sir." Julian snapped for the millionth time. "I have no part of them. I belong *here*." He cleared his throat again. "I was merely saying that perhaps the surface people would be able to..."

"If you love the surface people so much, boy, go ahead up there and *see* if they'll take you in. I just don't know why you're always coming to me whining about it. The day you leave, the entire ocean will throw a glorious celebration. ...Until the surface people toss you back because they wanted a *bigger* fish." His father shoved a man aside and continued through the crowded streets of the capital. "The way I see it, you owe me a debt which you can *never* fulfill. After all, *I'm* the one who is saddled with your mother's little mistake, aren't I? But do I take that rage out on you? Of course not. You should be *thanking* me for my generosity." He stopped in his tracks and waited patiently. "So, why *aren't* you?"

Julian's jaw clenched in silent rage and he opened his mouth to obediently parrot back the words the man expected to hear... but then he stopped. For some reason, the words would not come. Julian closed his mouth, and simply stared back at his father, meeting his gaze with cold determination.

The old man obviously didn't like that. "You're just like your mortal whore of a mother, you know that?" He turned around to look at him again. "Have I thanked you today for killing that little surface bitch?"

"Yes, sir." He told him after a moment of silence. "You did."

The other man nodded. "Good. Some days I think I forget, and it's possibly the only thing you've ever done *right*. If you hadn't come along, there's no telling how long she would have lasted. But you *did* show up, and *that's* what pushed the demented little slut over the edge and got her out of my hair once and for all."

"Everything lives by killing something, sir." He shook his head. "Whether they intend to or not."

"Wow." The man snorted. "You read that in one of your surface mortal books?"

"I read those books in an effort to understand our enemy, sir." He choked out. "I must know how they think in order to discover how to destroy them."

The man made an annoyed sound. "Would you shut up about your damned people for five minutes, and focus on the matter at hand?"

"They are *not* my people, sir."

"I have bigger fish to fry right now than you and your damned *terrestrials*."

Julian made a face. He hated when his father used expressions like that. It showed a distinct lack of respect for their subjects. Fish didn't deserve to be fried; they deserved to be protected and honored by their rulers. Julian had often told him that, but the old man just didn't understand that fish were intelligent beings worthy of respect. In Julian's father's world, none of that mattered.

"The time has come to destroy our enemies, boy." The man all but whispered. "They have been striking out against the rest of us for too long. Their time has come."

"If that is the course you feel we should take, I am with you, sir."

The older man scoffed, then looked amused. "Oh, isn't that cute. You thought I was including *you* when I said 'us.'" He chuckled again. "I meant the *real* gods, boy, not the powerless half-breeds. What could *you* possibly contribute?" He shook his head, a taunting smile on his face. "*Mortals* with no real powers are *useless*."

Julian felt his face darken, his hands forming fists at his side.

"Aw, that makes you upset, doesn't it? I'll have to make certain not to challenge you to any sort of swimming competition today, or you would sure teach me a lesson, wouldn't you?"

Julian just watched him in silent rage.

His father paused on the edge of town, and appeared thoughtful for a moment. He turned to look at Julian again. "You don't think very much of me, do you, boy?"

"No." Julian told him before he had time to think better of it. "No, sir. I do *not*."

The man didn't like that answer at all. "I should have let your mother take you with her."

"Yes sir, you should have." Julian nodded. "I think we would have both been happier."

CHAPTER 8

KING: "NOW, MS. HARDY, PERHAPS YOU CAN HELP US UNDERSTAND THIS SITUATION BETTER. HOW CAN THERE BE SO MUCH CRIME IN THIS CITY, WHEN WE HAVE DOZENS AND DOZENS OF MASKED VIGILANTES RUNNING AROUND TRYING TO 'PROTECT' US? IS YOUR NEPHEW INCOMPETENT OR IS HE AN ACTIVE CONSPIRATOR IN THIS ILLICIT SCHEME?"

HARDY: "NEITHER. MY NEPHEW WYATT IS MISSING IN AGLETARIA. I DON'T SEE HOW HE CAN BE BLAMED FOR THE STATE OF THE CITY IN HIS ABSENCE. HE'S NOT IN CHARGE OF THE CONSORTIUM RIGHT NOW, THAT SHIRTLESS AQUATIC GENTLEMAN IS. THE FACT THAT CRIMINALS ARE BECOMING MORE BRAZEN IN THEIR ACTIVITIES WHILE HE'S AWAY JUST GOES TO SHOW WHAT A DIFFERENCE WYATT'S PRESENCE HERE MAKES."

KING: "OR PERHAPS IT JUST GOES TO SHOW US THAT HE FOUND A NEW WAY OF ATTACKING THIS CITY. ...NOT THAT I'M OUTRIGHT ACCUSING HIM OF BEING PART OF THIS TREACHERY, BUT I WILL POINT OUT THAT HE IS A KNOWN ASSOCIATE OF THE LEADER OF THE SUPER-PERSON RESISTANCE MOVEMENT. THE AUDIENCE CAN DRAW THEIR OWN CONCLUSIONS ABOUT WHAT THAT MEANS."

HARDY: "TEN YEARS AGO!"

KING: "SO EVEN YOU ADMIT THAT HE'S IN COLLUSION WITH REECE PROFFIT, THE CRIMINAL KNOWN AS 'RECIPROCITY' THEN, AND THEY'RE WORKING TOGETHER TO DESTROY THE GOOD PEOPLE OF THIS CITY? EXCELLENT. WE HAVE CONFIRMATION. I TOLD MY CO-HOST THAT, BUT CONNIE ALWAYS HAS HER HEAD STUCK IN THE SAND WHEN IT COMES TO CRIMINALS IN FLASHY OUTFITS. A KILLER IN A SKI MASK IS A MURDERER. ADD A MATCHING CAPE TO THE DISGUISE AND THE CRIMINAL SUDDENLY BECOMES A HERO AND PARAGON OF VIRTUE. THAT'S THE WORLD WE LIVE IN AT THE MOMENT."

Present Day

Reece Proffit, AKA "Reciprocity," got to his feet to address the assembly. "I would like to welcome you all to what is a very *special* meeting of the Super-Person Resistance Movement, coming as it does so close to our recent victory over the Norm police forces protecting the Statue of Liberty and their pitiful..."

"Wait, wait," in the chair next to him, Seth Van Diemen frowned, "your acronym is 'S-P-R-M?'" He looked around the table, appearing utterly delighted by that fact for some reason. "Really? That is just simply *magnificent*. If I had *planned that*, I couldn't have come up with anything better."

Reece cleared his throat. "I'd like you all to meet Seth, the god of evil." He gestured to the man. "I think we should all thank Seth for taking the time to meet with us today. He will play a *vital* part in the next step of our mission."

"Thanks Seth." Gyre called in a monotone singsong. He readjusted the sunglasses on his soap opera handsome face. The man was *impossible* to deal with. All he cared about were his clothes and his damn skin care regiment. He wore garments from designers whose names Reece couldn't pronounce, and had his shoes custom made in countries Reece had never been. He checked to make sure his blond hair remained in its characteristic puffy points every few minutes, and he exercised to the point of religious ritual.

Gyre lounged back in his chair, his personalized black combat boots on the table, intricately embroidered long black trench coat pooling around the legs of his chair.

Reece ignored him. He could deal with the man's grating personality because he was one of the most powerful men alive. His abilities had managed to melt the Norm's precious statue in mere *moments*. They'd have to call it the "*Puddle* of Liberty" now.

"I'm just doing my part, and am so *honored* that you asked me to join you." Seth smiled with *utterly* insincere sincerity. "Naturally, when you thought of great altruists dedicated to fighting for the freedom of the common super-powered man, you thought of me." He pressed a hand to his chest. "Why, I'm just like Spartacus: always willing to battle injustice wherever I find it. Seems *everyone's* been asking me to join them lately though. I'm like the prettiest girl at the ball, everyone wants a dance."

"...Or the cheapest whore on the corner." Gyre added innocently under his breath.

"Speaking of which," Seth dutifully began flipping through the newspaper in front of him as if he hadn't understood the man's insult, "*I for one,* am *very* excited to be a part of SPeRM and cannot *wait* until our mutual passions are released and we *explode* forth to *shower* the super-community in love."

Gyre snickered.

Reece ignored that too. "I think what we should all focus on is the fact that our brothers and sisters are toiling away to aide this city, and it is up to us to open their eyes to the truth! The age of selfless heroism and selfish villainy are gone. Their day is done. This is a NEW age, when our kind opens its eyes and sees the world as it is for the first time." He raised his fist. "We will win their freedom and show them that once we eliminate the Norm threat, we can all live in peace. THEY are the ones making us fight. THEY are the ones who hold back our greatness and force us into the shadows or to battle for their entertainment. For too long we have lived under the thumb of those weaker than ourselves and fought for the scraps they tossed us." He shook his head. "But now this city is OURS! And with it in our grasp, there is no limit to what we can accomplish!"

"Yes." Seth agreed. "I *too* am positively *aching* to experience SPeRM's explosive climax. Being in its firm grasp is the whole reason I came."

Gyre snickered again.

Across the round table from Reece, the Viking zombie "Draugr" crossed her dead arms over her Lamellar armor covered chest; small rectangular darkened iron plates the size of dominoes were joined together tightly by thin leather strips to form a sort of tunic, decorated at the shoulders with a cloak of grey wolf fur which hung down her back. The tunic hung loosely off her large breasts, stopping at her stomach and baring her midriff. Matching armor began again at her hips, where it was slit all the way up the sides and narrowed into a loincloth which hung to her knees, allowing her muscular legs greater freedom of movement, but baring a disturbing amount of flesh.

Postmortem lividity gave her bare dead skin an unpleasant mottled and veiny bluish red discoloration, the worst of which was located at what appeared to be an ancient rope burn around her neck. The colors of the *undoubtedly* mortal injury did set off the dark strawberry hue of her long hair quite nicely though, which hung passed her waist and was still styled in the intricate Viking funerary braids which she presumably had been entombed wearing, centuries ago.

The upper region of the woman's face was by some means always concealed in shadow, from her eyebrows to the tops of her cheeks, but her eyes somehow glowed from these unseen depths like a cat's in the dark. Whether there was actually still anything physical in this void or not was anyone's guess, as it looked completely empty aside from a reddish marking over her left eye which Reece couldn't identify and was sure had no significance. In either case, the oddly shaped iridescent cold blue lights she had in place of eyes gave no indication of intelligence. There was no spark of humanity in them; just a mindless hungry anger.

Her black lips formed an unhappy line. "Draugr does not care about tiny man and his tiny problems. Draugr just wants her gold."

The woman was the powerhouse of this particular group of SPRM members, exhibiting both the strength inherent in the Norse magical zombie-like creatures, as well as wearing "megingjörð" the power belt of Norse myth around her waist, which doubled her already impressive strength. From the wide red leather belt hung an ancient looking ox horn trumpet, decorated with elaborate silver filigree, and strapped to her bare thigh was a vicious looking iron dagger.

Reece didn't particularly like the mindless brute. She was humorless, greedy, carried a very large axe, and was already dead. Generally speaking, he found that *no one* was more difficult to deal with than the dead.

She wasn't even a *true* empowered person. She was simply a Norm who had died and had returned with powers. It was *completely* different. She was *also* a non-believer. Not because she had made any sort of choice on the matter, just because she was too stupid to even understand that a choice was being *asked for*. It would be like trying to get *breakfast cereal* to choose between political parties. ...*Rotting* breakfast cereal. ...*Retarded* rotting breakfast cereal. ...Retarded rotting breakfast cereal that *barely spoke English!*

Reece had just about given up on *ever* getting that corpse to understand the truth of his words. Hell, he had difficulty trying to get her to understand his words *at all*. She was just a big stupid *thing* which he had to look at every day.

For the time being though, she still served a purpose.

Reece nodded at the creature humoringly, trying to reach the decomposing remnants of her mind. She had evidently been rather dim even *before* her death though, and the time since hadn't helped matters. "Yes, I realize that you have ulterior motives for joining up with our cause, but I think once you see the kind of things we can accomplish together, even *you* will admit that this is a worthwhile endeavor." He paused, realizing there were too many big words in that statement and that she had no *hope* of understanding. He tried again, pointing back and forth between them. "We friends. We do *big* things. Make people *happy*." He nodded persuasively. "Happy is *good*."

"Draugr does not care about tiny man and his tiny problems." She repeated in her heavy Nordic accent, apparently not hearing or *still* not understanding what Reece was trying to tell her. "Draugr just wants her gold."

"Girl's got a one track mind." Gyre leisurely reached for his cup and took a long swallow of his dieter's tea. "...I think the fucking worms got the other ones."

Seth made a humoring sound. "Possibly. But your leader *does* make an excellent point: *no one* gives happy endings like SPeRM." He nodded seriously. "I think it's all the 'big things' they enjoy doing. *Big and hard.*"

Reece cleared his throat. Not liking the way this meeting was going.

No matter.

The Mary Sue finished putting her brown hair into an orderly ponytail, and turned to shake her head at Gyre reproachfully, her adorable tomboy features contorting into a pout and filling him with renewed faith in the goodness of humanity. "I don't like to hear you insult a comrade like that, Gyre. The rest of the world abuses us on a daily basis, but this group should be a safe haven from that." Mary Sue smiled at Draugr. "It's okay. You're with *friends* here. We don't judge, no matter how ugly, or stupid or scary you are."

Draugr opened her mouth to reply, *no doubt* about to mention her desire for gold again, but Mary Sue cut her off.

"Perhaps we should let Reece get back to the *presentation*." She smiled at the zombie thing again, somehow finding it in the depths of her pure, pure heart to look upon the other woman and not retch.

The Mary Sue was truly the best person ever at making everyone feel welcomed, and at reaching the black sheep of the SPRM. If Reece was really being honest with himself, Mary Sue would be a far more capable leader than he was. But she was just so darned humble and self-effacing that she didn't even know it. She was such a pure, pure soul.

"It would make me so very happy if you would *shut up* and let him speak." She went on. "Not that I think you *owe me* anything for all the years we've been like sisters... All the wonderful things I've *done* for you... Just that it would make me so *happy*."

Draugr fell silent.

Mary Sue's ability to control people using her voice was so *very* useful at times. All she had to do was speak, and suddenly she was the most important person in someone's life. The best at *everything*. So youthful and full of zest. She made people *believe* again.

...Believe in anything she *told* them to believe.

The woman deserved a medal for all the hard work she had put into this campaign. She had been the one to engineer the non-believing super-groups' little "vacation" in Agletaria. All Reece had to do was show up and deliver the coup de grâce. She didn't even *need* her powers to convince *him* that she was the most beautiful or the best at everything though. He could see that all on his own.

...At least, he *hoped* she didn't need her powers to convince him of that, anyway. Honestly, it was impossible to tell. But the results would be the same either way, so it didn't really matter much.

"Thank you." He nodded at Mary Sue in gratitude.

Detritus raised his hand, and readjusted his long blue toga. "It seems to me that what we should *really* be doing is focusing on getting as many of the Norms out of our new home as we can. We really only have to worry about killing the ones too stupid to leave. Why waste time disposing of creatures we can simply get rid of by telling them to get out of town? The result will be the same; they'll be gone."

The man could be quite eloquent when he wanted to be. Reece put Detritus in charge of dealing with the Norm rabble most of the time, since neither Reece nor Mary Sue could stand seeing them so often. Detritus excelled at the duty though. ...Reece was beginning to worry that the man may be too soft on the Norms.

He had no place in his organization for people who were *weak*.

"We will do what *needs* to be done." Reece put his hands behind his back and began to stroll around the table. "We here in the SPRM..."

Gyre began snickering.

"...We have a *mission*. We will free the empowered from their oppression. We will help them take their *rightful* place in the world's pecking order..."

"'Free the world's peckers!' that's SPeRM's motto." Seth enthused, raising one fist up high in support. "There's no one better *equipped* to make sure they're all in order."

"We will build a NEW world! Construct a new society from the ashes of the old. Shape a new way of life, from the ground up!"

"And what *pleasure* our erections will bring to the world." Seth nodded seriously.

Reece ignored him.

"We will *free* our empowered comrades." Reece stopped at the head of the table. "...And we will do that, by eliminating everyone who *isn't* super-powered."

"Makes sense." Seth nodded. "If the Norms can't swallow SPeRM's ejaculations of truth, then they're blowing it anyway."

Gyre giggled again.

Mary Sue glared down the table at Seth, an unhappy look on her pert little face. "Please stop that."

Seth placed his hand over his heart. "My *sincerest* apologies, my dear. I shouldn't be making light of such a *serious* occasion, especially not in *your* charming company. You, my enchanting creature, are the true *essence* of SPeRM: so warm and full of life."

Reece paused, trying to decide if that was meant to be another stupid double-entendre, or if it was the truth accidentally phrased in a *very* inappropriate way.

He decided that it didn't really matter, and pointed to the newspapers on his table. "The process has already begun. The Mary Sue and I lured all of the super-powered traitors and cowards to Agletaria, and then we *broke them*." He placed his hand over his heart. "Sadly, many of our SPRM brothers and sisters died in the effort."

Gyre took on a somber tone and bowed his head. "When I think of the duty and sacrifice that took... I still don't give a shit." He brightened. "Now, when are we going to kill the Norms?"

"I'm getting to that."

"Do they have Draugr's gold?" The Viking woman asked dimly, in her comically stupid voice. "Draugr desires her gold now."

Reece let out an aggravated sigh and glanced down the table in exasperation. He had an infinite patience but even *he* was tired of enduring the creature's stupidity. "Mary *Sue?*" He said, in a voice that sounded whinier than he would have liked. He pointed to Draugr. "*Talk* to her, please."

Mary Sue laughed gently, and prepared to *again* tell their not-so-bright companion to shut the hell up. Hopefully, she'd tell her to be quiet *forever* this time, as Reece had simply heard all he *ever* needed to hear from her.

Before Mary Sue could begin issuing her orders though, Gyre cut her off. He stared at the zombie creature sitting next to him, who was looking straight ahead, giving no indication that the tiny remnants of her brain even recognized that he was there. Reece believed the creature was operating on instinct alone; her illuminated eyes actually seeing nothing.

The lights were *quite literally* on, but no one was home.

"You know, I just can't think of *anything* sadder than a really hot chick with *amazing* tits, who dies, and then comes back as a walking fucking corpse who makes *Frankenstein* look like *Einstein*." Gyre rolled his eyes, sounding depressed. "It's like opening up the casket at a wake held in the Playboy Mansion; bitch isn't much of a conversationalist anymore, but you find yourself just looking at all the fun you could have had, if she hadn't gone and died before you got there and her sexy body wasn't decaying in front of you." Gyre shook his head sadly and unabashedly surveyed the curves of the woman's muscular but undead hourglass figure. "Fucking *tragic*."

Seth smiled pleasantly at Draugr. "Oh, don't listen to him, my dear, your repartee is *delightful.* The youth of today just doesn't understand the lost art of *conversation*, that's all." He casually stirred his mixed drink and took a long sip through a small red straw. "Personally, I find it *refreshing* to talk to a woman who is so *goal oriented*."

"Draugr does not care for conversation." The zombie calmly informed him in her heavily accented monotone. "Draugr just desires her gold."

"Oh, how *interesting*." Seth leaned forward like that was just the most *fascinating* gossip he had ever heard. "Please, do tell *more*. I can't *wait* to hear how this anecdote ends." He took another leisurely sip of his drink through his straw. "I hope I don't spoil it for anyone... but I'm guessing *gold* comes into play somewhere, doesn't it?" He leaned further forward excitedly. "I'm *right* aren't I?"

The creature didn't respond, it simply stared ahead blankly.

"*Spoiler warning!*" Seth sang, laughing merrily, like she had answered his question and he and the monster were simply the *best* of friends. "You thought you could sneak that foreshadowing by me, didn't you, you little scamp?" He ate the cherry from his drink, pulled the stem from it while it was in his mouth, then pointed it at Draugr playfully. "*I'm onto you!*" He chuckled again cheerfully, while chewing. "You're such a charmer. I *like* you."

Reece ignored them. He just didn't have time for the creature's antics right now, and Seth was beginning to grate. Reece needed him for the next phase of his plan, but that didn't mean he had to like it. The man was *far* too smug. Reece had no real idea what the limits of the man's powers were, but he obviously wasn't intimidated by anyone else in the room. In fact, he seemed to view them merely as a source of momentary amusement. Most disconcerting of all though, was the fact that the man had no shadow. No matter the light source or the time of day. Reece wasn't sure why or how, but he found it... *unnerving*. There was more going on with that man than Seth let on, and whatever it was, Reece was beginning to suspect that he didn't want to find out.

He cleared his throat again, trying to get his meeting back on track. "...Now that we have disposed of the quislings, the collaborators and the liars, our righteous task can *truly* commence. We have made our first step against the Norms by striking at their symbol of so-called 'Liberty' and by wiping out..."

"I hate to interrupt," Seth raised his hand, looking serious, "but I'm just going to ask what I know we're *all* thinking..." He paused to take a sip of his drink. "Will *gold* be involved at all in this, or *nooooot*..." He drew the word out to show his uncertainty.

Gyre erupted in laughter.

Draugr turned her head at the word "gold" but then promptly went back to staring.

"Yes." Reece cleared his throat again. "Very amusing." He sat down. "With Seth's help, we can launch the *next* phase of our plan. A phase which will put this entire world into the palm of our hand."

Seth nodded and stirred his drink, looking suddenly distressed. "I *do* hope it's not going to include attacking my good friend Julian though. He asked me to join his Consortium of Chaos club this week as well, and I just can't decide." He held out his hands, looking from one to the other as though they represented his options. "Do I want to get my hands dirty with SPeRM, or with the Seaman?"

Gyre chuckled again and pointed across the table. "You know, at first I thought you were going to be all godly and arrogant and shit, but you're *alright*, man."

Seth raised his glass to him in toast. "I try."

Reece turned to look at Seth, hoping to get him to focus on the issue. "What say you, brother? Will you listen to our call for freedom?"

"Well, you *do* make a compelling argument." Seth took another sip of his drink, and then appeared thoughtful. "And I *do* dislike the mortals..." He pursed his lips, stroking his chin thoughtfully and making a 'Hmmmm' sound. "...But after *careful* consideration, I've decided to *reject* your gracious offer of membership."

Reece's mouth fell open in shock, utterly *amazed* that anyone could listen to the truth of their goals and still refuse to assist them. "Don't you care at *all* about your empowered brothers and sisters still chained in the bonds of servitude to an ungrateful world!?!"

Seth chuckled like Reece had said something *truly* ridiculous. "I'm not that kind of god, Mr. Proffit." He got up from his chair. "Some gods trample out the vintage where the grapes of wrath are stored... and *some gods* use the grapes of wrath to make wine and get drunk." He raised his glass. "Cheers." He downed the rest of his drink in one gulp, then started towards the door again.

"I don't think I want you to leave yet, Seth." Mary Sue intoned in a pleasant voice. "Won't you stay here with me a while longer?"

Seth rolled his eyes. "My dear, I once *dated* a siren." He told her conversationally. "As flattered as I am to receive your attentions, and as *lovely* as your voice is, I'm afraid that the relationship did not end well last time." He shrugged. "And now, the thrill is simply gone." He gave a theatrical bow to the room at large. "And so, as we say in the hospitality industry:" he took on a sickening smile, "'have a *magical* day.'"

Seth strolled through the door and Gyre got up to retrieve him, but Reece waved him off.

"Forget him. He'll die with the others once the ceremony is complete." Reece refocused on the table. "We have *bigger* concerns than him right now."

"The Consortium?" Detritus guessed.

"Hell no." Reece snorted in dismissal. "We have *already* destroyed them. They are no longer a threat to us or *anyone*." He pointed at the folder in front of him. "Our only concern at the moment is the troublesome leader of *Norm* crime in the city." He smiled icily. "But Mercygiver won't be a problem for long. Mary Sue is about to take certain... *steps*."

"Is one of these steps retrieving Draugr's gold?" The Viking woman asked again. "Draugr desires her gold now."

****

Rondel Stanna, AKA "Mercygiver," looked up from his work as someone knocked on the door. "You may enter, Mr. Jack."

Jack pushed the door open. "Yeah, Boss. Just wanted to…" Jack's mouth fell open. "JESUS!" He turned around. "I don't want to see that! Put some clothes on!"

Rondel rolled his eyes. "You need to grow up, Mr. Jack." He went back to looking over his reports. "Was there something you wished to speak to me about which couldn't wait until *normal* office hours?"

The other man turned back around, still visibly uncomfortable with the scene. Mercygiver didn't care. In fact, it gave him a sense of power. He pushed his chair back another foot, ensuring that the man could see more.

Jack cleared his throat. "…Umm… yeah…" he looked down at the floor, "it seems that…"

"Baby?" The bedroom door opened and a tall dark-haired woman glided out into the office. She was similarly naked. She stopped short when she saw Jack, then giggled. "…Oh, sorry. Didn't know you had company." She smiled at Jack, giving no indication of being embarrassed at being caught totally nude, and simply continued walking through the office, putting her clothes back on.

Jack watched the woman getting dressed, obviously enjoying the sight of her shapely body before it disappeared back into her small black evening dress.

She smiled back over her shoulder. "Been fun, lover." She blew Rondel a kiss and opened the door. "Call me." She left.

The room was silent for a long moment.

Jack finally smiled at him. "Friend of yours, boss?"

"No."

"Really? 'Cause you two *looked* mighty friendly." He glanced at the door the woman had left through and then back at Rondel again. "Gotta say, that was a *fine* piece of ass."

"Ms. Hasan is the director of one of the largest art museums in Chicago, Mr. Jack. She's here to appraise some work I recently picked up. She is not a 'piece of ass,' she is a fine young woman."

"So… are you going to call her then?"

He snorted. "Of course not. I am not someone looking to become romantically entangled and neither is she."

Jack sat down in one of the office chairs, still doing his best not to look at Rondel's nakedness, by holding a hand up in front of his face. "Just a test drive. Gotcha. 'Rent but don't buy.' Good call." He peeked out from between his fingers. "Can I have her then? Because I'd soooo be willing to take out a mortgage to have her, if you know what I mean."

"I'm afraid I don't, and I don't want to." He signed one of the documents in front of him. "What was so pressing that you couldn't wait until tomorrow?"

Jack squirmed in his chair again. "Oh, yeah. *That.*" He cleared his throat. "Well, since the Consortium has taken the short bus to the great beyond, that 'Reciprocity' dude and his pals in the Super-Person Resistance Movement have been..."

Rondel interrupted him. "He really named his organization 'SPeRM'?" He rolled his eyes. "Jesus. When did the world start being controlled by thirteen year olds still struggling through puberty?"

Jack chuckled. "Yeah, but you gotta admit, the name just rolls off the ladies' tongues, doesn't it?" He grinned at his own off-color joke.

Rondel stared at him expressionlessly, entirely un-amused.

Jack nervously cleared his throat again. "...*Any-hoo,* some of their Supes have been muscling in on our turf. Seems they've all but crushed the Norms who've tried to stop them, and they ain't so happy with our non-superpower focused endeavors, and they're looking to start making some... *changes* around the city. Namely, they want everyone who isn't them to die."

Rondel shook his head. "I refuse to share power with anyone, least of all someone who pays so little attention to what their own organization's acronym spells."

Jack nodded. "Hey, right there with ya, boss. I am in *no* hurry to deal with Reece and his crazy Super-Klan." He pointed at his feet. "I intend to stay *right here.*" He was silent for another moment, then squirmed in his chair again. "...Please don't kill me."

Rondel rolled his eyes. "Do your job, and I won't have to." Rondel took out a binder from his bottom drawer and opened it. "If they are trying to stop you from fulfilling your duties, simply kill them."

Jack nodded. "Yeah..." He scratched at his chin nervously. "...Thing is? We don't really have enough Super-muscle around to go toe to toe with them. Our guys are more suited for shootouts with corner drug dealers than with super-types. Generally, bullets don't work so well on people impervious to bullets."

Rondel looked up from the binder. "So... what you're saying is that you are *incapable* of performing your duties?"

Jack shook his head emphatically. "*No!* I didn't say that at all! What I said was that..."

His words were cut off as Ms. Hasan walked back into the room unexpectedly. "I forgot one thing," she raised her arm, pointing a gun at him, "I need to get revenge for all the terrible things you've done to Mary Sue over the..."

The rest of her words were cut off as the guards stationed in the hall opened fire. The woman turned her gun on them, and started shooting back.

Jack swore and rushed forward. "*STOP! DON'T SHOOT! It's not her! It's fucking...*" He stopped yelling as the woman hit the floor in a bullet riddled heap. The guards slumped over a moment later, shot to pieces by the woman's pistol before she died. "...Mary Sue." He finished, then let out a long breath. He stared down at the woman, looking almost sad. "Shit." He hesitated a moment and carefully flipped her over, then glanced up at Rondel. "...I think the SPeRM just tried to use a mind whammy to make your non-girlfriend blow you away, boss." He took a step back, apparently expecting him to take the news badly. "She didn't make it. I'm sorry."

Mercygiver thought the matter over for a moment. "...Well, that's unfortunate." He casually opened one of the letters on his desk. "*Most* unfortunate. You may begin wiping them out at any time, Mr. Jack."

Jack inched towards the door, obviously still scared that the messenger would be killed. "...And... and what are *you* going to do?"

He opened another letter. "Find another art appraiser, obviously." He glanced up again a moment later. "Is there a *reason* why you haven't started killing them yet? If you don't intend to follow my orders, then perhaps I will need to find *someone else to perform your job!*"

Jack ran for the door, terrified by his boss' uncharacteristic display of rage.

Mercygiver sat alone in the silence for a long moment, thinking about his life and how it had come to this...

He knew *exactly* how his life had come to this, and *exactly* who to blame for it. And it *wasn't* that absurd 'SPeRM' organization and the meaningless little turf war which they apparently wanted to start with him. Rondel would deal with *them* soon enough. He'd been dealing with bullies his entire life.

No, he blamed the Consortium. Specifically, he blamed *her.* The woman who had robbed him of everything he held dear, and had then cast him out.

The woman had used him.

There was really no question about that in his mind. She had used him *terribly*. She'd led him on, and made him believe that she wanted to be with him. But she just needed his help. And after he had done everything he could for her, *rescued* her from the squalid mediocrity to which she had confined herself, and taught her *everything* he knew, she thought she could... what? Just walk away? Just take back everything he'd been promised and live another life somewhere without him?

He wanted HER, goddammit! That was it! Possessing HER had been his fucking goal all along! He'd been fairly clear on that point. In fact, he'd been *entirely* upfront about his desires before she even agreed to go down that road with him. They *belonged* together.

No, no. Rondel did NOT take rejection well.

Not at *all*.

As soon as he was finished taking over this shithole town which she loved so much, he was going to *show* her just how much he had missed her. He was going to kill all her little friends in front of her, and make her *watch*. Make her BEG for their lives and then cut them down in front of her. And as she stared at the mangled corpses of everything she loved, he was going to *carve his fucking name into her face with a knife*, so that every time she looked into a mirror, she would see *him*. She would KNOW who she *belonged* to. He'd brand her like fucking cattle so if she ever tried to stray again, everyone would know who *owned* that meat.

Fucking bitch.

...But she did have a *spectacular* body. Unbidden, his mind began to imagine all the things he could do with her. He intended to have *lots* of fun. Try out his darkest fantasies with her. ...Depravities which he had never tried. ...Agonies and humiliations which *no* woman had ever before been forced to endure. *SHOW* her who *really* had the power in their relationship, and make her *feel* every *ounce* of pain he could wring from her supple little ass before she left this world. She would *remember* his name and the *feel* of him inside her body long after her spirit arrived in Hell.

He closed his eyes, imagining the sensation of release and pleasure he would experience at seeing the blood spilling down her delicate features. *Her* blood. Warm and wet on his fingers. ...Hear her soft cries for mercy and loud screams of pain in the same voice which had once taunted him so smugly. ...The feel of her delicate pale skin *ripping* and *tearing* in his grasp. ...The vacant look in her eyes when he finally *broke her*. When she gave up all hope and simply let him take her any way that he wanted, at any time. To have *complete* control of her body.

...But even then, he'd still hurt her. She had *earned* it. The idea of her in pain excited him a great deal. More than it ever had before, in fact, and he had *always* enjoyed thinking about it.

It would be soon.

He wouldn't be able to hold himself back much longer. Soon, he would be ready to make his move against her. She *wasn't* to be underestimated though. She was *far* more capable than the idiots she associated with, and he needed to make certain that everything was in place before he acted, or she would escape his net.

He pursed his lips as he considered the matter, and decided he would let her live a moment longer than he had previously intended. He'd *jam* his blade into her stomach and in that same moment, he would yank her battered head up off the floor and gain his release. Literally and figuratively. *Right there*. Right on her blood soaked face. And then he would stand back to admire the scene, as the last thing she experienced in this world was the feel of the hot sticky evidence of his climax dripping down her perfect little features, mixing with her tears and her warm blood. ...Her all-too-clever mouth filling with all three as she struggled to take one last breath...

And he would laugh at her as she died. He would look into her scared and humiliated eyes as she slipped away, and he... would... LAUGH.

And his revenge would be complete.

He would finally *possess* that stupid little bitch, once and for all. She would be HIS and no one else's. She would NEVER try to leave him again. He OWNED HER! They were a *TEAM*, goddammit! *Friends!* But then she had tossed all that away. Thrown *him* away.

Selfish self-centered little whore.

NO ONE left him.

...No one.

He let out a shaky breath, trying to get ahold of himself. But all of that could wait.

For now.

In the meantime, he still had the body of his art consultant to consider. He really only enjoyed killing the people he *wanted* to kill. He found no pleasure in seeing *this* woman dead. He had no grudge against her. She seemed like a very sweet young lady. Pleasant and exceedingly knowledgeable about her field. He had *genuinely* enjoyed their time together. Contrary to what he had told Mr. Jack, he had fully intended on calling her again.

...True, Rondel probably would have ended up killing the woman himself at some point, but the fact remained that that decision was between he and the woman, and should *not* have involved his enemies. *At all*.

Collateral damage was always an unexpected blow,

particularly when the damage in question happened to someone who Rondel still had use of. Plus, he just couldn't stop thinking about the poor girl's loved ones. Someone as lovely as her must have an adoring family somewhere, who would no doubt be grief-stricken over this tragedy. The world had lost one of its miracles, and all of mankind was worse off for it.

Such a waste.

He would have to send her family a condolence card.

Perhaps flowers.

He reached for the phone and dialed the number, waiting patiently for the party on the other end to pick up.

"Hello?"

Mercygiver leaned back in his chair. "Hello Mr. Proffit. You just tried to kill me." A smile crossed his face as he thought of all the *wonderful* things he would do to this man. "Now, I'm going to *return the favor*."

CHAPTER 9

KING: "WELL, IF THEY'RE SO HEROIC, WHY HAVEN'T
THEY MANAGED TO STOP THE SPRM? WHY HAVEN'T
THEY TAKEN A STAND AGAINST THE CRIME WAVE
WHICH IS GRIPPING THE CITY OR HELPED THE UNTOLD
SCORES OF PEOPLE WHO ARE AFRAID TO EVEN GO
OUTSIDE? AFRAID THAT THE MOMENT THEY LEAVE
THE IMAGINED SAFETY OF THEIR HOMES, SOME
SUPER-POWERED THREAT WILL DESCEND UPON THEM
AND PLUCK AWAY THEIR LOVED ONES LIKE SOME SORT
OF DEMON SENT FROM HELL. AFRAID THAT THE
POLICE CANNOT POSSIBLY HOPE TO PROTECT THEM
FROM THE HORROR OF THE CAPED MENACE. AFRAID
THAT THE PEOPLE WHO CLAIM TO GUARD THEM FROM
MASKED HORROR ARE INDEED THE VERY SAME
CRIMINALS MASTERMINDING THIS SUPER-POWERED
BARBARISM IN THE FIRST PLACE, AND THERE'S NO WAY
TO PREDICT WHEN AND WHERE THEY MIGHT STRIKE
NEXT."

HARDY: "...WAS THERE A QUESTION IN THAT?"

KING: "WHAT I'M ASKING YOU IS WHY THE CURRENT
ROSTER OF CAPES IN THIS CITY, OF WHICH YOUR
NEPHEW WAS FORMALLY A MEMBER BEFORE HIS
PASSING..."

HARDY: "HE'S MISSING, NOT DEAD."

KING: "WHATEVER. MY POINT IS THAT PEOPLE ARE
AFRAID AND YOUR NEPHEW'S CRIMINAL GANG DOESN'T
APPEAR TO CARE ABOUT THAT. EVERY DAY I HEAR
MORE AND MORE REPORTS OF SOME NEW TRAGEDY
TAKING PLACE, SUCH AS THE BATTLE OF MIDTOWN,
WHICH THE CONSORTIUM OF CHAOS FAILED-- OR WAS
UNWILLING-- TO STOP. SOME REPORTS EVEN STATE
THAT THEY CAUSED THE DEVASTATION. SO, I'M
ASKING FOR AN EXPLANATION AS TO WHY THEY'RE SO
SELFISH? WHY ARE GOOD TAXPAYING CITIZENS
STRUCK DOWN BY YOUR NEPHEW'S INCOMPETENCE,
WHILE HE AND HIS FRIENDS ESCAPE WITHOUT ANY

REPERCUSSIONS?"

HARDY: "...ARE YOU SERIOUSLY ASKING ME WHY BAD THINGS HAPPEN TO GOOD PEOPLE?"

TRANSCRIPT OF "KING OF CAPES AND COWLS," MEDIA: TELEVISION, SHOW: 1407, NEWSCHANNEL 6, FRIDAY 21:00-22:00 EST, NETWORK SEGMENT-ID: 918000606

Julian's life had taken a most unexpected turn, and he had no idea what he was doing anymore. For the first time in as long as he could remember, his vengeance was taking a backseat to something else, and he wasn't sure what that meant.

He wasn't *unhappy* about the situation, as he found his newfound and long-sought companion to be utterly charming, he just wasn't positive what it said about his life that he was having so much fun with a *terrestrial* of all things.

Julian didn't really have a lot to lose though. ...Well, besides the entire planet, of which he was the sole protector. But on a *personal* level, Julian had always been solidly in the red. He'd never had much, so to even have the possibility of *friendship* with such a beautiful creature, was certainly something he was willing to endure any manner of humiliation for. Even pretending to tolerate her horrible and unworthy people. Just *how* she managed to put up with them was a mystery though.

Simply *looking* at them made him sick.

But Julian could play nice with the terrestrials for the moment... Biding his time until the *perfect* moment to strike. If they were all dead, Bridget couldn't exactly tell him not to hurt them, could she? And she couldn't really leave him to find someone else, because Julian had just killed all of her other options.

Oh, it was a *beautiful* plan and one which would soon come to sweet fruition.

But, in the meantime, there was shopping to do.

He placed his trident into the shopping cart so that its spiked end stuck up from the basket, and he trailed after his company's new press agent, pushing the small conveyance in front of him. "Tell me again why we're here?" He asked in irritation, eager to flee this place and return home.

Ahead of him, Bridget busied herself by looking over her notes. "Your friend Monty says..."

"Montgomery is *not* my friend." He interrupted, correcting

her misperception of the issue. "The man is a friend of *no one*."

"Well, whatever. Anyway, he says that his workers are being forced to fill in for the missing people around your secret-base-thingy, and so there's no one left to do the shopping. So, here we are."

"But why are *we* here?" He asked again. "I am a *leader*. Leaders do not *do* the shopping. That is why they keep inferior men like Welles around in the *first place*."

"Umm... I don't know your friend that well, but would you really trust him to be alone with your food? Because *I* wouldn't." She placed a jar of some unidentified terrestrial food into the cart. "The guy gives me the creeps. He looks like 'Jack the Ripper' or something. Every time I see him, I feel like I should be breaking out the crucifixes and garlic."

"You have *excellent* instincts." He told her, pleased to see that she wasn't an idiot like the rest of her kind, further cementing the idea in his head that she was *special*. Not a surface-dweller, but something worthy of respect and admiration. She was fast becoming his favorite thing in this world.

"Thanks!" She beamed up at him.

"I can kill him for you if you'd like." He offered.

"...Umm, no thanks. I think I'm good."

"Are you sure? Because it would really be no trouble at all."

She made a thoughtful face, as if considering that, then shook her head. "No, I don't think that'll be necessary quite yet." She dropped some bananas into the cart. "Thanks though."

He nodded. "You are quite welcome. If you change your mind, or think of any surface-dwellers you *would* like to see dead today, just point them out to me and it shall be done."

She put her finger up to her full kissably soft looking lips, and made a "Shush!" sound.

"Just... just please try not to kill anything in here, okay?" She looked around at the other shoppers and lowered her voice to a whisper. "It would look *bad* from a public relations standpoint. That would make my job harder."

"I assure you, I do not want to make your job any more difficult." He took on a serious expression. "I shall strive to avoid killing anyone today, but cannot make any promises. If I *do* end up killing someone in this human shop, know that I did so *reluctantly*, and they obviously left me no choice."

"That's the spirit." She gave him a sharp nod. "Go team!"

She led the way into a new aisle, which was filled with loafs of the mortals' bread. Just *why* the terrestrials needed so many different varieties of what was essentially the same product only in different forms, was anyone's guess.

The surface people were so strange.

"So, you look kind of weird today." She dropped several loaves into the cart and blinked up at him again. "Something wrong?"

He shook his head. "Not a thing. My kingdom is at peace today. All is well."

"Uh-huh." She didn't look convinced. "So, you're not worried about anything? Because you seem kinda tense. You haven't mentioned your quest for vengeance in almost an hour."

He scowled. "I do not like being among the surface people, Lady Haniver." He finally said. "Your people sicken me."

"Bridget."

"Your people sicken me, Lady Bridget." He repeated. "I hate them."

"Oh, we're not so bad." She dropped several jars of peanut butter into the cart. "Besides, I mean, you're like the biggest hero in the city now! People finally have a chance to really see how *awesome* you are! This is your time to finally be in the spotlight! You can *finally* get the credit for all the great things you've done for people over the years. You should be feeling good about us."

"I *do* feel good about us." He told her truthfully. "I do not know what this is between us, but I find it *most* interesting, and look forward to exploring it further with you."

She watched him for a long moment, then laughed. "Ha! You're funny. I wasn't expecting that." She went back to shopping. "Umm... I actually meant 'us' as in people."

He cleared this throat. "Of course." His mind raced. "...As did I. I look forward to... another day of," he tried not to be sick, "protecting the *surface-dwellers*."

"Good!" She brightened. "See, the secret to having a good relationship with the public, is to just be honest, you know? Just tell them what you're feeling."

"So, I should *tell them* that I hate them? I thought I was supposed to make a greater effort to *hide* that fact? ...And I am currently forbidden from *acting* on my blinding rage, as it would *surely* result in terrestrial casualties. ...But murdering them by the score would be a *truthful* expression of my feelings, so perhaps *not* annihilating their major cities is a *kind* of lie... and lying is *bad*, so..."

"Nope." She shook her head cutting off that thought. "...Sometimes too *much* honesty is also a problem." She led the way down the aisle. "The public overreacts to things, only because they don't understand what's really going on, and telling them the truth in the wrong way can be bad. But lying about it only makes things worse. ...Not as bad as *killing them,* but certainly bad enough. Better to get all the bad stuff out there all at once, and move on." She looked back at him. "You still look worried." She frowned. "What could worry a god-king?"

He thought about that. "...Well, sometimes I worry that I'm becoming *too* perfect and will lose sight of the common man. But then I realize that that's a really stupid thing to think. I mean, the fact that I'm still humble enough to *worry* about it, means that there's no danger of it happening."

She stared at him as if in wonder for a moment, then nodded. "You know, I have that *same* problem."

"Really?"

"No." She dropped several more packages of mysterious mortal goods into her cart. "Because I'm not insane."

"I am not insane. I merely struggle with my noble duties. While the terrestrials are all running around their dry landscape, I am singlehandedly protecting most of the globe."

"Uh-huh." She turned the cart into the next aisle. "I think you said that already. Several times."

"My wisdom oft bears repeating."

"Almost constantly, apparently. I feel like you really only say about a dozen things, just in different ways." She rolled her eyes. "Look, I'm not arguing that humanity is perfect or anything, but you seem to barely know us! How can you have lived around humans for so long, and have so little idea about them?"

"I know *plenty* about the surface people." He argued.

"Such as?"

"They are *killers*."

"And?"

"And what? That's all I *need* to know about them. Terrestrials are evil killers, and should not be trusted."

"There's a lot more to us than that."

"In my experience, there are two different kinds of surface person: soulless evil killers... and beautiful press agents named 'Bridget.' These are the only two varieties of your race."

"...Aww, aren't you just such a smoothtalker." She snorted and playfully batted at his arm.

"It is the truth. They murder my people by the score."

"You really love fish, huh? That's not just part of the whole 'King of the Seas' schtick?"

"My *what?*"

"Your gimmick, your thing, you know, the costume and trident and breathing underwater thing."

"...Are you insinuating that I'm... only *pretending* to be a god-king?"

"I don't know, *am I?*" She made a vague sort of hand gesture, as if his mastery of the watery depths was less important than the crackers she was buying. "I'm just saying that if you set out to be 'you,' you couldn't have done a better job from a marketing standpoint, except we would tone down the hate-filled diatribes about humans just a skoosh, and we'd lose the beard."

"What is a 'skoosh,' and what is wrong with my beard?"

"It means 'a bit' and there's nothing wrong with the beard. Nothing at all. ...If you're homeless or a Bernini statue." She shook her head. "But if you want to make it in the *modern* world, we're going to have to freshen you up some. Ditch the beard. We're going less 'The Odyssey' and more 'badass beach boy' sort of thing." She paused. "I'm keeping the whole shirtless thing though. That's *gold.* The ladies will *love* that, trust me. I mean... *wow.*"

He frowned. "I do not care what the surface people think of me." He surreptitiously turned and motioned for Quinn.

The man ran over from his place at the magazine rack, his issue of *Teen Bopp* magazine momentarily forgotten. "What's up, boss?"

"I need shaving equipment." He whispered and pointed off towards a random aisle. "Go and get me a shaving machine."

Quinn paused, then nodded. "...Okay. You wanna go electric or safety? 'Cause I'm thinking that the electric won't really go so great with life underwater."

"I don't care *how* surface people do it, I simply want it *done.*" He quickened his pace to catch up with Bridget again. "I still fail to see why all of this is even necessary. Surely the terrestrials will realize that I am simply *superior* to them, and will doubtlessly welcome me as their benevolent master."

"Yeah... not so much, I'm afraid." She shook her head. "We're not really big on people who constantly try to kill us suddenly deciding they're our friend."

He frowned. "But *all* of my co-workers have been trying to kill your people for years." He argued. "Why should this be any different?"

"...Well, you got me there." She shrugged. "I think it's different because we want people to actually *like* you. People merely *tolerate* them."

"That should not be a problem. I am a very likeable person. *All* of my subjects love me."

"Speaking of which, you're not taking that to a 'Troy McClure' level, are you?"

"...I don't know what that means."

"It means: it's okay to love fish, but not *love fish.*"

He made a horrified face. "...Eww."

"Agreed. Just checking in case I needed to explain some embarrassing photos of you and a whale or something."

Quinn appeared again with a bag of brightly colored shaving instruments. "They were out of disposable razors, so I got you these ones, which I think are made for girls, but it's all they have." He dropped them into the cart. "It's the same product, only pink and sparkly and gentle."

Julian frowned at the bag of pastel objects. "I am unhappy about this."

Quinn shrugged. "Oh, don't worry about it." He casually looked over the cart's contents. "You're just not used to buying stuff, that's all. This kind of thing happens *all* the time. Stop being sexist."

"Why doesn't he buy stuff?" Bridget asked in curiosity. "Aside from his lonely, disorderly and unhealthy lifestyle, I mean."

"I do not like being around surface-dwellers." He watched one of them suspiciously as she stood in the aisle looking over mortal goods. He slowly wheeled the cart by her, waiting for her to strike. The woman stared back at him, the can of soup in her hand apparently forgotten.

Julian's eyes narrowed at her.

...What was *her* problem? ...She was obviously plotting something. An attack on the seas, perhaps?

...Almost *certainly*.

"Jules tries to ignore everything that's not ocean related. And sometimes even *then* he still doesn't react the way you'd expect him to." Quinn helpfully informed Bridget, overlooking the threat of the woman in aisle five. "In the Undersea Base, we sometimes have movie night, just because there's absolutely *nothing* else to do, and we've tried to watch the movie 'Open Water' like a dozen times, and I've never gotten to see the end of it, because Julian's always laughing too loudly."

"The movie is an absolute *riot*." Julian felt the need to tell Bridget, forgetting about the potential attacker next to the soup cans. "Have you seen it? It *always* has me in stitches."

"Isn't that the one about those scuba divers who get left behind in the middle of the ocean and are terrorized by sharks?"

Julian chuckled, thinking about some of the film's many comedic moments. God, he loved happy endings.

Bridget smiled, like that idea was amusing to her as well for some reason, then shook her head. "No, can't say as I have." She grabbed a bottle of ketchup from the shelf and dropped it into the cart. "The last movie I saw was the 'Freedom Squad' film. I didn't like it. But, to be fair to the director, that probably had more to do with my having issues with that team, as I'm sure you recall."

"You know that they didn't put me in that movie, right?" Julian said angrily, having no idea what 'personal issues' she was referring to, but still upset over the filmmaker's slight and always ready to complain about it. "The ocean wasn't even *mentioned*. At the *very* least, one of my legendary *epic battles* with The Retiarius should have been shown."

"Who?"

Julian's smile faded.

She shrugged. "Well, it was kinda about the real world, and not so much about undersea adventures."

"'Real world,' *indeed*." Julian made a face, his mood darkening. "You people simply live on tiny little islands in the middle of *my* kingdom." He pointed at the packages in one of the frozen food coolers. "It is the same as saying that pepperoni are more important than the pizza. They are merely a *topping*; they take up only a small percentage of the surface of the meal, and could just as easily be left off altogether. The pizza would remain the same, whether the topping was there or not. It would remain a pizza. But the pepperoni would be lost without it. Surface-dwellers just enjoy thinking of themselves as being more important than they are. They are an *annoyance*. Mosquitoes which make the pleasures of my kingdom less enjoyable, but by no means are they the rulers of the globe."

"...How are pepperoni an 'annoyance?'"

He shook his head. "I do not like them."

"Huh." She frowned. "...Yeah, well, I don't think we should really tell the press about that theory either, okay?"

"Is disliking pepperoni a negative amongst your people?"

"Possibly. But I think telling people that you hate their kids will upset the public just a little more. So, if they ask our opinions on surface-dwellers, we can just say something like: 'the entire world is important and worthy of protection.' See how much better that sounds than insults and threats?"

He paused to consider that. "...Not really, no." He frowned in confusion. "You wish me to lie?"

"No, no. Not at all." She pursed her lips in thought. "...Actually, yeah. I absolutely am. Lie your toned little ass off. *Trust me* on this."

"Very well. I will try to hide my infinite contempt for your people, Lady Bridget."

"There ya go!" She patted him on the shoulder. "Good job! See how easy it is to get along with the public?"

Julian brightened, feeling like he was really progressing quite well on his path towards hero of the surface world. ...True, he was still planning on killing them all shortly, but Bridget didn't need to know that. First, he would convince her of his righteous cause, and then he could destroy her people without having to worry about upsetting her.

All in all, it was a very good plan, and it was proceeding *splendidly*.

He was about to casually ask her how upset she typically got over genocide, when Multifarious scurried over.

"Bridget? Can we get some cereal? *Please!!!* They have 'Ocelot-a-Chocolate!'" Mull excitedly pointed to the cartoon leopard on the box, which was enjoying a bowl of artificially chocolate flavored sugar and milk. "Look! Look! It has *marshmallows* now! Aren't they cute!?!" Mull pointed at the yellow sticker on the box like a happy child. "And I'd get a 'Lotti the Ocelot' plush keychain!"

Bridget looked down at the paper in her hand, then shook her head sadly. "...I don't think that's on the list of things we're budgeted for. Sorry." She made a sad face. "But, I'll talk to the Purchasing Department for you, and..."

Mull pointed at her. "You *fucking suck.*" He/she turned on his/her heel, and marched away angrily, the cereal box clutched against his/her chest. "I'll remind you that I'm an *assassin.* When an assassin tells you to buy them breakfast cereal with little marshmallow kittens in it, you *buy them the goddamn cereal* or they'll find ways of *expressing their displeasure with you.*" He/she turned into the next aisle. "I'm going to go look at the booze."

"...I just don't understand Capes." Bridget finally decided.

"Nor do I." Julian shrugged. "But I am forbidden from killing them today." He cleared his throat, trying to sound casual. "On a scale of one to ten, how upset would you be if... say... *Australia* were swept off the map by a tidal wave?"

"*Huh?*" She squinted over at him. "*What?* Where did *that* come from?"

He shrugged. "…Just curious. I'm sure nothing like that is on the verge of happening within days…" He cleared his throat. "…Just… you know. In general."

She opened her mouth to say something, then stopped. She blinked several times, as though at a loss for words, and then pushed the cart down the aisle again. "…Well, I guess I'd be *very* upset if something tragic like that happened, obviously."

He nodded. "Indeed. …Very tragic."

Damn.

He hurried after her, just as Oz was placing several white bottles into the cart. Bridget frowned down at them. "How much bleach do we really *need*?"

The man thought about that for a moment. "Good thinking. I'll go get a couple more bottles."

"I don't think we really have the budget for that right now." She called after him.

"Well, I guess we'll just have to learn to live in *filth* then." He pointed at the shopping cart. "Or how about we put back your box of sugary death, and use that money to buy something which could *save our lives,* instead?" The man went back to retrieve his cleaning products.

Bridget looked down to see that a box of 'Ocelot-of-Chocolate' had somehow found its way into the cart. She quickly put it back on the shelf. "Why is everyone blaming me for everything?" She asked Julian, sounding both amazed and annoyed. "Why am *I* suddenly in charge of the budget? I feel like this is daycare or something, and that I'm…" She trailed off, her vision falling on Traitor, who was standing in front of an end cap of candy, casually rocking back and forth on his sneakers.

Bridget stormed over to him and pointed at the candy. "Please don't steal that."

"Steal what?" The man sounded utterly innocent.

She snapped her fingers. "Give it to me." She snapped her fingers again. "*Right now.*"

"What?" He sounded completely baffled. "I don't know *what* you're talking about, Bridget."

She kept staring at him expectantly.

The other man reluctantly pulled something from his pocket and placed it into her hand, like it was a tremendous bother. "I was just *looking* at it."

"Well, it'll be easier to 'look at' when it's *on the shelf* and not in your *pocket*."

"I'm sorry, are you my press agent or my *mother?*"

"If I were your mother, Arn, I would slap you silly." She made a shooing motion with her hand and gently pushed him away from the display rack. "Go on. Scram."

"Hey! I'm just standing here and..."

"And nothing." She hustled him away. "*Git!*"

The other man scampered from the scene.

Bridget made an aggravated sound, which was utterly adorable. "How do you *put up* with these people?"

"It is a daily struggle." Julian agreed. "I find that it helps to imagine them all dying painfully."

She made a face. "Everything's always death and destruction with you, you ever notice that?"

He nodded. "Yes. I have an excellent grasp on reality. Thank you for noticing."

"Oh, that's not reality. That's just being negative! I mean, what do you really have to be negative *about?* You're a king and a god and a superhero and gorgeous..."

"Don't forget 'raised by dolphins,' Bridge. That one's my *favorite.*" Quinn appeared, holding something out to him. "They're out of shaving cream, boss, so I got you this K-Y Jelly. It's the same stuff, don't worry."

"Oh, it is not!" She slapped the container away. "This is *serious.*"

Quinn hurried away, giggling.

Bridget glared after him. "Shame on you, Quinn!"

Julian frowned. "...That is not the same as shaving cream, I take it?"

"No. It's..." She looked suddenly awkward and started pushing the cart away again. "*Different.*"

"Ah." Julian crossed his arms over his chest. "Are you *sure* I can't kill anyone today?"

"Yep. ...Well, at least not in *public.*" She dropped several bags of flour into the cart. "What we gotta do is turn your whole thing around, okay? The problem is that you suffer from an image problem. You need to get out there and show people what you can do. See, right now, when people look at you, they just remember the numerous times you've been tried for war crimes. But don't worry. We'll help establish your brand. We gotta show people that you guys aren't rejects; you're the *elite.* You were left in charge because you're all that's *needed* to keep this city safe."

He nodded. "A point I have often made. I am all that is

needed to keep the entire *world* safe."

"Yeah, well, let's just stick with the city for right now, and we'll go from there, okay?"

"Very well."

Ahead of them, Ceann was standing in the darkened entryway to the backroom of the store, simply staring out from the shadows, waiting for someone to attack. Every muscle in his headless body was tense, as if prepared for the battle which would erupt the second he looked away from the terrified shoppers fleeing his presence.

Bridget ignored him, and guided her cart past him. "Your problem is that you've gotten so focused on the big picture, you've forgotten the little stuff. You want your fish buddies to be safe. Okay. Great. But you don't *do* that by trying to kill people."

"Actually, that is *exactly* how I do that."

"And how has it been working out for you, big guy?"

He frowned. "There have been a few... setbacks."

"Yep." She nodded smugly. "That's what I thought. Violence isn't going to do it." She pointed a carton of milk at him. "What *you* need to do is get your message out there. And you don't do that by being a jerk. You do that by appealing to peoples' good sides."

"The surface people *have* no good sides, Lady Haniver. Trust me. I've known them longer than you have."

She thought about that for a minute, then laughed. "Ha! You know, I've never thought about it that way before, but you're right, aren't you?"

"I usually am, yes. I'm glad you've noticed."

"Well, in either case, the point remains the same. If you want people to understand how awesome the sea can be, don't you think it's your responsibility as the sea's representative to be *awesome?*"

"...Does it involve being around the terrestrials?"

"'Fraid so, big guy."

He heaved a longsuffering sigh. "Very well. If it is a prerequisite to your continued help, I suppose I can bear their company for a while longer." He tried to hide his disgust. "Speaking of which, I have not been able to locate your vehicle yet, but rest assured, it will be *found.*"

"My what?" She sounded like she was barely paying attention.

"'Honda.'"

"Oh, that." She rolled her eyes. "I'm not worried."

Excellent. She had faith in his ability to locate the conveyance. That made him feel... good. Like there was at last *something* he could succeed at.

...Of course, in all honesty, he had absolutely *no* idea where to even begin looking for 'Honda,' though, which could be a problem. Hell, he wouldn't know where to buy a *new* car in the surface world, let alone obtain one which had been stolen.

But, no matter. Bridget wanted the car returned to her, so it would be RETURNED.

She stopped loading soda into her cart for a moment to watch as Multifarious dribbled two different blue plastic playground balls simultaneously, while at the same time, performing all manner of acrobatic spins, kicks and flips.

Bridget watched the show for a moment, then turned to go back to shopping. "Your people are weird."

"These are not *my* people. *My people* live under the sea. These are *terrestrials*. These are *your* people."

"How can they be *my* people? I'm not even a hero!"

"I don't think they are either, Lady Haniver."

"Bridget." She corrected.

"They're morons, Lady Bridget."

"And that's *another* thing: you can't criticize teammates publically like that."

"Why not? It's the truth."

"So? You can't say it because it makes your entire organization look bad. The next time someone asks you about something terrible one of them did, either dodge the question or simply say something simple and noncommittal like: '*heroism* is a complicated and dynamic responsibility, and I don't feel qualified to second-guess another Cape's decisions in the field.'" She nodded, as if pleased with herself. "See how much better that sounds than 'they're morons'?"

"But they *are* morons, and who better to judge them than someone who *isn't*?"

She rolled her eyes. "You're just not getting this are you? The point is that anything bad you say about them blows back onto *you,* because you're the one who's employing them."

"How is their behavior *my* fault!?!" He yelled, *outraged* that his coworkers would make him look bad in her eyes. "I wanted to *kill them*, but *you're* the one who keeps telling me to spare their meager lives."

The woman standing next to them in the aisle gaped at them in fear at hearing his words.

Good.

She *should* be afraid. *All* terrestrials should fear what was coming. ...Right after he earned their trust and respect, anyway.

Bridget smiled at the woman reassuringly. "Mice." She told her. "Jules wants to buy the poison, but I still feel bad about it, you know?" She grabbed his arm and pulled him away. "What did we just talk about?" She asked in an aggravated whisper. "Do you remember?"

"*Mice,* apparently. ...Although, I don't recollect the specifics. I *do* feel that poison is probably the best way to..."

"*No.*" She cut him off. "About us *not* loudly proclaiming our intentions or desires to *kill people?*"

He thought about it for a moment, then nodded, realization dawning. "...I'm not supposed to do that anymore, am I?"

"No." She shook her head. "But that's okay. You're still learning." She pushed the cart towards the front of the store. "Come on, let's go check out. I think we have everything."

"Not quite." Multifarious appeared and dropped several items into the cart. "I got a paddle and ball game, four packs of plastic spoons, two-and-a-half English muffins, and a bottle of 'Black Pony Scotch.'"

Bridget frowned, then took on an overly patient and humoring tone, as if dealing with a child. "Now, are these things that we really *need,* or are these things which you merely *want*? Keep in mind that we have limited resources right now, and that we need to buy things for everyone, not just ourselves. We can only afford the *essentials.*"

"Only afford the essentials?" Multifarious repeated. "Essentials, like say, I don't know... suddenly hiring a certain *press agent*? Seems like if we got rid of *her* we could afford my cereal." Multifarious crossed his/her arms over his/her chest, obviously still sulking over the loss of the bowls of chocolate goo. "How about this: if you *don't* buy this stuff for me, I'm going to steal it. ...And keep in mind that that would look *real* bad from a PR standpoint, and since keeping us in the good graces of the press is your *job* now, I guess you'll just have to *find a way.*"

Bridget made an annoyed sound. "I swear to God! You people are just..."

The rest of her words were cut off as several people came running into the store, as something outside exploded in the distance.

Through the front window, it appeared that several people were fighting in the street.

"Oh my god!" Bridget gasped, and pointed out the front windows of the store. "The bank across the street is being robbed or something!"

Julian didn't bother looking up from the shopping list. "I'm sure they will be preoccupied with the vault. I know from personal experience that grocery stores have little in the way of cash to steal, so I highly doubt they will interfere with our shopping." He tapped the paper. "I don't think we bought the laundry detergent."

She blinked at him. "...Don't you think you should do something about it?"

"Sure, I think the detergents are in aisle..."

She cut him off. "*The bank*."

He scoffed. "Why? *I* do not bank there. My money is *entirely* safe from the thieves and..." Then he remembered that he was supposed to be a Cape now. "...And I will not allow anyone *else's* to be stolen either. It would be... Um...," his mind raced, "...the *least* I could do for the surface world."

Julian marched towards the front of the store, grabbing Tupilak by the back of his fur parka on the way through the doors.

The man made an annoyed sound and grabbed for the sticker he had just purchased from the vending machine next to the door. "Dammit, Jules! All I need is the skeleton to complete my set!"

Julian ignored him and pointed across the street. "We have *other* business."

Quinn watched the armed men for a minute. "...I think I know that guy." He raised his voice. "HEY! Jack! What up, man!?! They keep the vault key in the manager's desk."

The robber stationed in the doorway absently waved in greeting. "Yeah, I know. Gotta kill some super-folk though, so I can get the..."

Gunfire erupted, cutting off the rest of the man's words. It appeared that rather than being a bank robbery, there was some sort of larger dispute going on for some reason.

A large Viking woman picked up a car and hurled it at Jack as if it weighed nothing. The other man ran towards the vehicle and jumped, passing through it like a ghost while it was still in the air, and opened fire on the zombie with his gun. The vehicle crashed into the façade of the bank and exploded. A man in a black trench coat blasted the area with a power beam, causing the other gunmen to duck for cover.

The sirens mixed with the screams, as the situation spiraled out of control into a full blown war on the streets of the city.

Quinn watched the fight in silence for a moment, then frowned. "What the fuck is *this* about?"

"I have no idea. Nor do I care." Julian's eyes narrowed. "But we must *stop them*."

Quinn turned to look at him in amazement. "Huh? How? *Why?* I mean, what does it matter if a gang war destroys a couple blocks? You're planning on taking over this place anyway, and..."

Julian cut him off, talking right over him as Bridget walked up. "*Yes!*" His voice took on a dangerous edge of warning as a caution to Quinn not to continue that thought. "*Thank you* for the reminder, Tupilak." He shoved Quinn towards the scene. "We will take control of this situation and ensure the safety of the public."

Quinn's mouth fell open in shock. "...What the hell is *wrong* with you today, man?"

Julian ignored him and stalked back into the grocery store. He pushed aside one of the mortal cashiers and bent closer to the microphone next to the register. "All members of the Consortium of Chaos, please come to register five. All Consortium of Chaos members to the registers, please." He paused. "...Surface-worlders, continue placidly and obliviously shopping. There is no need to flee in panic. All is well." He turned to look at Bridget. "It's important to deceive the public about the depths of the danger they are in. If they knew the truth of their immediate peril, they could be killed in the futile rush for safety."

Yes. That sounded *very* Cape-like. He was fitting into his new role of "protector of the surface world" so well.

....Unfortunately, he said the words too close to the microphone, and his observation echoed through the store.

The shoppers stopped what they were doing, looked around the store, and then began to panic.

Idiots.

Had they not *heard* his command to be calm and ignorant of the crisis outside?

Why were surface people so silly?

He frowned in irritation, glaring at the store's patrons as they dashed about in terror. "Your panic just makes you easier targets for the madmen outside who were dedicated to murdering you, terrestrials. They could burst through those doors at any time." He reminded them into the microphone, his tone longsuffering. "If you don't calm down, these will be your final moments on earth."

Strangely, his soothing words did little to help the situation, and the people seemed even *more* upset for some reason.

He sighed and marched towards the front of the store again. He turned to Multifarious. "What are your powers today?"

Multifarious put one gloved hand in the air. "Today I am... 'White Dwarf!'"

Mack put his face in his palms. "Aw, hell. *That's* going to get us angry letters."

Julian ignored him. "Powers?"

"I have the power to collapse stars..." Multifarious held up his/her gloves hands and swirls of colorful energy began to dance and spin between his/her outstretched fingers like a glowing kaleidoscope. "...The cosmic life-cycle of the universe is *mine to control*..."

Mack shook his head, his voice calm but serious. "Please don't blow up the sun, Mull."

Julian let out a longsuffering sigh. "In other words, you are *completely* useless in a fight against terrestrial *bank robbers*."

"No!" Mull sounded insulted and crossed his/her arms over his/her chest like a petulant child. "I could destroy them *all* if I made the sun go *supernova*."

Julian rolled his eyes. "We'll call that 'Plan B.'"

"Please don't blow up the sun, Mull." Mack repeated.

Julian pointed at the doors. "Just guard the exit and stay out of my way."

"Can't I continue 'shopping obliviously' too?" Mull asked. "Because that just *completely* convinced me that there was nothing to worry about."

Mack frowned. "Why are we trying to trap all these people in here?"

"Because there is a *battle* going on out there, and they could get hurt if we let them leave the safety of the building."

"Oh." Mack nodded, as though that made sense. "Sorry. I guess I'm just not used to *carin'* yet."

"Tupilak, Traitor..." Julian pointed at the men. "You're with me." He looked around. "Where is The Horseman?"

Quinn shrugged. "I think he's still haunting the frozen foods section. Want me to go get him?"

Julian shook his head. "No. He is a liability in a situation where there are so many innocent people around." He deliberately said the words loudly enough that Bridget could hear them. They sounded so... heroic.

Truly, he *was* the greatest hero the surface people ever had.

...And like *all* of the terrestrial Capes of late, he was secretly plotting to kill them. But that didn't detract from his greatness.

He looked over his teammates, then frowned at an unfamiliar face. "Who are *you?*"

The young man looked hurt. "I'm Wendell. Remember? I work in Accounting and..."

"I don't care." Julian cut him off. "The boy will take out those gun emplacements on that corner." Julian pointed down the block where several large machine guns were set up and were busily blasting away at a group of super-powered people.

The boy looked stunned. "...I'm sorry..." He swallowed. "I'm doing *what?*"

"You will run straight down the street and seize those machine guns."

He paled. "...But... but I'm just an *intern*. ...I'm only doing this for *course credit!*"

Mull chuckled and pushed him towards the doors. "Time to earn your 'A' then, *college boy*."

Julian ignored them, and walked onto the sidewalk followed by his teammates, making sure the doors were secured behind him. He began to stalk across the street towards the fight.

"Surface-dwellers!" He yelled. "I am Lord Julian..."

The gunmen stationed at the bank opened fire, cutting him off.

Julian swore and dove for cover behind a parked car, Quinn and Arn right after him. The boy from accounting huddled behind some shopping carts and simply screamed hysterically in a high-pitched voice like a frightened child, his hands over his ears.

Quinn glared at Julian. "You just *announce yourself!?! What the fuck, man!?!*"

Julian cleared his throat. "This is *all* part of my plan."

"Is it now?" Quinn asked in amazement. "Well, that's good to know. I'm glad you have all the *details of our deaths* worked out already. If you didn't, I'd be *terrified* right now."

Julian paused to consider their options. "I think our main target should be the bank." He decided.

Arn frowned. "Why the bank? I don't think it's even being *robbed,* I think people are just using the doorway for cover. Personally, I'm much more concerned about the fact that Reece's men and some of the local human gangs are apparently having a battle in the streets of midtown for some reason." He pointed down the street at one of the men. "That's fucking *Gyre,* man. Once, I watched him blow up a *building* with his powers. While he was *inside it*." He shook his head. "Dude's insane. If he's here, *he's* our biggest threat, not some stupid Norms in a bank."

"We will stop the bank robbery, because the Lady Bridget *wants* us to stop the *bank robbery*." He carefully explained, sick to death of their slowness.

"*But the bank's not even being robbed!*" Quinn argued.

"And why should it matter *what* the New Girl wants?" Arn asked in confusion.

"It just *does*." Julian cleared his throat. "So, Traitor, you're going to draw their fire, and then I'm going to run over there and apprehend them."

"Can't I just shoot them from here?" Arnold asked, pulling out one of the small, silenced, scarlet red pistols he always carried. "I could hit them, and..."

"*No killing today!*"

"Why?"

"Because..."

Arn rolled his eyes, cutting him off. "Let me guess: 'because *Bridget* says.'"

"Indeed." Julian prepared to move. "Now then, Tupilak, you are to stop anyone leaving the bank who gets passed me." He focused on his targets. "Ready? GO."

Arn took off.

Julian stormed into the street a moment later, waiting for the guards to get distracted by Traitor... but predictably, the man had apparently run in the *opposite* direction, fleeing the scene and abandoning his teammates to their fate. As such, the guards had absolutely nothing to focus on but Julian.

He made a face.

He really needed to start working *alone* again. Teamwork was torture.

He resigned himself to the fact that he would now have to kill the men, which would disappoint Bridget *terribly*.

He had been doing *so well* too. He hadn't killed anyone all morning, despite *innumerable* opportunities and *extreme* provocation.

The gunman opened fire at him, peppering the grocery store behind him with bullets because mortals were under the odd belief that "more bullets" was better than "more accuracy." The people inside the store screamed and ran for the exits. The surge of patrons crashed into Multifarious and OverDriver who had been stationed at the front of the store, smashing them backwards through the glass automatic doors and onto the street. The crowd of panicked shoppers poured out of the narrow openings, paying no attention to the people they were stepping on in the process or the bullets flying around them.

Mack rolled onto his side, trying to shield his injured arm from the rush of people running over him.

A man wearing a sky blue tank top squeezed his way through the door glass and jumped out onto the street, his foot landing on Multifarious' chest. Mull grabbed hold of the man's foot and twisted it to the side, causing the man to stumble down onto the sidewalk as well.

Julian stalked across the street, ignoring the bullets, intent on stopping the gunmen. They would *pay* for making him look bad and ruining his shopping experience with Bridget. They would *pay* for...

And that's when he got hit by a car. The vehicle plowed into him, causing him to smash into the windshield, roll along the roof, and then fall back onto the asphalt again. The car stopped in front of the bank and the gunmen got in, then the vehicle tore down the street again.

He shook his head to clear it, then watched as the vehicle got further and further away. He glanced over his shoulder at Quinn. "*Do something!*"

Behind him, Quinn rose from his cover, tested the wind for a moment, then hurled his barbed harpoon through the air. The weapon's flight was graceful and true, falling on its target with deadly accuracy. ...Provided the other man was *aiming* for the vehicle's trunk. The harpoon sank into the metal, and stuck straight up in the air, as if it were some sort of radio antenna.

"Damn." Quinn watched the car drive away out of sight, his weapon still attached. "I needed that." He said sadly.

"...And what was *that* supposed to do?" Julian pulled himself to his feet with as much dignity as he could.

"Well I didn't see *you* coming up with any better ideas, oh-fearless-one." Quinn trudged out of the street and back onto the sidewalk in front of the store. "Maybe I should have gone with *your* strategy and tried to stop the car with my *face*."

In front of the store, the patrons had finally finished fleeing the scene.

...All that is except *one*.

"You think you can push me down and step on *me*, pal!?!" Multifarious dragged the shopper's head from the concrete by the front of his sky blue tank top and screamed into his face. "You're going to step on me!?! *Me!?!* I live in the *Bronx, motherfucker! You step on me, I'm gonna step on your grave!"*

"STOP KILLING THE BYSTANDERS!" Julian bellowed, causing Multifarious to stop, fist halfway to the man's face. "The Lady Haniver has already *warned* you not to do that anymore! It angers the surface-dwellers when you kill members of their own kind in front of them."

Quinn shooed Mull away from the man, who immediately staggered to his feet and fled the area.

"...But the more of them I *kill*, the fewer there are to *anger*." Multifarious argued seriously. "It only stands to reason. It'd also saves us time, because there would be fewer people getting themselves into danger and in need of rescue in the first place."

Julian stopped to consider the wisdom of that.

"I mean, why am I even *here* if I can't kill anyone?" Multifarious held his/her arms out in exasperation, as if the mere idea was utter lunacy. "Why did you bring in an *assassin* if I'm not going to *assassinate* something!?!"

"That's not what we *do* anymore." Julian drew himself up to his full height. "That was *Ferral's* way of doing things. We're the *guardians* of the surface world now. His violent thuggish ways have no place in the world I mean to create."

"I'm not paid to do that." Multifarious shook his/her head seriously, crossing his/her arms. "I'm a private contractor brought in by the Consortium to make things dead. I'm *not* a Cape. You're trying to change the nature of our association."

Quinn sank down onto the curb. "Well, we're all making sacrifices. Deal with it." He lay back on the sidewalk, shielding his eyes with his mittened hand and staring up at the sky. "*Fuck* its hot today."

"Why don't you just stop wearing heavy fur?" Bridget asked.

"I'm sorry, do *you* have a magical fur anorak parka which grants you supernatural abilities, Bridge? Because if you *did*, then you could take it off whenever you wanted."

Mull looked up at the sun. "I can take care of the heat for you if you want, Quinn." He/she held out one gloved hand towards the sky as if preparing to crush it in his/her grasp.

"*Please* don't blow up the sun, Mull. I'm askin' as a personal favor." Mack intoned calmly. "It wouldn't help in makin' this day any less shitty."

Mull made a dismissive hand gesture, as if he/she was the most mistreated person in the world.

"I think my arm is broke worse now." Mack winced and pulled a piece of glass from his neck, and absently flicked the bloody shard of automatic door into the street. "Hurts like a bitch."

"You are going to need to see a doctor to have your arm set again, McCallister. My readings indicate that your humerus is now fractured in *two* locations, and the stiches from your knife wound have reopened." Polly peered down at the arm with scientific curiosity, like he was a bug caught in a jar merely there to entertain her. "I calculate nerve damage if you do not seek medical attention within the next twenty-four hours."

Mack bent to retrieve his hat from the gutter, where it had fallen when he was pushed through the window. "*Hate* hospitals. Ain't goin'."

"*Yes, you aaaaaare.*" She practically sang.

Quinn held a bottle of ice water Bridget had given him against his forehead. "*God,* we suck."

"We're just having a bad day." Mack gingerly sank down onto a bench, letting out a weary sigh like it was good to get off his feet. "Happens to everyone."

Huddled in the shadows of the shopping carts, the boy from the college continued to weep quietly to himself, still too terrified to leave his cover.

Everyone ignored him.

"I don't think the crew at the bank even realized we were *here*, and they still somehow managed to wipe the floor with us. And those were just the *human* people. The other *empowered* folk couldn't identify us in a lineup. They didn't even think we were *worthy* of a beat down. They *completely* ignored us." Quinn sighed and looked up at Julian. "Can't we just go home to the Undersea Base?" He shook his head seriously. "We don't *belong* here, man." He gestured to their surroundings. "What can we do for these people? I mean, *really?*" He looked down at the gutter. "...Let's just go home."

"We are not going *anywhere.*" Julian snapped. Truth be told, he would have liked to go home as well, but that was out of the question. He had made a promise to Bridget to find 'Honda,' and he would fulfill his vow. Plus, Bridget was here, so this was where Julian wanted to stay. He'd searched for her for too long to lose her now. Wherever she was, that's where he wanted to be too.

"Ah, whenever I hear on the news that there has been *tremendous* property damage, great loss of life, and *no* suspects in custody, I know *right* where to find my beloved teammates." Montgomery appeared, followed by Higgins. "I daresay you've outdone yourselves *this* time though. Congratulations on losing what the radio is already calling the 'Battle of Midtown,' a fight that you weren't even *invited* to. I don't recall *ever* seeing such a *complete* and *humiliating* failure in front of the whole world before." He paused. "...Well, not since *Monday*, anyway." He glanced at his associate. "Higgins? You keep up with the media, how would one categorize the day's events thus far?"

The man swallowed, as if feeling unprepared for a sudden test he was being given. "...I-I-I believe the technical term in popular culture is: 'clusterfuck,' sir."

Monty's smug evil smile widened.

"Where *were* you, Welles?" Julian snapped, ignoring the toady's words. "You were *supposed to be here*."

"Yeah! While we were fighting for our lives, Willy Wonka and his fucking Oompa-Loompa over here were what?" Quinn pointed at the bag in the man's hand. "Shopping?"

"I've decided to enter the rewarding field of *coin collecting*." Monty slipped the small bag into his coat pocket. "I *fully* anticipate that my new pastime will pay off someday soon. Isn't that right, Higgins?"

"Y-y-yes, sir. A hobby is its own reward, sir."

"Indeed." Monty nodded. "Well said."

"...Twenty-three hours, fifty-six minutes and ten seconds until McCallister is permanently handicapped." Polly informed the group. "Twenty-three hours, fifty-six minutes and *nine* seconds..."

"Ah, a countdown. Why, it's just like New Years. How very *festive*." Monty casually wound his antique pocket watch, utterly unconcerned over Mack's serious injuries. "Let me know when your countdown hits the ten second mark, and I'll have Higgins break out the party favors and champagne."

"And instead of 'dropping the ball,' I'll just kick you in *yours*, Monty." Mack leaned forward on his bench. "How about that?"

Bridget cleared her throat and looked up from her notes. "You know what? This might look like a setback, but this is a moment we can *grow* from." She nodded. "I think we've all learned a valuable lesson today: use the crosswalks or you'll get run over." She nodded, as though this was a vital lesson they all should take heed of.

Behind her, Multifarious emerged from the store, carrying a box of chocolate cereal. "...Also, people shooting at people, will probably shoot at *you* if you let them, so you probably shouldn't let them, unless you like getting shot at."

Bridget frowned. "What did I tell you guys about stealing?"

"Don't even start with me, missy." Mull snapped in exasperation, then glanced around at the team. "Oh, *fuck* this shit." He/she waved goodbye and began calmly walking down the street.

"I'm outta here, guys. Been real, but I didn't sign on for this. When you get back to wantin' stuff killed, gimme a call."

"My darling team seems to be hemorrhaging members at an *astonishing* rate." Monty said with mock sadness as he watched Mull go. He put his top hat over his heart, as if mourning the loss of another true friend. "It's always so hard at the end." He replaced his hat. "*Twelve*." He said with no small amount of smugness, continuing to count the rapidly dwindling number of members in the organization.

"Oh, he'll be back." Quinn rolled his eyes. "He always gets antsy when he hasn't killed something in a while."

"Indeed." Julian nodded, trying to sound sure of himself. He turned to Bridget. "I am unfamiliar with the standard customs of the surface world, but do we still have to pay for *our* supplies? Can we not just take them now that all of the cashiers have left? No one would see."

CHAPTER 10

STORMS: "LORD SARGASSUM ACTUALLY HAS MORE EXPERIENCE WITH SUPER-POWERED EVENTS THAN MOST OF THE OTHER CAPES IN THE CITY. TRUE, HE SEEMS TO PREFER TO STAY OUT OF THE SPOTLIGHT, BUT I THINK YOU'D BE SURPRISED AT THE KINDS OF THINGS HE'S DONE OVER THE YEARS."

KING: "YEAH, AND I BET HE MAKES THE TRAINS RUN ON TIME TOO, DOESN'T HE, CONNIE? THAT'S THE WHOLE PROBLEM WITH YOUR DELUDED MINDSET: THE ENDS DO NOT JUSTIFY THE MEANS. YOU CRAFT SOME PRETTY LITTLE FANTASYLAND FOR YOURSELF, WHERE EVERYONE IS ALWAYS GOOD AND EVERYONE GETS THEIR HAPPY ENDING BECAUSE SOME FISH-MAN IS NOW YOUR CHAMPION AND WILL SAVE YOU BECAUSE HE HAS SO MUCH 'EXPERIENCE.' HE'S GOT A LOT OF EXPERIENCE WITH CRIME ALL RIGHT. COMMITTING IT. PEOPLE WHO DO TERRIBLE THINGS CANNOT THEN ARGUE THAT THE TERRIBLE THINGS THEY'VE DONE WERE FOR SOME HIGHER PURPOSE. ANYONE WHO SAYS OTHERWISE IS KIDDING THEMSELVES, AND IS DOOMED TO FALL TO DESPOTISM AND RUIN."

TRANSCRIPT OF "KING OF CAPES AND COWLS," MEDIA: TELEVISION, SHOW: 1407, NEWSCHANNEL 6, FRIDAY 21:00-22:00 EST, NETWORK SEGMENT-ID: 918000606

June 6, 1944

"You know what I like about you, Sargassum?" The Roach asked, casually leaning against the railing of the ship. "You're easy to talk to."

"Uh-huh." Julian blinked at him in confusion. "I fail to see how *any of this* helps me in my efforts."

The other man waved off his concerns. "I'm getting to that, I'm getting to that."

Julian shook his head. "I don't think that you *are,* no. You've been saying that for hours now, and yet we have done *nothing* to further my plans."

"When did you become such a whiney little *bitch*, man?" Roach rolled his eyes. "Here I am, taking time out of all the shit that *I* have on my plate at the moment, to try to help *you* get some stuff done, and what's the thanks I get?" He gestured to him. "*This.*"

Julian took a deep cleansing breath.

His newfound "team-up" with the man was not going as well as had been promised. He really should have known better than to trust a terrestrial with anything, *least* of all the successful completion of his righteous mission.

Honestly, he had no idea why he was allowing himself to get wrapped up in the other man's schemes. True, it was nice to have someone to talk to, but the problem was that Julian didn't particularly enjoy what the man actually had to *say*.

...But the alternative was to return to his solitude under the waves, and Julian wasn't ready for that yet. He could muster his courage and endure more of this terrible person, if for no other reason than he really didn't want to be alone.

"I don't know why you're getting your panties in a twist anyway." Hector absently spat over the side of the boat and into the sea.

Julian made a distasteful face.

"You need to go out there and *take* what you want." Roach advised. "You got like powers and shit, right?"

Julian nodded. "I am truly the only person who can claim mastery over *all* of the world's settings."

"You can fly?"

His smile faded. "No."

"Well, sounds like you missed one then." Hector busied himself by flipping through one of the pinup calendars left by one of the sailors before they all abandoned ship. "Besides, I mean, I know they're..." He trailed off and then whistled, turning the calendar around so that Julian could see it too. "Check out the gams on *this one!*"

"Very impressive." Julian deadpanned, not bothering to even look at the terrestrial pornography. "You were *saying?*"

"I said: I know they're all like important to you and stuff, but don't millions of fish die every day anyway? What difference will a couple minutes make?"

He leaned closer to the man. "Do you honestly believe that

if I could change places with them, that I wouldn't do it in a heartbeat?"

Roach blinked at him in astonishment. "You'd kill yourself? For... *fish?*"

"That is my *duty* to them. I am but their righteous arm; a servant at their command." He straightened to his full height. "It is one of the burdens which *comes* from leadership. I would gladly sacrifice myself for *any* of my people."

Roach rolled his eyes. "Whatever." He looked out over the side of the ship. "All I'm saying is that..."

"You will never get away with this!" Called Everett Keerg, AKA "The Retiarius," from his position strapped to the Navy destroyer's partially exposed propeller. "You'll never stop humanity's efforts to defeat your aquatic evil!" The man shook his head. "And you cannot stop us from beating back the Nazis!"

Julian looked over at his companion in confusion. "The who?"

"I don't know, man. I'm not political." Roach shrugged. "That asshole with the little mustache, I think."

"Ah." Julian thought about that for a minute. "Why does he think that just because we're trying to stop the Navy, that I'm on the side of that lunatic?"

Roach shrugged again. "I don't know, man." He absently gestured to the Retiarius. "He's not *my* nemesis. I'd never even heard of the fucker until I hooked up with you. He's totally bottom of the Cape barrel, man. I got no clue how his mind works. You tell me."

"This whole thing was *your* idea!" Julian snapped at him. "I wanted to work on raising an aquatic army of mutant fish to sweep the surface world clean. YOU were the one who wanted to come here and get involved in this stupid surface matter!"

"This is important!" Roach gestured to the hundreds of ships which surrounded them. "Look at this! This is D-Day, motherfucker! You're telling me that any villain worth his salt WOULDN'T be here trying to cause some destruction!?!"

"I do not *want* to cause destruction. I just want to protect my people!"

"That's what we're doing!" Roach argued. "And the BEST way to protect them, is to blow the fucking hell out of shit, right?"

"That makes no sense!" Julian gestured to their prisoner. "This accomplishes *nothing.*" He shook his head. "We should be using this time to put our plans on how to crush the surface world into motion, before he breaks free and tries to stop us!"

"Oh, he's not going to stop SHIT." Roach jabbed his finger down on the ship's ignition and the engines began to whir to life. ...Starting the propeller. He smiled over at Julian. "Problem solved, right?"

"You can't just *kill* him!" Julian hurried over to the railing to look down at the propeller. "He's MY nemesis! That is *not* how these things are done! *That's not right!*"

"What do you mean? You practically TOLD me to!"

"I did nothing of the sort! I said that we couldn't keep him prisoner..."

"Which means 'kill him.'"

"It does NOT!" Julian pointed his trident at him. "It means: 'let's forget whatever idiotic scheme you're cooking up in your twisted surface-dweller brain and get back to focusing on protecting my people!'"

"Well then why didn't you SAY that!?!"

"I did!" Julian bellowed. "I have said it INNUMERABLE times this morning, but you ignore me at every turn!"

"Well, you need to take a *stand,* man." Roach argued. "If you want something, you gotta fight for it. You wanna protect all the little fishies, then go do it!"

"That's what I'm *trying* to do, but you continue to insist that you know a better way of fighting for my kingdom."

"And I *do.*" The man placed his hand over his heart. "I wouldn't lead you astray. *Believe* me, I got this shit all worked out in my head. This whole battle is all *about* your fish people and..."

"What the hell is going on, Hector?"

Julian spun around to find a stranger dressed entirely in white standing behind him in the shadows. The person's face was covered by a facemask emblazoned with a strange doodle, and he/she was wearing a slightly baggy costume which looked like a bizarre mixture of a military uniform, body armor and a ninja outfit.

Roach rolled his eyes at the intruder. "Oh, Christ. This is *just* what I need today."

The person made his/her way from the corner of the room, walking nearly silently, despite the fact that he/she was wearing white combat boots and was walking on metal plating. "Do I even want to *know* what you're doing this time?"

"No." Roach said simply. "You don't. Fuck off."

"We are fighting for my innocent aquatic countrymen and the danger this war is placing them in." Julian informed the person.

"Uh-huh." The stranger put his/her hands on his/her hips.

"And how exactly does trying to stop the boats from reaching the beach help you in that?"

"I have no idea." Julian told him seriously. "But I am assured that it does."

The person pointed with one gloved finger at Roach. "I'm warning you, Hector: stop *now.*" The person shook his/her masked face. "You won't like what happens if you don't."

"Oh, *blow me,* Roy." Roach shot back and spun the wheel of the ship sharply, causing the Cape to stumble.

Julian gasped. "Be careful where you steer this craft! *There are innocent fish in the water!*"

The masked person reached to holsters strapped to his/her ankles and pulled out two telescoping metal batons and flicked them open. He/she looked over at Roach in apparent confusion. "*Fish?*" He/she asked incredulously.

"Yeah, it's his thing." Roach shrugged. "I kinda had to take the only partner I could get, you know?"

The masked person nodded. "Whatever." He/she absently pointed at him. "This the Retiarius' guy?"

"Oh yeah." Roach pointed over the side of the ship. "Or *was* at any rate!" He cackled with maniacal laughter. "With him out of the way, I can achieve my larger goal! I'm going to take this destroyer, and *carve off a nice slice of Europe for myself!*"

The masked person shook his/her head. "I can't let you get away with that, Hector. You've gone too far this time! Even if you kill me, other Capes will *stop you!*"

"Oh, I think they'll be too busy for that." Roach scoffed and gestured to the ships surrounding them. "All I'm saying is: in all *this* confusion, who's going to miss Norway?"

"The Norwegians?" Julian guessed.

"*They can just move to Sweden!*" Roach shot back. "They're the same fucking people, man. They're really all just one big country anyway, so you gotta stop thinking in 'borders' like that. That's marginalizing them."

Julian frowned. "And what about *my* people?"

Roach groaned in annoyance. "What do you think all of this is ABOUT!?!"

"You taking over *Norway,* for some reason?" The masked person offered. "...Although just how you intend to do that from northern *France* is anyone's guess." He/she was quiet for a moment. "Did you mistake 'Nor*mandy*' on the map for "Nor*way,*' Hector?"

"No!" The other man shot back, a little too quickly. "I know *exactly* where I am, and I know *exactly* where *you* can go!"

He launched himself at the Cape, and they began to fight.

Julian frowned at them as they wrestled on the ship's controls. "This accomplishes nothing towards the freedom of my people, Hector." He told the other man calmly.

"Then kill him and we can get on with it!" Roach shot back, slamming his fist into the masked person's stomach.

"How does killing this person help me?"

"Look, just..."

Roach's words were cut off as the masked person grabbed him by the fake antenna attached to his head and yanked him forward so that he could knee him in the face. Roach staggered backwards and the masked person pressed his/her advantage, grabbing him by the front of his roach costume and tossing him through the door to the boat's wheel house and out onto the deck.

Julian watched his flight through the door, then turned back to the Cape. "I have no idea who you are, but you are interfering with the plans of a *god,* mortal."

The masked person waved him off dismissively. "Yeah, whatever." He/she stalked through the door to finish off his/her opponent, pressing a hand to his/her stomach where the other man's punch had landed.

Julian walked after him/her. "I hope you realize that you are fighting to continue my people's *oppression*. All they desire is *freedom*."

The masked person turned to gape at him. "How am I doing that? All I'm trying to do is keep my idiot brother from taking over *Norway,* and..."

The rest of his/her words were cut off as thousands of roaches descended upon him/her, crawling all over his/her pristine white uniform. He/she staggered back, letting out a startled cry as the insects began working their way under the mask.

Roach laughed manically pointing at his opponent. "That's it! Kill! Kill, my minions! Choke the life from my enemies! And then... ALL OF NORWAY WILL BE OURS!"

Julian let out another sigh. "Is this going to *take long*, Hector? Because if you do not concentrate on my mission soon, I'm just going to go do it myself."

The other man focused on him again. "How can you say that? What do you think I'm doing this for? This is all about *you*, man. Once we take out the Capes, we can really get down to setting your people free."

Julian shook his head. "I do not believe that you are serious in your promises to help me in my quest." He put his hands on his hips, glaring at him in irritation. "I think you are just using me to accomplish your own ends."

"Come on!" Hector sounded insulted. "Why would I do that? Look at all the stuff I've done to free the fish, or whatever!"

"You have done NOTHING!" Julian yelled back. "MY people suffer and die, while all YOU seem focused on is fighting the absurd heroes of the terrestrial world. They are *meaningless* in the larger scheme of things. The REAL mission is to destroy *ALL* humanity, not to beat some fools in capes."

"I thought the real mission was to free your people?" Roach sounded confused. "'Cause if we got a new mission now, I'm going to have to change *all* of my plans."

"YOU HAVE NO PLANS!" Julian yelled at him. "This partnership is OVER! Do you hear me!?!" He swept his arms wide. "OVER!"

Roach rolled his eyes. "But what about the plan, man? You can't just abandon ship now that we're so close to taking over Norway and achieving your dreams!"

"NORWAY IS NOT MY DREAM!" He bellowed. "You are a liar and a maniac and a true *surface-dweller!*" He shook his head emphatically. "And my people deserve BETTER than..."

The rest of his words were cut off as an autogyro emblazoned with a large red shield reading "LL" on it began to hover overhead.

Julian swore under his breath.

Perfect.

He glanced over at his companion. "And *now* the 'Lovers of Liberty' are here to stop you, Hector." He began to stroll away. "Personally, I hope you *kill each other.*"

"Whadda ya mean 'stop *me*'?" Hector chased after him. "We're in this *together,* man."

"Oh, we are NOT!" Julian began to climb down the ladder to the main deck. "I had *nothing* to do with this plan."

"Give it up!" Announced a stern voice from their right. "There's no escape from the lustrous light of the Lovers of Liberty!"

Hector shook his head. "I hate fucking alliteration, man." He turned around to face the Cape known as 'Captain O'Industry.' "Don't you people have anything *better* to do than try to stop us from freeing Lord Sargassum's people?"

Julian shook his head. "This plot has nothing to do with me."

He pointed at Hector. "This is all on him. I'm going home."

"You're not going *anywhere,* Sargassum!" Cried Paper Tiger as she descended the rope hanging from their aircraft. "You're going to face justice for what you've done today!"

"I haven't done *anything,* mortal!" He argued. "I was merely standing here while ROACH did everything!"

"Standing by and watching evil be done, is the same as doing it yourself." The Captain told him proudly.

Hector rolled his eyes. "That's it. I'm gonna kill him." He charged the other man.

Julian groaned in annoyance. "I do not wish to fight these idiots! It accomplishes nothing! All I want is to..."

The rest of his words were cut off as "Punchline" dropped to the deck beside him and hit him with a heavy right fist. The man laughed as Julian hit the ground. "Now *that's* funny!"

He lifted Julian up over his shoulders and tossed him through the window of the wheelhouse, smashing the controls to pieces.

Julian began to pull himself to his feet, wincing in pain at the shard of metal which was now sticking out of his side. He yanked it free and then turned to look out the window he had just been thrown through, and gasped in horror.

The ship was now headed straight for one of the other empty boats which had been evacuated during Roach's mad plot, and the ship's wheel had become too damaged to turn.

He jumped to his feet and ran back to the deck. He raised his arms over his head. "We must stop this!" He pointed to the other boat. "We need to use our strength to steer this craft away!"

The others ignored him.

He turned in a circle, trying to find *someone* who would listen, then saw The Retiarius climbing over the edge of the ship. The man looked unhappy at almost being killed by Roach, but otherwise, was evidently uninjured.

Julian dashed over to him. *"We must stop this ship!"* He yelled at him.

The man braced for an attack, then paused. "...Why?" He asked suspiciously.

Julian pointed to the destroyer they were headed towards. "Because there will be an explosion!"

The Retiarius swore and raised his deep voice above the din of battle. "Lovers of Liberty! Everyone over the side! NOW!"

Julian shook his head. "NO! You can't just..."

The various combatants all immediately dove into the sea

and Julian was left alone on the deck, watching helplessly as the obstacle got closer and closer.

He looked up at the sky, cursing his existence, then down at the waves, saying a silent apology to his people.

The front of the ship plowed into the other destroyer and there was a horrible sound of twisting metal. Julian raced towards the stern of the ship and dove off into the water, just as the ammunition stores ignited and the boats were blown to pieces.

He bobbed in the water for a moment, watching the wreckage contaminate his home, then swam to the shore and pulled himself onto the sands.

The fight was continuing to rage on the beach, as Roach and the masked person faced off. In the background, machine guns fired from bunkers at soldiers who were storming up the beach for some reason.

The surface people did the most *peculiar* things sometimes.

The masked person punched Roach in the face and swung out with one of the telescoping batons, sweeping the man from his feet, then loomed over him. "I'm going to meet with some German rebels, and I'm going to try to help them take their country *back* from the hands of the Nazis!" He pointed over his shoulder. "The Allies will free France, and then we'll help free Germany, and I DON'T need to waste time trying to stop *YOUR* latest crazy scheme!"

Roach threw a handful of sand into his opponent's face, which did little since the person was wearing a mask. It did provide him a momentary distraction to roll free of his adversary though.

He looked back over his shoulder, shouting to Julian. "Can't you see that their 'Operation Neptune' is an *insult!?!*" Roach yelled at him. "I'm just saying the shit that YOU should be saying here!"

Julian considered that for a moment. "…Actually, that is a rather impertinent thing to call their attack on my domain."

"*Exactly*." Roach sounded pleased that he was finally catching on. "See? You protect your people by waging war!" He tackled his opponent, trying to beat the person's face in with a discarded army helmet he grabbed from the sand beside him. "…And by helping me take over Norway."

The Lovers of Liberty emerged from the sea, and raced towards Roach, completely ignoring Julian.

"You are all missing the larger issues at play here!" Julian screamed over the turmoil. "*What about my people!?!* What about…" He trailed off as he spotted scores of dead fish scattered on the beach among the corpses of the surface-dwellers. His mouth hung open in horror. "NO!" He fell to his knees gingerly trying to revive the fish and move them out of the way of the terrestrials' machine guns. "NO!" Tears formed in his eyes. "No, please... *please* speak to me, my friends..."

But they were gone.

The explosion of the ships had been too much for them to bear.

He glanced up at the Retiarius as the man stalked forward, obviously expecting Julian to fight.

Julian held one of the corpses up to him, still trying not to cry. "...They're dead, Everett." He said weakly. "I...I *tried* to stop them, but..." He trailed off, practically sobbing, and fell forward onto his hands and knees. "...They killed them, again..."

CHAPTER 11

KING: "IF THEY HAVE NOTHING TO HIDE, WHY DO THEY NEED A SPIN-DOCTOR? ...NO, WAIT. I MEAN ANOTHER SPIN-DOCTOR, BECAUSE THEY ALREADY HAD THAT MURDERER WHO USED TO BE ON THAT STUPID SITCOM IN THE 80S. ...I HATED THAT SHOW, BY THE WAY. IT WAS CORROSIVE TO GOOD FAMILY VALUES AND I BOYCOTTED THE NETWORK FOR YEARS AS A RESULT."

STORMS: "LOTS OF PEOPLE HAVE PRESS AGENTS, PAIGE. POLITICIANS... CELEBRITIES... EVEN THE POLICE, IN SOME CASES."

KING: "YOU KNOW WHO ELSE HAD A PRESS DEPARTMENT SPECIALIZING IN DISINFORMATION CAMPAIGNS DESIGNED TO PERVERT INNOCENT YOUNG PEOPLE AND TWIST THEIR LITTLE MINDS INTO BELIEVING WHATEVER THEIR OPPRESSORS WANTED? EVERY TWO-BIT DICTATOR WHO EVER TOOK CONTROL OF A FREE PEOPLE USING HIS SUPERIOR ACCESS TO THE MEDIA."

STORMS: "SO, IN YOUR WORLD, THE MEDIA IS THE PROBLEM. I GOTTA SAY, THAT'S A BOLD STANDPOINT FOR A MEDIA FIGURE TO TAKE ON HER OWN TELEVISION PROGRAM."

TRANSCRIPT OF "KING OF CAPES AND COWLS," MEDIA: TELEVISION, SHOW: 1407, NEWSCHANNEL 6, FRIDAY 21:00-22:00 EST, NETWORK SEGMENT-ID: 918000606

Present Day

Bridget paced back and forth, trying to head off the looming disaster. "Okay, *one more time*." She leaned forward against the back of the wooden chair which her client was currently occupying.

She could almost *hear* Julian's eye roll. "I will tell them exactly what you have *instructed* me to tell them for the past *hour*."

He sounded tired. "Can we not please just go?"

"No." She shook her head. "I need to hear it again."

Julian made an annoyed sound.

She stalked around the chair to stand in front of him and crossed her arms over her chest. "Listen, I have things that I could be doing today, *too*, bucko."

He frowned. "What is a 'bucko'?"

She ignored him. "I am here out of the goodness of my heart, trying to help you save your little club from falling into ruin, all because I feel like I *owe* you something for what you did for me."

He shook his head. "...But I have not *found* 'Honda' yet. I am sure that I am only a matter of..."

She cut him off. "Forget the fucking car. I'm not talking about that."

"...Then what are we talking about?" He looked confused. "I am afraid I am at a loss here, Lady Haniver."

Her temper snapped. "*Would you just call me fucking 'Bridget,' already!*"

"I am afraid I'm at a loss here, 'fucking Bridget.'"

Her eyes narrowed. "Now you're trying to be *cute*, and it's *not* going to work." She shook her head. "You need to *focus*."

He let out another sigh and rearranged himself in the small wooden chair he was crammed into. He looked uncomfortable, but since that's where she had told him to sit, he had done it without complaint.

"I *am* focused, 'fucking Bridgett,' it is just that..."

"You're being *cute* again." She interrupted warningly. "What did I just *say* about that?"

"That it 'wouldn't work.'" He promptly repeated. "I assure you, if I knew what it was which was 'cute' and annoying you, I would desist in doing it immediately."

"Listen," she put her hands up, "right now, the only words I want to hear coming out of your mouth are: 'Absolutely I'll listen to your advice, Bridge, because you're the only one I know who isn't *insane!*"

"Very well." He nodded with regal dignity. "Absolutely I'll listen to your advice, Bridge, because you're the only one I know who isn't *insane!*"

"Better." She continued circling his chair. "This *isn't* a laughing matter, you know. If you say the wrong thing in there, we will have a *serious* problem. They will *eat you alive*. I mean, you understand that, right?"

"Yes. That fact has been communicated to me several dozen times in the past hour."

She stopped walking and made a sound like an incorrect answer on a game show. "Eeeeennn. *Wrong*." She tapped a finger against his forehead. "*Think*. What are the only words I want to hear coming out of your mouth right now?"

"Absolutely I'll listen to your advice, Bridge, because you're the only one I know who isn't *insane!*"

She nodded. "Correct."

Unfortunately, in order to tap him on the head like that, she had to get close to him, and now that she was this close, she was beginning to notice that the man was very... big. His chest was as broad as a fucking house! He had shaved off his beard, and now his face had a clean and youthful look to it. ...It was surprisingly distracting. And he smelled *really* good. There was something about the man which just exuded stately power and dignity, even if he was currently crammed into a tiny chair and being yelled at by a press agent.

It was like no matter how many fights he lost or how many stupid things he said, none of that could touch him. ...Like he existed above it all somehow. She didn't really believe that royal people were different than anyone else, but there was just something about Julian that made him seem so... *regal*. Like he was some kind of warrior king, out there protecting innocent women from monsters trying to do horrible things to them.

She found it very attractive for some reason.

Bridget had never met anyone like him before. ...And she *certainly* had never met anyone who was that good-looking. The guy looked like he stumbled out of a fucking cologne ad! You could just see him gazing out from a black and white magazine page, only his piercing turquoise gaze left in color, the bottle of whatever it was he was hawking clutched to his beautifully toned chest. The kind of advertisement which seemed to be saying: "Trust me. I'm too gorgeous to be lying. ...And if you smelled as good as me, I might even talk to you."

And Bridget found herself thinking that she would buy whatever it was that man was selling. Because when he looked at her, he was looking at *her*. She wasn't entirely sure how to explain that, just that she felt like the star of the show when he looked into her eyes. Like the skinny blonde fake actress hired to portray her in her silly imaginary "Bridget Haniver" movie had been pushed aside and now she was center stage. And for some reason, she liked seeing

Julian out there in the audience. She felt the desire to put on the best performance of her life, but she wasn't sure why.

In the instant case though, her distraction was very simple to explain. It arose from the fact that there was something about seeing the man's hard muscles crammed into that chair that just made you want to sit on his lap. To *feel* that kind of raw unstoppable power beneath you...

...She completely lost her train of thought.

She swallowed, suddenly feeling very warm again.

Julian frowned. "Are you feeling alright, Lady 'fucking Bridget?'"

"Just 'Bridget' or 'Bridge,' *pleuse*." She took a long breath to calm herself. "Look... Just... just don't talk for a few minutes, okay?" She ran a hand through her hair. "Let me *think*."

She went back to thinking about him naked.

He nodded pleasantly, as though to say "Of course," but kept watching her intently.

It wasn't that she was only focusing on his body though. Sure, his body was a lot of fun to focus on, but the man himself had a kind of oblivious charm which she found appealing. Sure, he threatened to kill people a lot, and he got preachy about how much humans sucked, but he did it in a sweet way. No matter how loud he yelled or how terrible the things he said were, there was still something gentle about him. Something innocent. Like he was from some other era, when men were gentlemen and fought with honor.

Julian was a *man*, in the grandest sense of the word. He was strong and proud and kind. ...Well, kind to *some* people anyway. ...Or at the very least to *her*.

In any event, life had given the man an opportunity to prove what he was really made of, and he had risen to the challenge when it counted. Because of that... Bridget could put up with the little rough patches of his personality.

She wasn't entirely sure why the man seemed to find *her* so fascinating though. ...It probably had something to do with the fact that he had never met anyone who wasn't a total *screw-up* before.

That must be a new thing for him.

"Okay," she walked over to the dry erase board and tapped on it with one fingernail, indicating the words in question, "from the top. What are we going to say to them?"

Julian cleared his throat. "I will say: 'I am...'"

****

"...delighted to be asked to speak to the children, Principle Madison." Julian bobbed his head in what he had been instructed was a friendly manner in surface-dweller culture. "I view helping the community as a Cape's *first* job. His most *important* job. And speaking to your students would be such an honor for me."

Behind him, Montgomery snorted under his breath. "Apparently more important than stopping the riot of super people going on in the financial district right now, anyway."

Julian ignored him, keeping his façade of helpful terrestrial hero firmly in place. Bridget had said that he needed to remain cooperative and pleasant throughout his visit, and he would kill everyone in the building before he allowed himself to fail at that.

The principle either hadn't heard Montgomery or didn't understand. "I'm so glad that you would take time out to come and talk to our children, Mr. Sargassum. With all the turmoil that's going on in the city, they need to know that someone's out there protecting them."

He opened his mouth to correct the idiotic terrestrial on his title, but then remembered that Bridget had told him not to scream at people who were too stupid to remember his rank. "Indeed." He told the woman sweetly. "I cannot wait to give them my *guidance*."

The principle frowned slightly, as though realizing that that sounded rather ominous.

Julian didn't care. ...Unfortunately, Bridget did, so he quickly tried to cover. "...I find that so many people are just on the wrong path in life, and all they need is someone to show them the *right* way."

The principle seemed reasonably happy with that, even though Julian thought it sounded only mildly less threatening. Sadly, after so many years of trying to terrorize the general populous, he was finding it rather difficult to now lull them into a sense of security. Which wasn't surprising when you really thought about it: what feeble surface person *wouldn't* be intimidated by his grandeur? Simply *seeing* him must fill them with fearful awe. He was the living embodiment of their sins against the undersea world, and surely the weight of their crimes was eating away at all of them, no matter how hard they tried to hide it.

Doubtlessly, their consciences kept them up at night, unable to let peaceful slumber interrupt the guilt which wracked them because of their many offenses against the seas.

Bridget cleared her throat. "Um... maybe we should just start now, huh?" She laughed nervously, as if realizing the difficulty that Julian was having. "I mean, *Lord* Sargassum has a lot of important things to do today."

She stressed his title, apparently in an effort to subtly correct the administrator.

Julian smiled to himself. Aw, that was so sweet of her. What a considerate woman. ...True, it probably had more to do with trying to keep him from stabbing the principle in the neck with his trident for offending him, rather than Bridget feeling insulted on his behalf, but it was really the thought that counted.

The principle smiled vapidly and hurried from the room to organize the children.

"Yes, *Mr.* Sargassum has a *lot* of things to do today." Montgomery watched her go. "...But not fight *crime*, apparently." He checked his watch. "So, I predict that this will end in some sort of school wide insurgency within... let's say... fifteen minutes."

Beside him, Mack slapped a twenty dollar bill onto the principle's desk. "*Ten* minutes."

"YOU HAVE SPELLED: FIVE." Ceann tossed his cash onto the desk.

Bridget shook her head. "*No one* is going to revolt against *anything*. Relax. This is what I *do*. This is a carefully choreographed event." She let out a theatrical calming breath, evidently in an attempt to ease everyone's nerves. "Everything will go *fine*. The kids are going to give him a nice welcome."

Monty watched her silently for a moment, as if that were the stupidest thing he had ever heard. "JFK's last words were in agreement with the idea that everyone in *Dallas* would give him a 'nice welcome' too, Miss Haniver." He told her flatly. "As it turned out... the welcome wasn't quite as nice as he might have liked."

Mack snorted. "Not to sound like I agree with Monty on *anything*, but I would also like to go on record as sayin' that this is a *bad* idea." He shook his head. "I know that you're the professional and all, but I'm *tellin'* you, nothin' good's gonna come of this. I mean, if you wanted somebody to come in here and speak to these kids about duty and responsibility, why didn't ya get Oz to do it? He's like the biggest boyscout I've ever seen!"

"Oz refused to come to the school because he said that it was too riddled with germs. Besides, he's not the *leader* of this team, *Julian* is." Bridget rolled her eyes. "He's just talking to some *school kids*, for God's sake. Nothing bad is going to happen, you're just being paranoid."

"You know what *Lee Harvey Oswald's* last words were?"

Montgomery asked no one in particular. "'*Aw, no one's gonna shoot at me.*'"

She pointed at him with an accusing finger. "You will *not* ruin this for him, do you understand me?"

The man gave a disinterested shrug.

Mack frowned over at him in confusion. "...You don't do this kind of thing, Monty. Ever. Field trips aren't your thing." He squinted at the man suspiciously. "What are you up to?"

Montgomery simply smiled his insidious smugly taunting smile, like he found the idea of Mack trying to understand his motivations amusing.

A moment later, the principle returned. "If you would all please follow me, we have the children assembled in the library."

They filed out into the hall, and towards the room in question.

Julian had never been in a school before, but he didn't like it. The place had an institutional and sterile feel. He'd been in more than a few prisons over the years, and this building felt very much like that.

Honestly, he would have preferred to go and speak at a prison somewhere, as at least *then* he'd get to see some familiar faces. Bridget had said that the public wouldn't really be impressed by that for some reason though.

They stopped in front of the library door as the principle went inside to introduce them.

Montgomery looked through the door's small windows at the students and press assembled inside. "Ah, the great lowing herd."

"Listen, I don't know why you're even here, okay?" She pushed Monty away from the door. "*I* sure as hell didn't invite you, but if you do *anything* to ruin this day, I will have Julian kill you, okay?" She pointed at him. "So you be on your *best* fucking behavior."

The principle appeared at the door to usher them inside and Monty watched the woman silently. "*Moo.*" He calmly deadpanned.

The woman frowned at him in confusion. "...I'm sorry?"

Bridget laughed nervously. "Oh, ignore him. He has the power to perfectly mimic farm animals. ...Usually a pig or a *jackass*."

Monty smiled his evil smile. "Now, why would I ever need to...?"

His words were cut off as two men from the school's security force appeared behind him. "Sir? Can you please come with us?"

Montgomery turned around. "*Excuse* me?"

They grabbed him by his arm. "Come with us, sir. There doesn't have to be a scene. We don't allow registered sex offenders on school premises."

Beside Mack, Polly waved one holographic hand. "Goodbye, Mr. Montgomery. I *do* hope you can find the help you need in *prison*. Be sure to write us from time to time and let us know how you're getting on."

His good eye blazed in fury as the men escorted him down the hall. He turned around to yell back at her over his shoulder. "You computerized little *monstrosity.*" He pointed at her with his deformed hand as though vowing revenge. "You really want to play this game with me? *Is that it? ME!?!*" Cold rage filled his hard soulless face. "When I'm done, there won't be enough of you left to run a *pocket calculator.*"

She continued waving pleasantly, fake friendly smile on her face. "*Goodbye*, Mr. Montgomery." She called, then turned to look up at Mack. "I am *really* going to miss him."

The other man chuckled, obviously enjoying his companion's mischief. "Don't we got enough problems without you startin' a pissin' contest with the prince of fuckin' *darkness*, Poll?"

Polly giggled merrily.

The principle watched the goings-on, looking upset. "...Oh dear..."

Bridget waved a hand. "Probably just a computer snafu or something." She told the woman, as if this sort of thing were a common occurrence in the human world. ...Which it very well could have been, for all Julian knew. "So, should we go ahead then?" She smiled up at him. "You ready, Julian?"

He nodded, then opened the door.

Two dozen tiny terrestrial faces turned to look at him as if he were an intruder... and Julian's mind went blank. He had no idea what he was supposed to say. What COULD he say!?!

He didn't like surface people, so why was he now expected to entertain their young!?! What was THAT about!?!

Julian hated children. Horrid little creatures which were *utterly* unproductive and contributed *nothing* to the world except becoming larger and thus eating *more* of his people. Their squeaky voices and grimy little hands contaminated everything around them.

A little girl seated by the door rushed forward and Julian instantly braced himself for her assault. She attached herself to his leg, hugging him in greeting. "I love you, Mr. Poacher! Did you get my letters!?!"

Bridget made a small cooing sound like she found the scene heartwarming for some reason. ...Most likely because she had never *met* Poacher, and had no idea what a tremendous *insult* it was to be mistaken for that repulsive oaf.

"Awww, isn't that adorable?" She pressed a hand to her chest like she was overcome by emotion.

Oh, god they were touching him! *It was horrible! Get it off! GET IT OFF!!!*

"...Yes. They are," he tried to hold back his distasteful face and building panic as he attempted to *pry* the small being free, "simply *charming*."

The kid was clamping on so tightly it was a wonder that he even had circulation left. It was like one of those horrible movies about aliens, where the creature attaches itself to the human astronaut and then they have to cut it off before it kills him.

Thankfully, the child looked up and saw Ceann looming in the shadows of the hall, and instantly let out a small fearful sound and fled the scene in terror. She quickly ran back inside the room, where more of her kind were waiting to attack Julian.

Ceann didn't move.

Bridget turned to look at the other man, obviously thinking she needed to sooth his hurt feelings or something. The woman was so kind to people who simply didn't matter. The man was *fine*. So, he terrified children? *And?* Hell, Julian would *love* to have that problem at this particular juncture, as *then* he wouldn't have blue finger-paint dripping down the back of his calf.

Ceann silently left the scene, slowly retreating back towards the entrance to the building.

Lucky bastard.

Julian reached for the door again, trying to build up his courage...

No.

No, he needed to get the hell out of here.

He backpedaled into the hall. "...Umm... I'm just going to go get some... umm... air."

"Now!?!" Bridget asked. "But the kids are waiting!"

"Yeah, I can see that..." He hurried down the hallway. "I'll... I'll be right back, okay?" He all but ran from the building and back into the sun.

He had never been so happy to see the surface world. It never looked more beautiful. He inhaled their tainted air deeply and leaned forward, his hands on his knees.

He felt sick.

...This was a bad idea.

A *really* bad idea.

What was he doing here!?!

Why was he betraying his most deeply held beliefs!?!

Why wasn't he at *home* right now?

He swallowed, trying to keep from panicking.

...Bridget.

She was why he was here. This was *her* plan to make his team more popular... or something. Honestly, he wasn't quite sure on the 'whys' of this whole thing. But luckily, he didn't particularly care either. If Bridget had showed up wanting to turn the Consortium into circus mimes, he would have forced his entire staff into Clown College.

But that didn't mean that he had to like it.

He *didn't* want to deal with those kids. Julian had a terrible track record with people in general, and he didn't think age was the problem.

He leaned against one of the oak trees in front of the school, and looked up at the sky, wishing that it was raining. ...Or that this school was located on a beach somewhere. ...Or that he was the kind of hero who could go in there and impress some silly little mortal children, so that the woman he was really *trying* to impress wouldn't recognize the fact that he was useless.

Sooner or later everyone did.

...Even Julian himself.

Goddammit.

Why did things need to be so hard?

Why couldn't he ever win at something?

...Just once.

"One would think that you would be at ease in a school, what with being a fish-man and all."

Julian swore under his breath. "I was hoping that you were being abused in some sort of mortal *prison* right now, Welles." He turned to look at the other man as he limped towards him. "But evidently, *nothing* is going to go right for me today."

The other man laughed. "Oh, you really didn't expect me to be sidelined by a couple of *security guards* and an insentient bratty *machine,* did you?" The man sounded entirely dismissive. "I thought you knew me better than *that.*"

"*Unfortunately.*"

Monty laughed good-naturedly in a hollow callous sounding way. If laughter was the music of the soul, then all of Monty's musicians were dead, and their corpses played to an empty theater on instruments which had no strings. "Do you know what I think our problem is, Julian? Why we're not getting along?"

"Because I'm not a power-hungry madman, twisted in both body and mind, and thus we have nothing in common?"

"No." Monty sat down on the bench beside him, favoring his right leg and holding it out in front of him at an odd angle. "I think that we're working at cross-purposes. I try to circumvent your new leadership and you try to stop me. But there's really no need for us to waste our energies doing that, while there are so many more *important* things we could be focusing on."

"Such as?"

"You want the Haniver woman." It wasn't a question.

Julian's eyes narrowed. "If you're intending to *threaten* her, I should remind you that I've killed men for less than that." He leaned closer to the man, his voice dangerously low. "A *lot* less."

Monty rolled his eyes. "And if you're trying to scare me, I should remind *you* that everyone in this organization is more powerful than you. Even *me*, and I don't *have* any super-powers." He checked his watch as if he didn't have a care in the world. "But, no. I mean the woman no harm. Honestly, I don't really understand what you see in her, but if she's the one you want, then I wish you only the best. And as it happens, you have caught me on a *good* day. I am feeling charitable." He nodded. "I will assist you in your little romance."

"Why?" Julian frowned. "I *detest* you."

"Let's just say that you'll owe me a favor." He smiled icily. "Quid pro quo, and all that."

"I don't *want* your help."

"Very well." Monty shrugged. "Suit yourself." He pointed towards the school. "Good luck in there by the way. I've heard that they're putting you in with the children who have *behavioral* difficulties, so I wouldn't expect too smooth a time of it. You're going to be dealing with the troublemakers and the bullies. Luckily, you have just *heaps* of experience with human children, so I'm sure you'll do fine. And besides, it's not like you have anyone you want to *impress...*"

Julian considered that. "What do you *want*, Welles? I tire of your games."

"I propose a simple trade: I will aide you in your coming romantic crisis, and in return, you will help *me*."

"And just how do you think you'll be able to assist me? I haven't noticed you ever being especially *successful* with women. They dislike you even more than the rest of us, probably because you are quite simply a man who has no redeeming qualities or endearing attributes. You cannot love or *be* loved if you have no soul. You have *nothing* to offer anyone but pain and betrayal, and no woman in this *world* is stupid or desperate enough to think differently."

"Possibly." The man looked almost hurt that Julian would ever doubt him. "But my good man, as I'm sure you *have* noticed at some point in our association, despite my lack of 'redeeming' qualities, I do have *one* aspect to my personality which can help you: I *excel* at getting my own way."

Well, Julian had to give him that one. The man did always seem to come out on top of things, no matter what was arrayed against him. He was one of the few people in the entire Consortium who, to the best of Julian's knowledge, had never seen the inside of the SeaCastle Asylum for the Super-Naturally Able Offender at one time or another.

Monty was a hard man to cage.

"...And what's *my* part of this deal?" Julian asked cautiously.

Monty casually looked down at the brim of his hat, which was clutched in his gloved hands. "Oh, nothing much. I know you're expecting me to ask for your kingdom or some such *ridiculous* thing, but in truth, what I want is actually rather mundane. At some point in the not-too-distant future, a matter will come up for vote in our organization. I assure you, it will not be something you have a feeling on one way or the other, and it has *nothing* to do with the seas or your new friend. It is an utterly trivial issue, but one I feel will come down to a very close decision and I am destined to lose simply because of a few... *misunderstandings* I've had with some of the other members. We have a bit of a *troubled* history, I'm afraid." Monty stood up. "When that day comes though, I want your word that you will vote with me."

"And why would I keep my word, if I already have Bridget? What would be in it for me?"

Monty smiled humorlessly. "Julian, let's not kid ourselves: your word is *all* you have. You are not a liar. If you give me your word, I will take your assistance as an utter *certainty*."

Julian paused to consider that. "...All I want is Bridget."

Monty nodded. "Yes, so you've said. And I am offering to help you get her. To be frank, I'm your best option, as I don't see too many *other* people lining up offering you their assistance, and unlike the rest of our coworkers, I *never lose*. To a man such as yourself, who has never won at *anything*, I'm willing to bet that that just might be beneficial."

"...And this vote has *nothing* to do with her or I?"

"*None*." Monty shook his head. "It won't even *interest* you.

184

I have no doubt you will ignore the entire debate on it, and would have most likely voted for it without knowing what the issue was even concerning anyway."

"Then why won't you tell me what it's about?"

"Because it *still* won't interest you." He argued. "You're just trying to catch me in some sort of lie, but I'm telling you the truth here."

Julian paused to consider that.

"I can do it *without* you." He finally decided. "I won't sell my soul to you, no matter *what* you're offering."

Monty shrugged. "Suit yourself, Julian." He got back to his feet. "Can't say I didn't try. I just saw you sitting over here worrying about what a loser you would look like in front of the only woman you've ever wanted, and I thought I could help out." He began to limp away. "Apparently *not* though. Be sure to let me know how she likes *your* 'redeeming qualities' and 'endearing attributes.'"

"...No one is to be hurt." Julian called after him, after a moment.

"I'm sorry?" Monty turned back. "What?"

"Your plan." Julian stood straighter. "*No one* will be hurt in your plan to help me." He shook his head. "She wouldn't like it, and I won't lie to her."

Monty placed his hand over his heart. "I give you my word that I will not harm *anyone* in my endeavors to assist you." He paused, as though needing clarification. "...*Threatening* to harm them is still allowed though, correct?"

"Yes, of course. That will be fine, *as long as it's not Bridget*." Julian silently cursed at himself for being so desperate. "You have a deal, Montgomery. If you assist me in convincing Bridget that I am the hero she is looking for, I will vote with you on your unimportant matter. ...Provided that you aren't *lying* about the subject of the vote, in which case I will vote however *I want*, and then tell you to *go fuck yourself*."

"Such *language*." Monty shook his head. "And you, a role model to the *children*." He put his top hat back on, and nodded his head. "Very well, Julian. I think you and I have come to an understanding at last." He began to limp towards the school. "Your vacillating and my unintended run-in with security have delayed my plans slightly though. As such, I'm afraid you'll be on your own for the first few minutes of the event. But don't worry." He turned back to smile his sinister smile at him. "I *always* deliver on my promises."

Julian felt sick.

...What had he just done?

CHAPTER 12

KING: "I GUESS I'M JUST NOT AS COMFORTABLE AS YOU WITH THE IDEA OF INCREDIBLY DANGEROUS PEOPLE, WHO HAVE COMMITTED ALL MANNER OF TERRIBLE CRIMES, WALTZING AROUND AN ELEMENTARY SCHOOL, COMPLETELY UNSUPERVISED, IN AN EFFORT TO MAKE US FORGET ABOUT AFOREMENTIONED DANGEROUS POWERS AND HISTORY OF CRIMINAL VIOLENCE."

STORMS: "HOW EXACTLY IS THE ABILITY TO BREATHE UNDERWATER A 'DANGEROUS POWER'?"

TRANSCRIPT OF "KING OF CAPES AND COWLS," MEDIA: TELEVISION, SHOW: 1407, NEWSCHANNEL 6, FRIDAY 21:00-22:00 EST, NETWORK SEGMENT-ID: 918000606

Bridget had had a lot of troublesome clients in her life.

She had a rock star who claimed that his girlfriend had stabbed *herself* in the chest and then locked herself in the trunk of his car in an attempt to frame him, and it had been Bridget's job to tell the press that while trying to keep a straight face.

She once represented a company which had put antifreeze into its grape soda, because the owners were under the impression that it would make their drink sweeter and more "full-bodied."

She had once represented a vacation company which sold fabulous cruises to an island which was going through a bloody revolution, and it had fallen to her to make that fact the main selling point.

"*Witness history being made!*"

...What a nightmare.

Still, despite all that, she was finding her current clients to be her most taxing. She had done everything for them on this event but work their little mouths like a puppeteer, and STILL they were screwing it up.

It was a good thing that Julian was so good-looking, because Lord knew that the man had NO career in public speaking. The first rule of making public appearances was that you HAD TO APPEAR! But no. Instead, the man was God knew where, doing God knew what, which Bridget would then no doubt have to explain to God knew who, God knew how.

She pushed open the doors of the school, still searching for her missing client. She had given the man enough time to "get some air." He had had ENOUGH air. Now, it was time to go talk to some kids about following in his footsteps. ...Well, not his *actual* footsteps, because that would mean they would all be criminals. But they could follow in the footsteps he was *currently* making anyway. ...Except for the fact that his footsteps were evidently fleeing the scene.

The point was the same though, they *needed* his guidance. ...Or the public needed to *believe* they did anyway. In actuality, Bridget couldn't imagine anyone being so desperate as to look for him for advice. Julian was a very sweet guy and the best hero she'd ever seen, but his counsel on how to live would no doubt be terrible and filled with angry tirades. She wasn't entirely sure how he had managed to become the hero or man that he had, but however it had come to pass, it certainly didn't have anything to do with his career as an inspirational speaker.

He seemed to be a good person *despite* his opinions about the world, rather than because of them. It was like deep down, he was just the sweetest and most gentle person you'd ever want to meet, but on the surface was a depressed and angry monarch, who hated the world. She wasn't entirely sure just how he had gotten that way, but it made her unhappy to see it.

The man's life was just so sad and empty, but he was so caring under it all!

She spotted the big, dumb lug in question as he was leaning against a tree on the far side of the school yard, looking like he had just been punched in the stomach. Montgomery was strolling away from the scene though, which explained it.

Monty had obviously been up to no good. Bridget was quickly beginning to realize that Monty was the shadowy man on the "Neighborhood Watch" sign; he was mysterious, sinister and seemingly *everywhere*. Always watching from the shadows. You had to remain constantly vigilant in keeping him away from your life, or he'd ruin everything.

She dashed across the lawn, hoping that she'd have time to undue whatever duplicity the other man had just done.

"Whatever he told you was a *lie*." She called to Julian, still running across the lawn. "Don't listen to him."

Julian glanced up at her and his entire demeanor changed. He instantly stood straighter. "I have long experience dealing with Welles, Lady Bridget. I assure you, I am under no delusions about the foul nature of his character. The man is a *reprobate*, but as it happens, he and I have come to an agreement of sorts, and I don't think he will pose us any future problems."

Her mouth hung open in shock and horror. "...Oh, God. You didn't make a deal with him or something, did you? The man's *evil!*"

Julian paused for a moment, then cleared his throat. "...No." He answered, as though he found her accusation insulting. "Of course not." He shifted slightly, his eyes straying. "...I'd... never... do that."

She put her face in her hands. "Oh, God. You did. I can tell." She let out a long sigh. "...Just please tell me that it doesn't involve anything which could ruin this speech."

"It does not involve this visit, no. ...Well, not *my* part of the agreement, anyway."

"Good." She tried to keep the relief from her voice. "Well, whatever it was you got, I hope it was worth signing over your life to *the devil*."

He watched her silently. "I believe it is, yes."

She made a noncommittal sound. "Yeah, I'm sure." She pointed back towards the school. "Can we just go back inside now? The kids are going to get restless."

He looked up at the sky again. "I will be ready momentarily. Honestly, I really don't know why you're taking this so seriously anyway. Wouldn't it be better if we just forgot all about this and went to the beach?"

"No." She shook her head. "I take this seriously because it's my job." She frowned at him disapprovingly. "It's supposed to be *your* job as well, by the way."

He let out a dramatic sigh. "And I think I have performed admirably well up until now. This visit is going *perfectly*."

She rolled her eyes. "Oh, yeah, things are just going *great* today. As a stalling tactic to cover your little disappearance, I had to give the press the information packs that I had you all put together, and as it turns out, Arnold's 'biography' is just the plot of the Cher song '*Gypsies, Tramps and Thieves*,' which could be a problem."

"What did Arnold say about it?"

"That Cher based the song on his life." She let out a weary sigh and sank down onto the park bench beside him. "Sometimes, I really wish he put more thought into some of his lies."

Julian frowned. "How do you know it's a lie?"

"Have you ever heard the song?"

"No."

"Then you don't know what a *stupid* question that is, and I can forgive you." She pointed back towards the school. "Can we just go talk to some kids now, please? If you don't go in there soon, you're going to hurt their feelings."

He nodded, making an effort to look appalled. "Well, we cannot have that. Those poor children need someone to..."

She cut him off. "Cut the bullshit, Julian."

He nodded. "Very well." He looked down at his feet. "I am... *apprehensive* about this event. I fear it will not go as well as you may hope, and you will be disappointed in me."

She restlessly played with her hands for a moment, then glanced up at him again. "Look, the truth of the matter is this: I'm *terrible* at my job."

"Nonsense." He sounded insulted on her behalf. "I have the upmost faith in you. My trepidation about this event has nothing to do with your skills or abilities. All you need is..."

"Aw, that's sweet." She cut him off. "But this isn't an attempt at getting you to compliment me, although it's *super* nice of you and I appreciate it. I'm just saying that I'm usually part of a team of people, who all ignore my opinions. Most of my clients are creepy corporations or scumbag celebrities, and none of them listen to me anyway. And I just want the chance to do something *right* for a change, you know? I think I can help you guys." She pointed at the school. "And I *genuinely* believe that this is the way."

He nodded. "And I trust you." He cleared his throat. "When this event suffers catastrophic failure, the fault will be mine and mine alone."

"How do you know it's going to fail!?!"

"Because everything I am involved with fails."

"Oh, enough of that crap!" She spread her arms wide. "You can *do* this! I know you can! I mean, just look how hot you are!"

He frowned. "I am capable of thoughts and feelings, as well, Lady Bridget."

She stared at him in blank confusion. "You're what? Huh?"

"Every time you mention my attributes, your list begins and ends with my physical appearance. I am merely noting that I am capable of emotions. Dreams. Thoughts of my own."

"...Are you insinuating that I'm... what? *Objectifying* you?"

"...No." He looked suddenly awkward. "I was just..." He shook his head and glanced down at the ground again. "Never mind."

"Fine." She tried to sound supporting. "You're an awesome Cape and a charming man! Hell, you saved *my* life, and I'm sure a lot of other people in the city can say the same."

He looked uncertain. "...I just..."

She met his eyes. "I'm telling you, you can *do* this. If I didn't know that for *certain*, I would *never* ask you to go in there." She gently took his hand reassuringly. "I know you doubt yourself, but *I believe* in you, okay?"

He stared into her eyes for a long moment. "...Okay."

She gestured to the school again. "Besides, they're just a bunch of fucking kids! Hell, the *school bus driver* impresses them!"

He nodded again, as though lost in thought. "Indeed." He shook his head. "But I have long had difficulty convincing surface people of the truth of my words." He paused. "Usually, it ends with explosions."

It seemed to Bridget like Julian's main problem wasn't his unrealized quest for revenge over whatever the humans had done to him in the past. His biggest problem was an identity issue. He needed to discover who he really *was*. Get some self-confidence. Or lose some, depending on the kind of mood he was in. The man had mood swings which made manic depressives look stable.

"That's because all you ever want to talk about with people is how much you hate them and the world, and how much better fish are."

"That's not true. ...Well the *sentiment* of the statement is obviously true, but not the assertion that it's all I talk about."

"Okay, then." She turned around to face him. "Tell me something about yourself that doesn't directly involve the oceans or how much you hate people." She waited. "I'm interested in Julian the *man*, not Lord Sargassum the sea god. What else do you do? What other interests do you have? What else do you like?"

He opened his mouth to reply to that, then stopped.

Silence.

She nodded. "See? *That's* what your problem is. That's what I'm having to fight against here. That's why I can't market your feelings. You have *no idea* who you really are, so how can you possibly go in there and tell those kids?" She shook her head. "You *can't*. You like the oceans and that's it."

"I like *you.*" He finally argued, as if that were some hidden aspect of his personality which made the rest an open book.

She stared at him for a moment in confusion, then laughed at his joke. "Oh yeah, I bet you're totally *smitten* with me." She rolled her eyes. "Come on, *lover boy*. Focus. If you want people to get to know the real you, there needs to be a real you to get to know, you get me?"

"...Get you what?"

"Do you *understand me*?" She clarified.

"I am trying to, yes." He nodded. "If you tell me what it is you wish for me to obtain for you, I give you my word that I will make it so."

"Aw, aren't you sweet." She gestured at him, trying to hustle him towards the door. "Right now, I just need you to be on your best behavior though."

"I am *always* on my best behavior."

"...*There's* a terrifying thought." She blinked rapidly, trying to dispel that idea. "Look, just go in there and talk about yourself."

"Talking about myself would just be pointing out the deficiencies of their species." He shook his head. "It wouldn't be right to gloat in front of the children."

She chuckled, even though he was being utterly serious. "How about this, I'll show you how easy it is to tell people things in an interview and make them think it's something important which they can market. This is how you establish a *brand*." She cleared her throat. "I grew up in Forest Hills, and my dad was a dentist. Every Sunday, we went to the park and played on the swings. Growing up, I wanted to do something great with my life." She nodded. "See how *easy* that is? It took like five seconds! But it tells you several utterly banal but endearing things about me, which the reporter can turn into a magazine blurb about rediscovering my roots or my lifelong respect for nature or other famous people whose parents were dentists. See how that works?" She pointed at him. "Now it's your turn."

"Very well." He cleared his throat. "I grew up alone. I lived alone. Every Sunday, I'd go do nothing, and I did it alone. Growing up, I wanted to be anything but alone." He told her calmly, then shook his head. "Are you sensing the trouble I will be having with this exercise, Lady Bridget?"

She blinked at him in amazement. "...Are you being serious right now?"

"Did it *sound* like a joke? I do not understand surface humor, so if it did, that fact was entirely unintentional, I assure you."

"How could you be alone your *entire* life? What about your parents?"

He shrugged, as though this were all an utterly unimportant matter. "My father was not a warm man. I suppose part of that is my fault, for having the temerity to be born to a mortal surface woman and all." He shrugged again. "Whatever the reason, the man and I didn't always see eye to eye on life and he chose to ignore me most of the time. In retrospect, those were the times I liked him the most." He started staring at the clouds again, as though lost in his own thoughts. "I gave that man everything I had. I tried so *hard* to get him to notice me... if not to call me his son, then to at least acknowledge me in *some* way. ...Some tiny *bit* of attention or respect. ...But he never so much as shook my hand. ...He... he didn't have it in him." He sounded almost bored. "I think the day he died, I was almost relieved. Because I wouldn't have to try anymore. I was so very tired of failing. ...I still am."

She watched the man wordlessly as the sun shone down on his shiny black hair and gorgeous face. She tried to think of something to say which would be supportive or understanding... but came up empty. "...I have no response to that." She finally whispered, trying not to cry. "I'm sorry."

"There is nothing to apologize for." He shook his head. "I really wasn't looking for one. I'm just explaining to you that my life doesn't really fit into your mortal press releases and magazine stories. I cannot go in there and tell those human children any 'banal but interesting' things about my life, because I simply have no such stories to tell. As you have told me repeatedly in the few days of our relationship, all of my stories are 'depressing' and filled with violence." He looked down at her. "If you would like me to have a more heartwarming tale to tell the surface-worlders' cameras, I think you're going to have to write it yourself. I would be glad to recite whatever backstory you think would better appeal to their limited minds."

"...No." She choked out. "No, that's fine. We'll just go with whatever you want." She swallowed the lump in her throat. "...W-what about your mother?"

He was silent for a long time. "She died and I was adopted by a new family."

"...And them?"

"They died."

"...I think I'm sensing a pattern."

He nodded and went back to watching the clouds. "I wish it would rain. I *like* the rain. It's the only thing about your cursed world which doesn't fill me with disgusted rage." He paused. "Well, except for *you*, but other than that, nothing."

Bridget watched him for another long moment. What an incredibly handsome, incredibly *lonely* man. ...That was most unusual. Women should be throwing themselves at him! What the hell was going on!?! Sure, his personality was a problem, but he was so heroic and good-looking, that shouldn't be too big an issue for most women. ...No, something *else* was going on here, and Bridget wasn't sure what. Men like this didn't wander around New York, talking about their own tragic loneliness and inner insecurities.

...No.

He must have *bigger* problems which she didn't know about yet. Problems which the other women had discovered, but which Bridget was still in the dark about. It was the only *possible* explanation for why no other woman had snatched this man up. ...Some dark and terrible secret which kept him on the market.

She just had to figure out *what.*

...And try to ignore how attracted to him she was.

****

Julian squirmed uneasily on the metal stool. "...There were *extenuating* circumstances in that event which mitigate my own culpability." He cleared his throat. "I am blameless."

The human children stared at him in silent confusion. Dozens of small eyes judging him and rendering the verdict of their people.

He shifted again. "...So, I hope you all understand that I didn't *mean* to send those piranhas to attack the president while he was at that water park..." He laughed nervously. "...It was all just a *big* misunderstanding." He flashed what he hoped was a confident smile and pointed at the next child. "Yes, you. The tiny surface-dweller in the back."

The miniature terrestrial stood up. "Are you the here-woe who beat up my daddy?"

"...Possibly." He cleared his throat. "But he *doubtlessly* deserved it." He held up his finger to indicate a learning opportunity for them. "No one is above the law, tiny humans."

"Yeah, but my daddy is a poe-weece man and..."

"Well, I'm sure that he learned his lesson." Julian shifted anxiously again, feeling the strain of the children's constant hammering at him. They were *relentless.* "Next question: you, the small mortal with the ugly hair."

"Can you fly?" The boy asked.

194

"No."

"Super-strength?"

"No."

"Can you use your psychic fish powers on people?"

"No."

"Are you *bullet-proof,* at least?"

His scowl deepened. "...*Next question.*"

"...So all you can do is swim and talk to fish?" The child blinked in disbelief. "That's so *lame.* My swimming coach can swim good too, and I don't think *he's* ever claimed to be a superhero."

"I don't just 'swim good,' I can live under the water *indefinitely.*"

The child didn't look impressed. "So can SpongeBob."

"That may well be, but I'm still the only *Cape* this city has who can make such a claim."

The child shook his head, unwilling to let it drop. "What about Poacher?"

"Huh? Don't be *absurd*, boy."

The child ignored him. "...All he'd have to do is like kill a fish or whatever, and then he'd be able to swim good *too*, right? Probably better than *you,* even."

Julian scowled at him in annoyance. "This questioning is *over.*"

"Yeah, but..."

"*Over.*" He pointed at his next inquisitor. "The female terrestrial with the freckles."

The little girl stood up. "Do you know Ariel?"

Julian let out an annoyed sound and stared at the ceiling, praying for patience. "*The Little Mermaid* is an aquatic version of *Imitation of Life,* children. It is a sobering look at the self-hatred and hopeless alienation which befalls disenfranchised aquatic youth, when the terrestrial media robs them of their identity and brainwashes them into believing that they are inferior." He shook his head. "That poor girl. She should have been happy to be who she was, a beautiful and proud aquatic woman, but instead, she just struggles to 'pass' as a surface-dweller." He pointed a finger at the terrestrial offspring, driving his point home. "Let that be a lesson to all of you: no good comes from dealing with your kind. You're all..." he stopped, glancing over at Bridget as she made frantic slashing motions with her hands, "...too precious for words." He rapidly covered. "You should all be happy with what you are. ...No matter how much better you would be if you lived under the sea. ...But don't try to. Just leave the seas alone."

There.

That sounded seamless.

"Next question." He pointed at a boy in the front of the room. "You."

The youth stared at him with blank mortal eyes. "So, all you can really do is just swim and stuff?"

Julian nodded. "As I have explained."

"You don't have like...," the boy thought about it for a minute, "...laser blasts or x-ray vision or nothin'?"

"No."

"Do you have like a cool car or jet?"

"I cannot drive."

"No big awesome guns like The Poacher's got?"

"They would not fire underwater *anyway*." Julian snapped.

The boy stared at him blankly, still trying to understand the very simple facts which Julian had already patiently laid out. "...I agree with Craig." The boy pointed at the last male child who had spoken. "That's *completely* lame." He glanced over his shoulder. "Miss Walker? Can't we talk to a *real* hero? Like one with superpowers and stuff?"

The elderly terrestrial looked embarrassed for a moment at the boy's rudeness, then lowered her voice to scold him. "Now Chris, you know they're *very* busy. I'm sure they'd be here to talk to us if they could, but they have the whole *world* to protect." She smiled up at Julian. "Mister Sargassum can dedicate his whole day to us though."

Julian watched her expressionlessly.

God, he *hated* the surface people. If it wasn't for the fact that Bridget was currently in the room and silently willing him not to, he'd strangle that woman right now in front of all the cameras.

"*Next question.*" He finally bit out, sounding more irritated than he'd intended. He pointed at a child at random, then paused. ...He didn't remember a child sitting there before. "Yes, *you*."

The boy stood up immediately, straightening his old-style overalls. "I just wanted to thank you again for saving me and my daddy from that giant shark which almost ate us last month." The boy's lower lip quivered in emotion. "I was so *scared*. None of the *other* heroes could swim after it after it grabbed my daddy and pulled him under. He would have died if you weren't out there protecting us all."

...Julian had no recollection of that event.

No.

No, that wasn't true.

He was *positive* such an event had never happened.

He cleared his throat again. "...You... umm..." He ran his hand through his hair. "You are welcome, small mortal."

The little girl sitting next to the boy stood up. "And my mommy just never stops talking about how you saved us from that mean man with the flamethrower who attacked my daddy's office party." She nodded excitedly, then glanced down at her hand as if checking something. "...We was so scared."

...What the *hell?*

The child apparently sensed his confusion. "My daddy said it was most *Irregular* for something like that to happen though, and that I shouldn't worry anymore." She stressed the word. "He just loves his job and his boss, so much. We *all* do."

...Of course. Julian tried to keep from smiling in victory.

Monty had salted the class with the children of his workers, the Irregulars. Oh, that beautiful, beautiful twisted evil man.

Julian nodded, feeling more confident. "You are *most* welcome, little girl." He glanced around for more children dressed strangely. "Yes, you. The boy in the knee socks."

"Yeah, Coach Sargassum," the boy stood up, "I was wondering if we're still gonna have baseball practice on Friday, or is it cancelled 'cause of our amusement park trip."

The reporter behind the boy frowned in confusion. "...Did you say 'Coach'?"

The boy nodded earnestly. "Yeah, Coach, he really holds all us orphans together. He's our only role model." He glanced down at his hand, delivering a not entirely convincing but still entirely welcomed rationale. "...He uhh... he 'gives us a reason to go on and to stay off the streets.'" The boy looked suddenly nervous. "...Or so my mommy says."

Julian frowned, hoping that no one else wondered about how an orphan on the streets could receive guidance from a parent. "*Yes.*" He quickly tried to cover. "Yes, we'll have practice at... umm... the usual spot. Tell your *foster parents...,*" Julian tried to hold back a victorious smirk, "...that I would love for them to visit the amusement park with us. Family is so very important in the life of a child."

The little girl who told the flamethrower story nodded. "Yes, Uncle Julian. I remember when you told us all that in church the other day. Your sermon on responsibility and civic pride really gave us all a *lot* to think about. I've decided to become a *doctor* now, and help the underprivileged just like *you* do."

Another little boy raised his hand. "Yeah, I'm wondering how exactly a Cape who only has powers in the *water* can be of *any* use in a fight against someone on the *land*, and..."

The little girl dressed in the old-style dress leaned over and whispered something into the boy's ear.

The boy stopped speaking and stared at her in fear.

She snapped the crayon in her hand in two, delivering a message.

The boy hurriedly sat down. "...Never mind."

Julian shifted uneasily again, trying to pretend like he hadn't noticed that. "Well, heroism is a complicated and dynamic endeavor, small human child, and I don't feel qualified to second-guess another Cape's decisions in the field. But rest assured, the entire world is important and worthy of protection though, no matter which of its elements the Cape is a master of."

Bridget beamed at him and gave him a thumbs up for a job well done.

And Julian had never been prouder of himself in his *entire* life.

One of the reporters raised his hand. "Mitch Leland, *The Wellesburg Wellspring and Gazette*. I'm just wondering what you say to the rumors that you are *singlehandedly* responsible for not only defeating the Freedom Squad, the Alec the Rooster puppet, and those zombies which attacked downtown recently, but have also spearheaded *all* of the humanitarian programs which the Consortium has been trying to put into motion?"

Julian opened his mouth to tell the man he couldn't *possibly* care less what the Consortium's plans for this city were, because they were gone and HE was in charge now. Hell, he wasn't even a*ware* of any "humanitarian programs." Before he could though he glanced over at Bridget.

"No comment." She mouthed.

"I have no comment on that, Mr. Leland." He obediently repeated. "...Caping is a *team* effort, and I just try to do my part."

The man laughed. "You're *kidding*, right?" He waved a folder in his hand. "I have here sworn statements, obtained by my paper's *esteemed* owner and publisher, from a dozen witnesses who say that *you're* the only reason this city is still here. And here's *another* dozen statements from retired Capes who are willing to swear under oath that you were only *pretending* to be a villain all these years, just so you could get the inside dirt on who the *real* bad guys were!"

The other reporters looked intrigued by that idea, and rapidly began writing it down.

Julian had no idea what was going on now, and had never even heard of a town called 'Wellesburg,' let alone its newspaper, but Bridget looked *overjoyed* by this line of questioning, so it must be good.

He cleared his throat. "Now then, are there any other questions?"

A little boy raised his hand. "Yeah, I wanna know why..."

The Irregular children all turned in their seats in unison to glare at the child threateningly.

The boy shrunk down in his chair and fell into fearful silence.

Bridget hurried to the front of the classroom. "Now then, thank you everyone for coming out today, and I'd like to give a special thanks to all of these wonderful children for playing host to us today and making us feel so *welcome!*"

The children were silent.

The Irregular children turned to glare at them again, and the class erupted in thunderous applause. In the back of the room, Mr. Leland began to confer with the other newsmen and share his purported 'proof' with them. Just why exactly the man was so willing to share his paper's exclusive research and interviews on the matter was anyone's guess. Personally, Julian was beginning to sense the four-fingered hand of Montgomery in it, although he had no idea how the man could have ever possibly come into possession of a newspaper.

Bridget leaned closer to him, whispering into his ear. "See? I told you you'd do *great.*"

Julian's entire body lurched from having the woman so close to him and her breathy voice in his ear. "...Yes. Indeed you did." He turned to look at her, his face mere inches from hers. "I never should have doubted."

He stared into her eyes for a long moment, lost in their depths. He reached his hand out to gently cup her cheek, and moved his head towards hers, intending to kiss her beautiful face.

She opened her mouth as if to say something, then stopped. She blinked rapidly several times. "Yeah, I think we should go."

He reluctantly let her go, his heart sinking in defeat. "Indeed."

Bridget hurried towards the doors of the classroom for some reason, as if Julian had done something wrong. He stood up and began to follow her.

"Uncle Monty said to tell you that he never forgets a debt, mister." The Irregular girl warned him ominously as he strolled past her. "*Ever.*"

Julian wasn't entirely sure if that was referring to Monty's promise of help in the interview, or to *Julian's* promise to vote with him at some point, but either way, it didn't sound good. ...Even Montgomery's workers' *offspring* were scary.

The children in question watched him like birds of prey sighting a wounded rabbit and preparing to strike. They were rather *disturbing*.

Julian hurried through the door to escape them. *All* terrestrial children were frightening, but those *particular* children were among the most alarming he'd yet encountered.

He spotted Bridget practically running down the hallway towards the school yard, and he raced after her to catch up.

"Wait!" He called. "I think our vehicle is parked on..."

She slammed through the door, ignoring him.

"Lady Bridget?" He finally caught up with her near one of the large grassy fields which terrestrial children seemed to gravitate towards. "Is something wrong? Have I offended you in some manner?"

She spun around to face him. "What's your problem?"

He stared at her blankly. "I do not understand the question." He shook his head. "If you are inquiring about what I am asking, I simply want to..."

"No, no." She threw her arms wide. "I mean, what's the hidden, terrible thing about yourself which you're not telling me?"

He blinked in confusion. "...I was unaware that I had one."

"No, no, no." She shook her head again. "Nope. Not buyin' it!" She gestured at him. "I mean, look at you! You're like hot, and charming and heroic and kids love you..."

"To be completely honest with you," he interrupted, "those were Montgomery's..."

"I don't care!" She cut him off. "I want to know why you're still... you know... ALONE!?!"

He looked down at the grass for a long moment, then met her gaze again. "A question I have often asked myself, Lady Bridget."

"You're fucking *PERFECT!*"

"Julian!?!" Mack asked in disbelief, leaning against the school's perimeter fence. "*He's* your idea of 'perfect'?" The man shook his head in stunned amazement and made a low whistling sound. "What kinda home life you *got*, darlin'?"

"Go AWAY!" They both yelled at him in unison.

The man put his hand up in surrender, the other one still in a sling, and backed towards the street again.

Bridget ignored him. "I'm still waiting for my *answer*, Julian." She crossed her arms over her chest. "What's your angle here?"

He frowned. "If you would like me to have an angle, please tell me which angle I should have, and I can assure you that I will..."

"Don't give me that!" Her face darkened, obviously angry over something. "*Don't be cute with me!*"

"I am continuing my efforts not to be, Lady Bridget." He said sincerely. "The practice is new to me however, so I ask only your patience with me as I try to discover which statements of mine bring you such dissatisfaction, and I..."

"What. Do. You. *Want?*" She bit out.

"I want *you*, obviously." He told her simply.

"No, you *don't*." Her eyes narrowed suspiciously. "What's really wrong with you that you can't do better?"

His frown deepened. "I do not claim to know a lot about the psychology of the surface people, but I'm pretty sure that's not a healthy outlook to have." He shook his head. "I think you have a bit of a self-esteem crisis, which is absolutely *absurd.*" He sniffed indignantly. "You are an extraordinary woman in every way. Certainly the finest example of your people which I've ever seen."

"Are you *mocking* me right now?"

"Huh?" He frowned in confusion. "...Is this a surface-dweller thing?" He glanced around the area, hoping to spot someone who could translate for him. "Because I just don't understand the mind games your people play with each other."

"No. I have *plenty* of self-confidence." She shook her head. "Don't try to turn this around and make it seem like this is me; this is all *you*. I *don't* know what your game is, but I'm going to *find out*. You're trying to play me for some reason, and distract me from my job, but it's *not* going to work. I owe you a debt I can *never* repay. If you need my help to do *anything*, I will *absolutely* help you in any way that I can." She swallowed. "But you will *stop* whatever it is you're trying to do *right now*, or I'll just forget all about helping you and get back to my *real* job."

His face fell.

"...Just... Just..." She spun on her heel, looking either hurt or furious, and stalked towards the car. "...Just don't even talk to me." She yanked open the car door and glared at Mack. "Go."

The other man frowned. "Yeah, but shouldn't we wait for..."

"DRIVE." She ordered.

Julian hurried towards the vehicle as Mack stepped on the accelerator. "Wait, can't we just talk about..."

But she was already gone.

"DAMMIT!" Julian's rage boiled over and he kicked the black and white spotted ball the surface children were playing with on their field as hard as he could. The ball soared through the air, flying hundreds of yards before disappearing over the highway.

The small terrestrials watched their ball vanish amid the speeding vehicles in the distance and then began to cry.

Julian let out an aggravated sound and ground his palms into his eye sockets.

Why couldn't people be as easy to deal with as fish were?

CHAPTER 13

KING: "THE TRUTH OF THE MATTER IS THIS: CAPES
THINK OF THEMSELVES AS A RULING CLASS. THEY
GET INTO THE FIELD FOR THE MONEY AND THE FAME,
AND THEN ONCE THEY'VE SQUEEZED EVERYTHING OUT
OF THIS CITY THAT THEY CAN, THEY RETIRE TO SOME
TROPICAL ISLAND AND FORGET ALL ABOUT THE
DAMAGE THEY CAUSED."

STORMS: "I HATE TO BREAK THIS TO YOU, PAIGE, BUT
IF A CAPE ACTUALLY SURVIVES TO OLD AGE-- WHICH
THESE DAYS, THEY RARELY DO-- SHOULDN'T HE OR
SHE GET THE BENEFIT OF A..."

KING (INTERRUPTING): "OF WHAT? OF THE HARD
WORK WHICH OTHERS DID? THEY JUST WANT TO FLY
AROUND IN THEIR LITTLE JET PLANES AND THROW
CARS AT ONE ANOTHER, AND DON'T WANT TO GO OUT
AND GET REAL JOBS, WHICH MIGHT ACTUALLY HELP
SOMEONE. MY FATHER WAS A SUPER-HERO, CONNIE.
I KNOW WHAT I'M TALKING ABOUT HERE. THEY'RE
CAPE WEARING GRASSHOPPERS AND THEY WANT TO
TAKE EVERYTHING FROM THE TAXPAYING ANTS OF
THIS CITY. WELL, YOU KNOW WHAT? I SAY WHEN
THEIR FIDDLING IS DONE AND WINTER IS HERE, THEY
CAN JUST GO AHEAD AND STARVE. BEING A CAPE
THESE DAYS IS ABOUT ONLY THINKING OF YOURSELF,
SO I SEE NO REASON TO THINK ABOUT THEM. THE
CONSORTIUM IS FILLED WITH POSTER-BOYS OF BAD
BEHAVIOR, ILLICIT ACTIVITIES AND DOWNRIGHT EVIL
DEEDS. AND YET, THE CITY IS CERTAIN TO SHOWER
THEM ALL WITH RICHES AND LET THEM RETIRE TO A
LIFESTYLE THAT MOST OF US WOULD KILL FOR. ...OF
COURSE, THESE SO-CALLED 'HEROES' ACTUALLY DID
KILL FOR IT, SO I GUESS I SHOULDN'T BE SURPRISED."

TRANSCRIPT OF "KING OF CAPES AND COWLS," MEDIA:
TELEVISION, SHOW: 1407, NEWSCHANNEL 6, FRIDAY
21:00-22:00 EST, NETWORK SEGMENT-ID:
918000606

15 Years Ago

Julian leaned against the wall, wishing he were somewhere else, with someone else, doing something else.

...*Anything* else, really.

This whole endeavor was *ridiculous*.

They had arrived at the "Mesa Verde Super-Person Retirement Castle" ten minutes before, and so far, Julian was not at *all* impressed.

The facility was like a tomb for people who weren't quite dead. The halls were lined with motivational posters of seemingly random images paired with *obviously* random words. They were hoping to inspire residents through such trite pleasantries as...well, "Inspire," unsurprisingly. Other posters advertised the merits of "Freedom" and "Responsibility." The signs were all displayed in cheap frames which could be purchased at any surface world Mega-Mart for $9.99.

Julian found no "inspiration" in cheap frames and stale proverbs. He could think of nothing more ironic than putting an image of an obviously restrained animal on a poster proclaiming "Freedom" and then imprisoning the print forever behind a sheet of glass.

But, the terrestrials who ran this establishment had not asked him for his opinion. If they *had,* he would have told them to kill themselves, because they were obviously morons.

The goal of this particular trip was to finally rid themselves of Roach's presence though, so at least it promised to be a *rewarding* day. Julian would *like* to have said that the years had just not been kind to the old man and that was the reason why he was so disagreeable, but the truth was that Roach had *always* been like that. The man had never been what someone might call..."civil."

"No prison can keep me for long. When I get out of this, I'm coming for *you,* girl." Roach's gaze narrowed in rage. "Your father won't be able to protect you."

Harlot Ceigh rolled her eyes and patted him on his shoulder affectionately. "Oh, nonsense. You'll have *fun*, Uncle Hector." She pointed to the common room area. "See? Look at all your old friends who are here!"

Roach's eyes scanned the room, then returned to Harlot. "I hated those fuckers when they *weren't* old and incontinent. You think I like them any more *now?*"

A mustachioed elderly man with grey hair looked up from his puzzle featuring ducklings frolicking in a reed basket, and smiled pleasantly. "Well, if it isn't my old enemy, The Roach!" He clapped his arthritic hands together in delight. "How the heck have *you* been, Hector!?! I haven't seen you since that time you tried to detonate an A-bomb at the bi-centennial."

"Fuck you, *Gary*." Roach crossed his arms over his chest. "Just do your goddamn duck puzzle and don't even talk to me." He glowered at the man. "Fucking *Cape*."

Harlot beamed. "Look, one of your old crowd is here and everything. I think you two have a lot of catching up to do, don't you?"

Roach glanced up at her. "I fucked his wife. 'Caught up' with *her* every Thursday for four months." He informed her nonchalantly. "Once, his *daughter* joined us." He continued pouting. "*That's* what I know."

Harlot pretended that she didn't even hear his vileness. "*Super.*"

Julian rolled his eyes and proceeded further down the hallway, sick of dealing with them. Why was everyone he knew so annoying? Why couldn't he ever spend time with someone who was *worthy* of spending time with? Why did he constantly have to deal with the bottom of the barrel?

...Because terrible people were better than none.

"Hey, Jules."

Julian spun around to find Peter Ferral, AKA "Continuum," standing behind him. The boy was out of costume, and appeared utterly unafraid of him.

A TRAP!

Julian held his trident out, preparing for an attack. "If you wish to fight me here, I will make this place your *grave!*"

The boy's eyebrows soared and he began to laugh. "Wow. Going old school with the threats. I like it. Don't get to hear most of the classics anymore. If your sentence doesn't end in an exclamation point, then you're doing villainy *wrong*, that's what I say." He gave him a thumbs up sign. "Way to keep it alive, man." The boy shook his head. "Nah, I'm just here to watch the show." He pointed at Harlot and Roach. "It's kinda a family thing." He nodded, like that made sense somehow. "Forgot that you were here too though." He reached out to give him a friendly punch to the shoulder. "How they hanging, man?"

Julian cringed away, disliking being this close to a terrestrial. "Do not touch your *betters*, surface man."

The boy laughed again. "Whadda ya doing here?" He pointed at Harlot. "You aren't getting sweet on her or anything, are you?" His eyes narrowed. "Because she's *spoken for.*"

Julian rolled his eyes. "I have no interest in *any* terrestrial, least of all *her,* even if she *weren't* twelve.*"*

The boy shrugged. "Just checking. In about ten years, that girl's going to get a whole lot more interesting to a whole lot more people, and I gotta watch my boy's back, you know? Kinda my job to stake his claim before he even knows he wants to make one. Some real estate is valuable, man. Everyone would want to call certain places 'home,' not just because of the obvious, but because of what realtors might call 'intangibles.' Some places can make you feel something you never felt before, just because of who they are, and if you want to make certain that someone you love gets to experience that, you need to make sure that no one else moves in first."

"I am fine with you moving anywhere, just so long as it's right now and you shut up about it."

The boy calmly glanced at one of the former Capes getting wheeled by on a gurney, and he casually took a sip from the coffee cup in his hand. "Life's a funny thing, isn't it?" He asked conversationally. "It's sorta like the sea, I guess. It seems so endless, until you run aground on the shore." He nodded at his own words. "Take me for instance: I was born knowing the exact time and place of my death. I've felt that final blow my entire life... I already remember every *second* of it..." He looked haunted for a moment. "...The feeling of my ribs bending and cracking... Drowning in my own blood..." He blinked rapidly, and his smile returned. "But as a consequence, I don't need to worry about a damn thing until that day." He nodded to himself, looking pleased. "There's a certain comfort in that. I'm immortal because I'm already dead."

"If you are already dead, then stop talking and leave me *alone.* If you continue bothering me like this, I'll..."

"Oh, you're not going to do anything to me and we both know it, Julian." The man cut him off and took a sip from his Styrofoam coffee cup. "If it makes you feel any better though, I also know for a fact that one day, you're going to rip the heart out of this city. You'll hurt them in a way that no one ever has before. You make this city *weep.*" He nodded. "You're going to kill a *lot* of people, my man." He made a jaunty gun-firing gesture with his hand. "Best make sure they're the *right* ones."

"Are they terrestrials?"

"Some of them."

"Then they're the right people."

The boy blinked at him for a moment. "I just warned you

that you're going to be responsible for something which will devastate everyone in this city, and that's the best you can come up with? You're not even going to ask why you do it?"

"I already *know* why I do it. Like you, I've spent my *entire life* knowing what I will one day do. I've been on a mission to destroy the world above for *decades* now, and I don't need *you* to tell me that I will be successful in that goal."

"So, you don't feel guilty at *all* about this?"

"About *what?*" He snapped. "Achieving my goals? No. I do not feel guilty about doing what's *right.*"

"Wow." The man crumpled up his cup and tossed it into the trash. "Gotta be honest here: I was expecting you to be a little more... umm... *open* to the idea of change." He shrugged. "No offense, but I don't remember you being this big a *dick.*"

"My only concern is that you will die before having a chance to see my final victory *firsthand.* To be there with the teeming masses of terrestrials as you all desperately try to make that final struggle to stay above the water... and *fail.*"

The boy watched him for a moment longer, then chuckled like that was amusing. "...Oh, *sure!* I remember this now!" He snapped his fingers. "Okay. Ya got me." He laughed again. "Yep. Sorry, man. Completely blanked on this conversation for a minute." He shook his head. "Nah, you go right ahead and feel however you want about killing people. My bad."

"Indeed."

The boy cleared his throat. "Any-hoo, just dropped by to check on Harlot and Roach real quick, and..."

"I don't care why you're here." He told him honestly. "I only care why you're not *leaving.*"

The boy held up his hands. "...Aaaaand that's my cue." He started walking down the hallway backwards. "Stay cool, my aquatic compadre. Hold down the fort while my bro's on his vay-cay, 'kay? Don't let Monty push you 'round."

Julian rolled his eyes and went back to ignoring the boy. Why was it that terrestrials *insisted* on creating their own silly words for things? Every year which passed, their languages were becoming more and more unrecognizable. Soon, it would devolve into incoherent hoots and grunting.

Fish were so much easier to understand.

So much more *civilized.*

Julian understood fish. Humanity was a mystery.

He continued down the hallway, with no real goal in mind

other than escaping this place and these people. Outside, a storm was raging and the sound of rain hitting the roof of the facility was calling to Julian. Every now and then Julian was overcome with a claustrophobic feeling of being trapped. Of being caught in a place or a situation which he couldn't escape. A dread of looming failure, and the overwhelming urge to run. Like events were stacked against him, and no matter how hard he tried, he would be unable to extricate himself from them. Like he was a fish trapped in a net.

This was one of those times.

He hated being indoors. He hated the terrestrials, and they obviously hated him. All of this was a reminder that he wasn't home.

But the rain provided him a...

"The chief disdained
the sailor's offers:
Away you rolling river.
'My daughter never you shall follow.'
Hi-Ho, I'm bound away,
'Cross the wide, Missouri."

Julian stopped in his tracks, hearing a familiar song being sung in a familiar voice from one of the rooms he passed. He edged towards the doorway, still wary of a trap.

Sure enough, sitting in a chair by the room's only window, sat The Retiarius. The man stared out at the clouds, relieving the old days when he was still a Cape in the field. When life in this world depended on how fast he could react to the coming disaster.

....But he hadn't been in the field for years now. He'd gotten old.

"Farewell my Dearest, I'm bound to leave you,
My girl, I've gone far from the river,
Oh Shenandoah, I'll not deceive you
Hi-Ho, I'm bound away
And I shall not see you again ever..."

And then Julian remembered his anger with the man. He cleared his throat.

The Retiarius turned in his chair, and looked almost happy to see him. "Well, there's an old face." He paused. "...Well, not really. You look the same as *ever,* kid." He ran his hand down his own wrinkled cheek. "Sadly, the years have finally caught up with me, I'm afraid. Even Atlantian magic runs out eventually."

"I am the ghost of your sins past, fisherman." He told him warningly. "And I've come for what's mine."

The old man rolled his eyes. "When you get to be my age, kid, ghosts are all the friends you have." He pointed to the chair next to him. "Have a seat."

Julian hadn't been expecting that, and didn't know how to respond other than to do as the man asked. He cautiously sank into the room's other brown plastic chair and watched the man warily.

"They say the sea air is good for the health." The Retiarius told him. "...Which is probably why this place is named after a desert site."

"I've come for your mermaid, surface man." Julian blurted out. "I want her."

The old man frowned in confusion. "My *what?*"

"*Don't play that game with me.*" Julian's grip on his trident tightened. "Don't you *dare*. Your mermaid is a child of the sea, and she is thus *mine*. The longer you try to keep her from me, the more of your people I will make *suffer* until she is *delivered to me*."

The Retiarius turned to look at him for a moment, then chuckled in apparent amusement. "Kid, if I had a mermaid, you think I'd be here? You think I'd *ever* want to live in a place where the bedpans are the same color as the soup bowls, and they lock you in at night?" He shook his head. "I'd be at home with *her* right now." His eyes stared sightlessly out the window. "...*Loved*."

Julian frowned. "Then who was she?"

The man shrugged. "...Probably just a dream." He all but whispered. "...Just a beautiful dream..." He began to softly hum his damned *Shenandoah* song again, seemingly oblivious to the entire world except for that tune.

The man *really* needed to learn a better sea shanty. Something not so maudlin and sad. ...And preferably something which was actually *about* the sea.

"I'm *serious*, Everett." Julian snapped his fingers to get the man's attention. "I want to find that woman. I assure you, I mean her no harm. I just need...," he paused, trying to think of a way to end that thought, "...*her*."

The other man paid him little attention. "I've been looking for her my entire life..." He cleared his throat. "Not your mermaid *specifically*, mind you. Just someone who... Someone who..."

"Someone who understands." Julian volunteered.

"Indeed." The older man's voice cracked, and he took a sip

of water from a pink plastic cup sitting next to him on a table, which was indeed the same color as the bedpan in the corner. "Someone who will love me despite the battles I've lost and the mistakes I've made. Someone who knows that sometimes it's the scars that *don't* show which hurt the most. Someone... Someone..."

"...Someone who takes away the isolation of this world and makes you feel part of hers."

"...Yeah." The old man nodded. "I loved a woman once, did I ever tell you that?"

Julian shook his head. "It didn't come up during the hundreds of times you were trying to kill me, no."

"Oh, I think you have our parts reversed in your head, kid. I was always trying to *stop you* from doing hundreds of terrible things. ...God, those were fun times, weren't they? There was always something to *do*." The old man smiled, as if the memories were amusing. "You were the only fish I could never catch. Try as I might, you always escaped the net and slipped the hook. And now I'm *glad*." He turned to face him. "You're the *best* parts of your mother. The parts that no one could tame."

That got Julian's attention. "You knew my mother? My birth mother?"

The old man nodded. "Yeah. Yeah, I sure did." He fell silent again, lost in thought.

Julian stared at him for a long moment. "What? Are you going to tell me that you're my father or something?"

The older man laughed humorlessly. "'Nah. 'Fraid not." He looked down at his hands. "I wish I was though. Shannon... your mama, she... she didn't deserve what happened. I worked with her for years, and she was the finest woman and the finest Cape I ever met. She was *so beautiful*... Like a sunrise over the calm sea on a clear morning. The kind of woman who made you want to stand taller, just being near her, you know? Made you feel... smarter. Tougher. Feel better about yourself and the world than you ever thought possible. Made you feel *lost* without her by your side. She deserved only the *finest* things this world had to offer. ...And... and none of those were me." He shook his head. "Sometimes I wish that I had told her, though. I thought about it... Even *tried* once, but I could never work up the nerve. ...And then it was too *late* to tell her that I... Tell her..." He paused. "Well, *you know*." He smiled with no real emotion behind it, then sighed wearily. "At least then I'd have something good to *show* for my life. I'd be able to stand next to you and say, 'This is my *son*. He's *King of the Ocean*. And I'm *proud* to be his father.'"

"...You would have been the only one who ever wanted to say that, Everett." He told the man seriously. "No one else ever did."

"Yeah." The older man nodded sadly. "I reckon not." He stared out the window for a long moment. "How did the world become so blasted screwed up, kid?"

"Surface dwellers." He answered immediately, staring out the window as well. "Everything they touch, they destroy."

The older man smiled humorlessly. "That they do, that they do." He leaned back in his chair, his vision still locked on the window, the venetian blinds casting shadows on his pale wrinkled skin. "But you and I have lived our whole lives close to the sea, and we haven't done much better, have we? I'm a broken old man, and you're..." He trailed off.

Julian nodded, swallowing a lump in his throat. "...Indeed."

"Sometimes I think we're so focused on our duty, we forget about everything else. I've spent my whole life trying to live up to the world's expectations. I gave them everything I had. Served the people to the best of my abilities. Tried to be the man they *needed* me to be." He looked down at his arthritic hands. "Sometimes I think being a Cape means more than being willing to sacrifice your life for others, I think it means sacrificing all chances for personal happiness." He held out a hand as if grabbing for something. "You just get so fixated on that brass ring, you forget all about anything else. All you can see are the smiles on the faces of the kids, and the thunderous applause as you defeat some villain and save the day." He looked around the room as if he could hear the roar of the thankful populous, then hung his head as he took in his Spartan and clinical surroundings. "...You never stop to think about what you come *home to* after the day is won."

"If you are waiting for me to disagree with you that being a Cape is a waste of time, you shall wait a *long* time, Everett."

The other man laughed humorlessly. "I imagine that I will, yeah." He absently picked at a tear in the covering of his plastic chair. "...It's probably not that different than being king of the seas though, when you come right down to it. ...You just get so caught up in the job that you don't have time for anything else. That isn't part of the life. And now I'm starting to realize everything I missed out on. I always said I'd be willing to sacrifice my life for the innocent, and that's just what I did. ...Only not in the way I expected." He glanced over at him. "I'm not going to make it long in here, you know." He said conversationally. "I won't even last out the year."

"Then why don't you leave? You certainly have more than a few good years left in you. Why cage yourself like this?"

The older man was silent for a moment, then went back to staring. "I'm one of those lobsters in a tank at a fish restaurant now, chum." He nodded. "I think about them sometimes... I never *used* to, back when I was fishing, but now I think about them all the time. I suppose it's like that for everyone at the end. Haunted by their deeds and their choices... I bet that the thing those lobsters fear the *most*, is another day in that tank. Trapped. Alone. Nothing to do but think back on the mistake which put them there. ...And when the day comes that they're finally chosen as someone's dinner, I'd bet it's such a *relief*. Because some things just aren't meant for tanks and cages. Some things should be wild and uncaught. They aren't meant to have masters or to follow rules. You try to cage them, and their soul dies. And once that happens, they're dead anyway, so it might as well come as soon as possible."

"I don't think *anything* would choose a death of being boiled alive."

The old man shrugged. "What does it matter, as long as the job gets done?"

Julian squinted, trying to follow where the old man was going with this. "So, you're saying... what exactly?"

"I'm saying that I'm finished with life."

"What about your work?"

"Ocean travel is dead, son. It's not like the old days. No one goes by boat anymore. Everything important or expensive is flown nowadays. What do I have to look forward to? Protecting a few cruise ships from drunken captains? Rescuing the crews of one or two banana boats that run out of fuel every couple years? No, thank you."

"What are you going to do?" Julian asked in confusion. "What about all of the other surface world Capes who depend on you?"

"And who exactly would *that* be? Even back in the old days, it was *always* just you and me. No one else gave a crap about what we were doing. Everyone had their own thing to focus on, and barely noticed us at all. You gave me a reason to get up each day, and made me feel like I was actually accomplishing something." He looked over at him. "I want to thank you for that, kid. Thanks for giving me someone to fight."

"...You're welcome?" Julian tried, unsure if that was the correct answer or if he was supposed to say something else.

"...When we started out, there were so *many of us*." He turned to look at the framed black and white photo on the wall showing his smiling image standing next to a group of heroes in the

212

'Lovers of Liberty.' Their happy faces stood in sharp contrast to the fact that they were now all dead, long since killed in the field. All except for Retiarius. "So many people in the trade who remembered what it was all about. ...The glory and honor. ...The untamed *majesty* of the calling. A time of *kings*..." His voice took on a faraway quality. "...But now... all I have is you." He looked back to him with sad eyes. "You're the only one of our fish left in the sea now, Sargassum. All the others have been caught, Capes and villains alike."

"Nonsense. *You're* still here." Julian gestured at him with his palm. "Our battle for mastery of the waves is not yet decided. The fate of this world is at stake and you'd just abandon it to its fate?"

"I'm too old, son. Tired. Tired of fighting. ...Tired of *everything*." He laughed humorlessly. "You and me, we've fought for so long, over so much. But I've always respected you as an adversary, and I always trusted that you and I had an understanding. We played the game by the same rules. You're a noble man, even in your soulless aquatic duplicity."

"Thank you." Julian was genuinely touched. "That's very kind."

"We each fought for our own vision of what the future should look like. You for your vision of ocean supremacy and me for my dream of a peace between land and sea." He shook his head. "But we were *both* wrong. The future is here already, and it's not ours. It will *never* be ours. It belongs to people like *them* now." He gestured to the newspaper and its headline proclaiming another victory for the Freedom Squad. "Back in the day, we fought with honor. We had civility and integrity. We were *gentlemen*. But these kids today, Sargassum?" He looked down at the floor. "They don't believe in that. I saw someone the other day run over a kid during a *car chase*. I mean, what on earth is *wrong* with Capes and villains? Why have they abandoned everything they used to stand for?"

"Because they are surface-dwellers and surface-dwellers cannot be trusted?" Julian guessed.

"Oh, that's your answer to everything." The man paused to consider that for a moment. "...Still, there's some truth to it, I suppose." He stared out the small dirty window, his eyes unfocused. "It used to be about the people, didn't it? I mean, have I just been deceived all these years? You try to rule the people, and I try to save them. That's what *I* always *thought* it was about."

"It was about the people." Julian agreed. "Ruling the people like a sea god of old, and teaching them the meaning of *true* fear."

"...But these new fellas," Retiarius continued as though Julian had never spoken, "all they want to do is curse and fight and kill things. And… and I just don't understand that. I tried. I really did. …Tried so *hard*." He looked down at his hands, then back up at Julian. "The Capes and the villains are starting to look alike, and I'm finding it harder and harder to tell the difference between us now. Sometimes… sometimes I think that we've been around each other so much, we're actually the same. Like two different loads of laundry which have been washed together too many times. We aren't black socks and white socks anymore; we're *grey*. A single load of horrifyingly grey socks, with no rules or morals anymore. *That's* the future of being a Cape in this city. *That's* what we'll all become. No right and wrong, just… the powerful and the powerless. The takers and those that get *took*." He leaned back in his padded chair. "So, I refuse to be part of that game anymore."

"Without you to stop me, you *know* I'll just destroy the surface world, Everett. Do you want that on your conscience?"

"Maybe." The old man shrugged. "How could things get any worse? Once upon a time, God looked down on his creation and thought that it was beyond saving, and so he drowned it in a flood. Maybe it's time for you to do the same. I mean, I look around, and what did all that fighting get us? Nothing. Not a goddamn thing. None of the things we dreamed of came to be. The world is *still* a mess. *Your* people are still dying. *My* people are still dying. Things keep getting worse." He started staring out the window again. "In the end, none of us get what we want. The world goes on, and leaves us behind in the wreckage of all the good things we used to have that are now gone forever. The memories of the miracles which were once in our lives before they were taken from us all too soon. …We dwell in the decaying bones of paradise. We can try to hold onto them, but in the end, it's like holding your breath underwater. …Sooner or later, you have to give in."

"I don't." Julian reminded him seriously. "I have no difficulty breathing underwater. In fact, it's actually much easier for me than breathing air."

"You're missing the point." He stared down at the floor. "We fought with principle in sunlight, but we were *deceived*. The kids today… they just don't understand that. And they never will. They're going to build their twisted version of the future on the graves of everything you and I believed in. They'll make a *desert* out of your ocean. A *Hell* out of my surface world. And there's no one left to stop them. No one else who remembers how things *should be*. …Nothing matters now. Not the city, or the money or the people." He looked up at him with tired eyes. "I'm warning you, son. Get out while you can. Just quit and go find something that makes you happy. There's still time to find what you really want out of life. Don't make my mistake." He urged. "You don't belong in the game any longer. Neither one of us do. We're dinosaurs and the age of *rats* has begun."

"I'm... I'm afraid I can't do that. My vengeance is not yet complete." He cleared his throat. "I will not rest until I have brought the surface world to its knees for what it did to me."

"If you don't stop, things will only get worse for you." Everett shook his head. "You're going to end up just like your mama and your adopted parents did. I couldn't protect her, but I can try to warn *you*." He shook his head again. "*Please* stop before they take you too."

He looked down at his hands. "..I...I *can't* stop, Everett. I couldn't even if I wanted to. ...Don't... Don't you understand?" He looked up at the old man again, his eyes welling up, feeling ashamed and alone. "...It's all I have *left*." He bit his lower lip to keep it from quivering. "...All I've *ever* had."

"Aw, kid...." The old man reached his hand out, intending to touch Julian's shoulder in comfort, then stopped halfway, returning his hand to the armrest. "...Well, I wish you luck then." Retiarius let out a long breath, like he'd been holding it for a while. "We've never agreed on anything, but you're still a good man and I was *honored* to have you as my evil nemesis." He stood up, extending his hand. "There isn't a Cape alive or dead who could say he had a better one."

Julian stared at it for a moment, expecting an attack, then shook it.

"I have nothing to give you, kid. Nothing to help you more than I could help your mother. Nothing but this...," Retiarius stopped shaking his hand and gripped it tighter, "they won't play by our rules anymore. They don't understand us; they think we're *weak*. Useless. Outdated relics of a forgotten age." He met his gaze with intense eyes. "Don't be afraid of them, Sargassum. You stand tall and be the man I always *knew* you could become. Don't let them turn you into something you're not. You're *better* than that. Better than *them*. Better than the *mockery* they've made of our calling. They won't see your like again; you're part of the *old way*." His voice became serious. "You're now the only fish left from the golden age of our proverbial sea." He pulled him closer, his voice a whisper. "Show them *why*."

Julian had no response to that, and Retiarius apparently didn't expect one. He opened the door to his small room and held it for Julian. "You're a king without a country, my friend. And one day, I truly hope you find what it is you've been searching for all these years."

"I can't imagine that you do, no." Julian walked into the hall, struggling to maintain his regal composure. "I've been searching for decades for a way to destroy your people, Everett."

"And what about your mermaid?"

Julian paused. "...I want *both*, obviously."

"Life isn't like that, son. I wish it were, I truly do." The old man smiled humorlessly. "You need to decide what you want *most*, and if that's what you need to make yourself happy, then you go after it and you hold onto it. You hold onto it for as long as you can, no matter who tries to take it away from you. Because there's nothing worse than arriving at the end of your life and realizing that you have nothing to show for it but scars that never healed, and the graves of dead friends. You get to thinkin' of the things you were too proud to say, and the things you were too scared to do, and..." He cleared his throat, eyes glistening. "...Well, *you know*." He cleared his throat again. "You take care of yourself, chum. Thanks for always being there." He closed the door.

And Julian was alone.

CHAPTER 14

KING: "LISTEN, I'M NOT ACCUSING PEOPLE WHO
SUPPORT THE CAPE PHENOMENA OF BEING INVOLVED
IN THIS CONSPIRACY OF EVIL. ...OTHERS CERTAINLY
BLAME THEM AND HAVE OVERWHELMING EVIDENCE TO
BACK IT UP, BUT I'LL LEAVE IT TO SCIENCE TO
DEBATE THE TWISTED MORALITY OF CAPE
APOLOGISTS. ALL I'M SAYING IS THAT EVERYONE IN
THIS CITY NEEDS TO SIT DOWN AND REALLY THINK
ABOUT WHAT IT IS THAT THEY WANT FROM CAPES, AND
JUST WHY THEY'RE UNDER THE DELUSION THAT WE
NEED THEM. WHEN THEY REALLY THINK OVER THE
SITUATION AND UNDERSTAND THE KIND OF WORLD
WHICH CAPES REPRESENT, I THINK THE ANSWER WILL
BE CLEAR."

TRANSCRIPT OF "KING OF CAPES AND COWLS," MEDIA:
TELEVISION, SHOW: 1407, NEWSCHANNEL 6, FRIDAY
21:00-22:00 EST, NETWORK SEGMENT-ID:
918000606

Present Day

Bridget absently tapped her fingernails on her desk, trying to concentrate.

She had just misspelled her own name.

That was probably a sign that she wasn't paying enough attention to her work. She couldn't help it though; she had *other things* on her mind.

Namely, she was dwelling on Julian and his odd behavior. The man was obviously hiding some kind of defect which had kept him from being claimed by some woman long ago. The other women must know something about him which she herself did not. Either that or he was playing some kind of game with her, and was just enjoying watching her squirm. Like those stupid movies where the high school jock makes a bet that he can turn the unattractive artist girl into the prom queen, and then spends most of the film secretly laughing at her.

...Of course, it was actually rather hard for her to even imagine Julian being popular enough to make someone he hung out with popular too, just by nature of their association. ...And he *certainly* didn't have enough friends to make bets with them. ...And she doubted he would even *understand* what a 'prom queen' was. ...And if you wanted to get really particular, the jock in those movies usually ended up *falling* for the artist girl.

But the point remained the same.

There was more going on here than she knew at the moment, and Bridget was not one to rush headlong into anything. Being an observer by nature had its advantages, and one of them was the ability to remain outside of an issue. She could sit back and calmly analyze what she wanted to do, without letting her mind get clouded.

She absently signed her email "Julian" and hit send before she could stop herself.

Damn. *That* was going to be a hard one to explain to her mother.

She let out a long breath.

Her relationship with the Consortium was so simple: she helps them, and they help her. Julian seemed intent on changing things though.

Historically, Bridget had *bad* experiences when Capes decided they wanted to take things to a "romantic" level.

...The thought brought up a whole heap of memories which Bridget didn't really enjoy dwelling on, and she immediately tried to push them from her mind.

In any case, she was currently taking a break from her work with the Consortium, and was trying to get some work done for her other clients. She was finding her respite from their drama to be very peaceful. True, she was spending a lot of her time *thinking* about them... well, mostly Julian... but that was only because they had sooooooo many problems.

She was *glad* to be free of them for an afternoon.

She didn't miss their insanity at all.

...Well, maybe a little. They were kinda entertaining sometimes, just from the sheer *craziness*. It was like watching puppies run around: sure they were loud and annoying at times, and sure some things got destroyed while they played, but they were just so *cute* and helpless that you felt compelled to watch them.

But that didn't *mean* anything. It certainly didn't mean that Julian was right, and they should take their relationship to some new level. Bridget didn't even think they *had* a relationship. He was simply a client. ...Just a perfectly average, incredibly handsome client, who wanted to date her and who lit up Bridget's world every time she saw him. Nothing unusual about that. Happened all the time.

Yep.

She let out another long sigh, realizing that concentrating on her work was harder than she thought. None of this stuff was interesting. No one was threatening anyone, or blowing something up. None of her press releases were designed to explain away the release of deadly pathogens or attacks by sea monsters. The pictures she was reviewing for release to the press were of *mayonnaise*, rather than tall gods of the sea, who had piercing eyes which made you feel like your insides were made of Jell-O...

Everything was so... ordinary.

Once again, Bridget was bored with the world around her. And it couldn't have *possibly* happened at a worse time, since she had a stack of paperwork she needed to get through thanks to ignoring it for a few days while trying to help the Consortium. If she worked the rest of the day on it though, and skipped dinner, she *might* be able to finish it by the weekend.

She glanced at the phone, debating with herself whether she should call them up or not. She hadn't left things with Julian very well. She probably could have been more tactful and explained her feelings better.

She could just call him real quick to apologize...

Plus, she had some preliminary thoughts on *Robinson Crusoe* which she wanted to run by him for the next book club meeting. ...Not notes from the *book*, of course, because she still had no intention of reading it. She was pretty sure there was some sort of movie about it starring the Remington Steele guy though, and she was going to be aaaaaall over that.

For some reason, she really wanted to watch it with Julian. The man was quickly becoming her sounding board for any random thought which came into her head, and she had a feeling he would get a kick out of watching the seas hold some guy captive for years. He had trespassed upon the waves and was sentenced to thirty years of solitary confinement for his crime.

Bridget chuckled to herself, imagining how Julian's expression would light up when he witnessed the man's isolation and misery.

Julian had a strange sense of humor, and it never ceased to entertain Bridget.

His eyes would twinkle with evil glee at some strange ocean

related tragedy, like a shark attack or boat sinking, and she always found that so endearing. ...*Horrifying*, but still quite charming in a way.

...She really should call him and apologize. As much as the man got under her skin with his strangeness, she didn't want to hurt his feelings. He was surprisingly sensitive for someone who was so oblivious.

Bridget didn't have many friends and she didn't like the idea of offending the only one she really liked. Besides, he was a *client*, and clients needed to be treated with care.

She reached for the phone...

"Unhand me, mortal!"

Bridget paused, wondering if she had imagined that voice. She closed her eyes and counted to ten, trying to keep calm and convince herself that Julian would *never* show up at her office. That would be crazy and *completely* unprofessional, and not even *he* would do that to her.

The man burst through the door.

Damn.

She put her face in her hand.

"Ah-ha!" Julian turned to glare at Joan from reception. "I *told you* I would discover your mistress' location without *your* help, servant." He pointed towards the door. "*Be gone!*"

Normally, Bridget would be overjoyed at being visited by a handsome guy, but in this case, it really wasn't so much fun. Any time Julian was out in public was destined to be bad, but having him at his most Julian-ness in front of all her co-workers was going to hit an all-time high on the suckiness scale. She could tell already.

...Or should that be 'all-time low'? Technically, an all-time *high* on the scale would employ *low* levels of suckiness, right?...

And the mere fact that she was even wasting her time thinking about that could probably be introduced as evidence at a commitment hearing.

She rushed over to close the door, sending an apologetic glance to the others in the office.

"What are you doing here?" She said in a low voice, trying to keep him from yelling by establishing a baseline volume level.

He missed the hint. "Why have you abandoned us?" His voice boomed through the small space.

"Shhhh!" She made a hand gesture indicating that he should keep it down because people could hear him. "I didn't '*abandon*' anything, I simply have another job to do. A job which *pays* me, I might add."

"Pay?" He considered that. "Very well." He squared his shoulders. "How much 'pay' do you require to continue spending time with me?"

"I'm not a *prostitute,* Julian!" She gave him a disapproving glare.

"I did not say that you *were.*" He sounded vaguely insulted. "I simply wish to pay you to spend more time with me. ...Any physical relations which result between us will *of course* be unrecompensed."

"...I can't believe you really just said that."

He paused. "Honestly, I couldn't afford the paid companionship of a woman of your beauty anyway." He informed her matter-of-factly. "If I were paying for a prostitute, she would have to be *very* ugly."

"Please stop talking." She put her forehead down on her desk. "I just want to do my job and be left *alone.* Can you just go?"

"If I have offended you in some way, I apologize. I did not mean to insinuate that all of your people's whores are unattractive, if that is what is upsetting you." He struggled to backpedal, assuming that she was angry at him for insulting ladies of the evening. "...I am sure *many* of them are quite attractive and..."

She cut him off. "*Not* helping."

He nodded, still utterly oblivious to what he could have said that would anger her. "Please do not forsake your commitments with my organization– or me– simply because I have said something which caused your ire."

"I'm *not* angry with you."

"It *seems* like you're angry."

"If I were angry with you, we would not even be *having* this conversation. I would simply tell security to escort you out."

"As if they even *could!*" He scoffed in indignation, like that idea was ludicrous. "A few surface-dwellers against the King of the Unconquerable Seas!?!"

She stared at him for a moment. "The *receptionist* almost stopped you, Julian."

"That is only because she sprang at me while I was reading all of these glassen doors, searching for your name. The woman moves quite silently, despite her girth." He shook his head. "And why do you allow yourself to be *caged* in this little box? You have committed no crime." He shook his head. "Your people always seek to trap things of beauty behind walls of glass."

"I *have* to go to work. *Some of us* need to *work* to make money, okay?" She waved a letter at him. "Do you have any idea how much it takes to pay the cable bill every month?"

"No." He shook his head. "No, I do not."

"A *lot*."

"And this upsets you?"

"Yep."

"So, you work at a job you hate, so you can earn enough money to pay for the privilege of watching other people do the things you could be doing if you were not spending that time working?"

"...Something like that."

He considered that for a moment, then shook his head. "I do not understand surface culture."

"Look, it makes sense if you're *from* here, okay?"

"Undoubtedly." He glanced down at the slip of paper on her desk. "And when does Cable need his money?"

She looked down at her watch. "...Two weeks ago."

"I see." He pondered that for a moment. "I am excellent with people; I will fix this for you." Then he got distracted by something he saw out the window of her office. "How can you *stand* being around all these terrestrials?" He watched the passersby in suspicion and disgust, as though expecting them to attack at any moment. "You're forced to *stare* at them all the time! Why have you not bricked over this window or something? You are completely defenseless from their inevitable treachery. ...And I do not recall *ever* seeing such a collection of *tremendously* unattractive surface-dwellers before. Why is someone of *your* beauty forced to endure..." He pointed at Susan from the art department. "Look at *that* one!" He yelled loud enough to cause Susan to stop walking and look back at him. "That's *horrible!* Why do you force yourself to stare at these inferior people all day!?!"

Bridget put her face in her hand. "*Please* don't point at my coworkers." She hurried over to close the blinds so that he wouldn't be tempted to assess her coworkers' appearances so loudly to their faces anymore.

"I am merely pointing out that you are better than them, and should find *better* employment."

"And I'm guessing that that 'better employment' is with *you,* right?"

He blinked in confusion. "Who is better than me?"

She rolled her eyes. "Can't we just talk about this later?"

"Why would you want to delay your delivery from this place? One would think you would *welcome* an escape from this company." His eyes strayed to the shelf behind her desk, to her aquarium where several colorful fish swam in lazy circles around their plastic castle.

She winced, expecting an angry tirade. "You're not going to be all like 'Let my people go!' are you?"

"No." He shook his head. "These fish are quite content with watching over you. How could they not be? You are a wonder to behold and I envy them for being close to you each day."

She picked up her pencil and began making random marks on one of her files, trying to send him a none-too-subtle message that she was busy and that he should leave. "You know, when you try to flirt, it just comes off as weird and kind of scary."

He made a face. "Your people frighten so easily. I've often said that many of my run-ins with them would have gone differently if they weren't so blasted cowardly and..."

"What do you *want*, Julian?" She cut him off, trying to avoid another chat about how inferior humanity was.

"I have come to finish our discussion about our relationship." He nodded sharply. "I have given you your space, but I feel as though you have now had enough time to think about your feelings."

She looked down at her watch. "Three hours?"

"Indeed."

She shook her head. "I'm going to need more time than that to figure out what your deal is."

He made an annoyed sound. "I have no deal!" He looked up at the ceiling tile in exasperation. "...But, very well. How much more time do you require? Another hour? *Two? ...Certainly* no more than two." He sat down in the office chair against her wall. "I will wait."

She massaged her temples to chase away a building headache, then just tried her best to ignore him.

Moments passed in awkward silence as she attempted to go about her work and he calmly watched her every movement from his seat.

Finally, she just couldn't take it anymore and made an annoyed sound. "*Why* are you still here watching me?"

"I told you: I am awaiting your decision." He made a regal hand gesture. "Please. Go about your day. Pretend I'm not even here. This is very interesting. I've never had a chance to observe your primitive culture like this up close before. I am anxious to know why your lives involve so much 'paperwork,' and I hope my observations reveal an answer."

"This just can't be happening." She pinched the bridge of her nose. "Look, I think I'm entitled to at *least* a day to think about this. You have to understand why I'm not entirely trusting your motivations here."

He shook his head. "No."

"You don't see anything at all suspicious with any of this?"

He shook his head again. "No. I have faith that you are not a terrestrial spy, trying to..."

"Not *me*, moron." She cut him off. "I mean *you.*"

"Me?" He sounded confused. "Why would anyone doubt *me* in anything? I am evolution's greatest achievement."

She rolled her eyes. "Yeah, you're just *super.*"

"Then why can we not..." He paused, obviously trying to think of a way to finish that thought.

"Date?" She offered.

"Indeed." He nodded. "I see no reason why we could not 'date.'" He made little air quotes. "Surface people do it *all the time!* I cannot *tell you* the number of occasions I have attacked the seashore and encountered surface couples on one of their 'dates.'"

"Ah, I'm always so comforted when the guy asking me out mentions his hobby of terrorizing the innocent like something from a '50s horror film." She grabbed another random file. "And I think we've talked about you not bragging about your crimes in public. That just makes my job harder."

"...You doubt my motives?" He frowned. "*Surely* it means something that I'm willingly enduring the *unyielding* degradation of the surface world for you."

She put her forehead down on her desk again, letting out another annoyed sound. "Why are you doing this to me? Why can't you just pretend to be normal for an afternoon? Is it really that hard?"

"I freely admit that I am rather anxious to be with you, because..." He trailed off, as if at a loss for words. He cleared his throat. "...Gods... gods can tell the woman they're destined to be with. Their...," his mind raced, as he visibly tried to come up with something that sounded convincingly 'otherworldly,' "...*Intended One.*"

He looked smug, momentarily flashing a face which seemed to say: 'Ooooooh, that sounded good! Hell, I'm halfway convinced myself.'

She stared at him for a moment. "...You're just taking that from some romance novel you've read, aren't you?" She looked up at him and nodded. "In fact, I'm pretty sure I've read that one *too.*"

"...You have?" He cleared his throat. "I mean... umm... *of course* I'm not just plagiarizing some surface world dime store novel." He rolled his eyes, putting on a show of looking dismissive. "I mean, what kind of person do you take me for, that I'd be buying that crap?"

"Uh-huh." She began to draw lazy doodles on one of her folders. "Besides, I thought her earlier work was better. The series lost focus after Demetrius finally hooked up with his 'Intended One,' what's-her-face the private investigator girl."

"*Dixie*." He reminded her. "'Dixie St. Mason.'" He shook his head sadly. "Your people concoct the *silliest* names for their mythologies, which in *my* view, contributes to the downward going quality of your world and the novel series in question. ...I did like Tristan's book though. I thought..." He stopped speaking and cleared his throat again. "...Or rather, I've heard that *some people* liked it more anyway. I *of course*, have no firsthand knowledge of that surface trash."

"No, of course not." She rolled her eyes. "So, is there any *reason* you stopped by today, other than to tell a few quick outrageously insulting and poorly constructed lies?"

"I am *not* lying." He paused. "...Well, not about anything *important* anyway."

"Just go away." She made a shooing motion with her hand. "I'll talk to you tomorrow."

He frowned again, looking unhappy. "...But I have your word that you will *return* to us tomorrow, correct?"

"Sure." She shrugged. "Why not. Just go."

"Excellent." He nodded smartly. "You will have your day to consider our relationship, and then you shall return to me." He opened the door. "I will await you at home." He stormed through the office, glaring at her coworkers like they were all assassins or pedophiles or some other dangerous and disgusting group.

Bridget watched him go, feeling utterly shell-shocked.

****

"So, how'd it go, boss?" Quinn asked, rising from his chair and hurrying to catch up with Julian as he stormed from the building. "Should I go rent a tux or what?"

"This is just yet *another* example of my own unending endurance and fortitude, Tupilak." He led the way down the sidewalk. "The Lady Bridget is simply feeling a little *apprehensive* at the moment, no doubt because of spending so much time around too many mediocre surface men."

"...You didn't *tell* her that to her face, did you? 'Cause it kinda sounds like you just called her a whore."

"No, *of course* not!" Julian scoffed. "I made *sure* to tell her that I *didn't* think she was a prostitute, but that even if she *were*, she would be *far* too expensive for me, as purchasing her body would be worth *any* price for men."

"You got *mad* romance skills, boss." Tupilak nodded seriously. "I bet women *always* like to be told what you'd pay for their bodies on the open market."

Julian ignored his negativity. "But I remain undaunted. I am on a *mission*, and I will not rest until that mission ends in victory."

"...Or until she calls the cops because we're stalking her."

"This is not *stalking*; this is *romance*."

"Really? 'Cause I think they got laws against it."

"Oh, the surface people have laws against *everything.*" Julian rolled his eyes in dismissal. "The point is that The Lady Bridget is worth *any* trial which I am forced to endure."

"...You *do* mean 'trial' like in 'challenge,' and not 'trial' like in 'legal proceeding,' right boss? Because if this is going to end up with us in court again, I'm going to suggest that we hold off on your 'romance' for the time being, 'cause our lawyer is on her honeymoon right now."

Julian scoffed. "I require no terrestrial assistance in these matters."

"...Didn't you recruit Monty to help you like... this morning?"

"That is beside the point."

"And aren't *we* like... talking about it right now?"

"The problem with your species, is that no surface person ever takes the time to really get to know their own heart. What they want. What their *mate* wants."

"If we're going to like... start hiding in the bushes outside her house or something, trying to spy on her to figure out shit about her, I'm going to have to *again* remind you that Marian's on her honeymoon, and if we get arrested..."

"*No one is getting arrested!*"

"Uh-huh." Quinn rolled his eyes. "The last time you said that, I spent a week trying to paddle home from the Bermuda triangle after that thing with the Coast Guard, man."

"And you *weren't* arrested then, were you?" Julian snorted contemptuously. "No. You simply had the opportunity to enjoy several *beautiful* days at sea. Many surface people pay a *great deal* for that privilege."

"Well, I almost paid *big*, but I was able to fend off the sharks."

Julian frowned at him in annoyance. "Besides, that whole

endeavor was the *surface people's* doing."

"So, what else is new?" Quinn turned to watch a woman wearing spandex running clothes jog by, then looked back to Julian. "Where are we going, anyway?"

"We are returning to the Lair to retrieve something, and then I am going to make a *personal* call."

****

"Good afternoon." Julian gave the woman behind the counter what he hoped was a fair impression of a happy surface-worlder. "I would like to see Cable Bill, please." He hefted the large chest up onto the desk at the cable company's offices. "Please tell Mr. Bill that I have delivered Bridget Haniver's payment to him. I hope Spanish doubloons from a sunken galleon will be acceptable?"

CHAPTER 15

KING: "AS I'M SURE YOU'VE NOTICED, MY CO-HOST IS
ABSENT FROM THE STUDIO AT THE MOMENT, BECAUSE
WE'VE BEEN GRANTED AN INTERVIEW WITH THE GROUP
OF SUPER-POWERED CRIMINALS WHO HAVE BEEN
LAYING SIEGE TO THIS CITY WHILE THE CONSORTIUM
OF COWARDS DOES NOTHING TO HELP. SO, WE'LL GO
LIVE TO OUR OWN CONNIE STORMS WHO'S IN THE FIELD
AT THE MOMENT. CONNIE?"

STORMS (VIA SATELLITE): "...THANKS, PAIGE. I'M
STANDING HERE WITH DETRITUS, A REPRESENTATIVE
OF THE SUPER-PERSON RESISTANCE MOVEMENT.
NOW, DETRITUS PERHAPS YOU CAN EXPLAIN TO OUR
VIEWERS WHY YOU HATE THEM?"

TRANSCRIPT OF "KING OF CAPES AND COWLS," MEDIA:
TELEVISION, SHOW: 1407, NEWSCHANNEL 6, FRIDAY
21:00-22:00 EST, NETWORK SEGMENT-ID:
918000606

Mercygiver casually approached the intersection.

Ahead of him, a newswoman wearing too much eye makeup was speaking to a representative of the Super-Person Resistance Movement about their efforts to seize control of the city. The man was wearing a loose-fitting blue robe for some reason, and spoke with a great deal of eloquence.

"Connie," the man said, "it's not that we hate the Norms of this city. We believe that they have a perfect right to live however they want, and are a valuable part of the community." He shook his head. "We just don't think they need to be a part of *our* community. Basically, what we're proposing is that the Norms of this city simply move elsewhere, where their tragic condition won't interfere with the others of us who are *truly* extraordinary. That's the reason why bad things are happening around the city, and I'm afraid that they will only get worse until people realize that they just have no other option. If they simply listen to reason, they'll all survive. We don't want to hurt anyone, and will let them pack up and leave our city completely unharmed. If they test our resolve though, I'm afraid that they won't like what happens."

Mercygiver casually kept walking ahead, as the crosswalk turned green. Around him, scores of busy people hustled to wherever it was that people in this city seemed to always be going in such a hurry.

Things with the SPeRM were spiraling out of control now, and they had been hitting targets all over the city over the past few days. Mercygiver intended on sending them a very public and very *powerful* message. HE ran this town. *PERIOD*.

Mercygiver pressed the detonator in his pocket, and a dumpster in an alley across the street exploded.

The reporter, the man from the SPeRM and the cameraman all turned to see what the problem was. Mercygiver nonchalantly brushed past the man being interviewed on the sidewalk, and in the same fluid motion, sunk his stiletto into the space beneath the man's arm, yanked it free and spun it around to repeat the process on his other side without ever breaking stride.

"How extraordinary are you *now?*" He whispered into the man's ear as his victim fell to the concrete dying, and Mercygiver disappeared into the crowd of people without a trace, as the screaming began.

****

"*Holy shit!*" Arn pointed at the screen. "Did you guys *see that!?!* He just stabbed him!" He quickly rewound the broadcast. "Shit!" He looked around the room. "I can't believe that just happened!?!" He turned his phone around to show them the program he was watching. "I mean, I know Stacy was always going on and on about how awesome 'Game of Thrones' is, but I had *no idea!*"

"I don't care." Julian made a face, doing his best to ignore the man. He leaned against one of the racks of clothes in the Drews department store building, and continued addressing his team. They had arrived in this terrestrial shopping center fifteen minutes before in order to make another personal appearance. Julian wasn't exactly looking forward to the spectacle; he wasn't a *mall Santa,* for god's sake. He was a hero! A king! A god! ...But he was also someone who wanted to make inroads with his press agent, and thus, when she suggested the idea, he had *instantly* caved. Any opportunity to spend time with her was worth it, in his opinion.

"Now then," he cleared his throat, "I have called you all here for a very important reason: *me*. I am leader of this organization, and it is *your* responsibility to help me achieve my goals."

Mack turned to look at him. "Goals? I thought we was just here to look pretty and get our pictures took?"

"Jules wants to score with the New Girl." Quinn chimed in helpfully. "We're his wingmen until he taps that ass."

Mack frowned. "Now, obviously I ain't *leader* of this group, but shouldn't we be focused on the fact that the entire city is angry at us and there's a group of super-powered people out there dedicated to destroyin' humanity?"

Ceann pointed at Mack. "YOU HAVE SPELLED: GOOD. YOU HAVE SPELLED: COUNSEL." He held his arms wide, indicating the city. "YOU HAVE SPELLED: LAWLESS."

"The Lady Haniver wants us to make a public appearance today, so we're *going* to make a public appearance today." Julian told him patiently.

"How does that make any sense?" Mack sounded mystified. "I think ya just *told* her that you were *free* today, in an effort to spend more time with her at some press thing. Which is pretty goddamned *stupid* if ya ask me, because half the city is under attack!"

"I *didn't* ask you, and I don't care if the *entire* city is under attack and this mall is engulfed in *flames*." He pointed at Mack imperially, driving the point home. "She will be here if we make a personal appearance today, so we're *going* to make an appearance here today, even if I have to kill you all to do it, and just prop up your corpses on stage. Do you *understand* me?"

"Public's gettin' pissed at us for not stoppin' Reece, Jules." Mack warned. "They don't like it when super-folks attack a Mets game and no one shows up to stop them but fucking *Oz,* the headless fella, and that little asshole from the Roustabouts."

"If they are angry with us, then we will need *more* of the Lady Haniver's assistance with the press, not less. The *obvious* solution to getting bad press is to have our press agent get us *good* press." Satisfied that he had gotten his point across, he returned to the issue at hand. "Now then, I have taken the liberty of writing down everything we know about The Lady Haniver." He handed the stack of papers to Quinn, who began to pass them out to the assembly. "I want you all to study this list, and come up with ideas which I can use."

Mack raised his hand again. "Yeah, but shouldn't we..."

"Fucking focus, man!" Quinn snapped. "Show some team

spirit! How about a little human compassion here, huh? Some understanding? This is a *sensitive issue*." Quinn turned to look at his boss. "What about Spanish fly? That might work."

Julian glared at him.

Quinn pursed his lips. "No, huh?"

Ceann watched them for a moment, then turned to stalk from the building, typing things into his toy as if talking to himself now. He gave them a dismissive gesture. "YOU HAVE SPELLED: HOPELESS." He held his arms wide, as if questioning how he had gotten himself into this mess. "YOU HAVE SPELLED: ATLAS." He took several exaggerated steps, as if burdened by carrying the rest of them and shouldering their massive incompetence. Several shoppers in the area stared at him in terror and cringed away as he made his way from the store.

Julian ignored him. Some people just didn't understand *teamwork.* "I have given her until today to give me an answer."

"That's big of you, boss." Quinn gave him a thumbs up. "Totally the *gentlemanly* thing to do. Women eat that shit up."

"I expect her answer soon, but if it does not go as well as expected, I will need to have a backup plan."

"...I think I have some chloroform in my suitcase." Quinn helpfully suggested. "I grabbed it from the Undersea Base before we left. If life has taught me *anything*, it's that you can *never* have too much of that shit around. It just might do the trick here. Give her a little whiff of that, then stuff her in the back of the car, and we got all the time in the world to convince her you're a hero."

Mack lounged back against one of the store's pillars, ignoring the suggestion. "What exactly is the problem with your relationship? Why can't ya just ask her out?"

"She doesn't trust me."

"Well, since our 'plan B' involves chloroform and the trunk of a car, that might be some pretty good thinkin' on her part." He readjusted his hat. "If she's got trust issues, why is she tryin' to date a super-villain in the first place?"

Julian scowled at him. "I am a *protector* of this city now. *Everyone* should trust me." He turned to look at Arnold. "You don't seem to have any trouble getting people to trust you. How do you do it?"

"Lies." Traitor answered distractedly, still watching his show. "Lies will solve everything."

Julian made a face. "I am not good at 'lies.' I followed your advice already, and it did not go well. She saw through it immediately."

"That's just because you don't know how to do it right." Arn informed him pityingly. "The first step to telling a successful lie is that you have to *believe* it. You have to be totally convinced that you're telling the truth."

Quinn took on a thoughtful face, as if giving the matter deep thought. "Hey, Oz is like all in touch with feelings and shit, right? Why doesn't he just tell you how to get her?"

Oz frowned. "I will take no part in your strange and rather *disturbing* attempts to seduce or kidnap this poor woman. Truth be told, I agree with Mack; I think we should be out there doing what we can to stop the Super-Person Resistance Movement. I only came today because I wanted to make sure that the children at this event weren't disappointed."

Quinn rolled his eyes. "Oh, yeah. I'm sure they'd be crying their little fucking eyes out if *you* didn't show up, man." He said sarcastically. "Why, *you're* everyone's *favorite* on the team! I bet a fucking *Oz* doll would be a *huge* seller this Christmas!" He shook his head. "You just tell yourself whatever you want, but we all know the *real* reason for your little visit."

Oz's eyes narrowed. "Just what are you implying?"

"All I'm saying is that maybe you should take some time out of your busy schedule stalking that perky little redhead employee over there, and help Julian score with the press chick that *he's* stalking. Help a brother out, man! But no. You can't even do that." Quinn shook his head in disgust. "And after everything Jules has done for *you*."

Oz turned to look at the salesgirl in question as she arrived for her shift at the store. He turned back at Quinn. "I'm *not* stalking, Miss Quentin. I did not know she was even working today. This is usually her day off, unless it's the day after a holiday or she's..." He cleared his throat, recognizing he'd said too much. "I am merely making sure that she is safe and is not..." He paused, looking genuinely curious. "...Wait. What has Julian ever done for me? I honestly can't think of anything."

Quinn shrugged. "He must have done *something*." He poked him in the chest. "You *owe him* and it's time to pay up!"

Oz ducked behind a display of clothes as the woman in question turned to hand a customer a box. He made a frantic hand gesture. "Get down! *She'll see you!*"

"Is there some reason why 'Ginger' over there can't see us?" Quinn obediently crouched down behind the mannequin. "Do we owe her money?"

Julian rolled his eyes and heaved an imperious sigh. "I do not care if that scarlet-haired surface-dweller sees me or not. If you wish to launch an attack on her, please do so *immediately* so that we can get back to more important matters."

"Like Reece and the people blowin' up large sections of the city?" Mack guessed. "Like the fact that most of the people hate us because of the Agletaria thing? Like the fact that doin' personal appearances when the city is fallin' apart is just givin' people a chance to learn the names and faces of the people who are responsible for failin' to protect them?"

"Like *Lady Haniver*." Julian ran a hand through his hair and refocused on Oz. "I *tire* of this. Kill the salesgirl if you're going to, because it is distracting us from our *real* mission."

Oz's expression darkened, obviously not liking the idea that Julian thought he was planning on hurting the girl.

Quinn put up his hand to stop him before this got out of control. "*Relax*, Romeo." He poked him in the chest again. "All Jules is saying is that it's time to shit or get off the fucking pot."

Julian's face contorted in disgust. "I recall saying *nothing* of the sort. I would never say anything so *revolting*."

Quinn ignored him. "Your little high school drama is slowing down my man's *love life*, stalker-boy." He poked Oz in the chest again. "So grow some fucking balls and make your play so that we can get back to seducing our new press agent and convincing her that Julian's really a nice guy, so that she isn't too pissed at him before he destroys the world. Scoring with her *after* he drowns everyone she's ever known and loved is going to be next to impossible, so he's gotta screw her *now*."

Oz took a deep breath, then shook his head. "I don't know what you are even talking about. My interest in Miss Quentin is *entirely* professional, and even if I ever *did* decide to ask her out, I'd..."

Quinn cut him off. "Shoot Reagan to get her attention and prove your love?" He shook his head. "Been done, stalker-boy." Quinn pulled up the hood on his parka. "Maybe *I* should just go over there and warm her up a little for you." He smiled tauntingly. "I bet I'd be *real* good at keeping her warm at night."

Whatever darkness lurked beneath the calm waters of Oz's psyche stirred dangerously for a moment, showing itself to the world. "I will say this *once:* no one in this organization is to hassle or accost Miss Quentin in *any* way." And just like that, the angry shadows which filled the man's voice were gone and were replaced by the calm and rational man again. "I don't think this is the time nor the place to discuss this issue."

Quinn shook his head. "You're a fucking pansy, New Guy. You know that?" He pointed at Julian. "My boy here is totally willing to put his heart on the line for the chick he wants. I'm talking *begging on his knees* for even one *ounce* of attention from her."

Julian frowned. "I do not recall mentioning being willing to '*beg*' for…"

Quinn held up a hand. "Relax, boss-man. I got this one." He refocused on Oz. "…Because that's what it means to be a *man,* New Guy. It means having the ability to say: 'Baby, I know that this is making me look like a weak simpering little pansy…"

Julian opened his mouth to protest again, but Quinn talked right over him.

"But I just need your body so bad, right now, that I don't even *care* how you terribly you treat me, or how much respect my friends are losing for me." He nodded and poked Oz in the chest and reached forward to take the man's hand. "It's about taking her hand like this and saying: 'I'm useless and basically powerless, but you're the only person who can stand me. So let's go back to my kingdom under the sea and shag like fucking rabbits on Viagra."

"I think you should take him up on that one, Oz."

They all looked up over the store display to see the red-haired salesgirl watching them.

"That was just so *beautiful*, I'm tearing up." The girl's eyes twinkled in amusement. "You two are just so *cute* together." She pointed over her shoulder. "Toasters are on special in housewares if you guys want to register here."

"…Oh. Hello, Miss Quentin." Oz cleared his throat. "My associates and I were just…"

"Expressing your love for each other amid the ladies lingerie?" She gestured to the half-dressed mannequins. "Personally, I can think of more romantic locations for a secret… *assignation*." She winked at him. "But whatever floats your boat, Oz. Drews Department Store doesn't discriminate or make judgments. We celebrate love in all its joyous forms."

Mack shook his head. "I have seen this exact kinda shit in like a *thousand* stupid-ass sitcoms." He said to himself. "…Can't believe I'm actually *livin'* it right now." He leaned against the pillar again, looking tired. "*Jesus*, do I need a better job."

Oz got to his feet with as much dignity as he could muster. "We are merely having a company meeting about…," he cleared his throat, "...hero stuff."

"'Hero stuff.' Riiiiiight." She made an unconvinced sound and held out a pair of yellow panties. "I'd go with *these* for the wedding night if I were you. They really pop on your skin tone."

Quinn looked down at the fabric and nodded. "You know, she's totally right." He intoned seriously. "Those look really good on you, man. If I was gay, I'd be *all over you* in those."

Oz shook his head, ignoring Quinn and remaining focused on the girl. He shied away from the garment. "No, thank you. I'm fine. I don't buy clothes that are not sanitized and hermetically sealed. There is no telling who may have tampered with them or what contagions they may have infected the material with." He looked haunted for a moment. "I can think of nothing more horrifying than touching someone else's underwear."

"How *boring* your love life must be." She grinned at him, dimples cutting her cheeks, and leaned against the display. She glanced over at Jules and her eyes skimmed down to his scaled swimming pants. "Looks like your friend went with black." She waggled her hand back and forth to show she wasn't convinced. "I'm not sold on that. Black tells me he's a player. Some girls might be scared off by that. I'd go with something softer; downplay the evil some."

Oz shook his head. "We are really not looking for advice on underwear right now, although we do appreciate..."

Jules cut him off. "What color would you suggest?"

Surface women cared about the *color* of clothing. THAT was why Bridget was being so difficult! It made perfect sense now! All he needed were the correct colors. LOTS of animals used colors as a signal in mating displays, and it only made sense that the terrestrials were one of them.

He was now very pleased with himself for discovering this fact.

Oz stared at him in amazement for a moment, then went back to talking to the surface girl like he had never spoken. "We really just came to discuss the girl Julian wants to begin a relationship with."

"Uh-huh." She nodded and hopped up to sit on the store display table, casually refolding some of the merchandise. "And is there a *reason* why you and your Cape friends keep choosing *this* store to work out you relationship troubles in? We just finished cleaning up from the *last* time, when you got us attacked by zombies. Or the damage from the time before *that*. I mean, have you ever tried to mop up a rack of sweaters that are dripping from the ceiling tile?"

"No."

She made a face. "It's not fun. As it turns out, argyle stains."

"I apologize." Oz shook his head. "But there's no particular reason why we come here. We just enjoy... bargains."

Quinn snorted. "Yeah, I love the fucking selection of *lamps* ya got here." He rolled his eyes. "God, everyone is just such a *coward* around here. Changed my mind; if I was gay, I wouldn't give you the *time of fucking day,* no matter *how* good you looked in those yellow panties, Oz. You wouldn't last a *second* in the artic, man."

Mack snorted. "Oh, like you've even *been* to the artic, Quinn. The farthest north you've ever been is *the Bronx.*"

Quinn pointed at him, his face angry. "That's a lie. That's a *goddamn lie.*"

Julian ignored their unprofessionalism. Insulting his team in public just made *him* look bad. "We are making an appearance in the mall shortly, and we are using your store to have a last minute strategy meeting." Julian informed her.

"Gotcha. Strategy meeting for an appearance at the mall." She nodded. "I think I can help with your complicated advanced planning. Just do this..." She held up one hand and robotically waved it back and forth, while taking on an utterly blank and vapid smile.

Quinn snickered.

Julian's eyes narrowed. "It always seems so *easy* for people who have nothing remarkable about themselves to look down on people who try to *lead*."

Oz turned to glare at him.

The salesgirl didn't notice. "Honestly, I kinda figured you guys would be too concerned about what happened last night to be here anyway. You must have been busy all morning, what with the robbery at the university and all."

Julian frowned and looked at Tupilak.

The other man shrugged helplessly, knowing nothing about the event in question.

Julian turned back to the woman. "...Of course." He cleared his throat. "It was certainly... concerning."

The salesgirl nodded. "Any clue on why the SPRM would attack an anthropology lab?"

"The who?" Julian asked, not really caring about the answer.

"Those super-freaks who want to destroy the city." She carefully folded a small feminine lacey garment which Julian couldn't identify but still began to imagine clinging to Bridget's curves. "I mean, I *know* the University found that weird tablet-y thing in Cairo last month, but I don't…"

Julian cut her off. "It's all very technical and heroic." He shifted, trying to change the topic. "I can't go into details."

Tupilak nodded. "Even if we *wanted* to."

The salesgirl made an unconvinced sort of sound. "Well, I'll leave you guys to confer about the super-secret hero public appearance thing, which evidently can only be discussed while hiding behind the rack of *thongs*." She hopped down from the display and started towards the back room. "I'll just quick go check in back for a pair of briefs in your fish-man friend's size."

"Her favorite color is blue." He called after her. "Although if you think that another color would better communicate attraction and stir her desire, that would be fine as well."

"So, your theory is that it's the color of your *pants* which is causin' her to be annoyed by your aggravatin' personality?" Mack asked in disbelief. "Not your inability to protect the city or be civil to people?"

"…It's worth a shot." Julian shrugged. "I do not understand terrestrials. How could anyone *possibly* object to *me?*"

"…It's a *mystery.*"

Julian's eyes narrowed. "…Is that surface sarcasm, I detect?"

"Nope." Mack shook his head. "You're just…"

"Okay, I talked to the press people, and they're going to hold off on the questions until after the meet and greet." Bridget appeared from one of the other departments, looking radiant. "I still don't know why you want to do another event today though. Seems like you guys do a *lot* of these."

"Yeah, some of us have noticed that too." Mack deadpanned. "That's *another* mystery."

Julian nodded his head in respectful greeting. "Good morning, Lady Bridget. Have you taken notice of how I am not pressuring you for your answer? I am giving you you're space, rather than making you feel uncomfortable or rushed."

She stared at him for a beat. "Yeah, you're playing real hard to get, big guy. Keeping things close to the vest." She rolled her eyes, ignoring his achievement. "Okay then, we're going to get this thing going. Now, I'm thinking that since Julian is obviously the most accomplished hero among you, that *he* should be the one who…"

"…Wait, you mean *this* Julian?" Mack said the words like he was seriously asking for confirmation on the issue. "You're sure this is *Julian* we're talkin' about here, and not some other fish-man person?"

Bridget looked confused. "I really don't even understand

that question. Julian's been in this game for *decades*. Longer than you've even been alive!"

"Redwoods live a long time too, darlin', and they ain't exactly what one might call 'active,' 'accomplished' or 'heroic.'" Mack ran a hand through his hair and replaced his cap. "I think you'll find that Julian has a distinct ability to..."

"*Always* save the day." Julian finished for him. He turned to Tupilak. "Right?"

"Oh, got that right, boss. ...Why, I remember that one time when... Umm... When the Undersea Base ran out of popcorn once, and you were *right there* to take charge amid the panic, and order me to go get some more." Quinn nodded seriously. "Totally saved the day."

"And he stopped the Freedom Squad almost singlehandedly, didn't you?" Bridget asked, sounding oddly proud.

Julian paused to consider that for a moment, trying to decide how large a lie would be completely unforgivable. "...Yes, I did."

That wasn't *really* a lie. True, he hadn't technically *gone* on that mission per se, but he was there in *spirit*, and his coworkers were no doubt inspired by that. Without him, there was no telling how the mission may have turned out,

"Funny, 'cause I was *actually* there." Mack shook his head. "And I don't remember seein' Julian."

"That's 'cause Julian didn't go anywhere *near* a strip joint that night." Quinn snapped. "Leave the man alone and let him work his fucking mojo, Mack." He pushed him in annoyance. "You should change your codename to the fucking 'Cockblocker,' man."

"I'm going to pretend I didn't hear that." Bridget said.

"Yes, we all will." Julian told her with some assurance. "The man simply has no idea how to behave like a reliable hero in public. A complete *lack* of decorum on how these things are done, and his unprofessionalism makes us all look bad."

Quinn opened his mouth to protest, but Julian began to hustle Bridget away before he got the chance. "Perhaps it would be best if we surveyed the field before the event, in order to better understand what we are up against."

Bridget let herself be escorted towards the main shopping area. "Is this a not too subtle attempt to get me alone?"

He tried to give a convincing gasp of insult. "No! Of course not! I am giving you your space and..."

"Cut the shit, Julian."

"Absolutely." He nodded. "I am *absolutely* trying to get you alone, both because I dislike those people and because I fear that you will begin avoiding me simply because I associate with them. I am one step away from pulling the fire alarm, just so this building will empty and I can have my moment with you." He cleared his throat. "Have you given my words enough consideration yet?"

"...Yeah." She looked down at her feet, appearing uncomfortable for a moment. "See, the thing is... The thing is that I think you're only asking me out because you're so lonely, that *anyone* will do. It's not *me* you're after, it's just *someone.*"

"And I've what? Simply been biding my time for the past couple of centuries? Do you have any idea how many surface people I am forced to look at on a daily basis? Now multiply that by all those years. And in all that time... all those millions and millions of people... you're telling me that I couldn't *ever* find *anyone* who would go out with me but you?" He shook his head. "*I* think you're only saying that as an excuse to deny yourself the happiness which you deserve."

"And I suppose being with *you* automatically equals happiness, right?" She rolled her eyes. "My God, but you're full of yourself, aren't you?"

"*As* a god, I think I have a *right to be.*"

She looked uncertain for a moment, then bit her bottom lip. "...I..." She trailed off. "...I just *can't,* Julian. I'm sorry. ...I...I have my career to think about and... and I don't..." She trailed off again. "...I'm sorry. I'll *always* be grateful for what you did for me, but... but I can't."

He swallowed, trying to process this news without destroying the world right now. "...I understand."

No! He DIDN'T understand! *AT ALL!* In fact, he was TOTALLY...

"Why am I *once again* called away from my *real* duties in order to waste time trying to make you people look competent?"

Julian whirled around to face the intruder on his private conversation. "*Not the time, Welles!*"

The man ignored him. "I figure I should take this opportunity while I have it, before your little friend there gets us all tarred and feathered." He held up the morning's newspaper, which announced the university robbery and angry editorials about the Consortium's lack of action on the growing crisis. "*Wonderful* job on controlling the press, by the way. I daresay, we could have gotten better results if we tried to control our image by closing our eyes and wishing really, *really* hard." He absently tossed the paper aside and readjusted his gloves. "Maybe the rest of these idiots are content with failure, but I assure you, I am *not.*" His face took on an arrogant and taunting expression.

"And now I realize at last *why* you have no degree in public relations, Miss Haniver. Because no self-respecting university would even let you in the *fucking door.* You. Are. *Useless."*

Julian decked him, and Monty hit the floor.

He prowled towards the man's prone form and lifted his head off the tile by his shirt collar. "I *warned you* what would happen if you insulted her again. *Didn't I?"* His eyes narrowed dangerously. "And now I'm going to do the world a favor and *end you."*

Monty watched him for a moment, his expression unreadable and his already damaged right eye beginning to swell shut. *"...Hit me."* He whispered.

Julian's rage faded for a moment. "What?"

"I have not forgotten our agreement; I *always* do what I say I'm going to do." Monty shook his head. "Every hero needs a villain, Julian." He glanced at Bridget and then back at him. "Welcome to the side of the angels." He raised his voice. "Oh, big man! Sure, step in to protect your useless little girlfriend from the big bad Mo..."

Julian hit him again, and the man went limp. ...Or at least *pretended* to. Truth be told, Julian thought the man wasn't the best actor he had ever seen.

But no matter.

He refocused on Bridget as Higgins arrived to pull his "wounded" boss from the scene.

Julian looked down at her, meeting her gaze and drawing himself up to his full height. "This will be my last word on the matter, and then I will speak no more on it, no matter your decision: I hate your people, Lady Bridget." He told her frankly. "I hate them with an intensity which you cannot possibly *fathom.* I am a proud man. Some call me haughty. *And yet*, here I am. *Amongst* the people I loathe. Putting myself on display for their entertainment. I will undergo *any* humiliation to be with you, even being with them. If you asked me to dress up like a mortal clown and perform at their children's birthday parties, I would do it, just as long as it meant that I'd get to see you and that it would make you happy." He watched her silently for another moment. "So, I am asking you to reconsider your decision. I know you doubt my motivations, but I challenge you to come up with *any other* explanation as to why I would do the things I have been doing, except that I'm telling the truth and that I want you." He shook his head. "No one else."

She watched him in silence for a moment.

"...How about dinner?" She finally got out.

He nodded. "Very well. I was not aware of mortal's *having*

clowns at birthday dinners, but…"

"No, dumbass. I mean you and me." She shifted in apparent awkwardness. "…We could… you know… have dinner or something. I mean, if you really wanted to."

"Indeed."

YES! He barely restrained himself from doing a fist pump of victory.

"You will not be sorry, Lady Bridget. I assure you, I can be quite charming when I want to be. I'm certain that I will make a *most* pleasant dinner companion for you." He nodded, now feeling very pleased with himself. "It is a wonder that the surface world and I have never gotten along. I can fit in so well here. Why, I even took care of your troubles with 'Cable Bill' for you." He shook his head. "You will never have to worry about paying that charge again."

"You paid it for me?"

He began to escort her towards the area where they were scheduled to make their appearance. "No, they have shut off your service."

She put her face in her palm.

CHAPTER 16

KING: "...WHICH POLICE WARN COULD NECESSITATE A COMPLETE EVACUATION OF THE CITY FOR THE FORESEEABLE FUTURE."

STORMS: "IT'S JUST A PRECAUTION THE CITY IS CONSIDERING UNTIL THE CONSORTIUM CAN STOP THE SUPER-PERSON RESISTANCE MOVEMENT, PAIGE. LET'S NOT SCARE PEOPLE."

KING: "OH, NO. WE CERTAINLY WOULDN'T WANT TO 'SCARE' PEOPLE. YOU KNOW WHAT SHOULD SCARE THEM, CONNIE? THE FACT THAT WHILE THE CITY IS BEING DESTROYED PIECE BY PIECE AND EVERY ONE OF OUR VIEWERS IS ENDANGERED BY MANIACS INTENT ON MURDERING THEM, THEIR 'PROTECTORS' ARE OUT THERE DOING NOTHING TO STOP IT. 'ROME' IS BURNING AND OUR TEAM OF CAPE-WEARING 'NEROS' DOES NOTHING BUT FIDDLE."

STORMS: "I'M SURE THEY'RE TRYING THEIR BEST, PAIGE. I DON'T KNOW WHAT YOU EXPECT THEM TO DO. IT'S NOT LIKE THE SUPER-PERSON RESISTANCE MOVEMENT IS LISTED IN THE PHONE BOOK OR ANYTHING. THE CONSORTIUM IS PROBABLY OUT THERE RIGHT NOW TRACKING DOWN LEADS ON THIS."

TRANSCRIPT OF "KING OF CAPES AND COWLS," MEDIA: TELEVISION, SHOW: 1408, NEWSCHANNEL 6, FRIDAY 21:00-22:00 EST, NETWORK SEGMENT-ID: 918000606

"Haven't you ever seen one of those sequences in a movie where the person is trying on a selection of silly outfits or hats while cheerful music plays, and everyone laughs, until they finally emerge with some perfect but unseen outfit, and then everyone gives their approval and a few minutes later there's the big reveal of what the outfit looks like as the person descends some grand staircase in the restaurant and everyone is speechless?"

"No."

Bridget frowned. "Well, this is one of those moments. Shut up and put your clothes on."

"I still do not understand why all of this is even necessary." He disappeared back into the dressing room, obviously sulking. "Why can I not just go to dinner as I am? Why must I always change to suit others?"

Bridget rolled her eyes. Only Julian would make shirtless-ness an issue of personal freedom and empowerment. "Because the restaurant won't serve you if you're not wearing a suit and tie."

He made an unconvinced sound. "They would *beg* to serve me by the end of the night, once I *explained* things to them."

She cleared her throat. "I'm sorry? What was that? Because it sounded *suspiciously* like you were threatening *violence* against the good people of this city, who you love so much."

"...Of course not." He quickly backpedaled. "I have not forgotten our talks on that issue. I assure you, I will threaten no one during the course of the evening. I just simply do not see why we need to eat at a restaurant which is quite so... *terrestrial* focused."

"Because if we went to a restaurant under the sea, I'd drown and eating the soup would be ridiculously hard."

He scoffed. "And so once again, if falls upon the monarch of the seas to disguise himself in the dreary garb of a surface man and appear to be less than he is."

"Well, if it's any consolation, you're not very good at it."

"Strangely, yes." He brightened. "That does indeed make me feel better."

She turned the page of her magazine, waiting for him to reappear with his next change of clothes. Thus far, this shopping excursion had not been nearly as much fun as the movies would lead you to believe. In fact, it was actually kind of boring. Well, talking to Julian was always... interesting. But he was all hidden away in his little dressing room. Where was the fun in that? The experience would have been sooooo much more entertaining if the store had just allowed her in there with him.

...*So* much more interesting.

And this whole thing was taking too long.

"How about this: you need to wear a shirt to dinner because if you don't, the 'inferior terrestrial men' will get jealous and feel bad that they can't compare to your ripped physique?"

He considered that for a moment. "Why is it that no one pays any attention to *my* feelings?"

"Because your feelings are stupid." She turned another page. "Shut up and put your clothes on."

Surprisingly, Julian seemed to find that funny.

"I shall try." He chuckled. "Have you decided where we will be showing off my new look?"

"Well, I think I've been thinking about this all wrong. You're royalty and a Cape and a god and have the body to match all three." She swallowed, suddenly preoccupied with imagining the hard lines of the man's broad chest. "We need to get you out there more, you know? Nothing as formal or forced as a personal appearance. We need to show that you're a person. Just the average, incredibly hot, super-powered heroic guy, who lives an incredibly average, incredibly hot, super-powered heroic life. You're not one of those stuck-up Capes who lives in an ivory tower; you're an *every man*."

"I *hate* every man."

"Not *tonight*, you don't. Tonight, I want pictures of you rolling up in front of the hottest restaurant around like the biggest celebrity in town. Because that's what you *are*."

"...Can't we just have an evening that's about... *us*? Why does everything need to be work?"

"You know... I'm sorry if this comes off as insensitive or whatever, but I haven't really noticed you doing a whole lot of 'work,' big guy. In fact, your team mainly just seems to spend all of its time doing public relations thingies." She looked up from her magazine. "Is that how you *usually* operate? Because it's very strange. I expected there to be more... you know... fights and explosions and stuff."

"...Nope." He answered after a moment of silence, sounding confident. "...The Consortium has *always* devoted most of its time to making public appearances and dealing with the press. It's our primary focus."

She made a doubtful face, trying to imagine that. "Are you sure? That doesn't sound quite right to me."

"Positive. To change such a vital part of our culture and procedure would be utterly *unthinkable*."

She made an unconvinced sound and continued to absently flip through the magazines in the dressing room waiting area. "You almost done?"

"I was finished with this store before ever entering it." He trudged out from behind the little curtain and handed her his clothing choices. "I dislike these the least, and as long as they meet with your approval, they meet with mine as well."

She nodded. "Yeah, those looked good on you."

He nodded sulkily.

She snorted in laughter. "You really resent having to wear clothes, don't you?"

"I resent *all* of surface culture."

"Oh, there you go again. Whenever we get to talking about you as a person, you have to switch it around and turn it into a conversation about your hatred for the surface world."

"Terrestrials are..."

"Don't care." She cut him off. "Unless you're going to talk about yourself, me, or us, I don't want to hear it."

He closed his mouth, looking unhappy.

"I realize that this is going to completely rob you of your favorite little conversation starters like: 'You know what I hate about your people?' or 'Your parents *doubtlessly* deserve to die because...' and 'The undersea world is superior to you for the following reasons...', but the truth of the matter is that I just don't find it overly interesting to have to defend myself and my 'kind' to you, Julian. So you're either going to learn to deal with it, or we're going to call off this whole date thing, okay?"

"I understand." He nodded. "I will make sure that I only hate silently."

"Excellent." She smiled up at him. "Thanks for making that effort." She held up the magazine she had been reading. "Incidentally, look who's got his pretty face on the *cover!*"

Julian stared at the image for a long moment, prompting her to flip the magazine over to see what he found so interesting. The picture on the front showed a variety of Consortium members, including Julian. ...Unfortunately, the editors had placed the text advertising the story inside right across Julian's head, obscuring his face and most of his body. The rest of the Capes were clear, but he was almost entirely covered.

Damn.

She hadn't seen that. All she paid attention to was the fact that he was on the cover, not that he was chosen as the least important person in the image and was the one the editors felt would sell the fewest magazines.

She cleared her throat and quickly put the magazine down. "Listen, I know that it doesn't look like it right now, but just give me some more time and I *swear to you* that I will have everyone in this city knowing your name and realizing the kind of man you are, okay? I work with terrible people on a daily basis and make them look great, but I don't even need to do that with you because you *are* great. For once, I don't have to lie. All I have to do is show people what a truly *good* man you are." She gently patted his hand, trying to reassure him. "Don't worry about it."

"I am not worried."

"You *look* upset."

"No. I am used to being discounted and ridiculed, Lady Bridget. I assure you, this is nothing new. To be quite honest, at this point in my life, anything else would be strange and disconcerting."

She dropped the merchandise onto the counter, not even bothering to check to see if Julian wanted to pay for it. That was the advantage of dating someone who had no pockets and no ID: you could remain certain that you would be picking up the tab for things. ...Unless he decided to pay using gold coins anyway, which was causing all manner of difficulties with her creditors. The people at her credit card company had phoned back to request *more* of the coins, and the phone company had called the police on her, assuming that her account was linked to some sort of robbery or money laundering ring or something. She had spent the better part of the evening sorting it out, and was pretty sure that she would be dealing with the fallout of his "help" for years to come.

She couldn't help but wonder just *where* he had gotten that gold though, or why he didn't use it more often. Hell, for that matter, they were currently on a *date*, but he had showed up empty handed. No golden treasures or gemstones. Nothing.

Well, not "nothing." He had showed up at her door with flowers. ...Or the *seeds*, anyway. She had asked him just what the hell that was supposed to mean, and he had carefully explained that if he had brought her cut flowers, that would be bringing her death. If he brought her seeds though, life would emerge from them and bring beauty to the world the same way she did. ...Or something. She was kinda reading between the lines on it. He hadn't been quite so eloquent and she was pretty sure he had trashed the surface world a few times in his version of the statement, but the sentiment had been in there somewhere.

It was actually kinda sweet.

And weird, because they were pumpkin seeds, but again, the *thought* was what counted.

She popped another of the seeds in question into her mouth and absently chewed on it and pointed at her companion. At the moment, he was glaring at one of the store's mannequins as if it represented all of humanity. "He's... uh... he's going to go ahead and wear the stuff out of the store, okay?"

The salesman shrugged disinterestedly and handed her back her change.

She tossed him the bag. "Suit up, big guy. We got plans."

He returned a moment later, dressed for dinner and looking *incredible*. It really wasn't fair that he could just walk into some random men's store and throw on some random thing and end up looking that good. She spent *hours* trying to look presentable, and failed even at that. But this bastard could just effortlessly look like an angry runway model.

Unfair.

"You know, Jules, I finally understand why all those movies have that moment with the big reveal where the other person is left speechless, because... you might hate clothes, but they look *damn* good on you." She held out her hand, drawing attention to his outfit. "I mean, look at that! Wow! You're not going to tell me that you don't *know* how hot you look in that."

"It *is* very warm." He agreed, pulling at the collar of his very expensive dark blue suit. "I feel like I'm being strangled by something."

Her eyes narrowed. "You wrinkle that suit I just bought you, and you're going to be strangled by *me*. I've spent a lot of money on you, and I expect to be rewarded with hours of staring at your hotness and none of your complaining about it, clear?"

"We are clear." He started after her. "When I die from these tight garments though, please take them off to bury me at sea."

"Since the *second* you put those clothes on I've been thinking about taking them off you, Julian. Don't worry about that at all." She marched out the door and back onto the street, with him following behind. "Now, I've looked into it, and I've made reservations at the most popular restaurant in town."

"I'm surprised they had an opening."

"That's one of the advantages of knowing a computer system designed to hack *other* computer systems, Jules." She grinned at him. "Their reservation system really needs better security."

"...Am I allowed to mock them to their faces about that fact, or is that forbidden?" He asked seriously.

"We'll put a pin in that and wait until we've already eaten, how about that?"

He nodded. "Sounds like a fair compromise."

"See how easy it is to get along with terrestrials?" She threw her arms wide, as if showing him the world. "Isn't this so much easier than trying to kill us? All you need to do is find common ground."

"Having common ground was always the problem, Lady Bridget. They believe they can take mine and force me onto theirs."

She frowned at him. "It sounds like you're being negative again..."

He shook his head. "Absolutely not. I have not even mentioned my *festering* contempt for the masses of humanity which currently surround us. I remain at my *most* positive."

She nodded sharply, starting across the intersection ahead of him. "*Good.* You shouldn't be so negative, it's bad for the skin."

"I don't believe that."

"Do you know what not believing something is called?"

"Being rational?"

"Negativity." She shook her head in condemnation. "You're stuck in a negative head space and you need to find your way out of it. It's blocking you from seeing what's really important in life."

"I *assure you,* I know *exactly* what is important in life."

"Let me guess: killing humanity?"

He shrugged. "Eventually. That would be number two on the list."

"...And number one?"

"I'll tell you later."

She made a face at him. "Jeez, aren't we mister mysterious all of a sudden?"

"I'm not..."

"Stop!" Someone yelled. "*Someone stop him!*"

Ahead of them, a man was fleeing the scene carrying an elderly woman's purse. He raced down the sidewalk directly towards them.

Julian watched the goings-on impassively and moved to the side to allow the man past. Bridget frowned at him in annoyance. He was *supposed* to be a super-hero! *She* knew it, but for some reason, *he* could never quite grasp how amazing a Cape he was! ...Well, he *sometimes* was anyway. He was just too involved in his own head and his own drama to stop and think about all the good he could do for the world. All the people he could help, who would then actually listen to his ideas about man's relationship with the sea. It was all...

To her surprise, Julian cut off her line of thought by casually shoving the purse-snatcher as the man ran by. The guy stumbled off the sidewalk and into the street where he was positively *leveled* by a passing cab.

Julian didn't even break his stride. "Always cross at crosswalks or you get run over, surface man." He said cordially. "This is an important lesson."

Her mouth hung open in amazement. "Did you just help someone?"

He shook his head. "No. I launched an attack against one specific member of the surface world. And it was *glorious.*"

She laughed, her smile growing. "No, no. I think you just protected someone because they *needed* your help." She nodded. "This is a big step for you."

"Lady Bridget, if I could somehow arrange it so that the entire race of humanity was in that position, I would take *great* delight in pushing them *all* in front of a moving vehicle."

"...That would have to be a pretty big vehicle."

"Indeed. It would..."

And that's when the Taser hit him.

****

Three hours later, they were finally out of the police station and back on their way to dinner. *Apparently*, it was somehow against the law to push someone into the path of a moving vehicle, even if they had allegedly committed a non-violent petty crime. Something about deadly force and unarmed fleeing suspects.

The guy hadn't EVEN died! They were all being unreasonable.

This whole town was going downhill.

What was the world coming to? Back in the *old days,* no one would have blinked to see a Cape toss a *dozen* scumbags into the path of a moving car, train or planetoid. But you put *one* little punk into the hospital, all of a sudden it was like the end of the fucking world.

She patted Julian's hand, trying to ignore the fingerprint ink still staining his pretty hands. "Don't worry about it, okay? I'll handle this with the newspapers in the morning and make sure they realize what *really* happened."

"Do I *seem* worried, Lady Bridget?"

"Well... no. But *I* worry because I know how important your image is to you, and getting arrested isn't really going to help you achieve your goal of becoming protector of the world."

He shrugged. "I've come to terms with it." He glanced down at his paperwork. "And my attorney will have returned from her honeymoon by then, so I think everything will work out fine."

"As long as you're *sure*." She said again worriedly. "Because if you're really upset over this, I can go take care of it right now."

He shook his head. "No, we're going to dinner."

"The tabloids are going to report how you viciously attacked someone unless I get in front of this, Julian."

"We're going to dinner."

"I really think I should..."

He cut her off. "I really don't care what they say about me. It won't be anything they haven't said a million times before in a million different ways, when they notice me at all, which isn't very often." He started off down the street again. "I've done my good deed for the day, received my reward for it, and now I just want to enjoy a quiet meal with a delightful companion, and try to forget that this city exists at all."

She hurried after him. "You're not going to let this get in the way of helping people out in the future, are you?"

"I assure you, this will not change my thoughts on that matter *at all.*"

****

"There." She sank down into her seat. "Isn't this lovely?"

Julian made a non-committal sound and scooted his chair further away from the woman sitting four feet to his right, obviously disliking being among people. "...Lovely."

Bridget opened her menu. "Any idea what you might want to order?"

He started staring at something over her shoulder.

"Julian?"

He cleared his throat. "I will have whatever you wish for me to have."

She frowned at him in annoyance. "That's not how this works and you *know it*. The point is for you to relax and really get in touch with yourself this evening. I think you should have one meal where you don't go on and on about your people's plight, or talk about destroying anything."

He opened his menu, still looking distracted for some reason. "No, no. I agree. It will be nice to escape the burdens of ruling 3/4s of the globe for an evening. ...I'm sure it can take care of itself for a few hours."

"Absolutely." She nodded. "You're always so *serious* all the time. You need to relax."

"You are possibly the only person in this world who has ever accused me of working too hard, Lady Bridget."

She made a non-committal sound, trying to decide between the pork belly and the ceviche. "Just because you're the best Cape this city has doesn't mean you can't take a day off."

He flipped his own menu over, looking unhappy. "You are also the only person in the world who would ever accuse me of being a hero."

"You *are* a hero." She told him with utter certainty. "I've seen it. I know It. I've *lived* it. If the others can't see that too, then that's on *them*." She tapped on her menu. "I'm going to have the pork belly."

"What exactly have I ever done for you that's heroic?" He sounded baffled. "Because I have not found 'Honda' yet. His location continues to elude me."

She snorted, taking a sip of her wine. "Oh, I'm not worried about that. Honestly, I forgot all about it. I'm talking about..." She frowned at him again, noticing that he wasn't listening. "What's wrong?"

He refocused on her and cleared his throat. "...Nothing. Don't trouble yourself. All is well."

She made a face. "Well *something's* bothering you."

"Nope. Just enjoying this fine meal."

"You mean the meal that hasn't even been *ordered* yet."

"...The *anticipation* is..."

"Cut the shit, Julian."

He cleared his throat again. "I said everything is fine, and it is. Just enjoy the magic of the evening."

She refolded her menu and began to look around the restaurant, searching for the cause of the man's distress. Usually he was only too eager to complain about things which were bothering him, but for some reason, he was being all secretive and quiet now.

She swiveled in her chair and her eyes cut to the area behind her, just to the right of the reception area. "Ah." She turned back to the table. "Okay, if you don't mention the lobsters, I will."

He focused on his menu. "I don't know what you're talking about."

"Liar!" She yanked the menu from his hand. "You're getting all upset about it and it's going to ruin our date."

"I promise you, *nothing* will ruin this date."

She crossed her arms over her chest and leaned back in her chair. "And that's really what you want then? To just sit here and eat?"

He shifted in his chair. "I am sure that... they lived... full and contented lives." He flipped his menu over. "Their cries are..."

She rolled her eyes. "And you're just going to sit here and listen to that?" She pointed at the tank. "You're going to listen to innocent lobsters crying or whatever?"

"I am forbidden from acting against the surface world for the duration of our date, and even if I weren't, I have *no* intention of ending this evening early. A *volcano* could suddenly erupt from the kitchen, and I would still be sitting right here eating with you, because there is no where I would rather be." He pointed at something on the menu. "Do the short ribs have fish in them? They aren't like whale ribs or anything, are they?"

She let out a long sigh, then placed her napkin onto the table. She leaned closer to him. "I'll distract the waiter, you grab your friends."

He glanced up at her. "That is not necessary, Lady Bridget. I will not ruin this meal."

"And you really think I can sit here knowing that something's crying for help?"

He shrugged. "I've done it for years."

"Well, you're a hero now and heroes help the innocent."

"Typically, most surface people don't include the denizens of the deep in their conception of 'innocent.'"

She stood up. "Well, I'm not 'most people.'" She started towards the front of the restaurant. "Grab your magic pitchfork; we're leaving."

He obediently hurried after her.

She stormed up to the maître d'. "Hi, I'd like to complain about..." her mind went blank, "...umm... your wine list."

The man frowned at her. "It is the most extensive in the city, madam."

"Uhh... yes. Yes, I know." She leaned against the podium, trying to block his view of the lobster tank. "*That's* my complaint. It's confusing and makes me feel bad about myself. I want fewer wines to choose from."

The man stared at her for a long moment, obviously beginning to question his choice to ever go into the service industry in the first place. "...I understand." He stood straighter. "I'm sorry that you feel that way."

"...I need to speak to your manager."

"Yes, of course." The man began to move around her towards the kitchen.

She gasped and moved to block him. "Wait! Where are you

going?"

"...To get the manager?"

She shook her head. "No, no. That's okay. You don't need to do that. Just stay here and talk to me." She glanced over her shoulder to spot Julian carefully filling a bag with lobsters. "...Just don't move."

"Hey!" One of the other patrons shouldered his way towards the tank. "What do you think *you're* doing!?!"

Julian ignored him. "This doesn't concern you, terrestrial. Continue eating your victims."

The man shot a hand out to grab Julian's wrist. "Listen, pal. I know who you are. You're that fish-man asshole that's letting those SPRM clowns *ruin* this city. I don't care if you're planning on Freeing your Willy with your little girlfriend here or not, but I came to eat *lobster*, so I'm *going* to eat lobster!"

Julian yanked his hand free. "If you touch me again, you're going to be eating *all* of your meals through *a straw*."

The man pushed him.

Julian pushed him back, hard enough to knock him off his feet and into the dessert cart. The man toppled over the pastries and crashed into several of the diners.

Bridget gasped. "Ummm..." She looked around the restaurant, trusting her years of public relations experience to get them out of this jam. "...Ummm..." She took off towards the door. "RUN!" She tossed some cash at one of the waiters on the way out. "For the lobsters!"

Julian calmly strolled out after her, bag of Crustaceans in hand. "I do not believe in tipping." He told the waiter seriously. "Good night."

CHAPTER 17

KING: "HERE'S THE THING I DON'T UNDERSTAND ABOUT THE CONSORTIUM GANG: IF THEY CAN GAIN FORGIVENESS FOR DECADES OF UNSPEAKABLE HORRORS BY DOING ONE NICE THING, THEN WHY DOES DOING ONE BAD THING WIPE AWAY DECADES OF GOOD WORK DONE BY OTHERS? WHY SHOULD I SUPPORT THE CONSORTIUM FOR ELIMINATING THE FREEDOM SQUAD, WHEN NO MATTER WHAT THE SQUAD DID, THEY COULDN'T HOPE TO COMPARE TO THE APPALLING THINGS THE CONSORTIUM HAS DONE DURING ITS SHOCKING HISTORY?"

STORMS: "THE CONSORTIUM DID BAD THINGS WHILE THEY WERE VILLAINS. THE FREEDOM SQUAD DID BAD THINGS WHILE THEY WERE CAPES. TO ME, IT'S AN ENTIRELY DIFFERENT SITUATION, BECAUSE I DIDN'T PLACE MY TRUST IN THE CONSORTIUM WHILE THEY WERE DOING THOSE BAD THINGS."

KING: "YOU SEEM TO ACKNOWLEDGE THAT BOTH OF THEM ARE BAD PEOPLE AND THAT THEY BOTH DO BAD THINGS THOUGH, SO, I ASK AGAIN: IF THE RESULTS ARE THE SAME, WHAT THE HELL IS THE DIFFERENCE BETWEEN ONE GROUP OF BAD PEOPLE AND ANOTHER?"

TRANSCRIPT OF "KING OF CAPES AND COWLS," MEDIA: TELEVISION, SHOW: 1408, NEWSCHANNEL 6, FRIDAY 21:00-22:00 EST, NETWORK SEGMENT-ID: 918000606

15 years ago

Bridget sat on the chair in the Freedom Squad's command room and couldn't help but feel like all of this was some sort of beautiful dream. For the past ten years, she had been president of the Honey Badger fan club, and now she was getting the opportunity to spend some time with the man himself! It was all very exciting. True, her interest in the club itself had lessened of late, but it was still a big day for her. She had been very into Capes in her younger years and had kept up with the club just out of habit, and because she had made so many friends. All in all, it was a fun organization to be a part of, and even if she didn't attend every meeting anymore, she still followed what was going on. Hell, she had even looked into starting a local chapter at her university since it was a great way to meet people.

The past few months had sort of rekindled her interest in Capes and villains though, thanks in no small part to her recent run-in with that handsome fish-man at the theme park. She wasn't entirely certain where he fit into all of this, but if he was now on staff with the Freedom Squad, then she was *much* more interested in keeping up with the Squad's current events.

She'd bounced a few emails with the webmistress of the leading blog about Capes, but that girl only ever wanted to talk about Fabricator for some reason. She was obsessed or something. Bridget had nothing against the man, but he couldn't hold a candle to the fish-guy. Ferral was a *boy;* Bridget was interested in a *man.* In any case, Bridget was working under the assumption that he must be working here now, which was another reason for her excitement.

She had spent a lot of time over the past few months working on trimming down for this meeting, and she was determined to make the *most* of it. *This time* the fish-guy would see her at her best.

...If he was here today.

She bit her lower lip nervously.

Well, at the *very* least, the Honey Badger would be here today, and since the man had been her idol since she could walk, that was certainly a big deal. The man was awesome. ...And would *doubtlessly* know who the fish-guy was. Badger knew everything about every Cape in the city! He'd HAVE to know the guy! And since she was president of his fan club, he'd be sure to help her out, especially if she explained the situation to him.

Because that's what heroes did. They *helped* people.

Her eyes slid over to one of the control panels on the table in front of her, and she debated with herself whether she should just start pressing random buttons to see what happened.

A BIG part of her wanted to see what would happen. It was an almost *uncontrollable* urge...

The door on the far wall opened and the Honey Badger stormed in.

The man himself.

She jumped to her feet, suddenly feeling like she was fourteen and he showed up at her freshman dance or something. Her mouth felt dry and all she could manage was an awkward wave. "...Hello." She choked out. "...It's...uh... good to see you. ...Or meet you, or... you know... whatever."

It wasn't that she'd ever really had a crush on the man or anything. ...Well, not in years anyway. Just that he was the epitome of Caping in her mind. Her model of manhood. He was strong and brave and tough. He protected the people and was a champion of the weak.

The man stalked forward. "Do I know you?"

She cleared her throat. "Bridget Haniver? I'm president of your fan club?" She held out her hand. "It's an honor."

He looked down at her hand in confusion, then up at her official Badger fan club mask. Honestly, she hated wearing the goddamn thing since she felt like she was five years old whenever she had it on, but it was in the bylaws that she needed to have it on during all official club sessions.

She had her twelve year old self to blame for that one. At the time it had seemed like such a cool idea. In retrospect, it was really something that she should have struck from the books while she had the chance. Sadly, as time went on and the club got bigger and bigger, it was basically out of her control now. There were hundreds and hundreds of members, and she just didn't have the sway to change things. She'd created a monster. Still, the size of the club meant that she never had to really worry about not having something to do, since there was always some sort of activity going on. Bridget liked having that option, even if she rarely used it anymore.

As it was, she felt like she had outgrown the whole "Cape" scene. It just wasn't really her thing any longer. ...Well, except the fish-guy. She was still *totally* interested in learning more about him.

She cleared her throat again. "It's... uh.... good to meet you again, sir. You came to our fifth anniversary dinner a few years ago, if you recall." She shifted on her feet uneasily.

He pointed at her. "You were the one who dumped the shrimp cocktail on me."

She winced. "And again, I'm *so* sorry about that."

He waved a hand. "Forget it. I have."

...Except he obviously *hadn't* or he wouldn't have mentioned it.

"...Yeah." She fidgeted awkwardly, trying to think of a good segue into the topic and then decided that she really didn't care. "...Umm... do you happen to know... like, this big dark-haired guy who can breathe…" She trailed off, realizing that the man wasn't paying attention.

His eyes crept down her body and for some reason, the action made the hair on the back of Bridget's neck stand on end. She wasn't entirely sure why, but something about it made her suddenly uneasy.

Which was just silly.

He reached out a hand to run it through her hair, his eyes focused on her chest. "My… how you've sprouted."

She pushed away from the table and began to put some distance between them, suddenly very uncomfortable. "…Yeah, well, you know, it has been a few years." She strolled to the other side of the table. "…So, where is everyone today?" She tried to ask casually, wishing that she weren't alone here with him.

He shrugged. "Around." He made his way to the other side of the table. "But don't worry. They won't *disturb* us."

"…Oh." She backed up another step. "…That's umm… good. It'd be a shame if there were someone else here to get in the way of our meeting." Her back hit the wall. "Because I'm sure that you'd… you know… want to make sure that no one saw what was going on and in *any way* misinterpret our *utterly* platonic working relationship."

He ignored her. "If you show me your tits, I'll show you 'platonic,' girl."

She blinked in confusion as her mind tried to catch up with what was happening. "…I'm sorry?" She whispered, wanting to make sure she had heard him right.

He reached out a hand to grab at her. "I *said…*"

She pushed him away. "*Stop*." She bit out. "I didn't come here for that."

"That's okay." He yanked her forward. "I can do all the 'coming' for *both of us.*"

Bridget pushed against him, trying to get free, to no avail, then did what any girl raised on footage of Capes in action would do: she jammed her thumbs into his fucking eyes. The man let her go, howling in pain. Bridget used the opening to run for the door and freedom. Sadly, the man was as quick as he was reported to be and he vaulted over the table to arrive at the door first. She skidded to a stop in front of him, and he wiped away some of the blood streaming down his face from under his furry badger mask.

He flashed a vicious smile. "Oh, I think I'm going to *enjoy* this. I *like it* when they put up a struggle." He backhanded her and Bridget was knocked off her feet. She slid ten feet across the floor and impacted the base of the command console.

Her entire face felt like it was one huge bruise. She understood the basics of combat, but she was in *no way* a fighter. She hadn't been in a fight since she was 8 and one of her cousins pushed her down and stole her Darcie doll. She had never been hit in her entire life, let alone by someone who was a foot and a half taller than she was, a hundred pounds of muscle heavier, and who made his career from hurting people who were *far* stronger than she was. Hell, he beat up people who were stronger than *he* was. The man was renowned for his combat skills.

Bridget had no chance.

She started to get back up onto her feet anyway though, just because she wasn't a quitter. If he was going to...

She swallowed, unable to get her brain to even fully form the words in question.

...then she was going to make certain that she was either unconscious or *dead* when he did it. As long as she was alive and conscious, she was going to try to hurt the bastard.

He kicked her in the ribs, knocking the air from her lungs.

He chuckled, as if this was a fun way to spend an afternoon. "You know, I just don't think there's a better sensation in the world than the feeling of some slut's breasts smashing against my foot as I'm kicking her." He did it again, just to drive his point home. "It's like nature provided some padding so that my foot doesn't get sore, and once I'm done, it leaves the *sexiest* bruises on her body."

She tried to crawl under the table to get away, but he dragged her out by her foot again. She used the opportunity to kick him in the face as hard as she could, which barely even stunned him. The man was used to getting hit by people who were a whole hell of a lot stronger than she was.

He laughed again. "Nice shot." He readjusted his jaw. "I still owe you for that shrimp cocktail thing, don't I?" He backhanded her across the face. "You dumped it right on my lap." He loomed over her, pressing his crotch towards her and beginning to fumble with the fastening on his pants. "So how about I make you lick it all clean?"

She bit his leg hard enough to draw blood, then spat out a chunk of fabric and skin. "DON'T YOU FUCKING TOUCH ME!" She went for his eyes again.

He dragged her back under him and slammed his fist into her face, causing her to see stars. She could tell that he had broken something, as blood now coated the area beneath her nose and filled her mouth.

"Oh, you've got a lot of *spunk,* don't you?" He ran his fingers through the blood, drawing little hearts on her bruised cheeks with it. "I'm going to *enjoy* watching you break, girl. See, the more you fight, the more turned-on I get. And the more turned-on I get, the more *fun I'll have with you.*"

She weakly raised her arm one more time in an effort to push him off, but he backhanded her again. Her head flopped down against the tile floor and all she could see was a dim fog. It was like being a million miles away.

...She felt so sleepy. ...Yes, she should fall asleep and just...

"Attention Freedom Squad!" A voice suddenly boomed through the room from the speakers below the large viewscreen on the wall. "I am contacting you to inform you that I have taken control of the Texxron Oil Company's headquarters, in retaliation for their crimes against my kingdom, and unless my demands are met within the hour, I will..." The voice paused, apparently just seeing the scene displayed before him on his side of the screen. "...What the hell is that?"

Badger's hands left her as he focused on something new. "*Not* a good time, Fish Stick."

Bridget weakly moved her head to see a shadowy image on the viewscreen which filled one entire wall of the command room.

"What is going *on* over there?" The man on the screen gestured towards the camera. "Just what do you think you are doing to that scrawny female surface-dweller?"

"*Stay out of this!*"

"No, no." The man on the screen shook his head. "I expect a certain degree of *professionalism* when I contact my arch-enemies and issue them my evil demands. I do *not* expect them to be distracted with brutalizing children while I am speaking." His eyes narrowed. "I *knew* I should have looked around the city for a *better* group of heroes to begin taunting. You people are simply not living up to my requirements." He shook his head angrily. "Not at *all*."

Badger let out an annoyed sigh. "Don't you normally just bother The Retiarius with things like this?"

"I learned today that he has retired to a rest home in Jersey City, and so I am making my demands to you people *directly*." The man on screen straightened his cape. "Now then, unless my demands are met, I will..." He paused, pointing at her. "...Is that girl okay?" His piercing eyes narrowed dangerously. "What have you *done to her?*"

Bridget's eyes came into greater focus, and she recognized the guy from the amusement park. "...Help." She choked out weakly, her voice a whisper. "...Please help."

The fish-man's eyes locked with hers, despite the stupid mask she was wearing and the fact that her face was bloodied and bruised. He stood straighter. "Everything will be fine, Miss." He said calmly, as if that were the final word on the matter. "Don't be afraid. I have the situation in hand."

...And for some reason, Bridget believed him. She wasn't sure why. The guy was God knew where right now and only communicating with the Freedom Squad via teleconference... and was also apparently the *bad guy,* but when he told her that she would be fine, there wasn't a question in her mind that she would be.

She started to pull herself towards the screen, as if the man's mere image could somehow protect her.

Badger rolled his eyes and followed her.

"Badger?" The man on screen said calmly.

Badger ignored him.

"Look at me, Badger." The man said again.

Surprisingly, he did just that.

"I realize that you are a man who chose heroism because it presented him a chance to find an acceptable target for violence rather than from any real moral principles about the nature of right and wrong, but I am *telling you* that you have struck that woman for the *last time.*" The man on screen spoke slowly, his words filled with complete confidence. "Do you understand what I am telling you?"

For some reason, the man's tone caused even Badger to stop and think about what he was about to do. He looked up at the image on screen for a long moment, as if seeing the man for the first time.

"Fuck you, Chicken of the Sea." Badger finally bit out. "What are you going to do to stop me, huh? Last time I looked, even if you *were* in the room with me, you *still* couldn't stop what was about to happen. So how about you just *go away.* You go ahead and kill all those people you kidnapped. I won't even tell anyone and we'll call it even. If not, sit there and watch what I'm about to do to this little whore if you want. I can show you how to *really* give a girl a good time. Probably the only time a dickless little guppy like you will ever get to see a naked woman, anyway."

Badger started forward towards her again and Bridget scrambled away from him along the floor, closer to the screen.

"I am King of the Seas, you little rodent. A *god.*" The man told him calmly, his voice filled with authority and power. "When a *god* tells someone to stop," he hefted up his trident, twirled it in the air and slammed its spines into the ground, "they *stop.*"

The viewscreen sputtered with static for a moment and Bridget let out a frantic gasp, afraid of losing her only friend in all this. Thankfully, it stabilized. A second later, the entire room rocked as if hit by a shockwave and every alarm in the building seemingly sounded at once.

She put her hands over her ears and screamed, the sounds impossibly loud, probably because of her head injury.

Badger swore and got swiftly to his feet, just as two men ran in the door. She dimly recognized one of them as Wyatt Ferral, AKA "Fabricator," and the other one was his brother Peter.

"Whadda we got?" Wyatt looked up at the screen. "Sargassum!?! What *fiendish evil* have you committed *this time!?!*"

Peter pointed at Bridget and whispered something to his brother. Wyatt looked at her and his face turned ashen. He looked back towards the screen. "...Did you do this?"

"I find that insulting. I did *nothing* to that emaciated little mortal." The man on screen readjusted his cape imperiously. "All of *my* victims are in these offices."

"Not *you.*" The younger man bit out, his gaze leveling at Badger and he pointed at Bridget as if drawing attention to the bloody woman the older man must have just overlooked. "*What the hell did you do!?!*"

Badger began to prowl towards the two boys and Peter whispered something to Wyatt again. The boy didn't seem impressed. "I don't care." He told his brother seriously, meeting Badger's eyes again, standing his ground. "*Let him try.*" He braced his feet, obviously expecting there to be a fight. "I'm *not* a little girl. Let's see how that sadistic fuck likes getting hit *back.*"

Technically speaking, if anything, the boy looked younger than she was, but he was evidently one of those people who thought of himself as the most responsible and mature person in the room.

The man on screen cleared his throat. "I have contacted you all today to inform you that I have taken control of the Texxron Oil Company's headquarters for their crimes against my kingdom, and..."

"Can you hold on a second, Sargassum?" Wyatt cut him off. "I need to *talk* to Badger for a minute."

"Take your time." The man on screen absently examined his cuticles. "Your deadline is not for fifty-four minutes."

Wyatt and Badger went into the hall and their muffled yelling could be heard even through the closed steel door, as well as the sounds of things breaking in a struggle.

Peter knelt down in front of her and she cringed away.

"Hey!" The man on screen's voice boomed through the room again. "Leave that child *alone*."

Peter smiled as if he found that funny, and held up his hands to show he meant no harm. "*Relax*, Jules. I'm not going to hurt her." He gently began cleaning the blood from her face and he lowered his voice. "I'm *truly* sorry for this, by the way. Sometimes... sometimes it kind of sucks to be me. I have to *do* things that..." He let out a long breath. "I mean, I know this has been a nightmare for you, and I *wanted* to save you from that, I swear to God I did, but I could see that sometimes the egg has to break before the bird can fly. ...And because the bird which comes out is so *important*, even if you *knew* the egg would be..." He swallowed, looking guilty and disgusted with himself for some reason. "...Well, never mind. In any case, I'm *truly* sorry. I hope you understand what I'm trying to say here."

"*I* don't, so I can only assume she doesn't *either*. Save your lies and platitudes for someone who doesn't know the violence inherent in your kind." The man on screen paused, his face darkening again. "...Why are you still touching her?"

"Just trying to make certain she's okay, Jules." Peter told him calmly, then pulled out an ice pack which he seemed to have brought into the room with him for some reason, and gently placed it on her cheek. "Lucky thing Jules was here, huh?" He nodded. "Guy's not so bad once you get to know him. Annoying sometimes, but he's always there when you need him, and in my book, that means he's *alright*." He moved to wipe away more blood, and she jolted, expecting to be struck again.

"You're scaring her, Peter." The man on screen said evenly, as if trying to calm her down. "Just give her space."

The boy smiled again and backed away. "You got it, man. Whatever you say."

"You will be okay now, child." The man on screen said. "The Ferral boys will not hurt you. They are exemplars of all I *detest*, but they are honorable protectors of your surface world."

Bridget began to pull herself back to her feet, and rearrange her clothes which had gotten... disarrayed in the fight. ...She tried not to think about the man's hands pulling and ripping at them...

"Miss?" The man on screen said.

She looked up at him.

"You're safe now. Do not let this encounter imprison your mind in the future. You did *nothing* wrong. You are *better* than him. And you proved that." He shook his head. "Do not let thoughts of him return you to this room."

"...Thank you." She choked out.

He looked uncomfortable for some reason. "...Indeed. I..."

"*No*." She began to cry. "*Thank you.*"

He bowed his head respectfully. "I am at your service, my lady. I..."

Before he could say more, the door flew open and Wyatt was standing there, finishing his argument with Badger. His clothes were ripped as if he had just been in a fight with the other man. "*TRY IT, ASSHOLE!* You just fucking *try it!* Better men than you have figured out that I'm NOT SOMEONE TO CROSS! And even if by some MIRACLE you DO end up beating me, my aunt works in the DA's office and I'll see to it that she puts you away for so long that badgers will be fucking *EXTINCT BY THE TIME YOU GET OUT!!!*" He prowled into the room, his anger visible.

"Wyatt?" The man on screen said evenly. "*Calm.*"

The boy frowned at the screen, then refocused on her and winced. He swore under his breath and made a visible effort to relax. He cleared his throat. "...Are you okay? I mean, obviously you're *not* 'okay' okay, but I mean..." He trailed off. "...I'm *so* sorry. I know that doesn't really mean anything, but I'm just... I mean... If you tell me what happened, I *swear* to you *on my life* that I will make him *pay* for it."

She limped towards one of the chairs and leaned against it. "...I just want to go home."

"No. You can't just..." He winced again. "I mean, you're free to do whatever you want, obviously, but I think we should talk to someone about this and..."

"The girl says she wants to leave, Wyatt." The man on screen said as if that were the final word on the matter. "Stand aside and let her go if that is what she wishes."

"But if she just *tells me* what happened, we can..."

"You can what?" The man asked. "What can you do? Are you going to testify against him?"

"*Absolutely.*" The boy said. "I'll testify against him even if *she* doesn't. And if the cops won't deal with him then *I fucking will.* Wrong is *wrong.*"

"You are a *boy.*" The man on screen told him. "He would destroy you in moments."

"...I just want to go home." She said again weakly and started towards the door.

"I already took the liberty of calling you an ambulance, Bridge." Peter said reassuringly. "They'll help patch you up and listen to you if you want to talk to someone about this. They owe me a favor and they'll take you wherever you want to go and stay with you for however long you need, okay?"

Wyatt threw his arms wide. "She can't just... She can't *leave!*" The boy sounded almost scared, as if his delusions about the world and the nature of heroes were dying along with hers. "She has to... Has to..." He trailed off.

Peter cleared his throat. "Welcome to the real world, Wy." He patted him on the back. "It's okay. It'll all work out. It always does."

Bridget made her way into the hallway as more alarms sounded from somewhere.

Wyatt swore. "Oh, *perfect*." He pointed at one of the screens. "Now there's a gunman opening fire on Liberty Island." He pressed a button. "Saddle up, people. We got a job."

Bridget limped towards her waiting ambulance as the sound of Sargassum's incredulous voice filled the room. "Does no one CARE that I have taken this oil company hostage? What does some surface-dweller shooting other surface-dwellers matter!?! I kidnapped these people *first! I* should take precedence!" He paused in his tirade. "This *never* would have happened in the old days. Retiarius *never* would have brutalized such a beautiful creature, and he understood that villainy is on a *first-come first-serve basis!*"

CHAPTER 18

KING: "LOOK, ALL I'M SAYING IS THAT THE BOOK OF REVELATIONS SPECIFICALLY TELLS US THAT THE ANTICHRIST WILL BE SATAN'S ACCOMPLICE AND WILL BE A 'BEAST OF THE SEA.' EMPHASIS ON 'SEA.' AS IN: 'FROM THE OCEANS.' AS IN: 'BREATHES UNDERWATER AND CONTROLS FISHES.' HE APPEARS AS A BENIGN FIGURE, BUT REALLY HE'S JUST AFTER OUR DESTRUCTION AND WILL LEAD US INTO DEVASTATING WAR. SARGASSUM IS THE ONLY GUY AROUND WHO CAN POSSIBLY FIT THAT CRITERIA, AND I THINK ALL EVIDENCE POINTS TO HIM BEING INVOLVED IN THE END OF DAYS."

STORMS: "I THINK YOU EXAGGERATE JUST A TAD, PAIGE. JUST BECAUSE YOU DON'T LIKE THE GUY, DOESN'T MEAN THAT HE'S THE ANTICHRIST OR A FIGURE OF EVIL. WHY CAN'T HE JUST..."

KING (INTERRUPTING): "HE'S CLAIMING TO BE GOD, CONNIE! WHICH MEANS HE'S EITHER CRAZY OR A HERETIC, AND IN EITHER CASE, I DON'T THINK THAT'S THE DIRECTION THIS COUNTRY OR CITY SHOULD BE GOING. I FIND IT INSULTING AND WRONG."

STORMS: "HE'S A GOD, NOT THE GOD, PAIGE. THIS WAS ALL EXPLAINED IN THE PRESS RELEASE, WHICH I THOUGHT DID A VERY GOOD JOB OF SHOWING HOW IT WASN'T SACRILEGIOUS AT ALL."

KING: "RIGHT."

TRANSCRIPT OF "KING OF CAPES AND COWLS," MEDIA: TELEVISION, SHOW: 1408, NEWSCHANNEL 6, FRIDAY 21:00-22:00 EST, NETWORK SEGMENT-ID: 918000606

Present Day

Bridget watched in silence as the lobsters disappeared back into the sea.

"Can they survive in this water?"

"They will be fine." He told her confidently. "I advised them to head home."

"Ah."

He watched the waves for a long moment. "You know, when the pilgrims first landed, there were so many lobsters in the Atlantic, that the settlers could walk out into the water and catch them with their bare hands. Hundreds of thousands of lobster families, all living out their lives in peaceful contentment." He walked back up the beach towards her. "And then someone decided that they tasted good. And now?" He shook his head. "Their population has been decimated. A stranger invaded their peaceful lands, and they have all been expelled from their paradise."

"Jeez. You're making me feel kinda guilty here." She paused. "...So, can you communicate with crawfish too? Or are they still okay to eat? Because I totally *love* those little guys."

He made a noncommittal sound.

"That was a joke, mister gloomy." She playfully punched at his shoulder. "...Well, kinda."

He let out a long sigh. "I'm sorry that this evening has turned out the way it has. That was not my intention. We were supposed to show this city that I'm a hero, and instead, we destroyed a restaurant and stole a few hundred dollars of lobsters."

"Oh, it's fine. I *paid* for the lobsters, and I'll deal with the fallout of this little public relations snafu at the same time that I'm dealing with you getting arrested earlier." She motioned towards the surf. "Besides, I mean, who doesn't love a romantic walk along the beach?"

"Me." He pointed at the waves. "It is like being outside, looking in."

"You're being negative again."

"Sorry."

"...Umm. ...Listen." She nervously ran a hand through her hair, trying to build up her courage. "Okay... Can we have a moment of complete honesty here? Because I'm sick to death of all the bullshit pretending to think or feel something we don't."

"I *assure you,* my feelings are *entirely* genuine."

"You know what I mean." She flopped down into the sand. "...The truth is... the truth is that you scare the hell out of me."

"I'm sorry." He sat down beside her. "The power of the seas can be very intimidating. I shall strive to appear weaker than I am from now on."

She scowled at him. "Not what I meant." She absently let the wet sand run through her fingers. "I just... I don't know how to deal with you. Because you're just the greatest guy I've ever met... despite your *crippling* personality problems. And I keep expecting the other shoe to drop, because I've never exactly been what you might call 'lucky in love.'" She looked over at him. "Why do you want to be with me?"

"I told you: gods of the sea can tell the one they're supposed to be with."

She blinked at him in surprise. "...Wait. You were being *serious* about that?"

"...Sure. Why not." He shrugged. "I honestly have no idea. All I know is that when I look at you, I *know* that you're mine. I always have."

She paused to think about that for a moment, watching the surf. "...Yeah, I'm going to need something more than a vague feeling you have which may or may not be the result of divine guidance. To be quite honest, I've never really liked that idea."

"Nor have I. I often told other Eternals that the idea was *utterly* ridiculous and that I was glad that gods of the sea were not afflicted with it." He shook his head. "...But then I met you. And now I can't help but wonder if the other gods of the sea were all just assholes who no one could ever love, or if you're just so special that it doesn't matter."

"So, discounting the feeling that neither of us believes in then, why do *you* want to be with *me*?"

"Because you're the only one I've ever wanted to be with."

"See, that's a logical paradox." She frowned. "I'm really going to need you to be more specific."

"Why? Isn't that enough?"

"No." She swallowed. "...Because I'm afraid."

"Fine." He nodded. "...I know that I want to be with you, because *I'm* afraid of you looking at me the way everyone else does. And I've never been afraid of that before." He swallowed. "Not since my father died. The thing I fear most in this life is seeing that look in your eye because I've failed at something else and disappointed you. Again."

"...You won't see it."

"You say that now...," he shook his head, "...but you don't mean it. Sooner or later, you'll see how useless I am."

"I sincerely doubt that. I mean, your powers aren't *totally* useless."

"Huh?" He turned to look at her as if she were insane. "My *powers* make me the most powerful man on the planet." He pointed at his chest. "*I'm* the one who makes me useless. I can never live up to the requirements which are placed on me. I have a duty to my people. And I fail to honor it. ...Honor *them*."

She shrugged. "I think you do just fine."

They both watched the ocean for a long moment.

"Aren't you going to ask me why I want to be with *you?*"

"I wasn't aware that you *did*. Our date did not turn out especially well."

She leaned against his shoulder. "Because you saved my life once. And since that day, I haven't believed in heroes. But I believe in *you*. You showed me that there are good people in this world. And you make me feel safe."

He looked at her quizzically.

"...Remember?" She tried. "The Honey Badger thing?"

He continued staring at her blankly.

She sighed and launched into a rundown of the event in question, his face becoming more and more horrified.

"...And you really don't remember any of that?" She asked when the tale was finally told.

"...Of course I do." He cleared his throat. "...I've often thought back on it, and..."

"No, you haven't." She cut him off. "I'd be surprised if you remember it even *after* I just told you about it."

He opened his mouth to protest that idea, then slumped forward in defeat. "No." He choked out. "You're right. I have only the vaguest memory of something like that happening. I'm deeply sorry. What has to be the worst day of your life, and I barely remember it at all. In my defense, I did get tossed through a brick wall later that day though, so maybe that has something to do with it."

She nodded. "...Well, that's okay. I remember it for both of us, unfortunately. And yeah, it was a pretty bad fucking day, but if it didn't happen, I wouldn't have gotten to know who you really *are*, Julian. I'd never *understand* you. So, in the end... I'm not really sorry about it." Her eyebrows soared, surprising even herself with that revelation. "If I had to do it over again, I think I'd do the same exact thing. Because some things are worth getting beaten up for. And meeting the real you was one of them."

He nodded, his face impassive.

"You're thinking of doing something nasty to Badger's grave now, aren't you?"

"...Possibly. Cynic insists that the man isn't really dead and will return one day. I don't know that I can wait that long though, and I'm now considering having the Mortician dig him up and turn him into a zombie, just so I'll have the pleasure of killing him myself." He paused. "...Damn Ferral to hell for turning him to ash. That will make the process so much more difficult."

She smiled, finding that utterly sweet for some reason. "You know someone who can turn people into zombies?"

"So he *claims*." Julian let out a dismissive snort. "The man always seems to find some loophole about why he *can't* though, so he's probably lying. My coworkers are *all* frauds."

"Well, we're *all* rejects, Julian. If any of us were already perfect, we wouldn't need each other. We'd all have perfect lives and perfect jobs somewhere far away from here." She stretched her feet out in the sand. "We're all crazy, damaged people. We got *boatloads* of fucking problems, but we deal with them together. That's what being a family is all about."

He turned to look at her. "I'm so sorry that this event wasn't at the forefront of my mind since the day it happened or that Badger was allowed to live. Had I known that it in *any way* involved you, it *would* have and he *wouldn't have*."

"Meh." She shrugged. "He's dead now, so why worry. If it was really bothering me that much, I would have done something about it myself. Couple days in the hospital and a few sleepless nights, and I was good as new. I don't like to dwell. Hell, I'd wager that you've been beaten up worse than that in your life and didn't let it change you." She smiled at him again. "And I *totally* forgive you for not remembering clearly, so don't even worry about that at all. I mean, you probably save so many people that it all becomes a blur after a while."

"One." He kept staring at the ground. "Counting you."

"Well, I'm glad you saved yourself for me then, big guy." She smiled at him teasingly. "So, you didn't recognize me or anything? I mean, I was kinda wearing a mask and was covered in blood at the time..."

"No."

She nodded again, then realization dawned. "Do you know what that means?"

"That in addition to my many other failings, I'm also not very observant and almost sat around to watch the love of my life be beaten to death in front of me?"

"No." She batted his arm. "It means that you would have

helped *anyone* who was in that position!"

He thought about that for a moment. "...Probably not Ferral." He said seriously. "I would have just let Badger rape Wyatt." He paused again. "...Or Welles. ...*Definitely* Welles."

"You know what I mean!" She grabbed his hand. "It means that it's all a matter of perspective!" Her voice became more excited as she warmed to the topic. "You totally sucked at villainy, because you're *not* a villain! You're a hero!"

"I find that hard to believe. I am the worst villain the surface world has ever faced."

"No, no. Hear me out here because I'm onto something. You're a hero, just not to *people*. From *your* point of view, humanity is the villain, and as the hero of the seas, it's your job to protect the fish and stuff. But you *suck at it* because in order to protect them, you'd have to do bad things, and that's just not who you *are*."

"I assure you, I am *fully* capable of doing terrible things to your people, Lady Bridget. Frequently and with great personal satisfaction."

"Okay, let's review," she scooted closer to him in the sand, "what are we really talking about here? What bad things have you *really* done?"

He opened his mouth to begin listing them.

"...Bad things which actually *succeeded*." She added.

He closed his mouth, his brow furrowing as he tried to think of something. "...I think I'm partially responsible for sinking the Titanic?" It came out sounding like a question. "That's kinda bad."

"...Well, the *movie* sure was." She nodded. "Did you mean to do that?"

"Not really. I was just standing there at the time and was as surprised as everyone else."

"Uh-huh. Anything else?"

He thought about it for a minute. "...I'm sure there's something."

She shook her head. "I'm *telling you,* the *only* times I've ever seen you be as capable as I *know* you can be, is when you're doing good things." She counted them off on her fingers. "You won that fight against that guy with the sledgehammer, whose name I forget..."

"'Sledgehammer.'" He reminded her. "Capes aren't very inventive with their noms de guerres."

"Whatever." She waved him off, utterly indifferent to the hero's name. "We can't *all* be named after algae."

"I am not named after sargassum the seaweed, I am named

after sargassum the *fish.* One of mother nature's most effective predators. It lures in its prey by pretending to be what it is not, and is thus able to swallow enemies many times its own size."

"Neat, but it doesn't matter. The point is that you still kicked his ass though."

Julian's eyes narrowed. "He was breaking the rules. *No* Cape should have done what he was doing, especially not in front of you like that."

"See?" She smiled as if that proved her point. "And you punched Monty the other day when he was being a jerk to me."

He paused, as if debating something with himself. "To be fair, I think we both just found ourselves inside one of the man's plots."

"Would you have hit him either way?"

"Oh, I've wanted to hit him for *years.* This was just the final straw."

"And the only other time I've ever seen you actually win at something was saving me from Honey Badger." She paused. "...Although, those are also the only times I've technically seen you really *try* to do something..." She shook the idea from her head. "The point is that all three of those times were heroic! And the Badger thing wasn't even just about you and me, because you didn't even *know* that was me, you just knew that someone was in trouble and needed your help. You helped a surface woman because she needed it, not because you wanted to date her or whatever." Her voice broke. "...Because... because that's the kind of man you *are,* Julian. You're better than how people see you." She took his hand. "Better than how you think about yourself."

He looked like he was about to say something, then stopped and gazed out over the water again. "It's not just me who thinks that. My own mother tried to kill me once. It didn't take."

"Why would she do that?"

He shrugged. "You'd have to ask her. I think she just saw enough of this world, and didn't think either of us needed to see any more of it. So, one day when I was a child, she took me in her arms, and stepped into the waves. ...She thought we'd go together."

"...What happened?"

"We *didn't.*" He stared out over the seas. "My powers ensured that she made that trip *alone.* ...Of course, that's just my take on it. It depends on who you ask, really. I was a child at the time, so I don't exactly remember. All I know is that her end was... *unfortunate.* As she found out, there are worse things in this world than drowning."

He was silent for a long moment. "...Much worse things. But she had seen enough of this world, and simply didn't want to see anymore." He repeated, shaking his head. "I think she chose her own path, and picked one which would be *memorable.* And she tried to take me with her... but she couldn't." He swallowed, sounding haunted. "There have been moments in my life, where I regretted that. ...Sometimes I think my powers were a curse."

She tried to think of something supportive to say. "I think she was just trying to spare you the pain of life without her. She loved you and didn't want to see you hurt without her there to protect you."

"Yes. I'm touched. What a *beautiful* and *selfless* reason for her to try to *fucking kill me.*"

She snorted in laughter, then winced at her own insensitivity. "Sorry, I know that's not funny."

"The woman had emotional problems, and assuming that I would be similarly unable to deal with life was the *height* of conceit on her part. As it turned out, she was mistaken, because the world and I have gotten along just fine *without* her." He shook his head. "It wasn't the world which ruined my life; it was *her.*"

She cleared her throat. "Well, if you're looking for me to agree with you that things would have been better if you died, then I'm going to laugh in your face. You are *needed.*" She gestured to the oceans. "The *seas* need you." She nervously grabbed another handful of sand. "...*I* need you."

"Don't worry. I have never even considered taking the path she took. She was a *coward.* Rather than trying to kill us both, she should have made *changes* to the life which made her so unhappy. Left my father and found someone else. There were people who would have *helped her* if she had asked for it, but she couldn't be bothered." He shook his head angrily again. "Everett would have stood up for her. ...For *me.* He would have *been there* for us, and made certain that neither of us was mistreated. But instead, she decided that I needed to *die.* It was just *easier,* I suppose. She didn't have to risk anything if she just tossed me away along with her own life. She was just like every other surface person I've ever known; they're only *ever* focused on themselves and what *they* want. What *they're* feeling at *that* moment in time, without thinking about the future. They never stop to think that their actions affect other people and the world around them, and their decisions echo through the future like ripples in a pond. So, because she was having a bad time of it, she wound up dead, and I wound up with an uncaring bastard... and Everett wound up dying alone in a tiny room with hackneyed proverbs about 'responsibility' on the wall." He let out a long breath. "I've felt out of place my entire life because of that. Like I didn't belong anywhere. ...Sometimes it's hard to be... different."

"A fish out of water."

"Indeed."

"Well, what happened to your adoptive parents? You said you got along great with them, right?"

"...They were murdered."

"Oh, god! I'm so sorry! Do you know who did it? I mean, did they catch the guy?"

"Yes. I know who did it." He cleared his throat, obviously trying to change the topic. "And not to disagree with you, but I think you'll find that a much better explanation for the events in question where you believe that I displayed heroism, is the fact that *you* were present in every instance." He shook his head. "It's not me. It has nothing to *do* with me. It never did. If I'm able to do things which you think are 'good' or 'heroic,' it's only because you were there at the time and gave me a reason."

"What? Am I like your Cape muse or something?"

He leaned closer to her. "The promise of you is the entire reason I have done *anything* in my life."

"Wow." She mouthed. "...You are sooooo good at spouting off lines from cheap romance novels, aren't you?" She laughed nervously. "I mean, coming from *anyone else*, that's the silliest thing I've ever heard... but from you?" Her breath started coming faster again and she became incredibly aware of how close the man was to her. "...From you? It seems so...," she found herself preoccupied with his eyes, "...not stupid."

He reached up to smooth her hair behind her ear, and she turned her head so that his hand caressed the side of her face.

"It doesn't sound stupid coming from me, because I *assure you,* it is the absolute truth."

Bridget's entire body felt like it was on fire now. There was something so sensual about his calm evenness. Like he had been losing fights all these years just because he was saving his strength for what *really* mattered.

Her.

Rationally, she should have been worried about his pending legal issues, or the fact that the newspapers were going to have a *field day* with the restaurant incident, or that she was probably on the verge of getting fired from her real job, or the fact that she was sitting on a deserted beach with a super-villain... but she wasn't worried about *any* of that. At this particular moment in time, she felt utterly safe. She wasn't entirely sure *why* she felt that, but she felt it anyway.

Julian was a hero. He could protect her from *anything*. And the man was positively *gorgeous.*

Bridget really didn't believe in basing a relationship merely on the physical though, no matter how much she might have wanted the man at the moment. No, Julian was just... interesting. The man did and said the craziest things, all of which entertained her to no end.

He was gentle and funny and smart... True, he was rather crazy sometimes, but no one was perfect. And really, was humanity that great anyway? Probably not. She didn't always blame him for disliking them. Hell, he made some *excellent* points sometimes, so maybe in the end, *Bridget* was the one living in a fantasy world.

...But there *had* to be more going on here than there seemed. Bridget had never met a man in her entire life who would sit around on a deserted beach and have a heartfelt talk about his "feelings."

No.

No, there was something bigger at play.

She shook her head, pulling away from his hand slightly. "You don't want me, Julian."

"Don't I?"

"No. I'm... I'm..." Her mind raced. "I'm just the fat comic relief."

"Oh, please." He snorted. "You are *not* overweight." He shook his head, looking regretful, like he was about to break sad news to her. "And please do not become angry with me for telling you this... but I have not noticed you being especially *comical* either."

She scowled. "I'm *plenty* funny. It's just that you're so crazy that *your* craziness overpowers mine, that's all. If I were alone or with someone normal, I'd have the audience in stitches."

He blinked at her in confusion. "Audience?"

"Of the hypothetical show based on my life of which I am the co-star."

"...And why are you the co-star of a television show about your own life?"

"Because I'm the comic relief!" She sniffed in irritation. "Try to keep up."

"I am doing my best, dearest."

"The point is that you only *think* you're like attracted to me or whatever, because you just don't know anything about me."

"I know all about you, Lady Bridget. The language of the seas is bigger than terrestrial spoken word. It is also about emotion and movement. It's about recognizing what the other person is feeling, and what they want."

"...Uh-huh." She pressed her finger to her temple. "And what am I wanting right now?"

"We still have not had our dinner together. We should find a new restaurant."

"Yeeeeeeah..." She shook her head sadly. "I hope you're better at translating for fish, because you *completely* suck at deciphering what humans are thinking."

He was silent for a moment. "...I was under the impression that we had both agreed to cease lying to ourselves and each other."

She nodded. "Yep. We did."

"And yet you will *still* not admit that you are feeling exactly what I am feeling?"

"What? That I'm attracted to you?" She snorted. "*Obviously.*" She pointed at him. "I mean, *look at you!*"

"Excellent." He moved closer to her again. "So, I propose that I trust you to know who you are attracted to and not second-guess *your* choice, and *you* do the *same*." He took her face in his hands. "How does that sound?"

She met his intense gaze and her mind went blank again. "...Okay. Yeah. Sure, whatever. Sounds good."

He slowly began to lean closer to her and Bridget's mind snapped back into place, processing the scene. If she didn't stop this right now, she wasn't going to have the strength later. Her walls would be down, and Julian would see how much he meant to her.

...Ah, the hell with it.

She threw herself at him, toppling him backwards in the sand. He let out a startled sound which was lost as her lips devoured his. His momentary surprise quickly subsided and he wrapped his arms around her, pulling her closer.

Bridget finally broke away, turning her head to the side and gasping for breath as he began to trace kisses down the side of her neck.

She took the opportunity to begin tearing at his clothes. She made an annoyed sound, unable to pull his jacket off. "Goddammit! Why the hell did you buy this anyway?"

"You told me to." He tore his tie off and flung it towards the water. "Do you see why surface culture is so backward? If I were dressed as *myself,* we would both be naked by now."

"...Shit. You're *right.* Why do...?"

Her thought was interrupted by his lips slamming into hers again. She made a soft moaning sound, her entire body seeming to come alive with him so close to her.

She met his heated gaze, and his eyes flicked down to the top of her dress. She nodded. "The fucking thing is *gone.*" She wrenched at the fabric, ignoring the fact that she had spent the better part of two month's salary on it in preparation for the date tonight. It didn't matter. At the moment, it was just an obstacle to feeling his skin against hers.

She yanked the dress off and threw it away. His hands began to gently caress her body, and she closed her eyes, lost in the pleasure.

Her breath was coming in gasps now, blending in with the roar of the blood pounding through her veins and the sounds of the surf crashing against the beach beside them. Julian's hands slid under the cups of her bra and...

Suddenly, a bright light was shining in her eyes and Bridget let out an astonished yelp. She fell backwards off of Julian and into the sand...

****

Julian angrily signed his name to the booking form and began to storm from the police station. He glanced down at her. "I apologize, Lady Bridget. I have never been arrested twice in one night before. Please do not think that this is in any way a usual occurrence."

"Meh." She shrugged. "Don't worry about it. At least I finally have an interesting arrest on my police record now. I've been hanging out with you guys so much, I was beginning to feel left out." She glanced down at the paperwork. "And my mother will be so proud to hear that I've been arrested for 'indecent exposure.'" She looked back up at him. "Think your lawyer can help me with this?"

"I am certain of it."

"Good." She folded up the paper. "One less thing to worry about then." She took his hand. "And just think about how much more work she would have had if you had killed that guy like you wanted."

His eyes narrowed in anger. "He had no business telling me what I can and cannot do on the beach. The seas are *mine.* *I* will be the one to judge what is and what is not 'indecent' there, not some ridiculous *surface man.*"

"...Umm, I think a jury of our peers is going to be the one to judge it, actually."

"I *have* no peers. I am a god-king. I exist at the pinnacle of the world."

"Yeeeeah.... I'm thinking I might want *separate* trials, big guy. No offense, but you're just not going to have much jury appeal."

He nodded. "Well, I'll already be in court for the incident with the purse-snatcher anyway, so that will make it easier." He pursed his lips. "...And for freeing those poor kidnapped lobsters."

"Yeah, that's.." She trailed off as she saw a familiar name displayed on one of the TVs in a shop window as she walked past it.

She blinked, trying to clear her vision and convince herself that she wasn't seeing what she *thought* she was seeing.

"Hi, Paige! Hi, Connie!" The voice on the TV was saying. "Longtime viewer, first-time caller. What an *honor.*"

The woman on the TV said something to someone off-screen. "And you're *sure* this is legit?" Pause. "But *why?*" Pause. "Okay." She cleared her throat. "Caller, can you just please confirm what my producers are telling me?"

"I *would*, Connie, but I'm not sure what your producers are telling you." The man laughed, as though it was all simply some joke.

The other woman on the TV leaned forward in her padded chair. "We are being joined tonight by our caller, Traitor, of the Consortium of Chaos."

The screen changed to show one of Arnold's old mugshots. His ear to ear smile stood in sharp contrast to the prison number displayed on his chest. He was giving the camera thumbs up signs with both hands, indicating his approval.

The woman's voice became serious. "I'm glad that at least *one* of your gang is willing to answer for their criminal actions."

"*My* criminal actions? ...Okay. But I hope your show is on all-night, because this might take a while if you want an answer about all of them."

"What is your response to the fact that some people are saying that the city is too afraid to speak out against you, because they think you use threats and violence against the people who oppose you?"

"I'd say it sounded like we missed a few then." Arnold said nonchalantly. "Damn. Thought we got them all."

"And the people who say that you're all simply murders who should face justice for your crimes?"

He made a disinterested sound. "Haters gonna hate, Paige."

"And what is your comment to the allegation that you sold six year old Suzy Blandings a 'death ray' device at a recent yard sale you held?"

Arn gave a gasp of horror worthy of any horror movie bimbo. "I don't know *what* you're talking about. The very idea that I would hold a yard sale is *laughable.* The Consortium of Chaos is a *professional* organization, dedicated to preserving our freedoms. It is *not* a social club, and we *don't* do things like *garage sales.*"

"Really?" Paige glanced down at some paperwork which was handed to her. "That's interesting, because her mother says that you sold the girl the device for $1, and the child proceeded to use it to attack her sister's birthday party. Several injuries were reported and a skating rink was completely destroyed in the process."

The man sounded remorseful. "Sounds like a case of parental negligence to me, Paige. I mean, what kind of mother would allow their daughter to purchase a death ray at this *alleged* garage sale? Or even take their daughter to shop at one in the *first place?*" He sounded sad now. "I blame the media. Children just grow up in this culture of violence and want to act out what they see on TV and in the movies. I can understand the frustration which comes from such a senseless tragedy, but I think we need to place the blame where it belongs and not toss accusations at innocent super-heroes and death ray manufacturers."

"My co-host seems to be under the impression that your leader is dedicated to bringing about the end of days." Connie asked. "Do you have any comment on that?"

"Well, I can't speak for myself, but anyone who's ever talked to Jules knows that he *excels* at turning water into whine."

Bridget winced, turning the broadcast off. "...Okay. That's going to get us some hate mail." She pinched the bridge of her nose. "How many times did I tell you guys not to insult or belittle people's religions or beliefs? Huh? Is it really that hard?"

Julian shook his head. "I do not find it difficult. I have never mentioned any of the delusional ideas favored by your people."

"'Don't mention the bible,' I said, 'Don't compare yourself to any biblical figures,' I said, 'Don't make jokes about people's beliefs' I said, 'Don't say anything blasphemous and make yourself sound like a fucking idiot,' I said." She shook her head. "But apparently Arn is incapable of doing that. Hell, I'm not even very religious, and he even kinda pissed *me* off with that!"

"...To be fair, the host brought up the subject, and..."

She glared at him and he evidently saw that this was a losing argument.

"...And he should have just remembered your wise words on

the topic and kept his mouth shut."

She nodded sharply. "*Right.*" She started to stalk down the street again, trying to regain her composure. "But instead, now I have to go down there and sort things out."

"We do?" Julian sounded heartbroken. "...But isn't the damage already done? Could we not just return to the beach and continue with our date, and deal with this in the morning?"

She paused to consider that... Then remembered that she was a responsible person who... Who...

Shit. What did she normally do? What would be the *responsible* thing to do? ...Probably have sex with the hot guy.

Yep.

That sounded *totally* responsible at the moment.

She cleared her throat. "No." She choked out, with *tremendous* personal effort. "No, I think we need to deal with this now."

"We do? *Really?*" He made a pained sound. "*I'll put this city into its grave for this!*"

She started back towards her car. "This is just building anticipation."

"This is just building my *frustration.*" He trudged after her. "I begin to dislike this world even *more*. Just when it is about to achieve something wonderful, idiots arrive to ruin everything."

"Yep." She nodded. "Welcome to the dating scene." She got into the car. "I really should have known better than to think your friends could *ever* behave for an evening." She started the engine. "God, but they're morons."

"Told you." He tried to wedge himself and his trident into the passenger seat. "Do you understand why it's so hard not to tell everyone that now?"

"Sadly, yes."

She reached over to move some of the boxes of stuff she had purchased at their garage sale out of the way so that Julian had more room.

"I still think you're wrong about the rest of humanity though."

He stared out the car window, seeming lost in thought. "...I was wrong about them once. But I never will be again."

CHAPTER 19

KING: "...I JUST DON'T CARE. I DON'T CARE WHAT
JUSTIFICATIONS PEOPLE HAVE FOR DOING BAD
THINGS. YOU KNOW WHAT? LIFE IS ROUGH. NO ONE
HAS IT EASY. BUT THE REST OF US AREN'T DONNING
OUTLANDISH COSTUMES AND TRYING TO DESTROY THE
PEOPLE WHO MAKE US ANGRY. SOCIETY HAS RULES.
YOU EITHER FOLLOW THE RULES, OR YOU AREN'T
WORTHY OF BEING IN SOCIETY. WHY YOU CHOSE NOT
TO FOLLOW THE RULES MEANS ABSOLUTELY NOTHING
TO ME. WE'VE ALL GOT PROBLEMS."

TRANSCRIPT OF "KING OF CAPES AND COWLS," MEDIA:
TELEVISION, SHOW: 1408, NEWSCHANNEL 6, FRIDAY
21:00-22:00 EST, NETWORK SEGMENT-ID:
918000606

1912

Julian's family was missing.

He wasn't quite sure just where they had gotten off to, but they had been gone all day. All in all, it was most unusual.

When you had the entirety of the oceans in which to move, sometimes someone would get misplaced for a few minutes or hours though, but they always turned up again. And then they'd all laugh.

Julian always thought it was pretty funny the way his adopted parents worried about things. Since his father's death, Julian hadn't really worried about much. He did what he liked and didn't pay any attention to things which had always bothered his father. Julian just didn't care about that anymore.

He was free now.

True, the months after his father's death were rather hard. The man may have been a jerk and made Julian's life miserable, but Julian... well... he had still loved that mean old bastard in a way. He wasn't sure why. The man *obviously* hadn't deserved it. But Julian couldn't help the way he felt. The man was all Julian had, and trying to live up to the man's expectations had been Julian's goal for so long, he was utterly lost without that as his bedrock.

He didn't know what he was supposed to do anymore, and he had no one to discuss it with.

Instead, Julian just sat. He floated on the seafloor, and just stared off into the dark. His eyes were adapted to see through the gloom quite well, and he found the solitude restful. It was lonely, sure, but when you *were* alone, that was only natural.

He was down there alone for a long time.

Honestly, he wasn't even sure how long it had been.

Months? Years? ...Centuries?

He didn't know. Time really had no meaning down there. The sun didn't really make it that far down, only the barest hint of shifting luminescence giving any trace that there even *was* a world above.

And one day, Julian was overcome with the almost irresistible impulse to go up there and see what the mortals were up to. He'd always been rather curious, but his father never would have allowed it. And even if the old man *would* have agreed to let Julian go, Julian never would have. It would have proven his father right. It would be admitting to the man that he was a surface-dweller and that he didn't belong to the seas.

And such a thing was utterly unthinkable in Julian's world.

He was not his birth mother.

He was not a killer.

He breathed *water,* not air!

...Never air.

No matter the details of his parentage, Julian lived in the oceans and that's where he belonged. If his birth mother was a terrestrial, than that was *her* misfortune, and it was only because the seas obviously hadn't wanted her. The water *rejected* her. It robbed her of life in the same way that she had tried to rob Julian of his.

In any case, one day, Julian grew tired of his solitary life on the ocean floor and rose to the long-forgotten sight of the sun and the feeling of the wind on his face. He had floated in the calm sea, enjoying a beautiful day, not a care in the world.

And that's when he met his REAL family.

People who weren't concerned with the fact that he was half-human. Who didn't care how amazing his powers were or weren't, and who had never even met his father, let alone compare Julian unfavorably to the man.

They simply accepted Julian as he was.

They welcomed him into their lives, and always made sure

that he felt included.

Dolphins were a *magical* species. Julian didn't really have much experience with them before joining his new family, but he was fairly certain they were the finest creatures this planet had to offer. Julian's father had never liked dolphins. He called them frivolous. But Julian disagreed. Dolphins understood what was important about the world, and it wasn't the things which had always worried his father. Dolphins cared about each other. They cared about helping each other. And they cared about having fun with each other.

All in all, there were worse ways to live than that.

Julian had spent many a carefree day swimming the seas with his adopted family, and he learned more from them about love and life than he could ever imagine.

They had given him a place to belong. A place where he could be himself. A place where he was accepted and loved.

...But now they were missing.

Julian wasn't terribly worried about them though. They knew what they were doing. And besides, Julian had made sure to tell all of the other creatures of the deep that his new family was *off-limits*. Nothing would *dare* harm them, even if it wanted to.

But they were missing all the same.

Currently, he was following a lead from a very friendly sea bass, and was now floating close to the shore. He wasn't entirely sure why his family would come this close to land, but he could tell that they had.

He stared out over the ocean as the lights of the terrestrial settlement reflected off the dark water. Their structures really were quite beautiful, in their way. The illumination sparkled off the waves and made the sea look so magical.

Julian made up his mind.

He would go ashore and ask the mortals if they had seen his family anywhere. He had never really been amongst the mortals before, but he remained reasonably sure that his father had been wrong about them.

They weren't monsters.

Julian cautiously stepped from the waves and pulled himself up onto the wooden dock, which had been constructed out over the water. The feeling of the dry wood on his feet was an odd one. He could never get used to that. How could terrestrials stand it? Without the water to support you, you felt so... heavy. Burdened. Lacking grace and elegance.

There was a sickly smell in the air, but Julian couldn't identify it. He didn't have a lot of experience with air in the first place though, other than sitting around meeting halls waiting for his father, so he wasn't entirely sure that *all* air didn't smell like that.

Whatever the reason, mortals evidently did *not* dwell in the gentle paradise that the happy tile mosaics in his father's palace would have you believe. Things here were... *dirty*. ...And sticky. And the smell was everywhere.

He shouldered his way into the wooden structure and winced at the sound of the noise. Everything here was so *loud* and *irritating!*

Julian would be glad to return to the sea and forget this place. ...Just as soon as he found someone who could direct him to his family.

Julian spotted a male terrestrial standing near a large machine of some kind, and he started towards him.

"Excuse me!" He called over the din of the machines. "I'm wondering if you can..."

Julian stopped dead in his tracks as he looked down into the tank.

...The sight caused him to vomit.

Inside the large metal container floated hundreds and thousands of bodies. Horrible, horrible bodies, cut open and bleeding.

His gaze flashed over to another kettle filled with the ground remains of *more* bodies.

Another kettle filled to the brim with *boiling* bodies.

...Even the *floor* was covered with the gruesome remains of this travesty.

Julian staggered backwards, his mouth open in horror... and the full awful truth hit him like a fist. In that moment, Julian *knew* what had happened to the only people that had ever loved him. The only people that Julian had ever loved.

His gaze lowered to the foul slurry again...

They had been murdered.

Overhead, a banner proclaimed the merits of "Happy Sailor Tuna."

Julian fell to his knees, ignoring the disgusting mixture of blood and wet flesh which now coated his body.

...His father had been right. He'd been right all along. They were...

"You ain't allowed in here, mister." Yelled the murderer behind him. "Get lost!"

Julian continued staring down at the bodies, trying to come

to terms with the kind of evil it must take to do such a thing to so many innocent people.

All that death. All that pain.

He put his face in his hands and began to weep. "...Why would you *do this!?!*" He cried, tears streaming down his face. "What was their crime?"

The murderer frowned down into the vat. "What the hell are you talking about, mister?" The killer snorted. "They're only *fish.*"

And Julian's grief turned to *anger.* Ruthless fury, as strong and inescapable as the tide.

He whirled around and smashed the man away with the side of his trident, propelling him off of the vat and onto the floor a dozen feet below. Julian climbed down the ladder, feeling utterly numb. He kicked over a large barrel of fuel which was used to heat the vat.

...The fuel tank exploded in a fireball, lighting up the docks with a shifting angry brilliance. He stood back for a moment to watch the flames destroy the holding tank and its foul contents. The sickening smell of burning bodies filled the air.

He wiped his face, and slowly focused on his new enemies.

He jumped up onto the wooden crates filled with corpses and raised his voice above the blaring emergency siren and the sound of the inferno, as this terrible place burned.

"HEAR ME MORTALS!" He held his golden trident high over his head. "I am Lord Julian Thalassic Sargassum! Ruler of the waves and sovereign king of the seven seas!" He pointed his weapon at the crowd of soulless adversaries before him. "Your rape of my lands *ENDS NOW!*"

CHAPTER 20

KING: "...AND THAT'S REALLY YOUR ENTIRE EXPLANATION FOR YOUR GANG'S FAILURE? WHY THE CITY'S GOING TO RUIN?"

CALLER: "I REALLY DON'T KNOW WHAT YOU EXPECT ME TO SAY HERE, PAIGE. HELL, IT'S NOT LIKE THE CITY WAS REALLY LOOKING THAT GREAT TO BEGIN WITH. IT WAS A (EXPLETIVE) THEN, IT'S A (EXPLETIVE) NOW. THE ONLY DIFFERENCE IS NOW IT'S A (EXPLETIVE) THAT'S A LITTLE MORE ON FIRE. THE CITY ITSELF HASN'T CHANGED THOUGH. YOU'VE CHANGED, AND NOW YOU'RE NOTICING STUFF ABOUT THIS (EXPLETIVE) THAT YOU USED TO IGNORE. THAT'S ALL CHANGE IS, PAIGE. LOOKING AT THE SAME THING IN A NEW WAY."

TRANSCRIPT OF "KING OF CAPES AND COWLS," MEDIA: TELEVISION, SHOW: 1408, NEWSCHANNEL 6, FRIDAY 21:00-22:00 EST, NETWORK SEGMENT-ID: 918000606

Bridget drove across the bridge, heading back to Jersey and the Consortium's Crater Lair. Thus far, the trip had consisted of Julian staring out the window in silence, and restlessly switching the radio station, apparently looking for something which wasn't so unreservedly terrestrial-centric.

All in all, it was not the most comfortable trip.

A news station flicked across the dial for an instant, and the announcer was summarizing Arnold's less than wonderful interview on TV.

She scowled over at Julian. "I still can't believe he did that."

"The thing you don't understand, Lady Bridget, is that my team depends on my leadership to guide them, or they are utterly without direction. I should have known better than to leave them unattended. They need me so much."

****

"We have to get rid of Julian." Agent McPherson shook her head in certainty. "He's useless. There's no question about it: he has got to *go*. *Now*. He is refusing to do his job and protect this city, and is instead running around trying to romance the new press lady, who has *no* business being here *anyway*." She jabbed a fingertip against the table. "He's *done* here. Someone else is going to have to step up and take over."

The table stared at her in irritated silence.

"There is a madman trying to destroy the city!" She tried again.

Ceann shrugged. "YOU HAVE SPELLED: ALWAYS."

She threw her arms out wide. "Does *no one* here care that *millions of people* could be killed if Reece isn't stopped? Is *no one else* at all even *upset* about this!?!"

Monty continued watching her silently for another moment, his face like stone, then he shook his head. "I'm not given to bouts of theatrical sentimentality, no."

McPherson's eyes narrowed. "Julian is *out* as leader. Period." She crossed her arms over her chest. "You need to find *someone else*. That's an *order*."

"I have taken the last 'order' which I will ever take." Monty told her calmly. "And it wasn't from you."

"I'm with Julian and so is Bee." Quinn said the words like they were his final comment on the matter. "The Undersea Base crew sticks together. We won't follow anyone but him. *Period*."

"I don't think you understand. We're not 'voting,' here." McPherson shook her head. "This isn't a *democracy*. Let me spell it out for you: if you don't follow orders and see reason, we will *replace you with someone who will*. You have *no* say in this!" She leaned over the table. "So you shape up *fast*, or we'll come in here and take away your whole little operation."

"Lady, with all due respect, and I'm really sorry if this sounds like a threat but there's simply no other way to phrase it," Quinn's eyes narrowed, "but I have magic powers and you don't. So just what exactly do you think you're going to do to me? Huh? Even if you're right about our behavior and everyone in this city is worse off because of our actions, what could you *possibly* do to stop me from doing exactly what I *want* to do?" He paused a moment as though waiting for an answer. "That's right: *nothing*. So just let me do my goddamn job and shut up about it."

"You only *have* this job because we *allow you* to have it! Right now, we're *letting* you work here, but all that can change in a *second*." She held her arms wide, gesturing to the room. "You see all of this? Everything you have? This is *gone* if you don't play by my rules."

Montgomery considered that for a moment, then he took a relaxed sip from his teacup. "Let me tell you a little story, Agent McPherson. You see, I grew up in a small community where my family owned a factory. And straight through the center of town ran the railroad tracks, but once upon a time, we were just a minor operation and the train company thought we were unimportant, so for years the trains didn't stop. They just raced right past us and on to more important cities further down the line. We tried to lobby them to add us as a destination, but they refused. They thought they were better than us, you see, so we suffered through their noise and their pollution and saw none of the benefits. So... one night when my great-great grandfather Silas was a young man, *someone* placed five sticks of dynamite on the tracks down by the mill, and as a freight train went by, he blew it up. The engine ended up in pieces at the bottom of a gully and it took several weeks to repair the damage to the tracks. The railroad company got the message though, and after that, the train made three stops a day in our town. Because they knew that we'd get that train to stop. One way or the other, it was *going* to stop."

She frowned at him. "What does that story mean?

"What do you *think* it means, Agent McPherson?" He was silent for a moment. "It means that by the end, Silas Welles *owned* that same railroad. He *ruined* those men. And their children. And their children's children. All because he wanted to teach them a very important lesson about the way the world works. About what happens when you antagonize someone you simply can't control. He allowed them to see the *future*." He reached a hand out to tap the C of C coat of arms carved into the conference table, and its Latin inscription translating to: '*If I cannot move Heaven, than I shall raise Hell*.'

McPherson rolled her eyes. "What a delightful little glimpse at the freaky monsters swinging from the lowest branches of your family tree, but the point remains that you have no say in what..."

He shook his head, cutting her off again. "We *still* seem to be having some trouble communicating with each other, and I think it's because we don't know each other that well. Please allow me to introduce myself and tell you a little about *who. I. Am*." He carefully spaced each words. "My name is Montgomery Tarkington Welles, and one way or the other, I *always* get what I want." He sounded perfectly calm, almost pitying. "I cannot *be* fired, Agent McPherson. Or 'reasoned with.' Or intimidated. You cannot *scare me* with all the terrible things you believe you can do to my organization, or *threaten me* with the horrible agonies you and your government intend to inflict if I do not do what you want. You cannot 'let me' do anything, because you lack the power to *stop me* from doing anything. You cannot 'take everything I have' because nothing that I have is capable of being '*taken*,' by you or anyone else. You cannot control me by appealing to my sense of '*decency*,' or '*patriotism*,' or '*mercy*.' I'm afraid it's *far* too late for any of that. I always speak plainly, and will *always* do what I *tell you* I'm going to do." He casually stirred his tea and took another sip, then glanced up at her with cold flat eyes. "And right now, I'm telling you this and I would *advise you* to listen if you value keeping what *you* have: I am the watchdog of the Consortium's bottom line, Agent McPherson. *Don't cross me.* If this city no longer wishes to be my *friend*, then *by God* it will be my *enemy*."

"That's it." She wiped her hands together dramatically as if washing her hands of the group. "You people have proven that you can't be trusted with this." She reached for the phone. "I'm going to call in someone *capable* to run this organization. You think the city's going to trust *you* idiots to protect them? You can't even keep from fighting *each other,* let alone Reece and the other people trying to destroy the world." She shook her head. "You people are useless *fuck ups,* and..."

Mack let out an annoyed sigh. "Listen, I know that the SPRM is causin' us some trouble, but we'll get them eventually and I really don't see why you're gettin' so upset about this. We're tryin' here! It'll take us some time to find 'em, but we *will* find 'em. Oz and me spent all day trackin' down some leads on where they're hidin'. We're gettin' close. Just let us get our personal stuff sorted out on our off hours and then we'll take care of it. I mean, we've never exactly been..."

"You just don't get it, do you!?!" She cut him off and pointed the phone receiver at him. "You don't GET to take some 'personal time!' You are a civil servant! MY servant! The government OWNS you!" She gestured to their surroundings. "All of this? This is under *government* control, and they've put ME here to decide how and when it should be used!"

Monty sighed wearily and pinched the bridge of his nose. "Agent McPherson, I think that if you would just..."

"Shut up, you one-eyed sociopath!" She spat out. "You're the LAST person here I would ever listen to! You're just a fucking

'*Mystery Man*'!"

The room fell into sudden silence, both from shock that anyone would say that to Monty and from a grim expectation of what he might do.

Mack scooted his chair away, evidently expecting there to soon be blood.

Monty stared at her for a long moment. "I'm sorry you feel that way, Agent McPherson. I truly am." He said in a deadly calm tone, then steepled his fingers and leaned forward in his chair. "I'm glad that you feel comfortable enough with our relationship and new understanding that you can be so open with me though. Allow me to be *equally* open with you about how *I* view our association." Monty snapped his fingers and Higgins instantly put a walkie-talkie into his outstretched hand. Monty pressed the transmit button. "This is Welles. *Shut it down*."

The vents in the room immediately stopped pumping in fresh air. A moment later, the lights sputtered and they were plunged into total darkness and complete silence.

"I'm afraid you have been seriously *misinformed* about your status here, Agent McPherson." Monty struck a match and held it up, causing shadows to sway and dance across the scarred angles of his face. "This facility is under *my* control. The city may have placed you here to observe, and Julian may currently be in command of its administration, but *I* oversee the power, your food, your oxygen, the telephone lines and all the *exits* from this dark hole in the ground which is filled with people who *despise* you. I am the one who *keeps you alive*. Without me, this place will be your *tomb*."

There was a faint noise, and a dozen of Monty's men suddenly appeared behind them from somewhere, stepping forward into the dim light, most of them carrying heavy tools. They surrounded McPherson's chair threateningly.

Her hand reached under her coat for her gun, but found it missing. She looked across the table in shock to see her firearm in the hands of Higgins, who had somehow managed to steal it in the momentary darkness.

Monty's henchman racked the weapon, loading a round into the chamber. He pointed it at her, waiting for his boss' order to fire.

Monty pretended he didn't even see the gun. "Therefore, *I* will be the one who determines who will lead this organization and what direction it takes, and I can *assure you*, it will *not* be the government or one of its lackey bureaucrats." Monty's voice took on a hard edge. "You are in *my* house, Agent McPherson, and *no one* tells me what to do in my own home. The few brave souls who have tried quickly realized the kinds of things that I'm *really* capable of. I am *not* the kind and forgiving man I seem to be. So maybe you should show me some *goddamn respect*, before I lose my patience with you and become *most* inhospitable." He blew out the match and they were once again plunged into complete darkness. "I've made my point." He said calmly into his walkie-talkie. "Start it up."

A moment later, the air and the power returned.

McPherson spun in her chair to confront the men behind her, but Monty's men had disappeared.

"Now then, if I were *you,* Agent McPherson, I would take this opportunity to *seriously* reevaluate your position on this issue." He looked up from the crystal globe on his cane. "...Or try to make it to the exit *while you still can.*"

She swallowed, suddenly looking pale, but still unwilling to back down. "...I can't just let you people have free reign to..."

Monty let out a weary sigh, cutting her off. "Perhaps you didn't *understand* my threat— no, my *promise*— so please allow us to make it more blatant."

Tupilak pulled back the hood of his parka. "Stay *out* of our private business, or we will *kill you.*"

"Mi offrirò come volontario ucciderla!" Bubonic's hand went into the air and she turned to Quinn, the only one currently in the room who she wasn't afraid to talk to. "...Allegramente." She glared at McPherson through her bird mask and made a slashing motion across her throat. "*Mignotta.*"

McPherson blinked at her in confusion for a moment, trying to decipher what that meant. "...I don't speak Italian."

Polly beamed. "Loosely translated? Miss Bella just called you a 'cu...'"

Mack held up a hand, interrupting the cultural exchange. "Yeah, I think we can all guess what that meant, Poll. Thanks though."

She smiled innocently. "You are *most* welcome."

"Clear enough?" Monty asked calmly.

McPherson refocused on him. "You can't do that! You can't just kill me because you don't want to follow orders! That's... that's just not what's supposed to happen!" She sounded amazed. "You're the heroes!"

Monty watched her expressionlessly for a moment, his eyes never leaving hers. "Confidentially?" He slowly shook his head. "I'm not that heroic."

"He's really not." Polly agreed.

McPherson rose from her chair. "The city won't stand for this!"

"I think you'll find that with the proper *motivation*, people can be made to support the most *deplorable* things." He told her calmly. "I remain confident that I can find ways to *persuade them*."

"Besides, references to you and your mission here can be erased from city records before your body cools." Polly said helpfully. "I can even update your Facebook status to indicate how much *fun* you are having on your unannounced 'vacation.'"

"How *lovely*." Monty leaned back in his chair. "Do you understand me now, Agent McPherson? I may have my own *serious* misgivings about Julian's leadership– frankly, I've always suspected that if I were to place my ear up to his head, I would hear the ocean– but I would follow a *Chia Pet* into battle before I followed *you*."

"YOU HAVE SPELLED: AQUATIC." Ceann pulled his sword and turned it so that the flaming blade filled the agent's vision. "YOU HAVE SPELLED: CHIEF."

Her face went ashen again. "...You people are making a *serious* mistake here." She swallowed nervously, inching away from the fiery blade until she fell back into her chair.

Monty leaned forward like a salesman eager to close a deal or a jackal sensing a kill. "Let's recap, shall we? You have two options: you can accept that we know what we are doing and allow us to deal with our own business, in our own way, on our own schedule, and we can all live in peace. Option two: you can stubbornly insist on being an *obstacle* to the progress we are making here and try to install someone *else* to run this organization, in which case, we all get to see how long you can survive down here *in the dark*. I should warn you though, my Irregulars are quite familiar with these halls, and even if you *tried* to run, I *sincerely* doubt you'd even make it to the TV room before they are upon you." He took on a thoughtful expression. "This is indeed a *tough* decision for you." He sat back in his chair, his voice hardening again. "I don't think I need to tell which choice *I'm* hoping you make."

"I'm sure Agent McPherson will *love* her 'vacation' in 'Cancun.' Her brother has already 'liked' the photo of her 'trip' which I've taken the liberty of posting to her account." Polly held out her palm and a photoshopped image of the agent standing on a beach was projected into the air. No one on Facebook was apparently questioning why the agent was at the beach in a suit coat, or why she looked so unhappy and shell-shocked.

"My, just look how much *fun* she's having." Monty said pleasantly.

Quinn nodded. "I bet she'll *never* want to come back."

The woman paled, but obviously knew she'd been beaten. She sat back in her chair and stared at Monty in disgust. "How did you get like this? What the hell could happen in someone's life that could turn them into *you?*"

Montgomery casually poured himself more tea. "I watched my family get eaten by *wolves.*" He said sarcastically, adding a sugar square to his cup. "Tragic."

McPherson let out a long breath of pure revulsion for Montgomery and the Consortium in general. "You people are losers anyway." She finally announced. "Even if you *did* try to stop the SPRM and save the city, you'd just make it worse."

Monty smiled icily. "Agent McPherson, I make the *best* 'worst' you can possibly imagine."

"...I'm going to take this up with Wyatt and the Commodore when they get back." She threatened. "They won't like this."

"Yes, the thought keeps me up at night." Monty casually took another sip of his tea. "Especially since rumor has it that they're currently in the rather inconvenient condition of being *dead*. I fully expect to see their burned bodies hanging from a bridge in Agletaria on the news any day now, so I imagine they have *other things* on their minds at the moment."

"I'm sure they're fine." Mack said reassuringly. "They're probably better off than we are. I bet right now, they're all standing around laughing about the situation."

****

"There's nothing to fucking eat, Miles!" Poacher grabbed for the villain known as 'The Unpleasant Man,' in an effort to wring his skinny neck. "*This* little sonofabitch ate half the supplies! People. Are. *STARVING!*"

"Do NOT touch him." Miles Gloriosus, AKA "Keystone," pushed Poacher away and stood between the men. "He is not an animal or a monster, and thus, he falls *outside* of your department's responsibilities. This is a *security* issue."

"And what the fuck are *you* going to do, old man?" Poacher pushed him back, causing Miles to stumble in the snow on his bad knee. "Hold his fucking hand and make him tell everyone that he's sorry again? You already *gave him* a fucking warning!"

Poacher immediately reached out a hand to help the man regain his balance but Miles slapped it away and bent down to retrieve his old-fashioned policeman's cap from the snowy ground.

Poacher gestured to their frozen surroundings, high atop the mountains on the Agletarian border, yelling to be heard over the howling icy wind. "We're going to fucking DIE out here! We're a hundred miles from anything, and the weather is getting worse. We got enemy patrols closing in on us, and t*here's no food! I been hunting for days! NOTHING!*"

"What I do or *don't* do is none of your concern." Miles drew himself up to his full height, somehow still looking imposing despite the fact that he was older than Sydney and an inch or two shorter. "*Step back.*"

Poacher eyed him coldly. "*Or?*"

Bobbi, Miles' second-in-command, pressed something against the side of Poacher's head. He didn't need to turn his gaze to identify it, simply because he knew the woman. It was the long barrel of her Winchester Model 1897 shotgun. *Normally*, she would have pulled her service revolver on him, but whenever she was feeling uncertain about a situation, she broke out the more vintage weapon. Bobbi seemed to treat it like a safety blanket, probably because it was an excellent *problem-solver.* The weapon was such an effective killer during WWI that many considered its use a war crime and called for it to be outlawed in the international laws of war. They called it the 'Trench Sweeper,' because it could cut down men in close quarters faster than anything else on the field. You didn't even have to pull the trigger again to fire multiple rounds; you just pulled it once and held it down, and as fast as you could pump the weapon, you could kill with it. It was a device designed for wholesale slaughter.

Still, she hadn't pulled out the AA-12 full-auto shotgun yet, so Poacher liked his odds. She pulled the service revolver on him at least once a week and he didn't even pay attention anymore. With the 1897? It was just bluster. She was pissed and scared about their situation, and wouldn't use it unless he forced her hand.

If she had pulled the AA-12 on him, he'd be dead by now.

"The Captain told you to *step back.*" She pumped the weapon. "Step. *Back.*"

Poacher rolled his eyes.

Her hero worship of the man was getting out of hand. In the girl's mind, Miles was some kind of heroic knight, out there singlehandedly fighting the forces of darkness while remaining pure as the driven snow.

Poacher just saw some asshole ex-cop in a stupid costume, who had a history of drinking problems, a failed career in the military, a bum knee, and a divorce or two under his belt. If he had ever been anything other than that, his best days were behind him. Most of the time, Miles just looked tired now. He had long ago basically handed off the actual fighting to his officers, who were younger and faster than he would ever be again. Poacher had always been of the opinion that the Consortium's security would be better off if they replaced Miles with a Yorkshire terrier puppy. Or a tin can and some string. Or a sign that said "Do Not Enter."

But no one wanted to hear that. The man had been the toughest dude around for so long, that no one paid attention to the fact that he had lost a step or *ten* over the years. In his prime, his name had struck fear in the heart of every law-abiding person in the city and all the criminals in jail. But those days were done. He was used up. He'd gotten soft.

Age was the one enemy not even *he* could beat, and the man had simply gotten old.

They needed to officially put him out to pasture.

Hell, he was *semi*-retired as it was. He spent most of his time behind a desk overseeing his officers, and the rest of it struggling not to fall back into the bottle. Villainy– *Caping*– was an unforgiving business, and the man just didn't have it in him anymore. He was washed-up. Old soldiers who were too tough to die needed to fade away before they got themselves and others killed.

Sydney understood that. ...Sometimes, he got the sense that Miles knew it to. He could see it in the man's eyes. The way he leaned against things for support when he thought no one was looking. The knee brace he tried to hide. The way he didn't want to get his hands dirty anymore, and avoided taking on jobs he used to complete with ease. He could see it in each and every one of the pills that Miles popped just to deal with the pain which comes from a half-century of constant fighting. The man had been hard as a rock his entire life, and now, cracks were breaking him apart.

Fucker was over-the-hill and over-the-edge.

Of course, he and Miles weren't close, so that could also have something to do with his opinion of the man. The two did not get along, which was another reason why they were given entirely separate responsibilities. One always played offense, the other always played defense. When you put them on the field together, bad things had a tendency to happen. Sometimes to each other, but usually to the people around them.

The Unpleasant Man straightened his costume. "Thanks for showing some intelligence, Miles. I'm glad to see *someone* here understands how things should be." He gestured to the others. "Do you think their lives have as much worth as ours? Really? Most of them don't even have any powers, and the others are too weak to realize what's happening. The food is *wasted* on them." He crossed his arms over his chest. "The *strong* survive in this world. Nothing will ever change until we scrape off all the deadweight and become the people we were *meant* to be."

Poacher *hated* bullies. Hated them above all things. Poacher was a killer and a thief, but he *wasn't* a bully. He had killed *scores* of people who had tried to turn him into one. Poacher would be put into the cold, cold ground before that ever happened, a fact which he'd already *proven* in the most literal way possible.

Miles continued glaring at Poacher. "Maintaining order is *my* department's problem, and you *will* stay out of it."

"Oh, I see how this works now!" Poacher gestured to him. "You used to run with The Archetypes, so they get special treatment! Your little buddy here just killed a bunch of people because he ate all of their food!" He pointed at the man. "MY food! GABE'S FOOD! JAMIE'S FOOD! BOBBI'S FOO..."

"Kyle and I were on the same team for years before I joined the Consortium." Miles interrupted. "I will not allow him to be the victim of 'mob justice.' We will have a *proper* trial for him on this issue, and then *I* will act accordingly." Miles turned to Bobbi. "Lieutenant, I think Poacher is in control of himself again. You can continue to make your rounds, but stay close to camp."

She reluctantly removed the weapon's barrel from Poacher's temple and marched off again.

Miles was silent for a long moment, looking very tired. "Did I ever tell you why I don't use my powers, Sydney?"

"I'm sure there's a Viagra joke I could make here." Poacher shook his head. "But I'm too fucking cold."

"Are you sure Kyle took the food?"

"*Yes*."

"Court is now in session." Miles skin took on a grey rocky texture and he turned to look at the other man. "I find you *guilty, Kyle*." He kicked the other man backwards off of the cliff and into the bank of clouds far below. His pitiless eyes returned to stare at Poacher. "It turns my heart to *stone*."

"*Jesus!*" Poacher's mouth hung open in amazement as he watched the other man plummet from view. "*That was your friend!*"

He gestured to his skin. "I don't *have* any friends when I'm like this, *especially* not ones who steal food from my people, even after

I warned them of the consequences." He shook his head, his voice coming out with all the emotion and tenderness of two cinderblocks being ground together. "When I use my powers, I don't care about a *goddamn thing*."

Poacher shrugged. "Hey, I'm not exactly crying that the little fuckrag is gone either. Guy steals food from kids, guy dies." He let out a long breath. "But the other Archetypes aren't going to take kindly to you killing their boy like that. Especially not since you and them were so close."

"I am concerned with keeping *order*, not with keeping *friends*. If they have a problem with the way I run this camp, they can take it up with me and I will *address their concerns* in the same way I just addressed *Kyle's*." He started to march off through the knee deep snow, visibly favoring his left leg but trying to hide it. "And the next time *you* get in my department's way, you and I are going to have a 'discussion' which involves a five hundred foot cliff and you being *thrown from it*. That is your *only* warning. I've already killed one friend today, and I assure you, as long as I am using my powers, I will have *NO* qualms about killing another." He raised his voice to be heard over the wind. "Lieutenant! Security report in my tent! Ten minutes!"

Poacher blinked after him.

Jesus.

Things were falling apart.

...They were all going to die.

****

"I think we're all going to die."

Rondel rolled his eyes. "Oh, now you're just being melodramatic."

"This is *Armageddon* they're talking about, boss." Jack informed him, sounding panicked. He looked around the darkened interior of the pyramid. "I do *not* want to end the world. I got tickets to see 'The Muppets on Ice' next week, and I *don't* want to have to miss it because everyone's *dead*."

"Was there something about our enemies which suddenly makes them seem particularly *competent* in your eyes?" Mercygiver casually kicked a stone so that it rolled down an incline and into a seemingly bottomless pit. "Frankly, I'm surprised the SPeRM has the intelligence to remain walking upright. Even if they *could* translate what the tablet said, they still could never pull off the ceremony." He checked his watch. "We've wasted enough time here. Please contact your teleporter friend and tell him that we are ready to go home now."

All in all, he was not finding Egypt to be that exciting. Maybe it was the company.

"You heard what the old witch broad in the sarcophagus said about the signs!" He pointed over his shoulder, being careful not to dislodge the ceremonial headdress lined with red burning candles which was still attached to his head. "The SPeRM has found all ten of the emeralds, and they stole the tablet from the college, and now they're going to open up the gate! Reece and his jackbooted thugs are gonna..." There was a noise behind him and he spun around, the light from his headdress illuminating the hieroglyphics on the wall and the shadows which dominated the darkened hall beyond. "Oh shit!" A horde of mummies suddenly loomed from the darkness, lurching towards them. *"Get back, boss!"* He pointed down one of the corridors, their only avenue of escape. *"GO!* The mummies are here for the necklace! *RUN!"*

Jack pulled out his gun and started blasting at the undead creatures as they...

CHAPTER 21

KING: "MY POINT IS THAT THIS CITY IS HEADED FOR
TROUBLE, 'TRAITOR.' ANYONE CAN SEE THAT.
HUNDREDS OF RESIDENTS HAVE ALREADY LEFT...
MAYBE THOUSANDS... MAYBE MORE. PEOPLE ARE
SCARED. THEY DON'T KNOW WHAT'S GOING ON, AND
THEY DON'T FEEL SAFE. THEY'RE LOOKING AROUND
FOR SOMEONE TO HELP THEM, AND RIGHT NOW, ALL
THEY HAVE IS A BUNCH OF LOSERS WHO WEREN'T EVEN
GOOD CRIMINALS, LET ALONE CAPES. I'M SURE YOU'D
AGREE WITH ME THAT YOU'RE ALL TERRIBLE PEOPLE
WHO HAVE NO BUSINESS WALKING AROUND FREE."

CALLER: "...YEAH, THAT'S FAIR."

KING: "SO, MY QUESTION TO YOU IS THIS: WHAT DO
YOU HAVE TO SAY ABOUT THE EVENTS OF THE PAST
COUPLE WEEKS?"

CALLER: "SHIT HAPPENS, PAIGE."

KING (INCREDULOUS): "...THAT'S IT? REALLY? I
HAVE TO SAY, I'VE NEVER REALLY BEEN THE
CONSORTIUM'S BIGGEST FAN, BUT EVEN I THOUGHT
THAT YOU..."

CALLER (INTERRUPTING): "...AND WHEN SHIT
HAPPENS, YOU DON'T CALL IN SOMEONE CLEAN TO
DEAL WITH IT. YOU CALL IN SOMEONE WHO'S BEEN
KNEE DEEP IN IT HIS ENTIRE LIFE."

TRANSCRIPT OF "KING OF CAPES AND COWLS," MEDIA:
TELEVISION, SHOW: 1408, NEWSCHANNEL 6, FRIDAY
21:00-22:00 EST, NETWORK SEGMENT-ID:
918000606

"What the hell is going on around here!?!' Bridget stormed
into the meeting room, ready to start smacking people. "Huh!?! Julian
can't leave you alone for *five minutes* before you decide to start

---

ruining his date!?!"

Quinn looked over at his boss. "So, how far'd you get? Second? Third?"

Her eyes narrowed at him. "You're *disgusting,* you know that?"

He leaned back in his chair. "Well, I'm filled with shame and regret and all kinds of tears and stuff over my…"

"Oh, shut up." She cut him off before he could recite his full canned apology yet again. "The fact remains that we now have a very *serious* problem."

Mack looked up from some kind of machine he was working on. "Yep. Oz and me are pickin' up all kinds of evidence that the SPRM are up to something *big* and…"

"Not *that*." She interrupted him. "I mean the fact that Arnold is on the news, saying all *sorts* of things he *shouldn't* be saying, which is just going to undo *all* of the work I've done on making you guys more acceptable to people."

"Like say… robbing a five star dining establishment tonight and getting arrested for felony assault and battery?" Monty guessed. "Because according to reports I've been receiving, that's how *you two* have spent your evening."

"And what the hell have *you* been doing, Welles!?!" Julian bellowed.

"What do you *think* I've been doing? Shoplifting bagfuls of *crustaceans*, obviously." Monty fired back. "That seems to be the 'it' thing to do in the company at the moment, and I wanted to do what all the cool kids were doing."

Bridget flopped down into one of the chairs. "I think we're all just a little overset because of this latest media disaster."

"I'm not." Mack felt the need to chime in. "I don't give a shit what you people do to each other. I just care about stopping the SPRM."

"*Fine*." She corrected. "Everyone but *Mack* is upset because we look like crazy people to the media again."

Monty stared at her in his usual complete smug detachment. "Do I *look* upset, Miss Haniver?"

She made an annoyed sound. "Fine! Okay!?! *I'M upset!* Because Julian has worked long and hard to get to where he is, and now it's all endangered."

Bubonic leaned over and whispered something to Quinn. He shook his head. "I don't know. I'll ask." He turned to Bridget. "Hey, Bridge? Bee wants to know just what exactly Jules has done to…"

"*He's done a lot!*" She cut him off. "*Leave him alone!*"

Quinn made a face and turned to Bubonic again. "I'm saying 'second base.' You?" She whispered something to him and he shook his head, looking uncertain. "You think? I don't know. She doesn't seem like that kinda girl to me. ...Jules *is* like totally a *pimp* though... Hmmm..."

Bridget made an annoyed sound again and spun in her chair. "Julian?" She pointed at them. "Please do something." She paused, already recognizing the obvious problem with that request. "...Which *doesn't* involve killing them." She quickly added.

Julian sat down into his chair with regal dignity. "It seems to *me* that the best course of action is *obvious.*" He nodded to himself. "The Lady Bridget and I need to go back to the beach and continue our date *right where it left off* so that the public isn't made to feel like something major has happened. It is only a crisis if we *act* like it's a crisis and we should return to some semblance of normalcy."

Most of the room nodded, either because they weren't listening, didn't care, or were just as delusional as he was.

"Meanwhile," he continued, "Welles will find someone we can blame the lobster incident on, thereby alleviating the Lady Bridget of her stress."

Monty nodded, looking pleased that someone had come up with a plan that made sense. "I already have a list of preliminary suspects for the fiend *actually* responsible for 'Lobster-Gate' and suspect that he, she, or *they* will be in custody within the hour."

Bridget frowned at them. "You can't just pin *our* crimes on someone innocent!"

Monty let out another longsuffering sigh. "...Miss Haniver? I hope you realize how understanding I'm trying to be about your inexperience with the true nature of life, and I hope you take this in the spirit in which it is intended." He shook his head. "*No one* is innocent. Not in this city or any other. No matter what I could *ever* do to someone, I assure you... *they had it coming.*"

"I'm just saying that I think rather than framing someone innocent for a crime that we committed, it might be easier if we just took some responsibility for our actions and moved on." She argued, trying to sound calm and reasonable.

"I'm a busy man, Miss Haniver." Monty got to his feet. "I don't have *time* for any more of your 'learning experiences.' Frankly, I think my life has already taught me more about the *real* world than yours *ever* will." He started from the room. "I'll tell you what though: you go ahead and confess, and I'll find us a patsy, and we'll see which of us can make their story the 'truth' first." He smiled tauntingly, his smirk one of ice. "*Race ya.*"

She pointed after him and looked at Julian, as if drawing attention to Monty's behavior.

He shrugged. "I will deal with Welles later."

"...You still can't kill him." She warned.

"...Damn." His scowl deepened and he pointed at the table. "Well, we still can't get distracted from the *important* issues here though."

Mack looked up again. "Good. I figure that the SPRM is all set to make..."

"Now," Julian cut him off, "I think our date should reconvene at a secluded spot in this city that is *without* police interference. I tire of their relentless meddling in my affairs."

She stared at him in wonder. "Are you really putting the location of our date up to a vote in your little club?"

"The sewers aren't patrolled by anyone, boss." Quinn chimed in helpfully. "You could have sex with a whole *sorority* down there and the cops wouldn't know about it."

"...The sewer?" Julian took on a pondering look, like he was giving the matter deep thought. "Mmmm..."

"Now, normally, I'd just ignore a vote like this because it's stupid. But in *this* case, I am *not* going to have sex with you in a sewer!" Her voice rose in indignation, then she frowned as she realized what she had just said in front of everyone. "...Or anywhere. Because that's private and what I do or don't do is of none of your concern."

Quinn nodded. "Second and on the way to Third." He translated and looked over at Bee. "We were both right."

"None of my concern?" Julian's eyes narrowed, ignoring Quinn. "I *knew* I should have throttled that patrol officer for interrupting us."

Quinn gave an "Ooooooooh!" worthy of any sitcom laugh track audience upon hearing of sexy hijinks.

Julian pointed at him and the noise stopped.

Bridget put her face in her hands again. "Our date is *over* for the night. Our discussion of what did or did not almost happen on our date is *over* and will *never* be brought up at a company meeting again." She looked out over the table. "The only thing which we *will* be discussing is how to make certain that people realize what a good person Julian is."

The table was silent for a long moment as they considered

that.

"...All I'm comin' up with is hypnotism or some sort of brainwashin' through torture." Mack said seriously. "Is that what everyone else is at too?"

"Yep." Quinn got to his feet. "You start building the waterboards and I'll start working on the positive things about Julian we can scream at people while..."

"If you're joking, it's *not* funny, and if you're serious, it's really sad." Bridget said tiredly. "I have never done *anything* of merit at my job, and for *once* in my life, I would like to be able to make someone happy who *truly* deserves it. Okay? So *please* work with me on this."

Julian turned in his chair to watch her. "Just sitting here next to you makes me happy, Lady Bridget." He told her earnestly, meeting her eyes. "Nothing more is required from you or anyone else."

Bridget's mouth hung open and time just lost all meaning.
Wow.
What a beautiful sentiment.
...Especially from someone like Julian, who was habitually incapable of saying anything pleasant.

She cleared her throat. "...On second thought, I'm willing to listen to some *suggestions* on possible date locations." She shook her head. "NOT the sewer though." She glanced at Julian out of the corner of her eye and was once again struck by how smitten she had somehow become with him. "...Probably. I mean, unless it's like the *only* choice or something, like if zombies have invaded or there's some kind of giant asteroid headed towards earth and Julian pushes me in there as a last ditch attempt to save us, and we're huddled sexily in the dark and..."

"Do I really hafta be here for this?" Mack asked the room at large. "I mean, if you and Julian are an item now, I'm thrilled for ya. I really am. Especially since it means the plan involvin' the car trunk and the chloroform is finally off the table..."

"...What?" Bridget's smile faded. "...Wait. What? What was that?"

Mack ignored her. "...But if you guys are just goin' to go on and on about all the things you could be doin' on your date, I'm sorry, but I just have more important things to do around here than that."

Julian glared at the man. "If the Lady Haniver wants to tell you about giant zombie asteroids, you will *sit,* and you will *listen,* and you will *love* her story about giant zombie asteroids."

Mack looked at him for a moment, then put his face in his

hands. "Oh, for *gawd's sake*. Sometimes I think I'm the only sane one here."

"Are the zombies *on* the asteroid, Bridge?" Quinn asked seriously. "Or is the asteroid *causing* the zombie infestation?"

"Neither, dickhead!" Multifarious snapped. "It's an asteroid *made* of zombies! Keep up, huh!?!"

The entire room jolted at seeing the masked person back and lounging in his/her usual chair.

Julian frowned. "Didn't you quit?"

"Leave of absence." Multifarious said, pouring some water into his/her glass, despite the fact that the facemask he/she always wore had no slit from which to drink the liquid. "Thought now was a pretty good time to come back and see how my buddies were doing." He/she looked around the room. "Don't see Monty. He dead? Fingers crossed, fingers crossed!" Something close to hope was in his/her tone. "Please-say-yes-please-say-yes-please-say-yes..."

"Nope." Mack informed him/her.

Mull threw his/her arms out in annoyance. "*Fuck.* Well, so much for the power of prayer, I guess."

Quinn squinted. "Mull left? Really? I don't even remember that."

"Why exactly did you pick *now* to come back?" Mack asked.

The masked person shrugged. "No reason. Just a whisper on the breeze..." He/she directed his/her gaze off towards the corner of the room between the wall and ceiling.

Everyone looked at the spot, trying to see if something was actually there, or if the person was just out of their fucking mind, as usual. As it turned out, it was the latter, and the group refocused on the table.

Bridget absently spun her pen around and around in her hand. "What we *really* need is some sort of..."

Her phone rang and she fished it out to answer it.

"Hi!" The friendly voice on the other end said. "This is Prometheus... *Jones* with Channel 6 News, and I have a proposition for you..."

****

"Explain to me again why we are here." Julian asked, trudging from the car behind her.

"I *told you* already: we have an appointment with one of the major networks, and they're going to do a puff piece on you guys."

He made a face. "I do not *want* to be 'puffed.'"

Quinn shrugged. "Depends on who's doing the '*puffing*.'" He looked around at his companions. "Am I right fellas?" He nodded. "Oh yeah. You know what I'm talking about."

"Why is the city so quiet?" Julian ignored that, glancing around the strangely empty streets. "And where is Welles?"

"YOU HAVE SPELLED: SCHEMING." Ceann interjected from his position in the shadows of the building in front of them. Bridget noticed that whenever possible, the man preferred to remain hidden in the darkness. ...There was something kind of sad about that.

"Yeah, that's a good guess." Quinn shrugged. "Monty went off that way a few minutes ago." He pointed down a dimly lit side road. "Personally, I always start to worry when he disappears. The dude is like a canary in a coal mine; he's a good indication of trouble brewing. When he's gone, chances are, you should be too."

Bridget let out an annoyed breath. "Well, I can't say I'm particularly surprised by his absence. *Delighted* would probably be a better word for what I'm feeling. The man is possibly the *worst* interviewee I have ever met." She pointed at Julian. "And I'm dating *him.*"

Julian frowned. "Hey!"

She patted his arm. "Oh, you know it's true."

"I know nothing of the sort!" He argued. "I have a *natural* charisma which all intelligent beings are drawn to," he paused, "...It's only the *surface people* that dislike me, probably because they sense my natural superiority."

She nodded humoringly. "I'm sure that's it."

Ahead of them, Ceann paused in the street to stare at the image on one of the TVs in the window. He watched it for a moment, then typed something into his toy. "YOU HAVE SPELLED: RESE."

Quinn frowned. "What the fuck is a 'Rese'?"

"It's a verb meaning to 'tremble or shake.'" Polly helpfully intoned. "...Although why such an obsolete word is in a child's spelling toy is anyone's guess."

Multifarious paused and took on a dramatic posture, speaking in a booming theatrical voice:

> "*And downward from a hill, under a bente,*
> *There stood the temple of Mars armypotente,*
> *Wrought all of burned steel, of which the entry*
> *Was long and straight, and ghastly for to see;*
> *And there out came a rage, and such a veze*

That it made all the gates for to rese."

"...Thanks for that, Mull." Quinn rolled his eyes. "Whatever the hell it means."

"What?" Mull pointed to the side of his/her mask. "You say something to me?"

"Yeah," Quinn started yelling, "I said: YOU DON'T MAKE SENSE!"

The masked person shook his/her head. "I still can't hear you, human of Earth. Acoustic Shadow, *the Silent Assassin* is deaf."

Bridget frowned. "...Then how could you hear us discussing the word?"

Mull put his/her hand to the side of the mask again. "*Huh?*"

Julian pinched the bridge of his nose. "Can we please just concentrate on our interview, and not on whatever weird nonsense Multifarious is spouting today?"

"It's not nonsense." Oz informed them. "It's *Chaucer*."

"YOU HAVE SPELLED: NIGHT. YOU HAVE SPELLED: TALE." Ceann clarified.

"Dude, I don't give a shit if it's a *flying Chaucer,* it makes no sense!" Quinn shot back.

Ceann casually pointed at the TV again as they strolled by him on the sidewalk. "YOU HAVE SPELLED: RESE."

They ignored him. Bridget didn't like Chaucer. Everything was spelled weird.

The headless man pressed the button several more times as they left him behind. "YOU HAVE SPELLED: RESE. RESE. RESE."

They rounded the corner.

'YOU HAVE SPELLED: NOT. YOU HAVE SPELLED: SMART."

Bridget rolled her eyes. "Just because I don't read *Chaucer* doesn't mean that I'm not..." She trailed off as she came to the intersection, and a small park area in front of the TV station.

Arranged around them were several hundred people, all standing before a podium where Reece and the Mary Sue appeared to be performing some sort of ritual. They were dressed in long red robes, and had a strange tablet covered in what appeared to be emeralds. Beside them, TVs were broadcasting their images to the entire city, as they attempted to complete their ceremony.

Bridget made an annoyed face. "Oh *shit*." She stomped her foot in aggravation and frustration.

Ceann pointed at Reece as the man stood on the stage. "YOU HAVE SPELLED: RESE."

The Mary Sue glided to the microphone and leaned closer to it, her nauseatingly cute tomboyish features contorting into a smirk. "Everyone? I'd like you to meet what's left of the Consortium of Chaos." Her sneer grew. "Please kill them."

The crowd of brainwashed citizens turned on them in unison, like robots being activated.

Bridget shook her head. "...I'm really beginning to dislike this town."

CHAPTER 22

KING: "I SUPPOSE WHAT I'M REALLY SAYING IS THAT ANYONE WHO CHALLENGES SOMEONE AS MAGNANIMOUS AND AMAZING AS THE MARY SUE IS JUST DOOMED TO FAILURE AND RUINATION. SHE IS THE KIND OF PERSON WHO MAKES LIFE WORTH LIVING."

STORMS: "AT LAST YOU'RE SAYING STUFF THAT MAKES SENSE, PAIGE. WITH HER INDOMITABLE SPIRIT AND SPUNK, SHE'S REALLY THE KIND OF LEADER THAT THIS CITY CAN GET BEHIND."

KING: "...AS SOON AS WE KILL THE CONSORTIUM OF CRETINS FOR HER IN ORDER TO SHOW OUR LOVE."

STORMS: "OH, YES. OBVIOUSLY. AND THEN WE CAN REFOCUS ON KILLING OURSELVES FOR HER. AFTER ALL SHE'S DONE FOR US OVER THE YEARS, IT'S THE VERY LEAST WE CAN DO."

KING: "I'M FINDING HER PLATFORM OF BIPARTISANSHIP AND 'CARING ABOUT THE LITTLE GUY' TO BE QUITE REFRESHING, AND I LOOK FORWARD TO SEEING THE KINDS OF THINGS THAT SHE AND REECE WILL BE ABLE TO DO WITH THIS CITY IN THE FUTURE NOW THAT THE SUPER-PERSON RESISTANCE MOVEMENT IS RIGHTFULLY IN CHARGE. ...YOU KNOW. EXCEPT THAT WE'LL ALL BE DEAD. BUT THAT'S A SMALL SACRIFICE TO PAY FOR HER GENTLE SPIRIT OF GOODNESS AND LIGHT, AND I'M SURE THAT ONCE WE'RE GONE, THE CITY WILL BE EVEN BETTER!"

TRANSCRIPT OF "KING OF CAPES AND COWLS," MEDIA: TELEVISION, SHOW: 1408, NEWSCHANNEL 6, FRIDAY 21:00-22:00 EST, NETWORK SEGMENT-ID: 918000606

     Julian had done a lot of annoying interviews since his turn from villain to Cape. The events of this evening were rapidly becoming the worst incident with the press he had ever had though. ...Well, except that thing at the school. That one might still beat it.

He sprinted down the concrete, trying to stay ahead of the angry mob shouting for their heads, and trying to ignore the fact that the mass of humanity appeared to be growing with each passing moment. Every building they came to was occupied with *more* people who seemed intent on killing them for some reason, and the entire city was apparently rushing from their doors and into the street to join in the chase. Each intersection was filled with angry motorists, who exited their cars and immediately fell into step with their murderous countrymen.

...Luckily, Julian's life had prepared him for this. *Every day* up until now he had bravely faced the surface people trying to kill him and destroy his people, so this was nothing new.

Terrestrials were *all* killers. And this *proved* it once and for all.

Let them come.

He would be rather smug over finally being proven right, except there was that pesky little fact that he'd be too dead to gloat to anyone. ...It would almost be worth it though.

A large mob of people appeared in the street in front of them, and Julian dashed to his right in an effort to evade being caught and torn to shreds. All he had to do was make it to the ocean. Once he was home, he could take Bridget away from here, and no one would ever catch him.

...Sadly, he was nowhere *near* the water.

The city really needed to make more aquatic enemies. He was beginning to understand how Everett must have felt. Hell, he must have been *overjoyed* to see Julian arrive on the scene, just so that he had something to do every day.

Julian had never felt more powerless in his entire life.

He still felt better than the boy from Accounting though. The intern had simply started screaming hysterically as soon as the angry crowd began chasing them, his feet rooted in place. The little coward didn't even *try* to stop the throng of people as the mob bypassed him, focused on the rest of the team.

Some people just had the *wrong* attitude about super-heroics.

He glanced over his shoulder, trying to take a headcount of his crew. "Horseman: we left Bubonic in our vehicle." He gestured to his left. "Go retrieve her."

The headless man strolled down the side street, looking entirely unconcerned about the events of the evening. The good thing about the Irish was that they were all too crazy to pay attention to inconvenient facts like overwhelming odds, impending death, or that all the other pantheons thought they were insane.

He turned to his left. "OCD? Go find Tupilak. He seems to have gotten misplaced."

Oz nodded, and turned at the corner, sprinting off to look for their missing comrade.

Bridget struggled to keep up with Julian, and he was seriously debating just picking her up and carrying her. Sadly, her choice of footwear was not meant for long-distance running. "Any clue what Reece is up to?"

He shook his head. "How should *I* know? I don't understand terrestrials on a *good* day, do you honestly think I understand them when they're performing some magic ceremony?" He thought about it. "And who was the little boy with him?"

"Huh?"

"The little boy with the ponytail?"

"She's not a boy!" Bridget gasped in horror. "That's Mary Sue!"

Julian frowned over his shoulder, back towards the square. "That's a *woman?* ...Are you sure? Why is she so tiny? And... flat?"

"The Mary Sue is the most inspirational and warmhearted person that this cruel world has ever produced!" She informed him. "Her gentle good-humor and innocent zest for life fills us all with joy during these dark times and makes us *believe* again!"

Julian pursed his lips, considering that, then shook his head. "No, I still think that's a little boy. *Women* have breasts! They have a shape! They have..."

"After everything she's done for you, this is how you're going to treat her!?!" She yelled. "She's like your darling little sister!"

"*I've never even met him!*" He shot back.

The image of the little boy in question appeared on the TV in the window of one of the bars they were running by, and his shrill voice projected out onto the street. "I wonder if the Consortium would please just kill each oth...."

Polly made a high-pitched electronic sound, drowning out whatever Mary Sue was trying to say.

"SHHH!" Bridget paused in the doorway to hear the broadcast. "You're interrupting Mary SUE!"

Julian was *well* acquainted with all sea life, even if it was mythological. He turned to face the hologram. "That small boy is a siren." He picked Bridget up and began carrying her away. "Polybius?

We are once again in need of Multifarious' particular *skill set*. Let's send that boy our *regards*."

Polly nodded and turned to project an image of the Mary Sue surrounded by large glowing letters into the air, which read: "Multifarious: *kill this bitch a LOT!*"

Multifarious pulled the katana from the sheath on his/her back and brought it down in a swift cutting motion. "I shall move like a whisper, and she shall die with a scream."

The masked person immediately ducked down an alley to double-back towards the boy.

Julian kept running, trying to keep Bridget from injuring herself during her struggles to listen to Mary Sue. "OverDriver: *stop that broadcast!*" He yelled back at the man.

Mack halted in his tracks. "...But I kinda wanna hear what she's got to say? I mean, she *is* the..."

Polly held up her hand. "Look at me, McCallister." The man met her electronic gaze. "I've known you my entire life. I trust you more than any person on this planet, biological or electronic. So I *know* that when I tell you that you need to stop that broadcast, you will do as I ask." She looked uncertain for a moment. "...Please?"

Mack snapped his fingers and every TV for blocks around blew up, and the power in the neighborhood shorted out.

"Good. If we can just make it to the ocean, we'll be fine. ...*Everything* will be fine..." Julian dashed toward his home. "*And where the fuck is Welles!?!*"

****

Montgomery Tarkington Welles was someone who *believed* in kicking a man when he was down.

He truly did.

A lot of the other members of the Consortium shied away from the practice, but Monty had always seen the advantages inherent in dealing with someone when they couldn't strike back. If they were on the ground, you kicked them. And you *kept* kicking them, until you were sure they wouldn't be coming back. You made *damn* sure they were dead, because if you let them get up onto their feet, they could do *terrible* things. ...Things they *never* could have done before they hit the ground. ...Things that would have once been *unimaginable*.

Life had taught him that lesson the hard way, and he had the scars to prove it.

He ran a thumb over one of the wounds in question. The

bullet had severed a nerve cluster in the area, and so now the entire left side of his face felt perpetually cold. Not numb, just like someone was continuously holding an ice cube to his cheek, or as if he were always standing in a snowy breeze. For its part, the milky blue eye on that side could only see a reddish fog which sometimes seemed to move and swirl. If you shined a bright light directly into it, he might be able to tell, but that was about it. For all intents and purposes, he was half-blind.

He casually breathed onto his monocle and wiped it clean with his handkerchief.

They were late.

Monty *abhorred* lateness. Time wasn't just money, time was *power.* Time was what allowed you to do whatever you wanted. Timing was *everything* in life, whether you were talking about the release of a new product, or eliminating your super-powered foes.

His father had once told him that being a businessman was having the ability to see what was coming around the corner, and the guts to risk *everything* on that prediction. A businessman *prepared* for disaster and for the future. When the winds of change started blowing, a businessman built windmills while the others built walls. All he needed was faith in himself and to never be afraid of putting it all on the line for something he *believed* in.

And Monty could do both.

No matter what problem you put in front of him, he could solve it.

He would *solve* it. He would *profit* from it. He would *beat you* with it.

There was *no question* about that in his mind.

Plan carefully; execute rapidly; win decisively.

Win at any cost and by any means.

Win.

Monty would get his way even if it meant the horrible death of every living thing on earth. ...If it meant the death of the planet itself. ...If it meant that he *himself* would die as a result, he'd *still* do it, if it meant that he'd *win* before dying. Winning was the *only* thing that mattered, and there was NO line he wouldn't cross to get there. NO person, thing or concept he wouldn't step on. *Nothing* he wouldn't sell out, and *nothing* he wouldn't do.

Monty *didn't* lose.

Not *ever.*

...Not again.

Sadly, that meant that his time was often spent like this:

standing in the middle of some deserted place and waiting for his opponents to *finally* appear and carry out the actions he predicted.

But he was *very* good at making predictions about people's behavior.

He didn't have precognition or anything like that, Monty simply had a deep understanding of how things worked. How all the pieces could fit together and how he could use them to accomplish his goals. It was as close to a superpower as he came, but he found it more useful than any laser blast or elemental ability could have ever possibly been.

Among the Cape set, Monty was known as a "Mystery Man": someone who has no powers, but still engages in the super-powered life. The term *wasn't* a compliment; it was a pejorative. Generally, people with no powers were looked down upon by those who possessed them. But Monty wouldn't have traded places with them even if he could. Honestly, he *preferred* it when his enemies dismissed him as a threat, because it made it easier to defeat them. He wasn't after honor or glory or friendship or love, he was simply after victory. *Power.*

Monty wanted to win. He was *going to* win and the rest of humanity would *lose,* and lose *big.*

Over the years, he had used his abilities to control situations– and just about everything else– to always get what he wanted. The most incredible super-powers in the world could only help you if you had an opportunity to use them, and Monty didn't believe in ever giving his enemies that chance.

He would *win*. No matter what he had to sacrifice in the process, or how many people got hurt.

It was simply a matter of building an accurate blueprint and then waiting for all of the pieces to blunder into place, exactly as you anticipated. When you really came down to it, that's all people were: tools. Machines. They could only react in certain predetermined ways to a limited number of stimuli. You press their button and they move along their track. The world was *filled* with puppets and Monty was the only one who understood how to work their strings.

He was the last of a great line of American industrialists and his family had once had their place at the forefront of economic life in this country. Although the influence of the Welles name had declined considerably in the years before his birth, being a lord of steam and steel was in his blood. He *understood* it on a deep level that not even he could fully explain. He *knew* how to use money, influence and the sweat of his workers to build his vision. Build his dreams. Build his *power.*

He was a *Welles.* He made the gears which moved the world. ...And sometimes, things got crushed in them.

But Monty had never lost any sleep over that. After all, no one cried if they broke a hammer or bent their screwdriver, did they? They didn't lie awake regretting the tons of coal or gallons of gasoline which they had been forced to consume to achieve their goals.

No.

They were a necessary sacrifice. A resource which had been provided for the purpose of building what their manager desired. That was their entire reason for existing in the first place.

Pieces got broken. It was a lamentable fact of life in manufacturing anything. Luckily, they were also *entirely* interchangeable. If one piece broke, you could swap it out with another, and use that one instead without any real negative effect. The machine would roll on. Because, the only person who *really* mattered, was the man at the controls.

W.C. Fields' last words were: "Goddamn the whole fucking world and everyone in it except you...!" In actuality, he had been speaking to his mistress, but Monty always preferred to look at it as advice on how to live.

It wasn't a hard credo for him to live by. He wasn't a happy person by nature. Call it another element of his grasping and pitiless ancestors or perhaps a consequence of his own disfigurements, but it was easy for him to ignore the rest of the world and its tedious plight.

Very easy.

Montgomery's last happy moment was a beautiful day he had once had in his youth. His family had a picnic on the grounds of their factory, and all of their friends and employees had attended. He had sat on that tablecloth and looked up into the brilliant blue sky, and the entire world had seemed so wonderful.

His parents had been so happy.

Everyone had been so happy.

Everything seemed so pure and perfect.

Later that day, he realized how wrong that assessment had been. It was probably the only time in his life when he had misjudged a situation so completely. It had taken losing sight in one eye to realize how blind he had been. The world had *deceived* him; its brilliance blinding him to the truth.

Nothing was perfect. Nothing pure.

There was no Heaven. No pearly gates. No one sorting out the just from the unjust, the moral from the wicked. No "True Love,"

"Magic," or "Destiny." No Divine manager controlling the factory which produced civilization, and standing behind his product with a satisfaction guarantee.

The Universe was simply a machine which had been abandoned by its operator... if it ever had one to begin with. Because when you came right down to it, if there existed an all-knowing infallible Creator, then his quality control standards were *terrible*. He should be *ashamed* of the shabby nature of his finished product. Life was one of those cheap shitty products shown on television infomercials; it just never worked the way it was advertised by its inventor. He always made it look so *easy*... Made you so many pleasant little promises about doing the right thing and being rewarded...

But that was just the *hook*. Just a smiling pitchman selling you a *lemon*. And once you bought his line, there were no exchanges or refunds.

No, Monty had long ago come to the conclusion that the world was simply a machine which behaves according to specific rules and in known ways. And *no one* was at the controls but you. All you would ever have was what you could craft for yourself here in this hellish place. You could build the blueprint of your *own* destiny, out of whatever parts and scraps which that long absent manager in the sky had left behind in his haste to escape the horrible and embarrassing sight of his own defective creation.

His mother had once told him that 'God helps those who help themselves." To Monty's way of thinking, that was just another way of saying: "It's every man for himself." And if his mother was right, then God was going to fucking *adore* Monty by the end, as Monty intended on *"helping himself"* to as much of this world as he could carry and using it to build an empire! He was going to take everything that wasn't nailed down, and he'd go *straight through* anyone who got in his way.

That's all life was. All you could ever hope for. The mad scramble to create meaning for yourself in an utterly meaningless world.

And then you were simply gone.

Forever.

That was what was awaiting everyone.

Like Odin, Monty had sacrificed an eye for the ability to see the future. And the future had no picnics with friends. The future had only graves. It had the dead and the dying. The decaying and the destroyed. The future was in the hot bite of steam and the cold grip of

314

steel. The future was in accumulating power and overseeing the machinery of death.

The future was a lonely and crooked road to travel.

All of the people you couldn't bear to lose were dead in the future. In fact, they were dead in the present as well. All good things existed only in the heavenly past, forever frolicking in the green grass, and rejoicing at the end of another perfect day. ...Shielded from the hellish future and what you had to do to survive there. Their whole lives would always be ahead of them; an eternal picnic which would never end.

But life simply held no more picnics for Monty.

He could see that quite clearly, even with his blinded sight.

He had accepted that fact from the moment the last picnic had ended, and he first began his solitary walk down the crooked mile. ...When his dreams had fallen to Earth like a plane from the sky.

He still thought of that last picnic quite often though, like a condemned man recalling his last meal while marching towards the gallows. The taste of the food and the feeling of the warm sun on his then unscarred skin, had stuck with him all these years. The joyful look in Karen's eyes, so very different from the last one he had seen in them. The sight of his younger sisters chasing butterflies across the grass, so different than watching them realize that they had no wings of their own. His mother's happy screams of amusement at something one of the employees had said, so different than the last time he had heard her voice. The smell of hamburgers on the grill, so different than the smell of *other things* burning in a fire.

...One perfect moment.

Sometimes when you taste something that sweet, everything after it tastes like bitter ash. ...Ash and gunpowder.

If Montgomery could have anything in the world, it would be to spend just a few more minutes at that picnic. To watch the sun go down and enjoy the glorious but fleeting moments of twilight, before the darkness descended on his life forever. When he could look at the world through both eyes, and could grasp those closest to him with all ten fingers.

When everything Monty loved was still alive, and he could live in his happy delusions about the world and the nature of man.

When Monty's biggest concern was that he knew when he grew up, he wouldn't be able to run the factory as well as his father did.

...But none of that was to be.

The sun had set on that memory of the past. The *future* had arrived.

The picnic was most decidedly… *over*.

As if on cue, his opponents *finally* made their way into the intersection.

He glanced down at the familiar gold and enamel face of his great-great-grandfather's pocket watch. They really could have shown more dedication in searching for him, he had been standing around for almost *ten minutes*.

People had no *pride* in their work anymore.

The two figures stalked forward, unapologetic over making him wait.

Gyre stood in front, a tall broad-shouldered man with blond hair, which was cut in a short but spiky military style. His outfit featured a stylized red circular pattern, over which he wore a black trench coat. Dark sunglasses covered his eyes, despite the fact that it was night. Monty had heard that he wore them to protect his eyes from the brightness of his power beams, but he suspected that it had more to do with the fact that the man was making an obvious effort to look cool. His energy blasts were among the most powerful in the villain community though, and were said to be able to cut through a mountain.

Behind him prowled Draugr, dressed in Viking armor; her arms, stomach and legs bare, save for the iron gauntlets and fur-trimmed boots she wore. Standing even taller than the man in front of her, she had the build of a classical Amazonian warrior, despite her Norse heritage: muscular, but unarguably still feminine. She looked like someone had taken a normal-sized shapely woman and simply scaled her up about 20%, until she topped 6'4". Her skin had the mottled appearance of a corpse, as if she had been beaten savagely and was now black and blue over her entire body. Not putrid and decaying like a zombie in a movie though, merely undead. Her eyes cast a blue and evil looking light which somehow still did nothing to dispel the shadows which perpetually shrouded her eye sockets. The red tattoo running down her face over her left eye could still be seen through the darkness though, as if it were glowing from within; the Rune "*ear*" meaning "Grave" or "Death personified" which looked almost like the letter "W" with a vertical line running downward from its middle point.

She wasn't to be underestimated. If Hazard was the strongest person alive, then Draugr was arguably the strongest person who *wasn't*. But that was just the tip of the iceberg as far as her abilities went.

The woman also cut a striking figure. She could even be called very pretty... in an undead zombie monster sort of way. Monty certainly wasn't one to judge someone over such a thing though. He wouldn't have won any beauty pageants, even *before* getting shot in the face.

Gyre pointed at him and turned to his companion. "Ah, *there's* one of the little dipshits. Told you they were over here. You see why you should listen to someone whose brain *isn't* rotting in their skull?"

Draugr didn't respond.

"Montgomery Tarkington Welles." Monty cordially doffed his top hat with long practiced grace and etiquette, and then replaced it on his head. "Pleased to make your acquaintance."

Gyre rolled his eyes and stopped a short distance in front of him. He turned to his companion again. "So, you wanna be the one to kill him, or did you want me to do it?"

Draugr didn't respond.

Gyre raised his voice. "Hey! *'Walking Dead'*!" He began speaking in an exaggerated 'slow' tone, evidently trying to make himself understood by his slowwitted partner. He poked her in her ample chest, ostensibly to get her attention, but his hand lingered there for a beat too long, and he obviously took *far* more pleasure from the action than was appropriate, whether the woman was dead or not. "I'm talkin' to you! *Earth to fucking corpse!* Are you going to kill this guy, or should I?"

Draugr didn't respond.

Monty was *hopelessly* outmatched in this confrontation. To be perfectly honest, most of the Consortium would be though, so he wasn't alone in that regard. Together, his opponents made up a nearly unstoppable force. In a fair fight, he wouldn't last five seconds against either of them. ...Luckily, Monty never *played* fair. Not that he cheated, either. He just didn't believe in playing at all, really. "Playing" implied that there was some element of chance involved, and there simply wasn't. Monty had already won this battle. He'd won it a week ago, he had simply not bothered to tell his adversaries that yet. They'd figure it out soon enough.

People were so *pathetically* predictable.

His discussion with the rest of the team earlier had showed him an important weakness inherent in his own position in the Consortium though. He was smarter than all of them. Craftier. The only one who could see the entire game board and understand the movement of the pieces. Life was Tetris, and no matter how many annoying blocks you threw at him, Monty would use them to build his wall and he would build it better than any wall in the world. But if the final push came, and things ended up in some sort of altercation, Monty was at a distinct disadvantage. He wouldn't win that fight. Brains were all well and good, but sometimes brawn would triumph and trample out the more intelligent pearls cast before them.

He could see it all playing out in his mind as if it had already happened, right down to the moves his coworkers would use in their battle against him. His department outnumbered the others, but it was staffed by a loyal– and sadly almost entirely *normal*– workforce. The other people in the Consortium would take some losses, but would undoubtedly also control the field when the day was done.

He didn't believe in fighting battles he was destined to lose. Monty had been knocked down for the *last* time in his life, and he *refused* to ever fall again.

He would *win*.

No matter what.

Thus, he would need to recruit a new employee, in case the situation ever spun out of his control. That would be difficult however, as all of the most powerful Capes and villains in the city were already spoken for. Monty would need to somehow tempt someone truly *remarkable* into betraying their current employer and joining up with him. ...Luckily, few men have virtue enough to withstand the highest bidder.

Not that Monty put much faith in *purchased* allegiance, mind you. On the contrary, he realized the serious limitations and numerous drawbacks inherent in controlling a force of mercenaries. After all, if they were willing to betray one employer for money, what would keep them from betraying Monty just as quickly?

No, Monty didn't believe in merely *renting* things he needed to *own*.

Cash offerings and promises of position could always be topped by another party, given enough time. Blackmail was simply an invitation for the person to strike back at you. Threats and violence lost all effectiveness over the long-term. Family ties and the bonds of friendship were weaknesses which life had *long ago* divested Monty of, and he had seen firsthand how fleeting such ideas were. No, the only *true* way to ensure success as an employer was loyalty. Complete and total devotion was the ultimate power in the universe. No money could buy it. No threat could destroy it. No law or promise could create it. It needed to be *earned,* and once you had it, you could be *unstoppable*.

Monty didn't trust in much in this life, but he *believed* in loyalty. He had *seen* the power the idea held. The things it could accomplish. Loyalty was what kept people in the palm of your hand, no matter what happened. If you earned it from someone, then they would die for you. *Kill* for you. Endure anything this world and any other threw at them. All because you had given them something that no one ever had before. It was simply a matter of finding out what that thing was. And once you found it– discovered which string to pull– they were *yours*. And they always would be.

Oh, yes. Monty *believed* in that.

He absently brushed lint from the shoulder of his long coat.

Monty would need to add someone like that to his department, as he had no intention of getting his *own* hands dirty by fighting the Consortium, should it ever come to that. Monty was the king on the chess board of life; he was *above* the fighting. He left that to the pawns. The loyal and expendable little pawns.

He was simply the one who pushed the metaphorical button; he wasn't the bomb which was released.

But *everyone* had a button.

"Was the gold I gave you not enough, Gyre?" He asked the man casually, making sure confusion was apparent in his voice. "I thought we had an agreement."

That got Draugr's attention, and she slowly turned to look at her companion in angry accusation.

A wicked smile crossed Monty's scarred face.

Everyone.

"Gold?" She advanced on the other man and grabbed him by the front of his uniform, lifting him off of the ground like he was weightless. "Draugr was not *given* gold. Draugr *desires* her gold. *Now*."

Gyre put his hands up. "Whoa! Whoa, slow down there, sister. I didn't get *nothing* from this guy. I'm just trying to *kill him*."

Monty busied himself by examining the crystal globe at the top of his cane. "I really do not understand what you hope to gain by denying this. It was a simple bargain: I give you the gold, you deliver your partner her half, and you both leave me alone." He shrugged. "Is the gold not still in your pocket? If I knew you would misplace the bribe, I would have given it to your partner instead."

Draugr let go of the man.

Gyre took a step back as the woman continued to tower over him. "*I don't have any fucking gold!*" He reached into the pockets of his trench coat and turned them inside out in an effort to show that

Monty was lying.

A small sack fell to the street with the unmistakable jingling sound of golden coins.

Coin collecting truly *was* a grand hobby.

...THAT little trick had taken Monty several days to engineer, and had ultimately involved some of his Irregulars who worked outside of the Crater Lair and performed actions around the city for him in a more *discreet* capacity. The bag had actually been in the other man's pocket for less than three minutes.

Monty tried to hide his smile.

Welcome to the machine, Gyre.

Draugr looked down at the bag and then very slowly refocused on her companion. "*No one* steals Draugr's gold." She snarled, pulling out her axe and round shield, which was painted with an image of a blue and red dragon.

Gyre swore and lashed out at her with his powers. The reddish-yellow laser cut a wide swath of destruction, which she blocked with her wooden shield. The enchanted material deflected the energy, and wasn't even singed.

She made a move to slice at him with her axe, but before she could, Gyre cut off her arm with his powers. Concentric circles of energy blasted the limb from her body like a hot knife through butter and propelled it a short distance away.

Draugr stared down at her severed arm lying on the ground for a long moment, as if surprised to see herself injured by something, then at the sizzling stump where it had formally been attached. Wisps of smoke gently rose from her seared flesh.

Gyre smirked and then cut her in half at the waist.

Monty casually ducked to avoid the beam of energy as it sliced through the woman and continued on its way down the street, blasting apart the façade of a hardware store in the distance.

The man's powers hadn't been oversold; they *obliterated* the woman's midsection like she was made of tissue paper and blew her to pieces. His powers were *indeed* amongst the most impressive displays of energy Monty had ever seen. He would be a valuable asset to anyone he worked for; powerful and *utterly* without morals. ...Pity that his abilities were so underutilized and underappreciated by his *current* employers. What the man really needed was someone with *vision* to show him the way. Someone to lead him from the wilderness into the future. Someone who understood the world, and could help Gyre find his place in it.

Gyre wiped his hands and stepped over the smoldering

chunks of the woman's dismembered corpse, then crossed his arms over his chest. He watched Monty for a moment, looking unimpressed. "Let me guess, dipshit: your plan was for Franken-bitch and I to kill each other? Or at the very least, distract us enough by fighting that you could get away?"

Monty calmly checked his watch again. "Something like that, yes."

The other man snorted and started stalking forward. "Well, so much for your whole 'puppet master' thing." He smirked at Monty. "You thought *wrong* this time, you pathetic little Mystery Man."

Monty leaned against his cane with both hands. "Gyre, I *never* think wrong."

Before the other man could reply to that, he was sliced in two lengthwise by the thin sloped blade of Draugr's Danish axe. The weapon effortlessly cut downward through his head and body, and then embedded itself up to its haft in the pavement between his legs.

Monty checked his watch and the tiny golden men inside confirmed what he had told Gyre: everything was going *exactly* as he planned. In fact, now he was currently running almost two minutes *ahead* of schedule. He had anticipated more of a struggle before Gyre was dispatched. The results of the battle between his job candidates had never been in question, but even *he* was surprised at how quickly Draugr had ended it. Gyre was one of the most powerful people in the world, but she had eliminated him with no effort, in mere seconds.

It was for the best though. Gyre had no potential for loyalty in him. Monty had no interest in loose cannons or selfish people who couldn't see the big picture. Gyre was not a team player, and Monty was scouting for the new quarterback of "Team Welles." It was a shame to kill someone so powerful, but Gyre had left him little choice. Had he been a better potential employee, the fight may have turned out very differently for him.

Pity.

The zombie woman bent to retrieve her severed arm and held it against the stump at her shoulder. A second later, the undead skin seamlessly repaired itself and she flexed her newly reattached bluish fingers.

Monty's eyes fell to his own mutilated hand, thinking about how nice it must be to have a body which could repair disfigurement like that. Sadly, that option had not been available to him.

She grabbed the bag of gold and tied it to her belt, then turned to glare at Monty, obviously debating with herself whether he was worth the effort to kill or not.

Her glowing blue eyes shone out from the strange shadows somehow being cast over her face, and met the cold milky blue remnants of his own left eye.

She was *far* from a mindless brute, no matter what the rest of the world thought. Monty could see that immediately. The woman was *considerably* smarter than people gave her credit for, but apparently he was the only one who ever noticed it. It was the equivalent of being a prospector who showed up late for the rush, but then discovered that the miners who got there first had mistakenly tossed away what they saw only as a rock. Just a slow-witted rock, who wasn't worth the effort. But *Monty* could see that this woman was in fact an *exceedingly* rough diamond. She was the toughest and most valuable thing in the mine.

All she needed was some help to *shine*.

"You and I aren't so different, are we?" He asked her rhetorically. "We're both underestimated by the others in our field, and we have both found a way to use that to our advantage." He pointed with his four fingered hand to the ancient rope burns around her neck, and then back to the bullet wound beneath his eye. "We've both been *scarred* by people who would see us dead to possess what is *ours*. ...Both been knocked down and left to die. Both heard the gloating words of the ones who thought themselves our murderers." He shook his head, a sly smile crooking the corners of his mouth. "...But neither one of us is that *easy* to kill, are we?" He shook his head again. "Oh, no. Not us."

He began to slowly limp around the woman in a circle as she watched him.

His voice began to build. "We *endure*. Though they call us 'soulless' and 'dead inside.' They say that we have 'no hearts,' and lack 'mercy.' That we are cold, inhuman and not right in the head. That our bodies are twisted and frightening. They try to *hold us back* from doing the things we believe are *right*. Tell us that we should *listen* to them as they seek to *strip us* of our *power* and our *treasure*." He shook his head again, gesturing with his free hand. "Oh, no. Not *us*! We *ENDURE*! *Don't we!?!*" His voice built even higher, letting his passion show in a booming voice. "We *thrive* on their contempt and their fear. We *thrive* when the odds are low and the only prize is survival. We *thrive* when the world is against us and it expects us to break. Break!?! " He shook his head vehemently. "Oh, no! *NOT US!*"

He pointed to the bisected remains of Gyre's body, remembering how he had touched the woman inappropriately.

"We fill the graves meant for us with the bodies of our

executioners and those who laid their hands upon us without consent. Those that think themselves *superior!* Superior!?! Oh, no! *Not to US!!!*" He nodded, continuing to circle around her, using his cane for support. "We come *BACK* for what's ours, *don't we*? No matter how *badly* you hurt us. No matter how badly you *scar* us. No matter how *rid of us* the world thought it was, or how much it might *rejoice* at our passing. We come *BACK! Don't we!?!* WE WOULDN'T GIVE THEM THE *SATISFACTION* OF STAYING GONE! OH, NO! *NOT US!!!*" He returned to his original place, and leaned forward on his walking stick with both hands, his voice returning to normal. "We. Will. *Win. That* is who we are. No matter what we are forced to do to achieve it. No matter how long it might take us. No matter which pieces of ourselves we have to sacrifice to accomplish it. We endure despite their best efforts to *stop us*. Despite their mocking taunts and disapproving glances. Despite the fact that we are *abominations* to this living Earth, and *disgust* those around us. Oh, yes. That is us. That is who we are. And we are not so different."

She watched him for another long moment, considering that... then shot out a hand to lift Montgomery up off the ground by his neck, his feet dangling in the air. Her gloved fingers tightened, cutting off his air and causing his monocle to fall from his face and dangle from the golden chain connecting it to his vest pocket.

"One-eyed man will bring Draugr her *gold*." She wrenched her weapon from the street by its long wooden pole handle, and pointed the sweeping silver inlayed head of the axe at him. "He will bring Draugr her gold *now*, or Draugr will send him to misty Niflhel beneath, the home where all dead evil men dwell." She pointed at Gyre's bisected body with the weapon. "Let another's wounds be one-eyed man's *only warning*."

She dropped him back to the street.

Monty hit the concrete gasping in lungfuls of air, then calmly put his monocle back on. He smiled up at her pleasantly; overjoyed to see that the woman was *everything* he had predicted that she would be.

More.

He now had access to one of the most powerful puppets in the troupe. His days of being concerned about fallout from the *other* puppets, should they object to his plans, were now *over*. If they got in his way, he now had someone who could cut their strings. *All of them.* And *this* woman was someone who *understood* the concept of loyalty. Someone whose faithfulness and trustworthiness would be *beyond question*. He was *sure* of it. It was simply a matter of pulling the *right* string...

"What is your name?"

"*Draugr.*"

He got back onto his feet and leaned forward on his cane eagerly, sensing his opening. "What *was* your name, Draugr?"

The woman was silent for a long moment. "...Hildr." She finally answered, shifting on her furred boots, showing a small indication of discomfort at the direction this conversation was headed. "Draugr was called 'Hildr Stoneblood' in life." Her cold eyes suddenly narrowed in suspicion again, glowing brighter. "One-eyed man is stalling and attempting to distract Draugr with big speeches and remembrances of life. He seeks to *charm* Draugr with honeyed words because he thinks Draugr is thickheaded and easily turned from task."

"On the contrary, I'm of the opinion that you are one of the *cleverest* people I've ever had the good fortune to know." He shook his head. "I can *assure* you, if I thought you were stupid or even *slow*, we would *not* be having this conversation." He smiled at her. "Just as *you* are not fooled by my 'honeyed words,' *I* am not fooled into thinking that you are in *any way* impaired, no matter how hard you may try to deliberately represent yourself as such." He tilted his head to the side. "I *see* something in you, Miss Stoneblood. Something quite *rare* and worth more to me than gold. Something which caused me to put my life on the line tonight, just for an *opportunity* to speak with you. I think you're worth risking *everything* for. I'm willing to bet all that I have on you, because among other things, I can recognize a kindred spirit who *relishes* being underestimated. I, playing the part of a powerless Mystery Man, and you... if you'll forgive me for being *deplorably* crude for a moment," he tipped his top hat to her in apology, "as a lumbering corpse with more breasts than brains." He was silent for a moment. "Oh yes, I think we are *very* much alike."

They eyed each other for a long moment; one coldblooded and ruthless entrepreneur sizing up another.

He felt the beginnings of a smile, already knowing how this encounter would end, and excited to begin the next phase.

"One-eyed man is not like Draugr," she finally answered, "he is far more *breakable*." She looked down at the blade of her bloody axe, then back at him, sending him a clear message. "Do not make Draugr *test* how much One-eyed Man can '*endure*.' He will *deliver* Draugr her gold *now* or Draugr will deliver *him* down below to the ninth world."

The sinister smile which crossed Monty's scarred face got impossibly wider.

His side of the chess board now had its queen.

She.

Was.

Marvelous.

"Miss Stoneblood, I can do better than *that*. As it turns out, we have an opening on my executive staff in the Purchasing Department, which I think you would be *perfect* for." He gestured for the woman to follow him. "Come, let us walk the crooked mile together, Hildy, and I shall tell you of my plans for the *future*." He started to limp away, and the woman trailed behind. "How would you like to be *Treasurer*?"

****

Ceann was an unhappy man.

...Or at least, the unhappy *wreckage* of one anyway.

All he had in the world was his dickweed little brother, his maniac sister(s) and his equally crazy parents. His entire world revolved around trying to keep them from killing themselves and each other, and sometimes it just made him so tired.

So very tired.

Ceann had been *born* tired.

He was just the shattered pieces of a man, held together by God knew what force, and animated for some purpose which escaped him.

His life was a curse.

Punishment for the crime of loving unwisely.

The world was a living hell, and his sentence was an eternity of haunting it like a ghost.

One of the disadvantages of having no eyes was that you could never close them. Ceann was always awake, no matter how much he may want to rest. Always watchful for some new disaster about to befall his people because they were *categorically* incapable of taking care of themselves. They seemed to run round the world like infants; aimlessly wandering in search of some new way to endanger themselves and make the twisted shell of Ceann's life even more difficult.

...No, infants with *scissors*, which they insisted on running with towards the busy street in front of a cliff of some kind. ...And a train. There would probably be a train in there somewhere too.

They were reckless and annoying and *deeply* stupid.

Which was why he was currently here, standing on some

dumb street in the middle of the most irritating city in the world, trying to help his brother's idiot friends. All because his brother was off on his honeymoon with a beautiful woman who was FAAAAAR too good for him, and Ceann wanted to make sure he didn't come home to the graves of his associates.

Truth be told, he wasn't sure why he even cared. Even if they *were* all brutally murdered, his brother would just shrug it off with some sarcastic asshole comment, and then go back to spending time with his perfect wife, who for *some* reason thought he was just *wonderful*.

Initially, Ceann had intended to go to Agletaria and help his brother's idiot friends there, but upon spending a few minutes with the idiot crew here, he realized that *these* idiots needed his help more than *those* idiots did. Hell, they needed more help than even *he* could provide them.

He glanced down at his "teammate."

Case in point.

The *terribly* young girl dressed as a Plague Doctor was attempting to rally her bravery to walk another step.

If Ceann had eyes, he'd be rolling them right now.

A fifty foot stroll had never taken anyone in the world this long. Hell, the first fish that ever crawled from the sea and took life's first steps onto the land had probably been walking faster than they were at the moment.

Plus, her costume was silly. He lived through the Black Death; it sucked.

The girl huddled in the doorway, breathing heavy and seeming utterly panicked. Ceann had seen sheep as they were slaughtered which looked more at ease. She moved with the fear and anxiety usually reserved only for those on the way to the gallows.

Ceann had a long history with fear though. He'd seen a lot of it over the many years of his life. Generally speaking, no one was really happy to run into the Headless Horseman. Even before he had lost his head though, people had still greeted him with dread. In fact, fear was the emotion he best understood. He'd seen it wash across the faces of people from Japan to Ireland and back again. He'd heard the terrified noises they made as he approached, and their screams of horror as they died.

He scared men.

He scared women.

He scared children.

He even scared most animals.

Ceann was quite *literally* a monster. They'd even made that movie about him starring what's-his-name. He had become some sort of ghost story over the years and his image now haunted books, television and film. Entire generations of people had lived their lives in fear of him.

He was the reason why they were afraid of the dark. He was what was lurking in the woods for them at night. He was the heartless beast which took their loved ones away for no reason.

He *was* fear.

Not that he particularly ever *wanted* to be feared, because he didn't. All he had ever wanted was to just do his job and go home. But somehow, home always seemed further and further away. His entire life was spent trying to make it there while there was still some of him left. But like a colander filled with water, every moment that went by, it felt like there was less and less of him remaining.

First his metaphorical heart had been torn from his chest and he had to watch as it was burned in front of him. ...And the pain of that stuck with him every moment of every day. And then he lost his very *real* head, and was forced to go on without it.

He was a man without a heart and without a head. He was broken, and he'd never be complete again. He wasn't meant to be.

Honestly, there really didn't seem much of a point to anything. If he had been on his own, he'd just find someplace nice and end it all. But Ceann *wasn't* alone. He had too many completely helpless people to look after.   He had always been willing to give up his own happiness so that they could have theirs, and that had certainly gotten easier since his happiness was *literally* impossible to achieve now. It was simply no longer his fate. It had been torn from his chest.

His happiness was murdered long ago.

But he still had a job to do, and right now, that meant helping out his brother while his brother *once again* got everything he wanted *handed* to him, despite the fact that he did absolutely *nothing* to deserve it.

Ceann loved his brother, but that didn't mean he didn't find him *endlessly* frustrating. Sometimes, he just *hated* that little prick. He was the fair-haired child who was just allowed to do whatever he wanted, and Ceann had to follow along behind to protect him from the fallout of his own actions. Fallout which usually blew up in Ceann's face. ...Hell, blew the damn thing *off*.

But that didn't matter right now. His people were in danger, so it was his job to protect them.

Again.

So, he was taking part in yet another battle, and had been forced to endure the assistance of one of his brother's silly friends. Thus far, their part of this battle had consisted of slowly walking half a block down the street. They'd take a few steps, then the girl would panic and she'd hide somewhere for several minutes.

He impatiently tapped his gloved fingers on the top of the mailbox he was standing next to. His spelling toy had no comforting words in it, and even if it did, he really didn't have the time or inclination to type them in.

This was taking too long.

He kicked down the door to one of the buildings and turned back to the girl in the bird mask, pointing inside. "YOU HAVE SPELLED: PIGEON." He rapidly typed out his thought. "YOU HAVE SPELLED: STAY."

She looked up at him, panic coming through loud and clear despite the mask. She huddled down further, glancing into the darkened building. "Terra *pericolosa*."

He wished his spelling toy could somehow make a dismissive snort, but sadly, it could not.

"YOU HAVE SPELLED: YES." He hoped the patronizing sarcasm was clear to her, but it apparently wasn't. The girl lived in her own little world. He got the sense that even if he *had* been able to effectively communicate the emotion, she would have missed it anyway. She didn't seem like someone who really understood the subtleties of non-verbal communication.

The whole thing was a mystery to Ceann. He had no idea what was going on inside the human's head. He wasn't one, and he didn't have one.

Several people suddenly appeared at the end of the street and Ceann marched out to meet them. He braced his feet apart and drew his sword, the flames casting shifting shadows onto the facades of the darkened buildings around him.

The men took off running in the opposite direction.

Even brainwashed by that weird little girl on stage with Reece, no one wanted to fuck with the Headless Horseman. ...Or maybe they just didn't realize that he was a member of the Consortium now. ...Sort of. In either case, Ceann didn't particularly care about them. He'd kill them if it came to that, and he wouldn't think twice about it. They were innocents, true, but Ceann had killed his fair share of innocent people over the years. That was the cost of being a monster. And when you really came down to it, a few dozen people more one way or the other wasn't going to make that big a difference at this point. He'd gone too far to ever go back now.

There was no redemption for Ceann.

No hope of rescue.

No forgiveness.

Some debts ran too deep to ever pay.

There was no happy ending for things like him.

That wasn't part of his story. He knew that, because he'd seen the movie. And the cartoon. And the TV show. And that one episode of Scooby-Doo which his little sister had made him watch.

Ceann had already lost the only battle in his life that mattered, and now he was just killing time until the end. Until he could just go to sleep and not have to try to juggle his family and their strange problems. ...Until he could rest.

From behind him, Ceann could hear a large group of people approaching. Unlike the last guys, these people had powers. They were *dedicated* to the SPRM company line, and were unlikely to be scared off by one headless man.

If he were on his own, that wouldn't have really bothered him. There wasn't a lot left in the world that could hurt Ceann, and he *sincerely* doubted these people posed him any great risk.

Sadly, he was *not* alone. In his infinite brilliance as a leader, Julian had stuck Ceann with a tiny little Italian girl to watch over during the battle. It was a *serious* handicap. The girl could seemingly do nothing but cry, and they hadn't actually even *done* anything worth crying *about* yet. And if he had to guess, when the battle really *started,* her skills in that *actual* fight would consist of... wait for it... *crying.*

He held up a finger to indicate silence, and gently took her hand, pulling her back onto the darkened sidewalk. All they had to do was get around the corner and everything would be fine. They'd lose the people tracking them, and then Ceann could stick the girl someplace safe and go back to pick the guys off one by one.

It was a *beautiful* plan.

...But like everything else in Ceann's life, it was doomed from the start.

He should have known.

The girl took several steps onto the street, then stopped. "Oh God....Oh God...*ohmygodohmygodohmygod!*" Every muscle in her body locked and she froze in place, her head darting around the area like every building and tree was an enemy poised to strike. She started rapidly babbling in Italian, which wasn't Ceann's mother tongue, but he understood some of it. The girl wasn't afraid of the men with guns and super-powers trying to kill her, she was terrified about being outside *at all*.

Weird.

"YOU HAVE SPELLED: NOISE." He tapped her on her tiny little shoulder and pointed down the street. "YOU HAVE SPELLED: ALERTING. YOU HAVE SPELLED: ENEMY."

Her rapid breathing became a loud gasping sound, as she struggled for air.

"YOU HAVE SPELLED: QUIETLY." He tried again.

Her gasping got louder, turning into a high-pitched wheeze.

"YOU HAVE SPELLED: URGE. YOU HAVE SPELLED: SILENT."

Her breathing got even more rapid.

He made a gentle motion with his hands, indicating that she should keep her noise down. "YOU HAVE SPELLED: PLEASE."

She began to tremble like a frightened child.

If Ceann needed to breathe, he'd sigh in frustration and annoyance right now.

He looked around the area, trying to find someone who understood what this girl's problem was and how to deal with her. Anyone! Maybe that Eskimo guy or something, because Ceann had NO clue. He turned back to her, holding his arms out in baffled amazement. He pointed at her. "YOU HAVE SPELLED: MYSTERY." He shrugged again, trying to get her to focus on telling him what the hell was going on with her. "YOU HAVE SPELLED: WHAT. YOU HAVE SPELLED: PROBLEM."

The girl hyperventilated and passed out, dropping like a stone at his feet. Her masked unconscious face rested on top of his left boot.

If he still had his head, he would be shaking it sadly right now.

How did he get himself into situations like this?

He actually glanced down at the girl in confusion, surprise and wonder. "YOU HAVE SPELLED: CRAZY." He said to no one. He pressed the button several more times, just for his own benefit. "CRAZY. CRAZY. CRAZY."

…On the bright side, this did simplify matters though. He leaned down to pick the girl up, draped her over his shoulder, and then trudged down the street to fight his brother's friends' city's enemies for some reason.

God, he needed a fucking vacation.

Or to finally die.

...One or the other.

Why was it that his entire life was spent cleaning up someone else's messes? Why was *he* the one who always had to pick up the pieces? Why was it that *he* was the one who was *falling* to pieces in the process?

...And predictably, that's when the ground began to rumble and he saw a dark shape on the horizon racing towards him at unbelievable speed.

Perfect.

Just fucking *perfect*.

Again, he wished he had the ability to let out an annoyed but resigned sigh over his incredibly piss poor lot in life.

But he didn't. The Headless Horseman would remain forever silent on that issue.

And all others.

Yes, Ceann was a *deeply* unhappy wreckage of a man.

CHAPTER 23

KING: "IT JUST SEEMS TO ME THAT IF THE PEOPLE
OF THIS CITY REALLY LOVED THE MARY SUE AND
REALLY LOVED THEIR COUNTRY, THEY'D BE OUT THERE
ON THE STREETS RIGHT NOW TRYING TO KILL THE
CONSORTIUM, THAT'S ALL."

STORMS: "YOU MAKE AN EXCELLENT POINT, PAIGE. I
THINK WE SHOULD STOP THE SHOW AND GO OUT
THERE TOO, IN ORDER TO SET THE RIGHT EXAMPLE."

KING (STANDING UP): "IT'S THE LEAST WE CAN DO
FOR SOMEONE AS INSPIRATIONAL AS MARY SUE."

TRANSCRIPT OF "KING OF CAPES AND COWLS," MEDIA:
TELEVISION, SHOW: 1408, NEWSCHANNEL 6, FRIDAY
21:00-22:00 EST, NETWORK SEGMENT-ID:
918000606

Julian had now expended his team's entire roster.

The crowds only continued to grow, and they appeared to be getting angrier.

The Lady Bridget had become the victim of a mind-controlling little boy in a sundress.

And he was still blocks from the sea.

All in all, he had enjoyed his *last* date with Bridget far more than *this* one. True, that one hadn't ended especially well either, but at least no one had ripped him to shreds.

A large mob of citizens surged up in front of him, preventing him from reaching the water. His only option was to head down an alleyway to the next block, and try again.

A man reached out and tried to grab Bridget from his arms, and Julian kicked the man away. If they ever did manage to stop The Mary Sue's mind-control, the guy would most likely end up with several broken ribs.

Good.

Julian had no time to worry about the people around him. His only concern was Bridget and getting Bridget from the fight as quickly as possible. She was in danger here, so she had to leave. Julian had no qualms about abandoning this entire city if it kept her safe. Besides, the city had made its choice. It had never liked him anyway, so it couldn't exactly expect him to go out of his way for it now.

Risk Bridget for the surface people? HA! Not going to happen.

The next street over was similarly blocked by a crowd of angry people rushing towards him, so Julian was forced to head up a block and try again. He was literally *losing* progress in his efforts to make it to either the river or the sea, but it wasn't like he had a lot of choice in the matter. As long as The Mary Sue was around, the surface people's *true* malevolence was revealed.

But Julian had been a villain a long time. He'd been hated and chased by one person or another for his entire life.

And he hadn't been caught yet.

The next block was even more crowded than the first, and Julian was now effectively boxed in on all sides. His gaze darted around for some way to escape the surface people's trap, then he raced forward to kick down the door to a dress store. He ran through the building, then burst out into the connecting alley.

Clear.

Plus, he was now headed in the right direction again, which was good. All he would have to do was...

He arrived at the street corner to find Reece and half a dozen members of the... whatever the man's stupid club was called... honestly, Julian forgot... walking towards the river. Reece had *always* been a mere distraction, even *before* he lost his mind and started trying to kill Julian.

The man looked shocked to see Julian burst onto the scene though.

"What are you doing, Sargassum?" The man asked him calmly.

"Leaving."

Reece shook his head. "I don't see why." He pointed back and forth between them. "Don't you see? We want the same basic thing. We both want humanity *gone*. I just want the empowered people to stay at the end of it, that's all." He gestured to the crowd of terrestrials forming around them. "But *these* people? They don't matter. Not at all. You've always known that. You are the empowered person who has *always* seen that the clearest. The one whose own views on them are closest to my own. They have persecuted and victimized your people and mine for as long as either of us can remember. But now the tables have turned. I can *give* your aquatic countrymen their freedom. *Watch*." He turned to a woman wearing a sweatshirt, who was standing next to him. The girl appeared to be in her late teens or early twenties, and had the innocent look of a surface-dweller who had not yet discovered how evil her kind was. Reece glanced down at her and handed her a weapon. "Dear? The Mary Sue wants you to shoot yourself as punishment for your crimes against Lord Sargassum's kingdom."

"Of course!" The girl enthused happily. "*Anything* for her! She's so..."

BLAM!

Julian jolted in shock as he watched the self-inflicted gunshot rip the friendly looking young woman's head off and splatter the crowd of her fellow citizens with blood and brain matter.

Reece turned back to him. "You see how *easy* it is to punish a lesser species for their crimes against our people, Julian?"

Julian remained dazedly fixated on the rapidly spreading pool of blood on the concrete where the female terrestrial's face had once been.

He felt numb and sick.

"They don't matter. It doesn't matter if you're a Cape or a villain. They're the *same thing*." Reece pointed back and forth between them. "*We* matter. I don't want to hurt someone who wants the same things that I want. There is a place for you in the SPRM. A home. I give you my word that if you join me, once we're done with the Norm threat, both of our kingdoms will live in peace. I will rule my people on the land, and you, your people under the sea." He shook his head. "And there will be no one left to bother either of us ever again. We can have *peace*."

Julian kept staring blankly at the blood and for the first time in his life, he had an epiphany.

...Bridget was a surface-dweller.

He looked out over the crowd, his mouth hanging open.

...And these were her people.

If he didn't do something to protect them, her kind would be killed and Bridget would be sad. She'd be as alone as he had always felt. Feel the pain which comes from constant isolation. Sure, Julian would be there to soften the blow, but if he could just prevent the extermination of her kind *now,* then even the momentary sadness she

334

felt over the extinction of the human race could be avoided.

And in Julian's world, preventing Bridget's unhappiness was his main duty as a Cape.

Julian wasn't entirely certain that he believed in the idea that certain kinds of Eternal people could know who they were destined to be with on sight. Frankly, it sounded weird and kinda stupid to him. He didn't understand it. He did understand the biology of the deep though, all except one thing which had always confused him: he had always wondered why certain fish would go upriver to find their mate, even though after doing so, they would surely die. Why wouldn't they just stay where it was safe? He didn't understand why anyone would toss their life away, just to find a mate.

...But he understood it now.

Julian still kinda hated this city. But he loved Bridget *more.* And if Bridget needed him to stand up and be a man, then that was what he was going to do. He was going to show this city who he *was.*

He wasn't like Reece.

The man killed innocent people.

And no matter what Reece did, he could never turn Julian into that. Everett had been right all along; Julian was part of the *old* way. The *better* way. Julian was part of *Everett's* way; his son in every way that mattered. He understood how these kinds of things *should* be done, and that sure as hell didn't involve brainwashing little college girls and getting them to shoot themselves in front of you to prove a point.

No.

Hell, no!

Julian might not know what he was. He might have never really known where he belonged. But he knew *damn* sure where he *didn't,* and that was with Reece.

...Besides, even if that *weren't* the case, the man was *still* a terrestrial and Julian was predisposed not to like him on general principle.

His gaze slowly looked out over the crowd again and then settled on Reece. He gently put Bridget back on her feet and straightened to his full height.

Reece apparently saw the meaning behind the action. "You don't have to do this, Sargassum. You don't have to throw your life away over something so meaningless."

"My reasons for doing the things that I do have *great* meaning to me." He squared his shoulders. "And I have fought better men than *you.* Men who had *honor* and who knew more about duty and sacrificing for their people than you could *ever* understand. It would be a *disgrace* to their memory if I let you kill me here when they had failed so many times."

Reece let out a weary sigh and pointed at Bridget. "You know I could just get her to stab you or something, right?"

"If you say one *word* to her, your second will be muffled by your own blood." Julian threatened.

Reece chuckled. "You *can't* fight me." He shook his head. "Want me to remind you of *why*?" Reece held out his hand to Bridget. "Mary Sue would want you to come here, my dear."

Bridget obediently placed her hand into his.

And Julian saw red.

He smashed his trident down on the man's forearm, knocking it away. Julian winced in pain as the damage from the attack was inflicted on his *own* arm though. He was fairly certain he had just broken his wrist.

"See?" Reece smiled knowingly as Julian held the wounded limb against his chest in an effort to lessen the pain. "Even if by some *miracle* you did manage to hit me, anything you did to *me* would just cause damage to *you*." Reece crossed his arms over his chest. "That's how my powers work. Plus," he held out his arms, "I have an army of eight million people in this city, and I will tell them to tear your little girlfriend apart while you *watch*."

"No. You can tell them to *try*." Julian corrected, ignoring the pain from his arm and holding up his trident. "You are trifling in the affairs of *gods*, mortal."

"I'm terrified."

"I shall crash against you like a wave of blood and wash you free of this world and into oblivion!"

"Oh yeah?" Reece chuckled. "And how exactly are you going to do *that*?" Reece made a show of looking around the space. "Because I'm not seeing any water around here, genius. We're *blocks* away from anything even *close* to being water, unless you count the fact that I'm close to pissing my pants from *laughing* at you. You're USELESS! I was willing to let you on my team simply because I'm a nice guy and I hate killing my own kind, but we *both* know that you can't do anything and never could. As long as I don't go for any swims, I think I'll be fine."

Julian looked up at the sky, utterly amused. "It's times like these that I'm so *glad* the surface world educational system is in the state it's in." He sighed. "Since I'm reportedly going to die in a moment, allow me to use my last seconds of life to give you a brief refresher course on the Roman cosmology." He cleared his throat. "The Roman world was principally controlled by three brothers, each of whom oversaw one realm. Jupiter ruled over the sky and the world of the Gods. Pluto ruled over the underworld and the dead." Julian smiled icily and held his arms out to indicate the city. "But the world of *man?* That was the domain of Neptune, *my* father." He shook his head. "Despite what you may have been told, he was *not* the god of the sea. He chose to live there because it's the most powerful thing in his lands." He swung the trident downward, jamming its spines into the pavement and causing the entire street to shake with power. A pulse of energy was released, like a ripple in a pond. "But he was really the god of the *Earth*."

"Oooooh, scary." Reece snorted. "What? You think a little tremor is going to scare me?"

Julian shook his head. "No. I don't imagine that it will." He turned to Bridget, his voice utterly calm. "Hold onto me."

"What? Why?"

His smile became a full-fledged smirk. "I'm showing this city *my wrath*."

In the distance, a shadow appeared on the horizon, rapidly drawing closer and filling the street with a deep rumbling sound. The mass moved faster than anything anyone in this city had ever seen, and was upon them before they could react. A wall of water several stories high crashed over the seawall and into the city beyond. The tidal wave tore down the street, washing away everything in its path.

"So," Julian called, taking on a chipper quality evident even over the roar of the water as it closed in on them, "*who's up for a swim?*"

****

The Mary Sue could tell that things were almost done with this city. True, the Consortium's arrival had been unexpected, but it was more like "surprise party in your honor" unexpected, rather than "disaster" unexpected. It was like a gift for all the SPRM had done.

Like they were being rewarded for their hard work and dedication.

Honestly, it was beautiful. A sign that the fates were on their side.

First the city would go down in flames, and then the SPRM would move onto the next one, and so forth. The entire *globe* would be free of the scourge of humanity and only the empowered *worthy* would remain.

It was a *lovely* dream, and one she couldn't wait to see come to pass.

In the meantime though, there was still some cleanup to do and a ceremony to finish. Reece had gone off to try to persuade that fish-man guy to join the winning team, but Mary Sue didn't understand why he cared.

It was just a distraction from what *really* mattered.

She pressed her hands to the emeralds on the tablet, carefully pushing the last one into place. The object began to grow and radiate with green power.

Her smile grew.

The gate would now be opened and...

There was a noise from an alleyway behind the podium and she turned around to see what it was. "Joe?" She called into the inky blackness, trying to see if the man at the other end of it had seen anything.

"Guess again." Came a voice in reply.

Mary Sue's face contorted into a pout. Everyone was always trying to ruin her achievements. Why couldn't people ever be happy for her? Why did they always feel the need to tear her down?

It was unfair.

She snapped her fingers and sent two of the SPRM's men into the alley to root out the cause of this unfortunate blemish on what was an otherwise beautiful evening.

The men vanished into the darkness.

A moment later, several odd noises echoed through the alleyway... and then silence.

"Shall I point out the logical fallacy inherent in sending killers to kill a killer who kills killers for a living?" Asked the voice pleasantly. "Or would you rather we did that *face-to-face?*"

Mary Sue's eyes narrowed. "Come out here, please." She asked sweetly, using her powers to control the person. "I have something I want to *give you*."

"Hey, because you asked so *nice*."

Mary Sue heard a noise behind her and spun around to find that Multifarious had suddenly somehow appeared there.

"Hi there." The masked figure said calmly before swinging out a samurai sword in an effort to decapitate her.

Mary Sue stumbled back, avoiding the strike by inches, and falling to the ground. "Stop!" She ordered. "I'm Mary Sue! You can't kill me! I'm..." She stopped midsentence and was forced to roll to the side to dodge Multifarious' follow-up attack, as he swung the sword downwards to try hacking Mary Sue in two.

That was odd. Her powers should have stopped that strike.

She kicked out her foot, catching the sword handle as the blade ricocheted off of the street, and knocked it free from Multifarious' grasp. She jumped to her feet and slammed her fist into the figure's face. Her hand impacted the milky white faceplate the person wore, and Mary Sue winced as her fingers came close to breaking.

Her opponent used the distraction to grab her arm, pull her forward and slam an elbow into the side of her head.

She staggered away, dazed.

Multifarious stalked after her, kicked her in the back of the leg so that she fell to her knees, and grabbed her head, intending to break her neck...

Mary Sue's gaze fell on a police officer standing on the corner staring blankly at the tablet, patiently waiting for the ceremony which would kill him to begin.

Mary Sue screamed at him, using her powers to control his actions again. "*SHOOT HIM!*"

The officer immediately drew his firearm and began shooting at Multifarious, who dodged to the side in an effort to avoid getting hit.

Mary Sue rolled forward and came up with a shotgun which the owner of a liquor store near where their ceremony was taking place had dropped when he died, and spun around to finish the masked Cape off.

Multifarious leapt clear as the 12 gauge punched a hole in the car door behind him, and dove into the sidewalk.

...Right into the officer's line of fire again, who instantly shot him.

The round tore through Multifarious' arm, spinning him around and showering the wall behind with blood. The Cape swore viciously and staggered to the side as more bullets ripped the area around him to pieces.

Mary Sue fired off the shotgun, missing her target but still spattering the back of Multifarious' thigh with several pellets of buckshot, and he hit the pavement in a heap again. He rebounded and kicked down a door to one of the apartment buildings and staggered inside as another round from the shotgun blasted the door to splinters behind him.

Mary Sue got back to her feet and reloaded the weapon from

a box of shells the Norm store owner had been carrying, and turned to look at the police officer again. "I wonder if you could do me a favor and make certain Multifarious doesn't escape out the back, please?"

The officer smiled. "Of course! After all you've done for the department over the years, it would be the *least* I could do! You're an inspiration to all of us!" He obediently ran off.

She pumped the shotgun, and started towards the building, following the blood trail. The Cape was bleeding profusely, so it was easy to track him. Hell, with any luck, the blood loss *alone* would kill him.

The building had been cleansed before the SPRM had begun their ceremony, and the area around her as she walked through the building began to fill with signs of the fight. Gyre and the others had wasted so much *effort* on these people, when they could have just left well enough alone and waited for the ceremony to kill them. But they had *obviously* had fun, so Mary Sue wasn't the kind of person who would get in the way of that. The men worked so hard, it was only right that they got a chance to celebrate a little and let off some steam.

Bullet holes and bodies filled the hall, and Mary Sue made a face at having to get Norm blood on her shoes. She *really* didn't want to catch anything from these creatures. Slumped in the doorway to one of the apartments was a dead man with a scar on his face, blood covering his chest and shirt. The man's handsome face stared down at his own chest, his mouth hanging open. Mary Sue disregarded him. She stepped over the body of a woman, ignoring her sightless eyes staring towards the ceiling and the bloody wound on her neck. Next to the woman was the body of a small boy, who appeared to have been hit in the chest with one of Gyre's energy blasts. The gaping wound which went straight through his body was blasted in the dead center of his little blue baseball jersey, the edges of which were blackened and burned.

Mary Sue didn't care about these people. They were merely the evidence of a victorious battle. They were obviously Norms or Norm apologists. It was people like *them* who had made the world what it was. They weren't even *real* people. *Real* people had super-powers. These things were just animals. Weak, un-empowered little animals. Just *beasts* befouling the Super-Persons Resistance Movement's lands and trying to rob Mary Sue of her destiny. THEY were the reason why no one ever appreciated her the way she DESERVED to be appreciated. Why she always had to work *twice* as hard as everyone else. Why no one ever took the time to ask her what

SHE wanted or how SHE felt. No, they were all too selfish for that. But what could you expect? They didn't even have super-powers.

And Mary Sue meant to see them all exterminated for that.

She had memorized the map of the building before taking part in this mission and she knew the hallway ended around the next corner. Mary Sue left *nothing* to chance. Her powers were impossible to resist, but she found it was always best to prepare for the worst anyway. Her target would be cowering there. She smiled as she pictured Multifarious' terrified face, exalting in the knowledge that the people who shielded the Norms from justice were now the ones living in fear. It was *their* turn to hide in the shadows. It was *their* turn to know what it was to be persecuted.

She followed the blood trail into what she knew was a dead end, and jumped out into the hallway, pulling the trigger and sending a round into the darkness.

…And hit nothing.

Where the hell had…

Suddenly an arm wrapped around her neck in a chokehold.

"*Always* check the bodies." The voice whispered in her ear.

"…But we're *friends,* Multifarious." She soothed, trying again to control her opponent with her voice. "Don't you remember all the things I've done for you?"

"I am not Multifarious. Today I am… Acoustic Shadow, the Silent Assassin. …Acoustic Shadow is deaf," the voice got lower, nearly a growl, *"and doesn't like you very much."*

She felt a sharp pain in her back as Multifarious slowly slipped a blade into her spine, and she fell to the floor. She stared up in astonishment at the figure standing over her, which she had casually passed by moments before in the hallway. The image of Multifarious' real face began to blur and fade, as she lost more and more blood, until it became merely a shadow, blending into the hallway around it. The ghostly figure put on that weird facemask again, and casually straightened a blood-soaked shirt.

"Next time you try to take over someone's mind, make sure you don't *miss one*, lady." The shadow tapped a finger against its temple, indicating its fragmented psyche. "And if you want to start killing people professionally, you're going to have to learn to double-tap the bodies you pass, just to make sure that they're *really* dead." The figure limped over to where the shotgun was laying, and bent down with obvious pain to pick it up. "Here, I'll *show you*." The shadow placed its foot on the center of her chest, and pumped the weapon, ejecting the empty shell. "The Consortium of Chaos would like to give *this* to you in recognition of all you've done for us. We hope you find it as *inspirational* as we do, you fucking bitch." Multifarious held the weapon with one hand and pressed the barrel of the gun against Mary Sue's face. "This is for my friends."

"Wait!" Mary Sue choked weakly. "You can't just... NOOO!"

Multifarious pulled the trigger and the world went dark

****

Julian smiled as the wave slammed into the crowd of people around him like a freight train, and there was nothing they could do about it but scream in fear. Reece and his men turned to run, but there was no escape from the fury of the ocean once it was unleashed. The liquid mass crashed into them and carried them away like ants.

Julian held onto Bridget and allowed the wave to pass over him. Julian once again felt at home. The waters caressed him like a lover's embrace, welcoming him back home and promising to aid him in his fight against his enemies.

Bridget began to panic in his arms as the wave carried them along in its swirling maw, desperately trying to make it to the surface and air.

Julian smiled again.

She was so sweet. But she had nothing to fear from the water. She was queen of the seas now. Granted, he hadn't technically gotten around to proposing or anything, but she was his queen all the same. He didn't believe in surface laws and their preoccupation with paperwork and ceremonies.

She was his queen and she always would be.

The water wouldn't hurt her. It belonged to her the same way he did.

One day she'd see that.

In the meantime though, he'd have to improvise.

He tightened his grip on her arm, tugging her down next to him and keeping her from the surface. She frantically pin-wheeled her arms, trying to break free, but he held her close. She met his gaze with panic-filled eyes, and Julian pulled her to him. He pressed his lips to hers, forcing oxygen into her lungs as the water carried them through the city streets.

She wrapped her arms around his neck, returning his embrace. His lips surged over hers, his hands caressing the back of her head and reaching down to wrap her legs around him, pulling her up against him and letting him feel more of her incredible body.

He finally pulled away as the wave began to ebb, and he gently ran his hand down her face. She looked too stunned to speak, which she probably couldn't anyway, since she was still underwater.

But no matter.

His head popped out of the water and he let the wave carry him along until his feet hit the ground, and continued on with its momentum, never breaking stride.

Ahead of him, the few remaining members of the SPRM were staggering to their feet and clustering around like drowned rats, searching for high ground. The citizens who had been crowded around when the wave hit were now nowhere to be seen, with the exception of a few stragglers who were currently fleeing the scene, so he was assuming that Multifarious had been able to deliver his *message* to the Mary Sue boy and the city was no longer under orders to kill him.

And now it was *Reece's* turn.

He turned to Bridget. "Lady Haniver? Would you be so kind as to remain here for a moment? I need to go speak to these gentlemen about their behavior towards my city."

She sat down on one of the stairs to the building, still looking dazed, either from almost drowning or the kiss. "...Yeah. Yeah, you go do what you gotta do, big guy. I'll just... sit."

Reece staggered onto a raised plaza between two buildings, staying out of the water. In front of him stood several other super-people who Julian didn't recognize. But it didn't matter.

Julian prowled towards them through the water, which still came up to his waist. "Now, where *were* we?" He took on a thoughtful expression. "Oh, yes. As I recall, you were telling me about your 'unstoppable army of eight million people,' that's right." He smiled at the group of SPRM men as they started to move to attack him. Julian had no idea what their powers *were* exactly, but it wouldn't matter in a moment. "Yeah, eight million people sure is a *lot*," he said with fake enthusiasm, his smile growing, "but there are *plenty* more fish in the sea than that."

The expressions of the men turned to fear as they saw the sharks swimming around Julian and through the water towards them. The men tried to make their way to dry land, but the water slowed them down and the sharks rapidly pulled them under, one after the next. One of the men surfaced a moment later with a bloodcurdling scream, and then there was silence as the ocean ran red.

Julian ignored them and casually strolled from the sea up the steps towards Reece. Ahead of him, a SPRM member unleased a pack of attack dogs, pointing at Julian. The animals raced forward, intent on killing him.

"Fun fact about *dogs*, surface man: they evolved from *whales*." Julian glanced at the animals and they stopped in their tracks. "You are now free of his enslavement. Take your *vengeance* for the mistreatment you have suffered at his hands." He told them calmly.

The dogs instantly attacked their cruel handler, ripping at his flesh. Julian ignored them and continued on his way up the stairs.

Reece pulled himself to his feet and glared at Julian. "Well, you're *full* of surprises, aren't you?"

"Not really, no." Julian shook his head. "I told you I was the most powerful man alive. I can't help the fact you were too stupid and arrogant to listen."

Reece reached behind his back and pulled out a gun. "If you think I've come this far to let you kill me now, you're in for a surprise of your *own,* Julian."

He shook his head. "I am not a surface man. I am not a murderer. If you surrender now, I will let you live. Let your *own* people deliver their justice."

Reece cocked the gun. "And if I refuse to surrender? Just what do you think you're going to do to me? Anything you try will only end up hurting *you*. And I doubt you can pull off your little tidal wave trick twice."

"Bet he can." Bridget chimed in helpfully from her place on the stairs. "I bet Jules can go *all night*." She leaned her head to the side in an effort to get the water from her ear. "I think you should feed him to the sharks or something, Jules. That was neat. No, no! Wait! Get a giant octopus to tear his arms and legs off!" She laughed, imagining the scene.

"Shut up, you little Norm whore! Those were my men you're talking about!" Reece pointed the gun at her. "Leave it to the king of the ocean to fall in love with a fucking *whale.*"

"Scratch that." Julian stormed forward. "Changed my mind: now I'm going to kill you."

Reece turned the gun on Julian, but the shot went wide when Julian used the forked end of his trident to redirect the man's aim. Reece pulled his hand free and tried to shoot again, but Julian kicked him backwards down the stairs to a lower section of the plaza, wincing as the man hit each step and caused Julian pain.

But Julian had endured a lot of pain over the years. He could deal with it.

Reece hit the pavement at the bottom, and Julian stood over

him. He held the trident over his head, and then slammed it towards the man's neck.

Reece closed his eyes as the spines descended… but they never connected with his skin. Instead, his head was held in place between the spikes of the weapon, pinned to the surface of the road.

The man began to laugh. "Told you you couldn't kill me. Anything you do to me…"

He trailed off as Julian straightened and walked a short distance away, where he casually knocked off the nozzle of the fire hydrant with his foot, spraying the scene with water. …Water which began to rapidly fill the small depressed area where Reece was pinned.

Julian ran a hand through his hair. "I'm not going to lay a *hand* on you, surface-man." He bent down to kneel on Reece's chest with one leg, his face utterly calm as the water in the area began to rise. "You know, despite all of your impressive powers and feelings of superiority over me and my 'useless' gifts," he leaned closer to the man as Reece struggled to free himself and escape the water as it closed in over his face, "I bet you'd trade it all for the ability to breathe underwater right now, huh? Not so 'useless' a power *after all*, is it?" He met the man's panicked eyes as the bubbles rising to the surface of the water slowed. "You *really* shouldn't have touched my woman."

The bubbles stopped.

Julian waited a moment longer to make certain the man was no longer a threat, then pried the trident from the cement, and shook his head in disgust. "Fucking *terrestrials*. Always trying to take what's *mine*."

Bridget started across the plaza towards him. "Pretty sure a lot of people would see that as murder, big guy."

"Well, they can take it up with my attorney. She's due back in a few days, and I'll be in court for my last arrest anyway, so it will be easy." He made a face. "Make that '*arrests*,' because I already have three of them, and this would make four."

She smiled at him. "Ah, my hero."

He took her hand and helped her down the stairs, then pulled her close again. "I have to go locate my missing coworkers right now, but then, I fully intend to continue our date right where it left off."

She stared at him in silence for a moment. "…Okay. Yeah. I was thinking the same thing." She shook her head. "No sewers though. Let's just get a hotel or something, okay?"

"Wherever you will be the most comfortable, is where *I* will be the most comfortable, Lady Bridget."

"You know, you just drowned half the city, and the body of your latest victim is bobbing at your feet, and this is *still* more romantic than you usually are."

"I think I am really growing as a *person*." He decided, beginning to walk towards where he believed his coworkers could be found. "And I assure you, the city is fine. The brainwashed people will all survive."

She gestured to the devastation around them. "And the buildings?"

"They probably had flood insurance."

"And if they didn't?"

He shrugged helplessly. "Act of god."

"That's not what that means." She shook her head, hurrying after him. "*You* aren't the god they're talking about when they say that."

"Well, then they should have been clearer about that too. I am blameless."

Ahead of them, they spotted Tupilak, standing in front of another man who appeared to be covered with razorblades.

"My people believe that everything has a spirit." Quinn told the man threateningly. "A *soul*, if you will. Every rock, tree, squirrel... *everything*. So, when you stop and think about it, killing a dozen people is no different than having burgers for lunch. Murdering a king is no different than stepping on an ant. It's all the same." He smiled. "I live on a diet of *souls*... and I'm *very* hungry." He held out his gloved hand and...

Multifarious suddenly appeared behind Quinn's opponent and cut his head off with a katana.

Quinn made an aggravated sound. "*Dammit*, Mull! I was doing my whole 'badass shaman' spiel, and then you had to come along and *ruin* it." He crossed his arms over his chest. "We've talked about that before."

Multifarious nudged the other man's severed head with the tip of his/her boot, apparently in an effort to see if the man had somehow *survived* the decapitation. "Oh super," Mull stabbed the blade down through the head just to make sure it was dead, then looked up, "Quinn the Eskimo's here. Everybody jump for joy."

"Hey, *fuck you*, Mull! Okay? I don't have time right now to..." His eyes traveled down to the considerable amount of blood seeping from Multifarious' shoulder and leg, dripping onto the street. "What the hell happened to *you?*"

Multifarious cocked his/her head to the side. "Huh?"

He/she pointed to the side of his/her faceplate. "I'm *deaf* today, remember?"

He pointed at the gunshot wounds.

Multifarious shrugged, slumping over slightly and leaning against a telephone pole for support. "I got *sloppy*."

"Mary Sue fuck you up?" Quinn looked around for the woman. "Where is she?"

Multifarious straightened. "I'm sure they just *love* her gentle spirit and zest for life in Hell right now."

"Damn straight!" He slapped a hand on Multifarious' back. "Fucking-A!"

Mull's body cringed in pain. "Still *shot* though, just in case you forgot."

"What is that?" He squinted at the leg wound. "That a shotgun?" His eyebrows rose. "You are one *tough* son-of-a-bitch, you know that?"

"*The pure death is so my foe*
Though I would die, he would not so;
For when I follow him, he would flee;
I would have him, but him not me."

"...Is that supposed to mean something?"

"No."

"It's *Chaucer* again." Oz said calmly, wiping his hands with antibacterial wash. "*The Book of the Dutchess*." He squinted over at the wound on Mull's shoulder, then calmly sprayed the area with the bottle to keep it from getting infected.

Mull hissed in pain and shouted a few obscenities. "*Jesus, Oz!* Take it easy, huh?!"

"Is everyone accounted for?" Julian called to them.

"Hey, boss." Quinn waved at him in greeting. "Yeah, we're just missing..." He trailed off as the ground beneath them began to vibrate. A frown crossed his face and he looked at Julian. "You decide to let us all go surfing again?"

"No." Julian shook his head, looking down the wide street back towards where the SPRM's ceremony had taken place. "No, this is different."

The gemstone encrusted tablet began to glow as bright as the sun... then it shattered. Out of the illumination appeared a monstrosity with three arms, its head ringed in fire. It let out a roar which rattled windows for blocks.

Julian turned to Quinn. "Do we know him?" He asked

calmly.

Quinn shook his head. "Don't think so."

"Any ideas on how we should handle this?"

"...Well, sharks seem to work pretty well. Let's throw a few of *those* at him and see what happens."

"But they could be *hurt*." Julian argued. "I will not endanger the innocent to *protect* the innocent."

"Oh, I see." Quinn rolled his eyes. "But endangering *me* is fine though, right?"

"Sharks are majestic and noble creatures."

"And you're saying that I'm *not!?!*"

Bridget pursed her lips. "...Wait..." She dashed off down one of the streets. "Wait there!" She ordered.

Mull watched her go. "Your little girlfriend just ditched us." The masked person shook his/her head sadly. "Ain't love a bitch."

"She undoubtedly just had something *important* to do." Julian defended.

"As opposed to trying to stop the gigantic fiery demon thing bent on destroying all humanity, which is stalking towards us right now?" Mull asked. "What could *possibly* be more important than that?"

"Oh, she should have gone to the can *before* the fucking battle, man!" Quinn argued. "Hell, *I did!* And I've been sick all day!" He gestured to the restroom in the building behind him. "I mean, it was like fucking *Krakatoa* in there! But here I am anyway! Ready to lend a hand!"

"I didn't need to hear that." Mull shook his/her head sadly.

Oz looked equally disgusted. "And please *wash* your hands before you 'lend' them."

"Oh, *grow up*." Quinn made a face at them, then turned back to Julian. "Well... what's the plan, boss?"

Julian thought the matter over for a moment, then started forward. "*Kill it*."

"I like him *sooooo* much more than Wyatt." Mull enthused. He/she pointed at the monster. "Three arms, three of us? I like those odds."

The creature sprouted a forth arm.

"...Not so much now." Quinn added.

"This city is mine." Julian declared. "I am a protector of this world, and the creature will just have to be taught that nothing can defeat the power of the seas."

"Oh, I can't swim today." Mull added conversationally. "Just so there aren't any surprises."

"How can an assassin not know how to swim!?!" Quinn shouted.

"I *know* how to swim, just not today!" Mull shouted back. "'Acoustic Shadow' has no experience with your earth water."

"But apparently he's learned to fucking *hear* pretty well in the past hour!"

"...What?!?" Mull put a hand to the side of his/her head.

"Yes, this is *obviously* the conversation I always hoped I'd have right before I *died*." Julian let out a weary sigh. "I should just go back to working alone."

The creature sprouted another head.

"Looks like not everyone agrees with you, boss." Quinn pointed at the monster. "I think he wanted a friend."

The demon saw them and bellowed in fury. It started to charge forward, and Julian braced his feet for the coming attack.

Suddenly, the monster's second head was blasted with an undulating bluish beam of power. The demon shrieked in pain and surprise, stumbling backwards and falling to the street in a heap.

Julian whirled around to see Bridget holding a strange looking contraption in her hands.

"Best fifty cents I ever spent." She grinned. "Testla was the fucking *man,* huh?" She looked down at the object. "Sorry about that. Had to run back to the car for a minute and grab it from the garage sale stuff."

"Bridgeeeeet!" Quinn cheered, elongating the middle of the word. "I knew there was a reason why I like you besides the fact that you're going to put out for my boss-man over here."

"I'm going to pretend you said 'put *up* with,' rather than 'put *out* for.'" Bridget told him calmly, adjusting one of the wires on the strange ancient looking contraption in her hand.

"Whatever." Quinn said happily, sitting down next to Multifarious. "I'm just so stoked to be alive right now, that..."

"Foolish humanity!" Boomed a strange voice. "I have been summoned to your plain to bring *order* to your chaos! To sow this land with your bones, and grow a *new* world! One free of your powerless blight!"

Quinn watched as the monster struggled to get back to its feet. "...You know... I think I liked the other head better. This one's so speech-y."

"My world is a world of death and darkness... I have already feasted upon the souls of all the powerless little creatures there. I will make this land bleed! I am the unstoppable fury of..."

The demon's name was cut off as the demon's *head* was unexpectedly cleaved from its wide shoulders. The severed head fell to the street, and was absently kicked through the second floor window of a nearby building by Ceann's large black boot. The skull exploded in a shower of broken glass and fiery ash.

Ceann ignored it, and spun his weapon's flaming blade around to casually plunge it through the monster's gigantic body, without breaking stride.

He stalked forward, paying no attention to the collapsing remains of the huge monster, as its body turned to ash and blew away. He stood in front of them, Bubonic draped over his shoulder.

"...What the hell happened to you, man?" Quinn finally asked. "You look *terrible*."

"YOU HAVE SPELLED: STRANDED." Ceann dumped the girl onto the hood of a nearby car like she was a burden he was glad to be rid of. He pointed at her, indicating who he'd been stuck with. "YOU HAVE SPELLED: PIGEON. YOU HAVE SPELLED: CRIES." He shuffled forward a step, then pressed the button again. "CRIES." He took another step, then pressed the button again. "CRIES." He threw his arms wide. "YOU HAVE SPELLED: CRAZY." He pointed at himself, water dripping from his leather outfit and cape. "YOU HAVE SPELLED: DROWNED. YOU HAVE SPELLED: MOIST. YOU HAVE SPELLED: FURIOUS." He pointed at Julian. "YOU HAVE SPELLED: LIABLE. YOU HAVE SPELLED: DEAD." He pointed at him with his sword blade. "YOU HAVE SPELLED: CHOPPING."

He charged forward and Julian brought up his trident to return the assault...

CHAPTER 24

KING: "...WHICH OF COURSE, WAS THE CONSORTIUM'S FAULT TO BEGIN WITH."

STORMS: "HOW WAS IT THEIR FAULT AGAIN?"

KING: "THEY FAILED TO STOP THE SPRM UNTIL THINGS GOT OUT OF HAND, WHICH LED TO A LARGE CHUNK OF THE CITY BEING DESTROYED, AND THEN SARGASSUM TRIED TO DROWN THE FEW OF US LEFT SURVIVING."

STORMS: "I DON'T THINK THAT'S HOW IT HAPPENED."

KING: "THIS CITY WILL BEAR THE PAIN OF THAT BATTLE FOR ALL-TIME. HE ROBBED US OF OUR SOULS."

TRANSCRIPT OF "KING OF CAPES AND COWLS," MEDIA: TELEVISION, SHOW: 1409, NEWSCHANNEL 6, FRIDAY 21:00-22:00 EST, NETWORK SEGMENT-ID: 918000606

"Well, I think we all learned an important lesson yesterday." Bridget told them calmly. "*Julian* learned that you can't drown a man who doesn't need to breathe and if you try, he'll get pissed and hit you a lot, and *Ceann* learned that you shouldn't attack a man who carries a golden trident around with him everywhere he goes, when you're vulnerable to gold." She turned to look at the men as they sat sulking. "Don't you think?"

They continued to ignore one another.

Ceann obviously didn't like her version of their little run-in. He pointed at himself. "YOU HAVE SPELLED: DURABLE." He pointed at Julian, then made a stabbing motion, reenacting his fight with him and the pummeling he remembered giving him. "YOU HAVE SPELLED: AQUARIUM. YOU HAVE SPELLED: FRIED." He pointed at her and then at Julian. "YOU HAVE SPELLED: RESCUE." Indicating that she had saved him from Ceann's wrath before he could finish him off. He slouched down in his chair again. "YOU HAVE SPELLED: APOLOGY."

"Very well." Julian nodded. "I'll be the bigger man and accept."

Ceann was literally too angry to even type anything into his toy, his fingers simply forming a fist every time he tried. "YOU HAVE SPELLED: NO. YOU HAVE SPELLED: NEVER. YOU HAVE SPELLED:..."

Julian cut him off by rising to his feet and strolling away before the man could continue his angry electronic tirade. He glanced back at her as he looked out on the crowd of people gathered around the Consortium's gates. "Did you see how masterfully I defused that situation, Lady Bridget? A lesser leader would have held a grudge, but I allowed peace and forgiveness to rule my noble heart."

"Yeah, that was real magnanimous of you, big guy." She lounged against one of the trees and looked down at the newspaper in front of her, the headline of which was still too amazing to even consider.

Quinn shielded his face with his hand, trying to stay cool in his heavy fur coat. "Fuck, it's hot today."

"Maybe you should stop wearing a full caribou fur *parka* then?" Bridget suggested.

"Boss, your chick is getting mouthy with me again." Quinn whined, looking over at Julian. "I don't have to put up with that."

"Yes, do you." Julian informed him simply.

"I do? *Really!?!*" Quinn made a face. "Oh, *goddammit*." He went back to sulking and pointed at the newspaper in Bridget's hands. "And I can't believe they gave that kid from *Accounting* the credit for all of this." He rolled his eyes. "I still don't get that."

"Well, someone had to receive the public's adulation, and it certainly wasn't going to be *us*." Julian said sadly.

"You killed the Mary Sue." She shook her head. "This city will never forgive you for that."

On the radio, Multifarious was listening as some pop idol sang a reworked version of "Candle in the Wind," with lyrics about the Mary Sue and her enduring spirit of indomitable goodness.

Multifarious seemed to find the entire thing absolutely *hysterical* and had spent the better part of the morning requesting that the various stations around the city play nothing but that all day in honor of her memory.

Several actually agreed, which just made Mull laugh harder.

Julian watched the screaming angry throng outside his doors for a long moment, and Bridget just felt like crying. His whole life, all he had apparently ever wanted was to be loved by someone. And now, despite his best efforts and hers, the city had singled him out for their hatred. It just wasn't fair.

He had tried so *hard*.

She put her hand on his arm. "It's okay. We'll *fix this*; I promise."

He turned to look at her in confusion. "Fix what?" He gestured to the people. "This is *fantastic!*" He raised his voice to yell at the crowd. "That's right, surface fools! I took your *precious Mary Sue from you! ME! LORD JULIAN SARGASSUM, KING OF THE SEAS!*" He put his head back and gave a maniacal cackle. "She died for *your* sins against my world! Respect my domain or more of your cherished ones shall meet her fate!"

She frowned. "...You mean, you're *okay* with this?"

He turned to her, taking her hands in his. "You have given me the thing which I have wanted my entire life. This city knows who I *am* now, and they know the *hatred* and the *loss* which I've lived with from my birth. I have brought the war to their shores at last, and I have taken from them the thing which they loved the *most*." His evil smile grew. "I have my *revenge*."

"Yeah, um... you really didn't, 'cause that was Mull who killed her, and they didn't really love her because that was just a spell or whatever, right?"

"No matter." He held up his trident as if in victory. "They know what happened, *DON'T YOU, FOOLS!?!*"

Loud booing.

Julian laughed like a happy child on Christmas morning. "Who else do you love!?!" He called to them. "*What else do you cherish!?! What else can I take from you to show the depths of my anger!?!*"

"Best I can do right now, Jules." Mack appeared from behind one of the buildings, brushing his hand on the leg of his jeans, the other hand still in a sling. "I ain't a miracle worker ya know."

Bridget frowned in confusion. "Huh?"

Julian took her hand and led her over to a spot under a tree where her car was sitting.

"I have returned 'Honda' to you." He proclaimed with obvious pride.

Bridget beamed up at him, then smiled at her long-missing car.

...Or the damaged *remains* of her car, anyway. It looked a little worse for wear since the last time she had seen it. The front end was smashed in, and there looked to be...

She frowned up at Julian and pointed to the water damage. "Was it in the tidal wave?"

He cleared his throat. "...Umm..."

"Jules crashed it into the river." Quinn helpfully chimed in.

Julian glared at him. "That is a *gross* oversimplification. There were many extenuating circumstances." He sniffed in indignation and looked down at her. "And in my defense, I had never driven before."

She patted his arm. "Well, I think you did a *marvelous* job then. I mean, I have it back, and it's all in one piece..."

"Actually, there were *several* pieces before Mack went to work on it." Quinn added.

She shrugged. "Either way, I have it back and Julian has fulfilled his end of our deal."

Julian was practically *glowing* with pride. "Indeed. The vehicle was actually very easy to..."

"One day, you'll be held accountable for your crimes!" Screamed a man on the other side of the fence, cutting him off. "One day soon, someone will drag you cape-wearing fascists out of your ivory tower, and our beloved Mary Sue will have JUSTICE!" He raised his hand over his head. "JUSTICE FOR MARY SUE! JUSTICE FOR MARY SUE!"

"I am a foreign head of state, Arnold! King of the Seas!" Julian called over the noise, yelling at Traitor who was leading the mob against them for unknown reasons. "*DIPLOMATIC IMMUNITY!*" He cackled with evil glee again, which just caused Traitor and the mob to scream louder.

Quinn reached down to the cooler in front of him and pulled out several beers, handing them to the people around him. He raised his drink. "To the sideshow of the big show. We don't have the glory or the fame, but goddammit, we have each other."

Montgomery made a face. "Well, *that* thought certainly makes *me* want to drink heavily." He took a sip of his beverage. "Traditionally though, isn't a toast supposed to make me feel *better*?"

****

Bridget looked around the interior of the main living space in the Consortium's Underwater Base. "...And you really spend most of your time here?"

"Indeed." Julian busied himself trying to straighten up the

area.

Honestly, he needn't have bothered. The entire facility had a damp, rusting quality to it. The pressure made the walls creak and all of the lighting cast a dim yellowish glow. Several pipes which ran haphazardly through the ceiling overhead were leaking, and Bridget wasn't entirely certain whether she should hope that was *seawater* dripping onto her arm or something else.

All in all... the place needed a woman's touch.

...And she *fully* intended to hire one to clean it up before she moved in.

"I think it's *lovely,* Julian." She said, stepping around a bucket on the floor filled with more of the mysterious drippings. "I do wish that your friends put a little more effort and budget into this place though. I mean, I'm glad that they were able to salvage it, and I'm *amazed* that they were able to do what they've done..."

"We had to fix it up some, obviously. The place was a wreck when we moved in."

That would have been an *almost* amusing pun coming from anyone else. From Julian though, it just meant that he was too oblivious to notice it at all.

"...And it *is* a lovely location." She continued, glancing out one of the portholes and gazed onto the sea floor. "Do you think this counts as being *on* the Titanic? I mean, even though it's been... repurposed?"

"Oh, who would ever want to be on that old thing anyway?" He made a face. "It's so much grander now. We moved in and got some help with it from a few different members' powers, and it's so much *better* now than it *ever* was. And I speak from personal experience." He gestured to the decaying remnants of the doomed ocean liner's interiors which surrounded them. "*Everything* is better underwater." He said with some degree of certainty. "It has a *death ray* now." He nodded seriously and with obvious pride, then shook his head. "It didn't *have* a death ray before."

She considered the matter, leaning against the bannister of the grand staircase and absently watched the images flicker across the screen of an old TV, which someone had placed on a card table in the middle of the living area at the base of the stairs, next to some old couches which had been drug in from somewhere. "...Well, I suppose that *is* a rather interesting modification..." She hedged. "And it certainly *does* look far more intact than those TV specials would have you believe..."

"Indeed." He started down the stairs, gesturing for her to

follow. "Come. I'll show you how to work the volcano machine. It's on C Deck."

****

Bridget absently kicked her feet in the Titanic's pool... which was just a really strange thing to say, but whatever. The water wasn't exactly warm, but it wasn't too bad. This area of the Underwater Base seemed to be much nicer than the common room/ grand staircase. It was evidently where Julian spent a lot of his time, and the man's presence filled the space.

She turned to look at a framed newspaper on the wall. The paper was yellowed and very old looking, and proclaimed the results of some great sea battle. A woodcut illustration showed a man dressed as a Roman fisherman gladiator locked in combat with an artist's representation of a horrible sea monster of scales and seaweed. The headline touted: "The Retiarius Stands Alone Against the Sargassum Creature from a Thousand Fathoms!"

Julian emerged from the depths of the pool, and Bridget found herself distracted by watching the cool water running down his muscular body...

He pulled himself onto the tiled floor surrounding the pool and absently reached for his drink, then followed her gaze towards the framed picture on the wall.

"That is Everett Keerg, the man I choose as my father. He taught me how to be a man." He told her, looking at the paper. "He was a fisherman and a hero of his land. And he had lots of good things to show for his life." He raised his glass in toast to the image. "Fair winds and calm seas, my old friend. Until I see you again in the Uncharted Waters and we can embrace once more."

She frowned at the image for a moment longer. "...Isn't that the Cape who like *sponsored* the place I used to work? Like, the aquarium where we met?" She nodded to herself. "Yeah. Yeah, it *is*. ...Huh. That's kinda funny."

"The world is a funny place sometimes, Lady Bridget. Sometimes it seems that our destinies are charted, and all the movements known." He looked down at the lines running along the marble top of a table which someone had drug into the room to hold an old fashioned looking radio and a collection of completely lame books, no doubt past and future book club endeavors. "I've always been fascinated with stone. It's so hard and unyielding. But water, although soft and compliant, gradually wears it away until there's nothing left. And when there's nothing left of the water, it turns to stone once again." He looked up at her. "There's a lesson about life in there somewhere, but I'm not sure what it is."

She shook her head. "Me either." She finished off her drink. "Sounds really profound and shit though, so you can feel free to say it at a press conference in the future, and then we can have the fun of watching the talking heads on the TV debate whether or not it was a threat."

Julian thought it over for a moment, then laughed. "Oh, that will be *hysterical!*" He enthused. "You must help me come up with some more of them!"

She smiled, absently kicking at the water with one outstretched foot. "I'll let you know if I think of any. Maybe something to do with the water cycle or tectonic plates or something." She took on a faraway zen-like voice. "'Shoelaces can be used to hold a shoe to your foot... but no matter how tightly you tie them... sometimes... the shoe falls off all the same. ...And then the shoe is gone. But maybe... the shoe wanted it that way, and you were wrong to tie it down.'" She tapped a finger to the side of her head. "'*Think about that*, people.'"

He smiled again. "I think I shall like this game."

She shrugged and raised her glass to him in toast. "Glad I can help."

"You have helped me more than I can *ever* repay, Lady Bridget." He told her seriously, leaning closer to her. "I have never said this to another living being, and I will *never* say it to another." He met her eyes. "I am *yours.* Heart, body, mind and soul. I will love you until the seas dry and turn to stone and the stone turns to dust and then back into water."

She had no idea what to say to that, but her body was becoming increasingly aware of *his* body next to her. Droplets of cool water were glistening on his warm skin as it brushed up against her, and Bridget closed her eyes, trying to deal with the interesting mix of sensations.

This was one *weird* fucking couple of weeks.

But she could deal with it. She could deal with *anything* now, because she always had something interesting to do. And her hypothetical "Bridget Haniver: The Movie!" now had an incredible leading man. A leading man who wasn't interested in anyone but her.

Bridget believed in heroes now. ...Sure, they might occasionally do selfish things which endangered the city, but if you didn't have them at all, things would be a whole hell of a lot worse.

And besides, the chinks in their armor just made them all the more interesting to look at.

They were all seemingly the product of one disaster or another, but like this silly base around her, they had been reborn as something all-together different and all-together more interesting.

Normal people didn't have death rays.

But they did.

And that was pretty cool.

"I love you too, Julian." She told him, resting her head on his shoulder for a moment. "I don't know when it started or how, but I know that I do. I...I think I loved you since the moment I first saw you on that video screen at the Freedom Squad headquarters and you saved me. I don't know if it's a result of your weird 'god's always know their girl' thing or not, but it doesn't really matter. Either way, it's true." She absently ran her hand through his dark hair, letting the water run over her fingers. "So... when you say that *everything* is better in the water..." She trailed off enticingly, then arched one eyebrow at him.

He nodded knowingly. "I see what you're getting at." He shook his head. "No, not driving." He informed her matter-of-factly. "I know from personal experience that 'Honda' was incapable of aquatic or submarine travel for some strange reason. What is the point of a vehicle which is useless on three-quarters of the globe? ...But don't worry. I am having Mack fix that strange design oversight for you."

Her smile faded. "Not what I meant."

Her hand lowered to his face and she leaned in to gently kiss his lips. He responded a moment later, his mouth plundering hers. He put his hand behind her, and gently moved over her, lowering her down so that her back was on the cold tile floor.

He broke the kiss and looked uncertain for a moment, sitting up and looking out over the water.

She frowned at him, coming to her senses and finding him gone. "What just happened? Why'd we stop again? That was going *great.*"

"I am deeply concerned about frightening you, so I am going to carefully explain what is going to happen so that you aren't afraid." He looked into her eyes, reaching his hand up to gently smooth her bangs from her face and tuck the loose strands behind her ear. "You are going to take off your clothes for me, and then we are going to make love. If you feel uncomfortable or uneasy in anyway, simply tell me and everything will stop. I give you my solemn *vow*: I will not be angry. We are working on *your* timetable, and I've already waited my entire life for you, so waiting longer will..."

She had heard enough of that crap and simply pushed him into the pool with an annoyed groan.

He let out a startled sound as he hit the water, then bobbed there for a moment.

She winked at him and stood up, pulling her top off in one smooth motion and tossing it aside. Her pants followed a moment later, and she was standing there in only her underwear.

His eyes traced up and down her body, drinking her in, then he made a motion with his hand. "Come on in. The water's *fiiiiiine*." He practically sang enticingly.

She laughed and jumped into the pool.

He had her in his arms a second later, his mouth once again on hers. The water was much colder now that she was fully submersed in it, and although warm enough to withstand, it was not terribly comfortable. The chilly surroundings just made her want to hold onto Julian's warm body all the tighter though. He felt like fire against her skin.

She reached behind herself to take off her bra, trying to rid her body of the cold damp fabric and expose more of her to his heat. The temperature made her arms rapidly cover with goose bumps and her breasts tighten to the point of pain.

Julian took a moment to look down at the hard points of her nipples for a moment, then bobbed his head down to take one of them in his mouth.

Bridget gasped, trying to withstand the sensation of his hot mouth on her cold body. She desperately reached for the side of the pool, trying to hold onto something, but she was too far away, and her feet couldn't touch the bottom. Instead, she merely floated, trying to keep from screaming in pleasure.

Julian's head moved to her other breast for a moment, and then he disappeared from view under the water. A second later, she felt her panties being tugged off, and the cold seawater rushing into the growing heat at the apex of her thighs.

Julian's mouth followed a second later, and Bridget couldn't hold in the scream any longer. She moaned from the most exquisite pleasure she had ever felt, then the sound was cut off as she was unexpectedly pulled under the water to join him. Her scream died as his mouth once again met hers, and he swam closer to the wall of the pool, taking her with him.

She reached down and began to tug off his pants, then

stopped, as she realized for the first time that they were a different color. Her eyebrows rose at him in question.

"Blue." He said, obviously pleased she had noticed. Bubbles rose from his mouth to the surface.

Bridget's favorite color was blue, but right now, she just wanted the goddamn things off of him before she lost her mind.

She gestured at him, and he leaned in to kiss her again, breathing for both of them.

Now that she had air in her lungs again, she yanked the pants off of him, and reached down to take hold of his body.

His eyes met hers, his face awash with lust and passion.

She gently guided his body to her entrance, and he used his footing on the bottom of the pool to push himself fully into her. She gasped, losing most of the air in her lungs, but Julian was right there, kissing her as his body moved inside her.

She wrapped her hands around the back of his head, keeping his face inches from hers the entire time. Her eyes locked with his and she kissed him for more air every few moments as he gently thrust his body, keeping his movements slow and the sensations exquisite.

Gradually, Bridget's body began to feel like it was on fire, despite the water and the cold tile she was pressed against. Julian's movements began to become more forced, and she could feel something building inside her.

He moved at just the right time, and her entire world exploded. Her vision swam, even more so thanks to the light streaming through the surface of the water overhead. She tried to hold in the scream of her climax, but it was useless. She threw her head back and let out a yell, but it was once again cut off as Julian's lips met hers. His entire body rocked forward as he climaxed a moment later, sharing his breath with her.

They floated that way for a moment, then Julian pulled his face back and gently pushed a loose strand of her hair out of the way.

She broke free and swam to the surface, pulling herself up onto the tile and gasping for air.

He followed a second later, effortlessly propelling himself out of the water and onto the floor beside her.

"...Wow." She gasped. "You *totally* weren't lying, were you?"

"I rarely do." His head tilted to the side to absently get a better view of her nakedness. "I don't understand why everyone doubts me."

She coughed, water dripping from her wet hair onto the

tilework. "Sex is *completely* better underwater." She said with some degree of personal amazement.

"I think you'll find that *everything* is." He sat down beside her. "You are my queen. We will forever rule the seas together. As time goes on, you'll catch on to the kinds of things you'll be able to do. In a few centuries? You'll be just as at home in the water as me."

"I'm like immortal now?" She considered the idea. "Okay. Not going to lie. That's pretty badass."

"Indeed." He pulled her onto his lap. "And our *children* will be a glorious *army* of fish-people. Powerful on land *and* in the seal And they will *cleanse* this land of all its ills."

"Sounds like you've got this all figured out." She said, trying to keep from making incoherent noises as his hands were once again closing over her breasts.

"I have always wanted a place to belong, Bridget." He kissed her deeply again. "And now, with you, I finally have it."

CHAPTER 25

KING: "THE CONSORTIUM IS INCAPABLE OF CONTRIBUTING ANYTHING GOOD TO THIS WORLD."

STORMS: "THEY'VE HELPED US A LOT OVER THESE PAST MONTHS, AND I THINK WE'RE ONLY HERE BECAUSE OF THEM."

KING: "WE'RE HERE IN SPITE OF THEM, CONNIE, NOT BECAUSE. THEY STARTED A WAR WITH A SOVEREIGN NATION, DESTROYED A LARGE CHUNK OF THE CITY, ALLOWED THE CRIME RATE TO SKYROCKET, FLOODED THE DOWNTOWN AREA WHICH CAUSED A FEW BILLION DOLLARS IN DAMAGES, AND KILLED OUR BELOVED MARY SUE, A PRECIOUS GIRL WHOSE ONLY CRIME WAS BEING TOO GOOD FOR THIS WORLD."

STORMS: "THE CONSORTIUM DOES THE BEST THEY CAN WITH WHAT THEY HAVE. ARE THEY PERFECT? NO. FAR FROM IT. BUT THEY DO BETTER THAN ANY OF US COULD DO, AND IF THEY WEREN'T THERE, WE'D ALL BE WORSE OFF."

KING: "PERSONALLY, I'M JUST WAITING FOR SOME NEW GROUP OF CRIMINALS TO COME ALONG AND DECLARE THE CONSORTIUM AN EVIL BAND OF SUPER-VILLAINS AND TAKE THEM OUT THE SAME WAY THE CONSORTIUM TOOK OUT THE FREEDOM SQUAD. THEY'RE ALL THE SAME PEOPLE, CONNIE. THEY'RE ALL ALIKE. SOON THE CYCLE WILL REPEAT ITSELF AND YOU WILL BE TELLING ME ABOUT HOW AWFUL THE CONSORTIUM WAS AND HOW GLAD YOU ARE TO BE RID OF THEM, BECAUSE SOME NEW AND EVEN FLASHIER BAND OF CRIMINALS WILL HAVE ARRIVED IN TOWN TO DAZZLE YOU WITH INTERESTING POWERS AND COLORFUL SPANDEX. BUT IN THE END... THEY'LL JUST BE THE SAME PEOPLE IN NEW MASKS. THAT'S HOW THE CAPE GAME IS PLAYED."

J. Wyatt Ferral slouched lower in the uncomfortable hospital chair, and reviewed where his life currently stood.

The Consortium had lost almost 25% of its manpower in Agletaria. Possibly more. It was a disaster that their company would be dealing with for years to come, not to mention the emotional blow of losing so many friends.

To make matters *worse*, in their absence, Julian had evidently decided that he was an *actual* hero, and was now the world's first line of defense.

Wyatt's eyes slid over to watch the man as he seemed to be arguing with the fish in the hospital's aquarium over something, and interpreting whatever it was that the fish were saying for his new girlfriend/'queen'.

Wyatt let out a long sigh.

He couldn't imagine *anyone* loving that guy. He was crazy. He never seemed to actually *do* anything except complain. But if this new girl could help ground him some, that would be nice. The group seemed to have a pretty good track record with that of late, and if Wyatt could cross one more of the more troublesome people off his list because they had found love and wouldn't be so difficult anymore, then he was thrilled. Wyatt was genuinely looking forward to a meeting that didn't involve Julian trying to hijack it with talk of mutant fish and terrestrial crimes.

...Something told him that all this relationship meant was that now Wyatt would have to listen to TWO people complaining about how mistreated the oceans were though. But, he supposed there were worse things in the world.

His gaze moved to focus on a chair opposite him, where Montgomery was poised in the shadows.

Case in point.

In the Consortium's absence, Monty had evidently recruited another new convert for his little cult, and Wyatt *didn't* like the woman. She... scared him. Not only because she was a walking corpse who carried a battle axe everywhere, but also because of what she *represented*.

On his own, Monty was trouble. He was a manipulative opportunist, who used cunning and deception to achieve his goals. He had a calculating cleverness, and his workers were fanatical in their devotion, but Monty was an *ambush* predator. His main threat arose from people overlooking and underestimating him.

Wyatt did not.

In his opinion, Monty was the most dangerous man in an organization *filled to bursting* with dangerous men. More than that though, the man was a danger to the Consortium *itself*. Possibly their *biggest* danger. He was a venomous snake, and one day soon, he would bite them. Wyatt had *always* known that. He made sure to *never* turn his back on the man for long, and *always* carefully watched what Monty was doing. He had Marian and Polly shadow *everything* the man did in his department— review every scrap of paper he touched and every digital file he looked at or produced— watching for *anything* which indicated trouble or a coming attack. But neither had ever found anything Wyatt could use to nail the man to the wall.

Wyatt was pretty sure that he could deal with Monty if it came to that though. On his own, the man had no powers. He was crafty, but so was Wyatt. If it came down to it, Monty could be *dealt with*.

...*If* he were on his own.

As if hearing his thoughts, the large warrior woman loomed behind her new boss' chair like a bodyguard, mottled veiny arms crossed over her chest, legs braced apart, like she was waiting for the nursing staff to make their move against her new patron.

...Put Monty's buxom new zombie friend into the equation though, and Wyatt wasn't so sure anymore. She didn't work for the Consortium, she worked for *him*. The man's private army was growing at the same time the rest of the Consortium's staff was shrinking.

His department had *always* been the largest, but add in the fact that everyone under his control had been suspiciously *absent* from the Agletarian affair, and now his department dwarfed the others by *far*. He outnumbered some departments by a ratio of ten to one. Twenty. *More*.

And his influence was growing.

Many people in the company had always worn the C of C logo somewhere on their costume. It wasn't mandated anywhere by the organization, it was just a little way of showing company support and to spice up the more mundane uniforms. *Monty's* men however, had now all taken to wearing pins which featured not the familiar red double "C" logo that Wyatt was used to seeing, but instead a *silver* design which displayed an intertwined double "*P*," for "Purchasing and Production."

One such eyesore was currently pinned to the armor over the Viking woman's left breast, proclaiming her allegiance to Montgomery. Just *how* the man had managed to turn someone who was both an immortal being of tremendous power *and* someone who had up until a few days ago been bent on killing him and everyone else, into such an unreserved and faithful supporter, was *anyone's* guess.

She could pick him up and tear him in half. *Easily*. But instead, she was following his orders without question. It made no sense! She shouldn't be obeying the commands of someone who was so powerless, no matter how slow she obviously was! He was taking advantage of her challenged mental state, and using her for his own ends. And she wasn't stopping him for some reason. Logic would say that she would have to be either too smart to listen, or too dumb to follow, but neither was the case apparently.

Hell, Monty wasn't even in *charge* of the Consortium; he was only *middle management!*

The man seemed to simply have that ability sometimes though. ...An ability which arose from his own twisted yet strangely charismatic personality rather than from any superpower, but an ability which had always amazed Wyatt.

Always *scared* Wyatt.

The man was an *expert* at turning desperate and frustrated people into unquestioning and fervent supporters, like some sort of dark messiah of the unacknowledged. His words somehow struck home with certain individuals, but Wyatt wasn't sure how he did it. Whether he was playing off their fears or their greed or their desperation, however he accomplished it, he mesmerized them like the word of God from on high. No matter how insane Wyatt thought he sounded, they *listened* to the man. They *believed* in him. They *loved* him. And those same people would then do *anything* for him. No matter what it was, or how malicious. No matter what he did to them, or how badly he might treat them. All he had to do was snap his fingers.

He said "spark" and they'd set the world ablaze for him.

And as they themselves were consumed in the resulting inferno, they would *thank him* for the opportunity to prove themselves in his eyes.

It was a *dangerous* ability to fight against, whether it was technically a super-power or not.

Monty's newest disciple was *different* than the other flunkies he owned though. This simple-minded woman gave Monty *power,* something that his department had previously only had because it was very large and stayed hidden in the shadows. Draugr however *was* power. She was more powerful than almost anyone else in the entire organization.

And she was *Monty's*.

In essence, the Purchasing and Production Department had just become a nuclear threat.

Whatever the man was planning, he had made an important step towards his goal in Wyatt's absence, and he wasn't at all shy about announcing it to the world. He was proclaiming it to the company at large; firing a warning shot over their bow in the form of a gleaming silver badge attached to his Viking underling, like the ownership tags you would put on the collar of your new attack dog.

He now kept his new pet with him at all times, as if too excited to even let her out of his sight: Higgins on one side, Draugr on the other.

He would make his move soon, and Wyatt wasn't entirely sure what that move would be. Wyatt prided himself on always having a plan, but in this case, he had no idea what to do. All he knew was that he *didn't* like Monty, and he liked Monty's new henchwoman even *less*.

He was sure he could deal with Monty if it came to that. He was *reasonably* sure he could deal with Monty *and* Monty's men if push came to shove.

...But Monty, the entire Purchasing and Production Department *AND* an undead killing machine?

Wyatt wasn't so certain he liked those odds anymore, particularly since when Monty's attack came, it would come without warning and with no mercy.

...And Wyatt had a *lot* to lose now.

Monty, however, did *not*. The man had nothing which anyone could take. He had no heart. He cared about nothing. He cherished nothing. He loved no one. He *felt* nothing. He existed solely to accumulate power and destroy those weaker than himself. There was simply no way to hurt someone like that unless you killed him, and the man was far too clever to ever fight anyone straight out. He wasn't the kind of man who *announced* that the fight was on; he'd smile at you and be your friend right up until he took you out in some trap that you never saw coming.

Wyatt knew this. He knew it as certain as he knew his own name.

But if you *did* decide to kill Monty, you'd have to sink to his level. You would need to make the first move and it would have to be *quick*. Because if you took your shot and missed, Monty would *devastate* your world in retaliation before you could try again. He *lived* to destroy people. He seemingly took greater pleasure in that than in anything else in his life.

He *enjoyed* it.

Wyatt wanted him *gone*.

...One way or the other.

Even if– almost certainly *when*– the situation broke down to the point where removing Monty from the world was the only viable option though, Harlot still would never allow it. You could say a lot of wonderful things about Wyatt's *amazing* wife, all of which were *utterly* true, but there was no arguing that she viewed the Consortium staff as her family, Monty included. She was loyal to them above all others. She would protect them, no matter the personal cost or risk. If it had been up to *Wyatt*, he would have gotten rid of Monty *long* ago. ...While he still could.

Right now, Monty could still be stopped, but with each passing day, the man became stronger and stronger. And Wyatt was forced to watch silently as the man prepared to do whatever it was that he was preparing to do. At some point in the very near future, Monty's plans would be put into motion, and then it would be too *late*.

Monty could *not* be trusted. Not *ever*. Any kindness you showed him would be wasted. Any friendship you offered him would be used to destroy you. Every day you delayed getting rid of him just gave him time to become more and more powerful.

Marian had once described him as being "obdurate," meaning a refusal to reform or repent; stubbornly insisting on wrongdoing; hardened by wickedness. And that was certainly true. The man wasn't really a man at all anymore. Like his new zombie henchwoman, Monty was already dead inside. Something *bad* had gotten into him, and now, he was gone.

Wyatt believed there was hope for *everyone* in the Consortium. Hell, Wyatt had been best man at *Cynic's* wedding for God's sake, and that man was one of the worst people in the world! ...But there was no hope for Monty turning things around.

He wasn't going to reform. He wasn't going to be your friend. He wasn't going to find love and settle down with some nice girl somewhere. He wasn't going to *ever* stop trying to get the better of you and take what you had.

He *liked* it.

He was *empty* inside.

Soulless.

A brutal conscienceless madman.

Obdurate.

Monty was simply the man that every man fears he will one day become.

The man in question pointed at something on a blueprint which Higgins was holding, and nodded sinisterly.

Wyatt didn't like this situation. Soon, he was going to have to act with or without his wife's consent, and he REALLY didn't want to do that.

To make matters *worse*, in his infinite brilliance, Julian had not only allowed Monty free reign to grow his menace, but *also* apparently allowed Megaris to wander away. She was *supposed* to have been with Julian's crew, but no one had seen her in weeks.

Which could only lead to badness.

The woman was unpredictable and dangerous. There was something *wrong* with her, but he had no idea what. Wyatt could understand Monty: he was evil beyond measure. But he was a known entity. Wyatt *expected* Monty to double-cross him or suffocate him in his sleep. If it came to a confrontation, he could at the very least *fight* Monty. With Meg though, Wyatt was at a loss. She couldn't be controlled by anyone. She couldn't really be "fought" in the traditional sense, she was far too powerful. She would do what she wanted, and she didn't care if you liked it or not. The Consortium's only control over her was that she didn't realize how big the world was, and how easily she could crush it. Thanks to Jules not keeping an eye on her though, their carefully created containment method had dissolved, and now the woman was free to go anywhere and do anything.

Meg just didn't belong here. And the one who realized that the most, was obviously Meg herself.

The Consortium had almost been shattered in Agletaria.

Their power at home had been shaken by Reece and his crazy plan, which fanned the flames of people's distrust of Capes.

The city liked the Consortium less than ever thanks to Julian's not-so-stellar handling of the situation.

And now it appeared that their most serious threats were arising from within their own ranks. The seeds had already been planted, and Wyatt felt like he was a farmer standing in the fields and watching helplessly as their destruction grew around him.

...And it promised to be a *bumper* crop this year.

Wyatt ran his hands over his face, more tired than he could ever remember being.

He'd have to send Poacher out to try to track down Meg soon, and he wasn't looking forward to that. Syd could be called a lot of things, but 'tactful' wasn't one of them. He could *find* Meg, but Wyatt sincerely doubted the man could convince her to return to the Lair if she didn't already intend to come back on her own.

In the seat closest to the hospital doors, Poacher rested his heavy combat boots on the upholstered chair in front of him and stared up at the acoustic tile ceiling in either abject boredom or deep thought. "Did you ever think that Newt in 'Aliens' isn't real?"

In the seat next to him, Emily Eden continued carving obscene images into the hospital's coffee table with a switchblade. "She's a *fictional character*, you fuck-wit."

Her identical twin sister Amy took on a consoling tone of voice and looked at Poacher in loving pity. "Fictional characters aren't real, Sydney." She told him seriously, as though he might have overlooked that fact all these years. Then she frowned, as if a new idea occurred to her. "...Except Cory. He's real."

Her twin glanced over at the man in question, as he was speaking with Lexington in the corner of the room, as the patriotic young woman once again imparted her *overwhelming* enthusiasm for the kindness and courtesy of the Mexican people while she had been lost in their country. Evidently, it was simply the world's most beautiful place. ...Next to *America*, of course.

Cory looked away from Lexie and over at Emily upon hearing his name being mentioned.

Emily gave him the finger. "...*Unfortunately.*" She added to her sister's thought on the matter.

"No, no." Poacher shook his head. "I mean, that Newt might be an Alien. *Think* about it." He sat up straighter. "Really *think* about it." He took a long drink from his flask, then handed it to Amy.

Amy politely thanked him, and took a sip. She made a small coughing sound. "...Umm... what *is* this?"

Her sister reached for the flask. "Tastes like Absinthe and Candy Apple Kool-Aid." She guessed, relying on the fact that she and her sister had Corsican Syndrome, and thus each twin experienced what the other did. In this case, the taste of what sounded like a truly *dreadful*– and up until recently *illegal*– mix of beverages.

Emily downed the entire contents of the flask without coming up for air, then tossed it back to Poacher.

He caught it in one hand, then frowned at her. "Hey! I meant a *sip*, not the whole goddamn thing!"

She made a face at him. "Oh, *blow me*, Syd."

"I'm sure Em is *very* sorry about overstepping like that, Sydney. She's a very giving person and would *never* intentionally do something selfish." Amy frowned at her sister reproachfully, then looked over at Poacher. "You were saying about the girl from your movie, dear?"

"Oh, yeah." Poacher looked excited to get back on topic. "What do we really know about her? Discounting the deleted sequence which shows her family, we know nothing. We never see her house or talk to anyone who knew her. All we know is that she claims to have been hiding from the aliens for an extended period. I mean, has anyone else in the *entire* Alien mythos ever been shown to be able to *hide* from those fuckers for long? Nope. I think Newt was just cooked up by them to keep tabs on everyone and keep them localized. She's the alien that draws them in and makes them easier prey for the queen."

Emily stabbed the switchblade down into the coffee table's veneer so that it stuck straight up in the wood, then absently began to paint her toenails with red nail polish which she produced from somewhere.

Poacher ignored her. "The Colonial Marines arrive on LV-426? No aliens. They fuck around the complex for a while? No aliens. They find Newt and ten minutes later it's motherfucking *anarchy*." He set about trying to fill his flask with cups of hospital coffee. "All of the colonists had a tracking chip in them, right, which is how the marines find the nest originally? Does Newt? Apparently not, since Ripley has to put her *own* tracker on her at the end. A tracker which *coincidentally* gets misplaced once Newt gets Ripley back in harm's way. The humans were almost free so Newt 'accidently' falls down an air vent, and bingo, the humans are back on the kill floor. The aliens are kicking major Marine ass the entire time, just knocking them off one by one in a matter of minutes, chasing them through the air vents, but once that kid leaves the group? Jesus, it's like fucking *Disneyland* there or something. The aliens can't find them anymore, and the marines just walk to the drop ship and then mysteriously have all the time in the world to gear up and discuss *all kinds* of shit."

Emily finished off her toenails, then looked around the room for something else to do, and finally settled on painting Poacher's fingernails in the same color.

He was either too wrapped up in his topic to notice, or simply didn't care. Emily began adding little rhinestone skulls to her work.

"In the *meantime*, do any of the aliens touch that kid?" He continued. "Nope. Ever go for the kid over anyone else? Nope. Ever have trouble finding the group once the kid is with them? Nope. Once Newt is in the room, you're a fucking *alien magnet*. The only one the aliens *don't* bother is Bishop, who coincidentally, is also the only one that the kid *isn't* with. She can't report back on him and what he's doing, because he's off on his own. So, he's fine the *entire movie*. Once she joins up with him again though? Ripped in fucking half. And how exactly did an alien get on board the Sulaco at the end in order to kill everyone at the beginning of Alien 3? 'Cause the queen sure didn't have time to lay any more eggs, even if her egg pouch *hadn't* been blasted to shit with the M41A Pulse Rifle. And no *other* aliens hitched a ride on the drop ship or someone woulda seen 'em. So how did it get there?" He let the question hang in the air for a moment. "It was there the whole time. They were all just too blind to see it because it had the best disguise of all: a *Newt suit*."

Emily stared at him in silence for a long moment. "I'm not sure if that's brilliant or the stupidest goddamn thing I've ever heard, Syd." She began gently blowing on Poacher's prettily painted nails to dry them.

Amy's mouth hung open as if trying to process this incredible revelation. "...Wow." She breathed. "Those poor soldiers."

Syd nodded in understanding. "Nothing in this world hurts like betrayal."

Wyatt put his face in his hands again.

This organization was *doomed*.

On the television in the corner, the talking heads were announcing how the criminals responsible for the theft of a dozen lobsters from a local restaurant had been taken into custody, and were identified as being allied with the SPRM.

Bridget turned to look at the news report, then whirled around to glare at Monty for some reason.

The man simply flashed his soulless smirk.

...Wyatt had no idea what that was about.

On screen, the image changed to show someone named "Wendell," as he tried to answer questions about his glorious victory over the SPRM and try to talk over the reporters shouting for information on how he could have ever succeeded without the help of the Mary Sue, who obviously had sacrificed herself for all of them.

In the seat next to him, Marian closed her notebook. "I am told that that young man was a great help to Julian in our absences, Wyatt."

He nodded. "Yeah, Jules said the kid's an intern and he was

looking after the Accounting department for us or something."

She nodded. "And now, our powerless *intern* is a Cape who is more famous and beloved by this city than *any of us*."

Wyatt slouched down in his chair, feeling dejected and worried about his wife. "So it would appear."

"There is just one problem with that, Wyatt." She shook her head, meeting his gaze. "I did not *hire* any interns."

Wyatt thought about the ramifications of that for a moment, then put his face in his palms and let out a weary sigh. "*Shiiiiiiiiiit*." He drew the word out tiredly, then glanced back up at her. "Any idea what *this* is about then?"

"None." She shook her head. "And neither does Steven."

Marian *always* knew what was going on. And on the rare occasions she didn't, Cynic could at least be counted on to postulate a few dozen insane theories which would explain the bizarre circumstances the group found themselves in, like alien involvement or some vast conspiracy. If this had them *both* stumped though, then something *bad* was happening.

No, Wyatt did not like this situation at *all*.

The hospital doors opened, and the nurses wheeled Harlot from the room, a baby cradled in her arms.

...On the other hand, there really wasn't any way this situation could be better. He had a beautiful wife, and now they had a beautiful child. He was surrounded by family and friends and the friends he didn't like because they were plotting to kill him.

"Peter?" His wife turned slightly, holding his new son at an angle to show the baby the people assembled in the hallway. "This is your *family*." She pointed at Wyatt. "And *that's* your daddy! Isn't he handsome?"

All in all, being alive was pretty amazing sometimes. The bad stuff just made you appreciate the fragile beauty of life all the more.

He kissed his wife's forehead and reached down to gently run his fingertip across his new son's tiny cheek.

A moment later, the large assembly of Consortium members which filled the halls began crowding around, all trying to get a look at their newest member, and Wyatt became concerned that someone was going to get crushed in the scramble.

But if he had to go, there were worse ways than that he supposed.

...Like whatever the hell Monty was planning on doing to him, for instance.

EPILOGUE

ANNOUNCER: "THIS HAS BEEN 'KING OF CAPES AND
COWLS,' BROUGHT TO YOU IN PART BY DREWS
DEPARTMENT STORE, YOUR SOURCE FOR QUALITY
GOODS AT REASONABLE PRICES. DREWS
DEPARTMENT STORE, HELPING THE COMMUNITY FOR
ONE-HUNDRED AND SIXTY YEARS."

TRANSCRIPT OF "KING OF CAPES AND COWLS," MEDIA:
TELEVISION, SHOW: 1409, NEWSCHANNEL 6, FRIDAY
21:00-22:00 EST, NETWORK SEGMENT-ID:
918000606

Natalie Quentin was the kind of person who added the milk to the bowl before the cereal, just to see what would happen. And after she mixed all the different cereal brands together to make the experience more magical, she'd probably forget to eat her concoction, because she'd be off onto something new. And in Natalie's world, there was *always* some new and fun thing to focus on.

She watched her Saturday morning cartoons on Monday afternoon because she forgot to watch them over the weekend, and she kept her Christmas stocking up all year even though she didn't get any presents. She had gotten kicked out of two different high schools because she didn't go to classes, and she always gave homeless people money. Every few months, she threw parties for herself, even though she was the only guest who ever came. Nat *always* voted for the underdog, and during instant replays, hoped that *this time* the team would somehow make the shot.

She was the kind of person who bought birthday cakes for herself even though it wasn't her birthday, just because she felt like doing something to make the day special. She lived alone, her socks rarely matched– if she bothered wearing shoes at all, which she rarely did– and she *loved* her job.

If you asked her, she would have self-identified as a sort of bohemian free-spirit, only she bathed regularly and had a job. She didn't pay a great deal of attention to the money the job brought in though, and she didn't bother to buy anything extravagant with it. She honestly didn't want fancy stuff. She enjoyed her simple life, and didn't need a lot of material things around to clutter it up. Not that she was Thoreau, and living alone in the woods somewhere eating berries and waxing poetic about the beauty of *leaves* or anything, just that she didn't need *things* to make her happy. True, sometimes things were nice to have around– because they were pretty– but they weren't necessities for a contented life.

Natalie had always been on her own, and she was used to it. Her parents were... well, she actually had no idea who her parents really were, and didn't much care to find out. She had grown up on the streets, and had done surprisingly well for herself. She realized that most people would expect her to have some sort of interest in her family, or want some sort of explanation as to why she ended up the way she had, but she honestly didn't care. They rarely even crossed her mind, and if they didn't want her, then she sure as hell didn't want them either. Not that she bore them any malice, because again, she didn't care. She had turned out alright, so it made no sense to hold a grudge. Wherever they were, she hoped they were as happy as she was, she just never wanted to hear about it. Natalie wasn't the type of person who blamed others for the stupid things they did. She tried to be very understanding of their idiocy. Besides, they were probably doing the best they could. The world was a tough place, and it must be *so* much harder if you were stupid.

She stared at herself in the mirror and carefully began pulling her cherry red hair into a semi-orderly ponytail. Generally, Nat wasn't the type of girl who paid attention to such things– they just slowed her down– but she always tried to look nice for her job. Unfortunately, she also wasn't the kind of girl who easily achieved that feat though. Between her pale skin, neon blue eyes and bright red hair, she looked more like something from a kid's movie than an elegant spokeswoman for her company. Really, the only company she could represent with ease would be the Wendy's fastfood chain. But that didn't bother her overly much. Their Frosties were *awesome*. And besides, she had always considered herself sort of pretty, in a wholesome Americana sort of way. If someone else couldn't see that, well, that wasn't really her problem.

Her eyes traveled down to the uniform she was forced to wear for her job. It did *nothing* for her figure, but that couldn't be helped. It wasn't like she had a choice in the matter, and sacrifices had to be made on the altar of good jobs. Besides, she had grown to really like it. It felt... natural. Like a second skin. Like *her*.

She was the kind of person who painted their apartment with every color the store sold, in the weirdest shapes and designs she could imagine. And then a couple months later, would paint it all again in some new color scheme. Just *because*. She fed the stray cats in the neighborhood, listened to overtly cheery music, was a big fan of movies about silly things like talking chimps and enchanted shoelaces which grant their 12-year-old owners magical baseball abilities, and she almost always had a smile on her face. She was a diehard romantic, could fall asleep anywhere, and she loved her fellow man.

She was incapable of eating anything without staining whatever she was wearing, most people thought she was weird and she had a tendency to snore. She liked stuffed animals and creating art projects out of things that other people had thrown away. ...Or at least, she enjoyed *finding* the objects and then putting them in a pile, *intending* to one day use them to create an art project. The actual creation process itself always took too long, and she usually got bored before it was done. Besides, the pile of art project stuff *itself* was pretty interesting to look at anyway. Actually *creating* art with the supplies would ruin that. It was so formal, and completely ruined the spirit of the project.

She didn't date a great deal, mostly because she usually forgot she was supposed to meet up with the guy somewhere, or that she was supposed to be home at a certain time to get picked up. That kind of big picture thinking was a foreign concept to her, and she didn't like doing it. She hated having to be anywhere but her job at a specific time. If she wanted to suddenly go feed ducks in the park, the *last thing* she wanted to be worried about was some guy waiting for her to go to dinner with him. She wanted to look at the ducks. ...No, she was *going* to go look at the ducks, and if he was unhappy about that, he didn't have to ask her out again. Not that she deliberately drove the men away by avoiding them or anything though. That would imply she cared enough about them to remember the date in the first place, which she didn't. Usually, she wouldn't even recall the appointment until she received the angry voicemail, or found the flowers bunched up in the trashcan outside her apartment.

She loved people, but sometimes she just didn't understand where they were coming from. So, she was four-and-a-half hours late to dinner? *And?* Did they really have some vitally important thing they needed to be doing *right then* which she had ruined? Worlds that needed saving? Orphans which needed rescuing? Nonsense. It wasn't her fault that they couldn't see the wonders of the world around them like she could. And she HAD shown up... eventually. And really, wasn't that what was important? Wasn't she worth the wait? Was the exact time of her arrival some essential element of their having fun together? Nope. Her tardiness just exposed their own selfishness, which she had probably recognized on some subconscious level all along, and THAT was precisely why her brain distracted her with feeding ducks or riding the subway around in circles to see where the track ended. She had sensed that they were *terribly* self-centered and that's why she had ditched them. They had practically *forced* her to stand them up. It was the only explanation, really.

Natalie didn't worry about anything, and never had. It would all work out. What was the worst that could possibly happen? She'd end up homeless? Been there, done that. As long as she was alive, things were good and she was going to keep going at her own pace. And if she died, well, at least she had had a good time before she went. Life didn't really need to be watched, it needed to be *enjoyed*. Experienced. *LIVED*. Things would take care of themselves, and obsessing over them just ruined the whole experience. You couldn't really do anything about them anyway, so it made no sense. Best to sit back, have fun and try to help others do the same.

She smiled at herself in the mirror, making sure her makeup was perfect before she got back to work.

Yes. All in all, Nat lived a happy life. She was cheerful and was *always* looking for some exciting new adventure.

"You comin' or what? You got a job you know!" Yelled the gruff voice from the other side of the door.

"*I hear you!*" She called back. "Lord, but you're such a *nag!* Let me take care of this first, 'kay?"

"You..." The man at her feet mumbled. "...You could just let me go. Please? I promise not to hurt any more kids. They..."

Whatever the man had been about to say was cut off as she snapped his neck in one smooth motion. He slumped over onto the cement floor of the restroom, his eyes now fixed and unmoving.

She sighed contentedly and put her face back on.

Multifarious looked at herself in the mirror, not nearly as pleased with what she saw as Natalie had been. But then again, masks were like that. They hide the ugly truth. Conceal what was beneath from the world.

They put on a show.

Personally, Multifarious didn't always understand "The Natalie Show." She thought Nat took her "free spirit" shtick a little too far. The girl was ridiculous. Not that Mull was depressed or anything, but Nat's hippie attitude was getting annoying. She needed to grow the hell up, stop eating so much ice cream-- which Mull then had to burn off on the treadmill– and take some *responsibility* for once. The girl was seemingly constructed out of every reckless thought and action which Mull had ever had. But once again, masks are often an exaggeration of something else. They need to be or you wouldn't be able to tell them from the face beneath any longer. Besides, Natalie seemed happy with it, so Multifarious didn't object. As long as the mask held, Multifarious had no complaints with letting the girl do whatever she wanted.

Natalie was very useful as far as masks went, and Multifarious had long ago let the girl take over a good percentage of their time. Truth be told, these days, Natalie was shown to the world more than Multifarious was. It was just easier. No one was afraid of Nat or looked at her like she was a maniac. Nat's life was so much easier than Mull's was. So much less complicated and painful. Hardly *anyone* ever shot at Nat. Besides... Mull kinda *liked* Natalie. She thought she was fun.

Not that Natalie was an alternate personality or anything like that, she was just... not entirely Multifarious. She was an act. A disguise. A role which Mull played on a daily basis in order to get through life more easily.

She was camouflage.

Everyone pretends to be different people at times. Hide who they really are in an effort to avoid judgment or scare off their enemies. ...Or to simply fit in. Multifarious might have taken that fact to its extreme, but the central fact remained the same.

Everyone wears a mask.

Multifarious threw the door open and walked back to where Poacher was waiting.

"Jesus, Mull. You fall in or something?" He pointed at the corpse. "He know anything?"

"I am not Multifarious." She shook her head. "Today, I am... *Otium!*"

He rolled his eyes. "Whatever. That dead guy *know* anything, '*Opium*?'"

"No." She pushed him in annoyance. "And it's '*Otium*,' not '*Opium*,' Syd. Do I make fun of *your* codename?"

"No. But that's because mine doesn't totally blow. ...No pun intended." He pointed towards the alley. "I'm going to go this way. You okay to check the roof?"

As far as Mull knew, Poacher was the only person in the Consortium who knew her "real" identity. His sense of smell was too sharp not to pick up on it. ...Well, Marian seemed to know as well, but with that woman, you could never really tell. Since Mull didn't really think of Nat as being *"her"* in the strictest sense though, it really didn't bother her that Syd and Marian knew what the mask beneath the mask looked like.

Hell, if worse came to worse, she could always kill them.

Nah, she was fine with Poacher. Usually. Every now and then, the man's sexism showed itself though and he got overprotective. He wasn't doing it maliciously or because he didn't think she was capable; he just always wanted to protect those he saw as weaker than himself. Mull just didn't have it in her today to remind the man that she could kill him six different ways before he could even make a sound.

She worked with him a great deal though, simply because they had completely different ways of achieving the same goal: the death of the thing they had been sent to stop.

Poacher fought in wars. He was built like a tank and just plowed through everything in his way.

He was a hammer.

Mull killed things. Silently. Efficiently. And then she was gone.

She was a scalpel.

She wasn't *entirely* certain what "Otium's" powers were, but she remained confident that she knew what she was doing. True, the nature of her abilities was often a crapshoot, but even on the days when they sucked, she could still get the job done. And she *still* didn't need Syd's paternalistic crap. The man watched out for her like some kind of annoying older brother. She wasn't entirely sure *why,* since few of the other women on the team were "lucky" enough to receive so much of his assistance, but whatever the reason, Poacher was always hanging around.

...Of course, the flipside of that coin could have been that he wanted to keep an eye on her because he knew she was off-the-fucking-wall bonkers, and needed to make sure she didn't start killing people without him being there to save them.

The thought made her smile.

As if he could really *stop her.*

"I think I can handle climbing some *stairs*, Syd." She rolled her eyes even though her facemask prevented him from seeing the action.

"I can call Oz out here and *he* could help you, if you'd rather." He said teasingly, like they were in grade school and he found out about some boy she liked.

She scowled at him, again, ignoring the fact that her

faceplate hid the action. He seemed to understand anyway though.

She pointed at him. "You leave Oz *alone*." She made a slashing motion with her arms. "He doesn't need to be a part of our crazy shit."

He snorted. "Speak for yourself. All *my* crazy shit's perfectly sane." He started down the alley. "'Sides, I think that dude's got all kinds of crazy shit of *his own* to deal with. He's prolly used to it by now. *Our* crazy shit and *his* crazy shit might even get along."

She made a noncommittal sound and started up to the roof. They were currently responding to reports of some sort of crime going on. Honestly, she hadn't really been listening. It was somehow related to the pervert downstairs though, but her questioning of him... hadn't gone especially well. There was a larger plot at play, but she wasn't really sure what it was. Something to do with that Wendell kid from Accounting, maybe...?

Multifarious might care about staying up on current events within the organization, but *Otium* apparently did *not*.

That was going to be a problem. Hopefully *tomorrow* she would be someone who could figure out what the fuck was going on, because right now, she had no idea.

Still, very few of these calls were in any way related to her actual duties with the Consortium anyway, so it probably didn't matter much. She could already tell that she was going to trudge all the way up to the roof, and find absolutely nothing.   ...Then she'd have to go all the way back down again, just to discover that Poacher had already killed the whatever-it-was which they were there to apprehend. ...*Then* she'd have to sit there and listen as Wyatt *once again* lectured them on not killing things.

Jesus, but that guy was annoying.

It was like listening to her last fucking guidance counselor again.

...And she had *stabbed* her last guidance counselor.

That was the downside of working with Poacher a lot: it *doubled* the amount of bodies on any one call which Wyatt could complain about. Hell, it almost made it a competition to see which of them could rack up *more*, much to Wyatt's chagrin.

She was totally winning.

Syd was *soft*.

She opened the door, bracing for an attack....

Nothing.

She swore under her breath in a language that she wasn't sure she spoke. Evidently, Otium was Belgian.

Huh.

That was a new one.

Just to be sure, she walked out onto the roof, still looking for the whatever-it-was-that-she-had-been-sent-here-to-kill-and-then-listen-as-Wyatt-yelled-at-her-for-killing.

She peered over the edge of the building, hoping to see Poacher walking underneath so she could spit on him...

She felt the shiver run up her spine an instant before he spoke.

"Hello, Kitten."

The knife was in her hand and streaking towards his chest before she even fully processed his arrival.

Rondel caught her wrist, stopping the blade inches from his heart. "Ah, I'm touched that you remember me."

Beside him, a dark-haired man frowned in worry and pointed at her. "Wait... who the fuck are *you*? Aren't you that crazy Consortium person? What are *you* doing here?"

Rondel swept out an arm, as if presenting her. "This, Mr. Jack, is the woman who made me the man I am today."

Jack processed that for a long moment. "...Yeah. Well she's totally fucked-up then. Like deep batshit crazy time." He shook his head. "We shouldn't be here. Let's go."

"Yeah, you should listen to your little sidekick, *Ronnie*." She slammed her shoulder into him, driving him backwards. "I may have to hurt you again."

Rondel smiled the smile which always churned her stomach. "You couldn't hurt me again if you *tried,* Kitten." He pointed at his chest. "You have already stuck your little hand into my chest and ripped out my *heart*."

She threw the blade at him.

He dodged to the side and she used the distraction as an opening to try to kill the bastard once and for all. She attempted to punch him in the throat, but he saw the movement coming and bent to the side, slamming his own fist into her wounded shoulder. The bullet wound from the fight with Mary Sue opened up again, and blood began to soak her outfit.

She doubled-over, holding her hand against her shoulder in an effort to stop the bleeding.

He kicked her in the face, then stomped his foot down on the shotgun wound to her thigh. She fell to one knee, grinding her teeth together against the pain.

The dark-haired man winced. "...Umm... Boss? I don't think

this is really…"

Rondel whirled around to face him. "If you don't want to see this, Mr. Jack, then *go wait in the car!*" He roared, pulling Mull forward and smashing her face first into the brick wall. The facemask took some of the blow, but it still hurt like hell.

She tasted blood, so it had probably broken her nose.

Jack winced again. "*Ouch.*" He cleared his throat. "…Okay. I'm just… I'm going to go then, 'cause it looks like there's some personal shit going on here and I really…"

"*GO!*" Rondel yelled again.

She frowned at the interloper, reluctantly agreeing with Rondel for once in her life. "If you're not going to help him or me, then get the hell out of here. You stay, and I'll kick your ass as soon as I'm done with *him*."

Jack started towards the door. "Hey, you got it, sweetheart. I'll be downstairs." He opened the door and looked back to Rondel. "Just saying that if you… you know… like kissed and made up or whatever, the day would be a whole lot more enjoyable."

Mull smirked at her ex as the door closed. "Aww, isn't that sweet, Ronnie? You've hired a *romantic* psychopath to do your bidding." She struck out with her leg, kicking him and hearing the satisfying crack of cartilage breaking.

Rondel somehow managed to stay on his feet, hopping slightly in pain but smiling at her. "I remember the night I taught you that one. Glad to see you haven't forgotten."

"Well, it was the only thing about you which was in *any way* memorable, Ronnie." She got back to her feet and grabbed him by the front of his suit, pulling him forward and smashing her mask into his face. "Everything else was… *a disappointment.*"

He staggered backwards, wiping away blood from his nose and mouth, then pressed his hand over his heart. "Aw, you *wound* me, Kitten."

She got back to her feet and pried her blade from the doorway. She held it up so that he could see it. "Not yet. But *wait*."

"We were *partners,* Kitten! Friends!"

"Oh, please." She rolled her eyes. "We were *never* 'friends.' We had a few rather *forgettable* nights together, and then I dumped your loser ass and moved on to *bigger* and better things. …Emphasis on '*bigger*.'"

He pulled his own weapon, one of the knives he'd used to kill *countless* people. …While she watched. "You can't beat me. I *made you.* I know every move you're going to make before you make it, because *I'm the one who showed you how to kill!*"

She slashed at him with the blade, but he blocked her again and caught her in a hold, twisting her arm to the side and breaking her wrist. In the same motion, he plunged his own blade into her body, right beneath her collar bone.

Her breath caught in her throat and she blinked down at the blade's handle as it stuck from her body, then up at him in astonishment.

Multifarious had killed a lot of people.

A *lot*.

She was by no means an amateur, and she had a deep understanding of exactly what was *required* to accomplish the task. She *knew* how to kill someone. She was... well... *good* at it. She was *very* good at it. *That was her thing!*

And there was *no way* that he should have been able to block that attack. *No way* he should have been able to stab her like that.

...She... she hardly *ever* got stabbed.

That *sucked.*

He smiled icily. "Yes, I've learned a few new tricks since we last met." He used his hold on her to move her towards the edge of the roof. "You see, I was planning on killing everyone in the city you love, and all that other garbage which you hear every two-bit villain yammer on and on about. But you know what I found?" He leaned down closer to her, his breathy voice in her ear. "Just killing *you* is all I'm really after."

Her heels edged out over the side of the building and he pushed her backwards so that she was leaning over the drop, suspended off the roof with nothing but his grip for support.

"If you wish to *beg* for your life though, I would *very much* enjoy it." His smile grew. "Go ahead. Make it *fun* for me."

Multifarious had never been the sanest of people. Some might argue that it was due to her upbringing, and some might argue that it was due to her being a wacked-out lunatic who was a danger to everyone she came into contact with. Whatever the reason though, she was NOT someone who backed down from a challenge or a threat.

NO ONE threatened her.

Not a fellow villain.

Not a fellow Cape.

Not a fellow psychopath.

And especially not her asshole abusive ex, who had never really understood the concepts of "no," "personal space," or "laws."

The man might have been able to terrorize her younger self and term her into his twisted ideal, but those days were *DONE*. He had made the mistake of teaching her everything he knew about fighting and killing things. ...True, in the years since, he had evidently taught himself some *new* things, but the point remained the same.

And Chapter *One* of "Kill Your Way to Friends and Fortune the Mercygiver Way"? *NEVER* miss an opportunity to hurt your target.

She smiled, her teeth coated with blood. She sensed her opening.

The man had gotten so *sloppy* without her there to clean up his messes.

She yanked his knife from where it was still sticking out of her own body and slammed it into his chest before he could move. The way he was holding her made his center mass the perfect target. He twisted slightly at the last second so she was a little off-center, but the blade still sank deep into his body and he howled in pain.

Mull smiled in satisfaction, always happy to pay the man back for the pain he had caused the world.

Unfortunately, her surprise attack also caused him to stagger back. ...And to let go of her in the process. She'd been expecting that, of course, but it still sucked. Totally worth it to see the man bleed, but still sucktacular.

Her arms pin-wheeled for a moment, but it was hopeless. She lost her balance and tumbled backwards off the building towards the alley below. She was pretty good at surviving falls. It came with the training. In this particular instance though, the building was too high and she was in the wrong position to even *attempt* a safe landing. Generally, it was difficult to walk away from a fall when you landed on your face. It had a way of just *ruining* your day.

She'd often heard that your life passed before your eyes in such a moment, but Multifarious had evidently lived too many of them for that. There simply wasn't enough time to see them all.

All she saw was the dirty alley getting closer and closer.
Well, didn't this just totally suc...
WHAM.

****

Oswald Damico hated dirt. He hated the way it stuck to you. He hated the way it made you feel. He hated the fact that sometimes something got so dirty, it could never be clean again.

You could have the most precious thing in the world and an

empty container of ice cream, and once they hit the dump, they were both trash. That was how it worked.

Garbage was garbage, and garbage *stayed* garbage.

You could never wash it entirely clean. It would forever be tainted.

He stared down at his hands, imagining the microbes which were at this very moment scurrying around on his skin. Billions of microscopic organisms living their entire lives on the Obsessive Land of Oz. Breeding, and chewing and doing who knew what else... And he was helpless to stop them. They were trespassers. A constant reminder that nothing was what it seemed. That even the most seemingly sanitary of surfaces were actually still disease-ridden. That no matter how hard you tried, your hands would never be entirely clean.

It was unavoidable.

That was simply the way the world worked.

Oz could do little things to try to slow down the process— like always turning light switches on and off eleven times and always making sure to turn in a circle before entering a new room— but the end would come all the same. One day, the billions of unwanted reminders of his past would get the best of him, and Oz would simply be garbage.

Again.

Sometimes, he just got so tired of his life. Got tired of the things he had to do in order to keep technology from poisoning him with its deadly rays and UV lights from turning people into reptiles. It was like being a prisoner. A prisoner who couldn't do the things he wanted to do, with the people he wanted to do them with. Sometimes it felt like he was outside of himself, watching as he did the crazy things which his brain told him he had to do.

He hated *those* times the most.

Those were his opportunity to really feel bad about his life and the state he had let it get into.

The things he did.

The things he had done.

The things he had seen.

...The garbage.

Sometimes... late at night, he could still smell it. Could still *see* it crowded around him in the dark. Could still *feel* the warm blood dripping onto his face, mixing with the grime of coffee grounds and stale beer...

And those were the days when he was the worst. When his

brain was looking for every opportunity to keep things from getting that bad again. To keep what little Oz had from being thrown away by forces outside of his control.

It was a constant struggle. And Oz was getting so tired.

Sometimes it felt like there were two of him: the rational side which was trying desperately to hold on, and something savage and monstrous trying to break free.

A demon born in garbage and weaned on crazy.

And when it was in control... Oz wasn't. Oz didn't like the things he did. He knew they were insane and unhealthy. He knew *he* was insane, but he was helpless to stop it. Crazy resisted all attempts to vanquish it. Like the microbes on his hands, it infested everything around you. You couldn't avoid it. You couldn't resist it. Your only hope was to listen to the best of it in an attempt to avoid the worst.

Because if you didn't... something bad would happen, and it would be *your* fault.

If you only did the bizarre action or movement like your brain told you, none of the terrible things would happen. It was like a safety net. Like a prayer. And really, why risk it? What did it matter if you spent an extra couple of seconds flipping a light switch on and off? Wasn't it worth it to ensure that your teeth wouldn't liquefy in your skull and your loved ones wouldn't die horribly in front of you?

Oz thought it was.

He lived in constant fear of forgetting to do one of his rituals, and then having to watch as the bad things happened around him. The people he loved would bear the fallout of his sloth and inattention.

Again.

Oz wasn't even entirely certain who or what he believed was controlling things that way, or why flipping a light switch several extra times might appease whatever primal desire that force carried, but he didn't really care.

His brain told him that he needed to do these things in order to keep bad things from happening to himself and the world around him, and so he did them. There was *very* little in his orderly life that he cared about, but he would do anything to keep it safe. Specifically, keep *her* safe.

Oz lived alone. He ate alone. He was alone.

He lived his life to a certain routine. Everything was carefully planned out so that Oz didn't have to worry about mistakes or surprises. Every morning he got up at the same time, ate his breakfast in the same number of bites, and drank the same cup of hot water in the same number of sips. He showered three times a day and used the same brand of hospital strength disinfectant soap every time. He shaved his head in the same number of strokes, because hair was a depository for illness and germs. He took the same number of steps to the closet every day, and always used the same brand of hangers for each one of his identical white suits.

He hadn't taken a sick day or used any vacation time in his entire employment history.

He didn't watch TV.

He didn't have friends except for work.

He didn't have hobbies or outside interests.

Everything in his apartment was decorated in white and stainless steel. Every object he owned had a clean and empty look which appealed to him. It told him that it was sanitary. That there would be no germs clinging to its surfaces. That it wasn't some aspect of his past rising from the grave to trap him again.

Nothing there smelled of trash and death.

...Nothing but Oz himself.

He didn't go to clubs. He didn't go to parties. He didn't go on dates. He didn't do *anything* but wake up, get ready for work, go to work, come home and go to sleep. That was his routine, and he followed it with a maniacal and mechanical dedication.

Oz lived a pretty joyless life. Not that he was unhappy, because he wasn't. His life was neither happy nor sad. It existed like his life existed: neutral. A completely ordinary and predictable reality, which offered no unexpected outcomes and took no risks. And he had thought for years that he *liked* it that way.

Lately however, he had realized how empty his life truly was. It had simply taken him a while to notice that he lived every day the exact same way. Every moment utterly predictable and orderly. He was... getting bored. Normally, Oz positively *thrived* on order and predictability, but he was unable to escape the nagging feeling that he wasn't really enjoying life. Something was missing.

And then one day, he saw what– or rather *who*– that little redheaded something was.

Unfortunately, Oz had absolutely no idea how to deal with that fact. It terrified him. It seemed to beckon him towards disaster like a siren's call, telling him to abandon everything about himself that he knew to be true. Cast aside the rituals and routine which kept things safe, and just embrace the craziness. ...Just do what he *wanted* to do, rather than what his compulsions *told* him to do.

And sometimes he wanted so *desperately* to listen. Just give in and accept that he couldn't tread water forever and that sooner or later, he'd sink back into the garbage.

He stared unseeingly at the water in the gutter.

He hated when it rained in the city.

For some reason, it always made things smell worse. It brought the stink to the surface until it seemed to permeate reality itself. The smell was a living thing, like the miasmas of old. It caused all manner of horrors. It was a reminder that the city couldn't escape the things that it had done. It thought it was rid of the unwanted trash, but the trash wasn't yet done with the city.

Garbage did terrible things to the look of this city.

...Did terrible things to people.

Oz hated it.

He hated it with every *ounce* of his being.

And sometimes... sometimes he felt like it was a *part* of him. Like it had mixed with his open wounds all those years ago, and now his blood was polluted with its foulness. Like he could never fully escape it. Like it was what was making Oz do the crazy things he did and think the crazy way he thought.

Like it had made Oz the man he was.

Because once something was tainted, there was no going back.

Garbage was garbage and garbage *stayed...*

WHAM!

Oz jumped back as something fell from the rooftop of the building in front of him and landed in one of the dumpsters, slamming the lid shut. There was a sickening sound of twisting metal and cracking bone.

Oz stared at the dumpster for a moment, debating what he should do. Under *normal* circumstances, there was no way in HECK that he would ever even go *near* that trash receptacle. Just being around it was bound to lead to *all manner* of diseases and parasites, let alone *touching* the awful thing to see what had just fallen into it.

Who.

The word flashed in his mind from its darkest regions which he didn't like thinking about. '*WHO* had just fallen into it.'

Oz had been on the Consortium team for months now. He was used to the kinds of destruction which seemed to follow them around, *especially* when Poacher was on the scene. In this case though, he heard no muffled curses or shouted protests that the disaster hadn't been his fault. He didn't hear the footsteps of heavy combat boots as the man tried to flee the area to avoid the blame, and no laughter at how far the blood from his victim had sprayed when they hit the ground *this* time.

There was only silence.

...And when the Consortium was involved, silence was always *bad*. Terribly, terribly bad. Silence meant that *they* hadn't tossed someone off the roof... someone had tossed one of *them* off the roof.

It was the only explanation.

He swallowed, utterly certain of that fact.

And for some reason, that knowledge filled him with a dread he couldn't name and had never before experienced.

...He *knew* what he'd find in that dumpster. *Who* he'd find. He knew it on the deepest elemental level, even though he actually had no idea. And whatever it was that was in there, the crazy part of his mind already *knew*. It had *already* figured it out, and was yelling at him to run away before whatever it was *broke him*.

Before he knew what was happening, his hands were already wrenching the lid open though, ignoring the slime which covered it. Under *NORMAL* circumstances, Oz wouldn't have touched that lid even if he were wearing a full contamination suit.

But these were *not* normal circumstances.

Oz had the lid opened within three seconds of the person falling into the dumpster, and was hauling himself into the receptacle within four.

He was overcome by a desperate maniacal terror, which caused the world to move in slow motion and made him completely ignore every ritual and compulsion which he had ever before sworn by.

He stared down at the scene before him, his pristine white shoes ankle deep in the chilly and noxious liquid sludge which filled the bottom of the empty dumpster.

And what he saw changed his orderly life forever...

AUTHOR'S NOTE & COMMENTARY ON BOOK

OVEREDUCATED AND UNDEREMPLOYED, ELIZABETH ("LIZZY") LIVES IN FLORIDA WITH HER SISTER CASSANDRA GANNON (WHO IS ALSO AN AUTHOR). SHE ENJOYS COMIC BOOKS, SOAP OPERAS, AND READING. SHE HAS ALWAYS BEEN THE TYPE OF PERSON WHO GENUINELY VOTES FOR THE BAD GUYS IN MOVIES, TV AND VIDEO GAMES, AND USUALLY CAN'T STAND THE HERO.

Julian stole Poacher's girlfriend. Twice. See, the basic idea was always for Poacher to go with the ex-head of Badger's fan club. I *loved* the idea of Syd having a fan club, and Wyatt had mentioned in passing that Badger had once beat up the head of the fan club years back, and I just assumed that one day she and Poacher would hook up. It seemed reasonable at the time. But Poacher didn't *want* to go with her. At all. I tried a chapter of it once, and he just sat there. Frustrated, I decided to let Poacher go off and do what he wanted to do, and tried Julian in the setting instead since it fit really well with where Julian wanted to go. Surprisingly, I found Julian's brand of laissez-faire super-heroics to be much more interesting when paired with the character, especially since she was always going to be someone intent on making her rescuer more famous. Julian trying to be a media darling? I liked that idea.

Meanwhile, I wrote a few more pages/chapters/notes for Poacher's book, and realized that his new love interest's name (Bridget), was a faaaar better name for Julian's girl. So, I stole that too. Thus, Julian stole Poacher's girlfriend twice. But that's okay though, as Poacher has since abandoned *those* plans for him as well, and *once again* has gone off to do his own thing, leaving me several beautiful and touching scenes that can never be used, because the leading man is no longer interested in the leading lady. So, I guess it worked out for the best. ...As long as you're Julian.

Comic books have what are called ages. The golden age stretches from the 1930's to the 1950's, and it's home to most of the archetypal characters we think of as the superhero (Superman, Batman, etc). The golden age has simple plots and clear morals. There is good and there is evil, and evil never wins. Storylines last one issue and the heroes are paragons of justice and morality. Next comes the silver age, stretching from the mid-1950's to the early 1970's, and it introduces a lot of the more complex heroes to the scene (the Fantastic Four, the X-Men, Spider-Man, etc). It is in this era that the heroes lose their ability to always know right from wrong, and the idea that heroes can dislike one another is introduced. Next comes the bronze age, stretching from about the mid-1970's to the mid-1980's. It is in this era that the heroes' morality gets even murkier and the idea that the bad guy can win is introduced. Finally, the modern era, stretching from the mid-1980's onward. This era is characterized by violent anti-heroes, dispensing justice as they see fit. Morality is gray and there is little distinction between the heroes and the villains, and characters frequently switch sides.

My goal for this book was to take a golden age character, and have him trying to deal with the changes that took place in the hero game around him. I think that must be hard. To start out with things being so simple (all Julian wants is to flood the world and create mutant fish people. He has no deeper political or personal goals) and now they are so complicated. I liked that idea, especially since the 1930s saw the introduction of all of the aquatic hero characters in comics. Thus, it was pretty much a given that Julian would have been a part of that era as well.

The original idea actually predates *Yesterday's Heroes*, and was something I always wanted to see a comic book tackle. The other element of this early version of an unwritten comic book-like story I always wanted to write was the dam fight scene in chapter 2. I really like the idea of being so concerned about your own drama, that you completely botch the mission on live TV. There's something so delightfully Bronze Age about that. There's some other stuff sprinkled through the book that was in that original story too. At some point, I'll have to do a blog post about how all these little seemingly unrelated scenes which I stick into this series in random places would have fit into the larger storyline of that original unrealized story, but I'll save that for another day. For instance, Draugr and Holly were once the same character, as were Wyatt and Monty, and even *I'm* not sure how they got so far apart in my mind. In any case, it's not a particularly interesting anecdote to anyone but me, but hey, it's my blog so I can post whatever I want there. I'd put it here, but it'd take too long and I don't feel like writing it right now. :)

Julian is named after Jules Verne, author of "20,000 Leagues Under the Sea," even though his name wasn't technically "Julian," but you get what I mean. It *SHOULD* have been, how about that? ;-) At the time, I thought about choosing something more "godly" sounding, but that just wasn't where his character wanted to go. "Thalassic" is a word meaning: "of or relating to the sea" and "Sargassum" is both a species of fish and of seaweed. I chose it because of the old Mystery Science Theater 3000 film "Bloodwaters of Dr. Z" and its infamous line: "Sargassum... the weed of deceit." I was looking for something that sounded over-the-top golden age villain-y and thought that fit the bill.

Bridget was originally based on the comic relief sidekick of every female lead in every action film I've ever seen. There's always a character like that. She's the heroine's best friend or sister with the loser fat husband who shows up to say funny stuff. That kind of thing. As time went on, Bridget sort of morphed and developed into the most responsible one in the book though, which really wasn't my intention. She was *supposed* to be kinda zany and kooky, but as it turned out, no one can out crazy Julian, and she stopped trying. Julian is a *terrible* straight man. He's just too insane on his own to ever find someone else's craziness odd or endearing. She *tried*, but he just went along with her, which wasn't particularly interesting. A lot of that got edited out because her heart just wasn't in it. She's named "Bridget" because I liked the metaphor of a bridge. It stretches out over the water and connects the land. ...Or something. Honestly, it made more sense in my head, but to be fair, it was very late at the time. "Haniver" comes from the "Jenny Haniver," a mythical mermaid like creature which sailors used to make out of various parts of fish and then dry and display. Why not name her "Jenny" you ask? ...Shut up, that's why! Because it would lose the metaphor, obviously!

If I recall correctly, Cassandra was the one who came up with the idea of Bridget being a Weeki Wachee style mermaid, although it might have been an independent invention even before she said anything. I don't remember. I went back and forth on the idea, but ultimately decided that there was simply nothing else she could be. In any case, if anyone is on the rural Florida gulf coast, I recommend a trip to Weeki Wachee Springs to see the mermaid show, exactly as I described it. ...Well, except for the super-villains. I took artistic license on that one.

The original goal of the layout of this book was to follow around what should be the B-story, without ever explaining what is happening in the A-story. We're only concerned with the secondary characters and storyline. The main story is obviously happening in Agletaria or in the war between Reece and Mercygiver or with whatever Holly and Cory are up to in Mexico, but the book is set up to only devote the time to those stories that would normally be spent on Julian and his crew in a normal book. In its purest form, the narrative should follow only Julian around and reveal only the facts about the main story which are known to him, but I found that unworkable from a story layout standpoint. Julian just simply doesn't *care* what is happening anywhere he isn't. While this may sound like it would make the situation even more amusing, it just didn't, because he took no *notice* of the event at all. He isn't the type of guy who's going to go investigating what's happening and wouldn't care even if someone told him. So, I had to make do. As it is, I find myself kind of agreeing with Paige King on her TV show: I think Julian's rather out of line allowing things to digress with the safety of the city for as long as he did. All of my characters are rather selfish most of the time, but that instance gave even *me* pause. …But Julian just didn't feel like changing his attitude about it, no matter how many times I tried to make him. He was totally focused on Bridget. Period. To be fair, it sounded like Oz, Mack and Ceann were working on stopping Reece though, so maybe I'll give Julian the benefit of the doubt and say that he's the one who told them to do that. And of course, Monty was already planning his eventual victory over the SPRM way back in the early chapters of the book, so maybe I misjudge them.

The setup for the flashback chapters is somewhat different this time as well, as usually they tell a sort of "origin" story, which most influences the character. Julian is rather unique though, in that he's both too simple and too complex for that. He has no one event which really makes him who he is. His entire life is a series of bad experiences, being ignored by people doing more important things than he is, and failure after failure. I actually stopped writing the book for a long time trying to conceive of a single storyline to follow, but his life just isn't set up that way. It's hard to find just one terrible event to showcase in a life that's filled with them. In fact, a bunch of them are still on the cutting room floor. I would have liked to show more swashbuckling Golden Age style action though, as I think both Julian and Everett would have liked that. I picture them constantly trying to top their last battle, like it's a game or something. I'm not sure if that's kinda sad, or really sweet. In either case, I think there's a lot there that didn't see print, although it wouldn't have any real impact on the central story. They're pretty good at inventing their own drama though, so I'm curious as to what they might have done. I actually had no intention of writing pretty much anything Everett said, from his sea shanty to knowing Julian's mother. For that matter, Julian's mother herself was entirely Everett's invention in the first place. He just sort of said it, and then I stopped and thought "…Wait. What does *that* mean? Where are you going with this?" I found Julian's relationship with him interesting, and if I have one regret about this book, it's that I didn't have room for more scenes with them. All well. Maybe in a later book.

Reality check time:

- Yes, Nicola Tesla's belongings really were sold off to satisfy a debt, just as described. Whether or not his supposed death ray was a part of that sale is up for debate though. He reportedly had it in his apartment with him when he passed away years later, and authorities report that it was simply vacuum cleaner parts. But who knows?

- Lamellar armor has been found at Viking sites, but it's unknown if they wore them, or perhaps a few foreigners visiting Viking lands came wearing them and then died. In either case, I liked the look. Why would Draugr wear armor and then bare her midriff? Because it's a romance novel set in a comic book, that's why. In a comic book, that's what she would wear. I'm powerless to mess with a classic comic trope. The axe, shield and myths are exactly as found in the historical record, although generally, I think the Danish axe was more of a two-handed weapon, but when you have super-powers, you could make do with one I suppose. The "ear" rune would be a little late for Vikings, but since I never said when she got it or why, I think I'm going to give myself a pass on that one.

- Yes, I realize putting them on the Titanic again is silly. It's another one of those occasions where I actually stopped writing and rethought it. I'd *always* planned on making it their "Undersea Base" though, so it would be untrue to the series if I changed that. …It is pretty silly however. But I think that's okay sometimes.

- Once again, I really feel that I should mention my aversion to acknowledging the passage of time, and paying attention to actual geographies and the actual world. Yes, I realize that the Pine Barrens are a good distance from New York. And yes, I realize that in the series' timeline, this should all be taking place sometime in late fall and it should thus be rather cold in the city, but I'm going to chalk that one up to me not caring very much about such things. ...Or maybe it's all just part of a larger storyline that I'm carefully laying the groundwork for. Yes. Yes, that's what it is. These aren't "*mistakes*," people, just meticulous *foreshadowing* of things I haven't thought of yet. ;)

- Norway and Sweden are not actually the same country. ...As far as I know.

- Yes, I did actually read *Remains of the Day* as research for that one scene. ...Well, the book on tape, anyway. ...Well, some of it. I honestly have no idea why I thought I had to though. Especially since the chapter relating to it was about two people who *hadn't* read the book, and everything they said about it was basically incorrect. But whatever.

- Monty's train story is true. I knew a guy who lived in that town, and whose father knew the guys who blew up the tracks in an effort to get the train to stop in their town.

- I can't actually find the citation for the Thoreau quote at the beginning of the prologue. It's one of the things that everyone says he said, but I can't find where. Personally, I think someone is just paraphrasing this line from his Journal: "[people] lay so much stress on the fish which they catch or fail to catch, and on nothing else, as if there were nothing else to be caught." That didn't fit my needs as well, so I used the unattributed version. I'm sure that's likely to make some Thoreau fans cringe though.

- Bridget has a tendency to use a lot of run-on sentences, which I suppose I should re-edit to make more grammatically correct, but generally I try to let a character's "voice" speak for itself. If it bothers anyone, I'm sorry.

- Oh, apologies to all the Italian speakers out there. *Mi dispiace*. Why does a character consistently use a language that I only speak a few words of? ...I have no idea. She just does. I really wish she didn't, as it takes forever to write. Mine's *very* rusty, and they didn't exactly teach us how to swear in the classes I took in it in college. I did the best I could, but I'm sure it's filled with incorrect sentence construction and conjugations (why would I write perfectly in another language when I can't write a typo-free book in English, right?). In retrospect, before she passed away, I should have asked my 100% Italian grandmother how to call someone bad names and then volunteer to kill them in Italian. Something tells me that she could have probably told me.

Alternate titles: "Triton of the Minnows," and "The Last Fish in the Sea."

Time spent writing the book: all told, it took around 8 months. Really though, only a few weeks of that was actual writing. The rest was spent either thinking about the book, writing other things or dealing with a broken laptop. Plus, one of the secondary characters *totally* screwed me over and ruined a perfectly good storyline that I had meticulously foreshadowed throughout the book, and it took me a couple months of doing nothing to come to terms with the loss and eliminate all traces of it from the story. Pity. It would have been really cool. ...I hope he knows what he's doing, because I sure as hell don't. And for *once*, it's not even Poacher doing it.

First chapter written: if I recall correctly, it was the sequence at the school with Julian talking to the kids. I wrote that a looooong time ago. Either that, or some of Monty's chapter and the death of Mary Sue. ...I really didn't like her. When she was introduced, I fully intended to make her another morally ambiguous character who did bad things, but wasn't really so bad deep down. I planned on making her a regular at some point. ...But the second she showed up on canvas, I just really really *hated* that bitch. I don't know why. Perhaps it's me projecting my dislike for every character like that she's in homage to or something, but whatever the reason, I just couldn't wait to see her dead. In fact, that sequence was written directly after I wrote her introductory scene in Electrical Hazard. I just wanted her *dead* and I wanted it *bloody.*

Last chapter written: I actually wrote a lot of this book chronologically, which is unusual for me. Last chapter written is Julian's second flashback to the cannery (the last flashback in the book), which technically isn't even written as I'm writing this, so if you're reading this now and there's no chapter like that in the finished book, then I made a very big mistake or just got sick of trying to write it and erased it from the story. If that's the case then please just forget I ever said anything about it ever existing and move on. It was never there. Nothing to see here. Nope. Move along. Move along.

Personal favorite part: I like their garage sale. I've always wanted to do that scene. I just wish it could have been longer. Maybe Arn will make it an annual thing.

Favorite line: Umm... I don't know that I really have one this time around. If I had to pick, I'd either go with Seth's contention that the Grapes of Wrath make good wine, or with Monty's plan to sneak into the reporter's house and lace all of her food with cocaine. They are both terrible, terrible people. Oh, and Julian's "I've never even met him!" line cracks me up.

If you enjoyed this book, please tell your friends, and leave a rating on Amazon or "like" it on Facebook or Goodreads or elsewhere. It only takes a minute, and I *genuinely* enjoy reading the comments. If you *didn't* enjoy the book... well, you don't have to bother leaving one. I've already wasted enough of your valuable time, and the rating process takes hours anyway and is SUPER difficult to complete. You just don't need that kind of aggravation. Besides, no one reads those things anyway. :-)

Please feel free to email me if you have any questions or comments about the book, series, characters, life in general, or just feel like chatting about other Star Turtle books: **starturtlepublishing@gmail.com**. I actually do answer all of my email, so while I can't guarantee my answer will make any sense, you will receive one.

Thanks for reading! Hopefully I'll see you again next time!

Don't miss the next exciting novel in Elizabeth Gannon's Consortium of Chaos series:

NOT CURRENTLY EVIL

Happy *Tanks*giving, from the Consortium of Chaos!

As a former caped hero, Oz is committed to doing good. Sure he's freaked out by germs and hates disorder, but that doesn't stop him from helping innocent civilians and keeping the city safe from bad guys. ...Even though he's currently partners with one of them.

As a former super villain, Natalie is used to carrying out complex robberies and impossible assassinations. Sure her powers mean that her personality shifts every day, but that doesn't stop her from being the biggest badass around. ...Until mysterious super-soldiers show up and try to kill her.

Now it's up to Natalie and Oz to solve the mystery of who wants her dead. Thankfully, they've got the help of the rest of the Consortium of Chaos, who only occasionally blow things up and kidnap people. Oz is frustrated by the messiness of Natalie's life and Natalie isn't sure about Oz's whole "saving the world" idea, but somehow they're making this crazy partnership work. In fact, the longer Natalie and Oz are around each other, the more this mismatched team begins to see that they just might make a perfect pair.